HER
LAST
GOODBYE

ALSO BY MELINDA LEIGH

MORGAN DANE NOVELS

Say You're Sorry

SCARLET FALLS NOVELS

Hour of Need

Minutes to Kill

Seconds to Live

SHE CAN SERIES

She Can Run

She Can Tell

She Can Scream

She Can Hide

"He Can Fall" (A Short Story)

She Can Kill

MIDNIGHT NOVELS

Midnight Exposure

Midnight Sacrifice

Midnight Betrayal

Midnight Obsession

THE ROGUE SERIES NOVELLAS

Gone to Her Grave (Rogue River)

Walking on Her Grave (Rogue River)

Tracks of Her Tears (Rogue Winter)

Burned by Her Devotion (Rogue Vows)

HER LAST GOODBYE

MELINDA LEIGH

Montlake
Romance

Published by Montlake Romance, Seattle

www.apub.com

Amazon, the Amazon logo, and Montlake Romance are trademarks of Amazon.com, Inc., or its affiliates.

ISBN-13: 9781542047968
ISBN-10: 154204796X

Cover design by Jae Song

Printed in the United States of America

To Mom,
for wallpapering the entire state of NJ in bookmarks

Chapter One

Digging a grave was hard work.

Moonlight gleamed on the shovel as he lifted a clump of dirt and dumped it outside the knee-deep hole. Despite the coolness of the October night, sweat dripped into his eyes. Pausing, he wiped his forehead with his sleeve. With a roll of his shoulders, he plunged the shovel into the earth like a spear and let it stand upright long enough to remove his flannel shirt. He tossed the shirt outside the shallow rectangle.

The breeze that blew across his bare chest cooled his skin. The scent of wood smoke lingered in the air. A carpet of dead leaves covered the trail, leaving the trees half-bare.

He leaned on the handle of the shovel and turned his face to the sky. Above the tops of the trees, the moon glowed, so low in the sky it felt like he could reach up and touch it. He lifted a hand, the position giving him the illusion of holding the moon in his palm.

The illusion of power.

Despite the failure he was literally burying, energy surged through him. He'd been careful, as always.

No one would find out.

No one would stop him.

There was no limit to what he could do.

He took a deep breath. The scents of pine trees and dirt drifted from the forest. Crickets chirped in the thick underbrush around him, and from the nearby river that cut through the forest and ran down the mountain, the sound of water rushing over rocks carried to his ears. Prey animals feared the dark, but he was a predator by nature.

The darkness was his friend.

And if he wanted to finish before dawn, he'd better get back to work.

Yanking the shovel out of the dirt, he returned to his task. Most people would have underestimated the length of time it took to dig a hole big enough for a body.

But then, most people hadn't done it before.

He scooped up another shovelful of dirt and threw it up onto the grass. At first, the ground was nice and soft. But the deeper he dug, the more packed the earth became. If it had been winter, the job would have been impossible. He stepped on the turned lip of the shovel, using his body weight to force the blade deeper into the ground. Time to get this done.

He had people to see. Things to do.

A replacement to choose.

He glanced back at the blanket-wrapped form on the grass next to the hole. The first rule of learning from a mistake was to accept responsibility. He'd fucked up.

He'd picked her, so this was his fault. She hadn't been hardy enough. Had she had some defect he'd missed?

Maybe. But now it was time to put this setback behind him and move on.

He threw renewed effort into his work. By the time he finished, his shoulders, back, and legs ached, but it was the satisfying kind of muscle pain, the kind that came from hard, physical labor.

He climbed out of the hole. It would have to be deep enough. Daylight hovered just below the horizon.

Crouching next to the bundle, he dragged it into the grave. The blanket shifted, exposing her plastic-shrouded face. Irritation washed over him as he flipped the cloth back over her staring eyes. She shouldn't have died.

But sometimes shit just happened.

She could be replaced.

He filled in the hole, stomping over the grave to compact the earth. Then he swept the ground with a branch, covering the freshly dug earth with dead leaves.

He stood and stretched his back, his gaze drifting over the dead leaves around his feet. The grave was practically invisible. Hikers could walk right over the body and never notice it. He returned to the narrow trail. He should have been tired from a night of hard labor. Instead, the cold night air—and his new plan—invigorated him.

He would leave his mistake behind. The opportunity existed to proceed with a clean slate. His strides quickened as he crossed the river at the wooden footbridge. The road was only a five- minute walk from there. He emerged from the state park and headed for his vehicle.

He wouldn't let this disappointment discourage him. He wasn't a quitter. Every failure could be turned into an opportunity.

It was time to start from scratch.

Time to pick the next victim.

Chapter Two

There wasn't anything ominous about 77 Oak Street. White with blue shutters, the compact two-story Colonial sat in the middle of a perfectly ordinary cookie-cutter development. Basketball hoops and hockey nets lined the street. Colorful chalk drawings decorated the sidewalks.

At nine in the morning, the neighborhood was quiet. Kids had gone off to school. Parents had left for work.

But a sense of foreboding trickled down Morgan Dane's back, along with a drop of sweat, as she compared the address with the paperwork in her lap. The numbers matched.

She squinted at the house. The October sun peered over the roof from a cloudless blue sky. Its rays cut through the chilly autumn breeze and shone on a maple tree in the center of the front lawn. It was a beautiful autumn morning, not that anyone inside would know. Every blind in every window was closed tight.

He was in there all right.

"This is the house," she said.

Lance Kruger tapped a finger on the steering wheel of his Jeep. "I don't like this one bit."

"Neither do I." Morgan flipped down the visor and used the mirror to apply fresh lipstick.

There was nothing fun about serving legal papers.

He drove past the house and parked at the curb two doors down. "Maybe it would be better if *I* knock on the door."

Morgan glanced sideways at the big man in the driver's seat.

Lance might have left the police force and joined a private investigation firm the previous summer, but he was still all cop—from his black cargo pants to the severe cut of his short blond hair. The blue flannel shirt he wore open and untucked concealed his weapon but did nothing to hide the impressive set of muscles that filled out the gray T-shirt beneath it. Below the rolled-up cuffs of his sleeves, his forearms bulged.

And if his physical appearance wasn't threatening, the flat glint in his blue eyes gave him away.

He looked dangerous, like he meant business.

If the lowlife they were trying to serve got one look at Lance, he'd run, and the firm would have to start looking for him all over again. It had taken them three days to track the rat down.

As a former assistant district attorney turned private attorney, Morgan owed Lance's boss big-time. Last month, Sharp Investigations had done her a huge favor and worked a criminal defense case without compensation. And if that wasn't enough, Sharp had offered to rent her an empty office in his duplex when she'd decided to open her own practice.

"He will *not* open the door to you," she said. "Which is why Sharp specifically asked me to help out with this case."

Lance frowned and turned his gaze on her. A deep sigh of resignation rolled through him. "You're right. But I don't like the thought of you getting within ten feet of that scumbag, not with his record."

Tyler Green owed his ex-wife thousands in child support. He was the deadest of deadbeat dads. He'd also been arrested multiple times for burglary and assault, though the charges had been plead down from a felony to a misdemeanor each time. To stay one step ahead of process servers and avoid paying his ex, he'd quit his job and moved out of his apartment, mooching his way through the households of family members and friends, never staying in one place long enough for the court system to catch up with him. But all good things had to come to an end. The ex had hired Sharp Investigations to find him so she could get him into court.

Lance's mouth flattened. "Maybe he won't open the door for you either."

"There's only one way to find out. I'm just your average suburban mom." Morgan hoped Tyler mistook her for one of the neighbors. She was crossing her fingers that he'd open the door, she'd hand him the subpoena, and the firm would get paid.

Lance's gaze raked over her. "You may be a mom, but there is nothing average about you."

She fluffed her hair, opened the buttons of her black trench coat, and reached for the tray of brownies in the back seat. "There's a much better chance Tyler will open the door with me standing on the doorstep."

"I know, but that doesn't mean I have to like it," Lance said in an unhappy tone.

Morgan stashed her lipstick back in her tote. Her coat sleeve rode up with her movement, revealing the edge of the fresh pink scar that ran from her wrist to her elbow: an ugly reminder that working with criminals could be dangerous. The stitches had been out for several weeks, but the wound still looked raw and ugly.

Lines deepened around Lance's mouth as he lifted his gaze from the scar to Morgan's face. There was more between them than a professional relationship. How much more was yet to be determined. He was the first man who had tempted her since her soldier husband had been killed in Iraq two years before. But with three young children, making time for a man was a challenge on a good day. And over the past few weeks, Morgan's eighty-five-year-old grandfather had been increasingly unsteady. Extra doctor appointments, tests, and worry were taxing Morgan beyond the normal level of crazy that was her life.

She touched Lance's thick forearm. She'd meant the contact to be reassuring, but the arm under her hand was tense. Who knew a forearm could be so masculine?

"I'll be watching," he said, grim-faced.

"I didn't doubt it for a second." She gripped the door handle.

"Give me a minute to get into position." Reaching under his flannel shirt, Lance checked the weapon at the back of his hip then got out of the vehicle.

Morgan wiped her damp palms on her jeans, took three deep breaths, and stepped out onto the pavement. Carrying the brownie tray, she walked toward number seventy-seven.

Lance crouched behind a shrub at the house next door. Peering through the foliage, he'd have a clear view of her on the doorstep.

She carried the brownies down the sidewalk and up the driveway. Climbing two concrete steps to the front stoop, she rang the doorbell. After a solid minute of silence, she raised the brass door knocker and rapped three times. For another thirty seconds, no one responded.

But she could feel someone watching her.

Footsteps sounded on the other side of the door. A few more seconds passed. Morgan imagined him looking through the peephole. She held her breath while the person on the other side of the door debated. Then the dead bolt slid with the quiet snick of metal on metal, and the door cracked with a soft squeak of its hinges.

Tyler peered through the opening. Barefoot, he wore jeans and a white undershirt very well. The photo in his file hadn't done him justice. His six-feet-plus frame was fit and lean, and he was good-looking in a scruffy, bad-boy way. The arrogant smirk on his face said he knew it. His gaze traveled from Morgan's face to her feet and back up again. He opened the door all the way, stepped into the doorway, and leaned lazily on the jamb.

"Who are you?" he asked her breasts. He dragged his eyeballs back to her face.

"I'm Morgan." She smiled, ignoring the giant *ick* in her belly.

"Hel-*lo*, Morgan." Staring at her mouth, he licked his lips, slowly, deliberately.

Slimily.

Was that a word?

"Who are *you*?" she asked.

He leered. "Whoever you want me to be."

What. A. Sleeze.

She tilted her head as if she wasn't very bright and didn't understand.

He grinned. "I'm Patty's cousin, Tyler."

"Oh. Great. These are for Patty and the kids." She held out the tray of brownies and smiled wider. She batted her eyelashes a few times, a clichéd but effective maneuver.

"Oh. OK." He took the tray in both hands.

Morgan pulled an envelope from her coat and set it on top of the brownies. "This is for you."

"What the fuck?" His body tensed. The leer slid off his face, and anger twisted his features.

Morgan stepped away, not willing to turn her back on him. But Tyler moved faster than she expected, his posture shifting from lazy to lightning in an instant.

He tossed the brownies into a bush and lunged forward. His hand closed around her throat, the pressure on her windpipe forcing her onto her toes. Morgan grabbed his wrist with both hands to break his hold. Gasping, fighting panic, she tried to peel his fingers off her neck.

But his grip was an iron collar. He was taller and stronger and furious.

"You fucking bitch. How dare you trick me." Tyler pulled her closer. "You can tell my ex-wife if I see her again, I'll kill her. That ungrateful slut won't get a nickel from me."

Stars blinked in front of Morgan's eyes as his grip around her neck tightened.

Chapter Three

Morgan!

Lance dug his feet into the grass and sprinted toward the man who held Morgan by the neck. She twitched like a rag doll, rising onto her toes. His vision tunneled down to the two bodies on the stoop. Fury added fuel to his legs.

If Tyler Green hurt her . . .

He watched as Morgan raised one arm over her head and spun in a quarter turn. She windmilled her arm forward and used the inside of her shoulder to break Tyler's grip on her neck. Then she drove the back of her elbow into his face. His head snapped back. Blood spurted. His hands went to cup his mouth and nose just as Lance hit him with a midbody tackle.

Lance and Tyler rolled in a tangle of limbs on the front lawn, coming to a stop with Lance on top. Flat on his back on the ground, Tyler swung out with a wild and weak punch. Lance swatted the fist out of the way like he would a gnat.

In the end, there wasn't much of a struggle. Tyler acted tough when he was attacking women but didn't know what to do with an opponent his own size. He was also bleeding profusely, and Lance wasn't at all ashamed to enjoy the sight. Tyler was a bully and a coward.

Lance rolled Tyler onto his face, pulled his arms behind him, and planted a knee in the small of his back.

Leaning close to the deadbeat's head, Lance said, "You wife beaters have one thing in common. You can't fight someone who fights back."

"Bitches all stick together," Tyler spat over his shoulder.

"She kicked your ass." Lance glanced at Morgan. "Nice shot."

Morgan was on her knees, one hand on her neck; the other held her cell phone. Lance assumed she was calling 911. After giving the dispatcher the address, she slid the phone back into her pocket, sat on her heels, and wheezed, "The police are on the way."

"Get off me," Tyler screamed into the grass.

Lance shook his head and shifted a little more weight onto his knee. The air—and the fight—went out of Tyler like a deflated tire.

"You just assaulted a lawyer, dumbass," Lance said. "She's going to put your sorry butt in jail."

With Tyler immobilized, Lance turned to Morgan. "Are you all right?"

She rubbed the base of her neck and swallowed. "Yes."

"You sure handled him." Lance massaged the achy spot on his thigh where a bullet had ended his police career the year before. The wound had healed as well as it was going to, but his sudden sprint had pulled at the scar tissue.

Morgan climbed to her feet and brushed off her knees.

Five minutes later, a sheriff's department cruiser arrived, and a deputy got out. Scarlet Falls was a small town. Its modest police force frequently relied on the county sheriff or state police for backup.

She showed the deputy the legal paperwork and summarized the incident.

The deputy handcuffed Tyler and hauled him to his feet. Blood smeared his face and soaked the front of his white T-shirt. The deputy loaded Tyler into the back of the cruiser and took brief statements from Lance and Morgan.

"I'll need you to sign formal statements." He nodded at Morgan. "I'll want pictures of those bruises too, but first I need to take him to the ER."

The deputy drove off.

Lance was quiet as they went back to the Jeep, but the residue of anger and worry rolled through his body as he steered her to the vehicle and opened the passenger door.

Turning to face him, she placed a palm in the center of his chest. "I'm all right, Lance."

He lifted her chin and swept her hair aside to examine her neck. "I'm sure you're hurting worse than you'll admit."

Red patches were already forming on her pale skin.

"Bruises heal," she said.

"That doesn't mean I like to see them on your lovely neck." As long as they worked together, Lance was going to want to protect her. Though she was tall, a slim frame and delicate features made her look almost dainty. Even with her attempt to dress casually, she was perfectly feminine, with little glittery earrings and black hair that shone like a shampoo model's.

But he'd keep his inner guard dog on a tight leash. She was no helpless female, even if her ability to defend herself always took him by surprise.

As did the ache in his heart every time he laid eyes on her. What he felt for her, even in this fragile, early stage of their relationship, floored him. They'd only shared a few—albeit scorching—kisses. But he couldn't deny his attraction went far beyond the physical.

Relief got the better of him. He moved suddenly, cupping her face in both hands and kissing her hard on the mouth. When he lifted his head, her blue eyes were dark and wide. "I know you can handle yourself. But I still wanted to rip Tyler's head off for hurting you. It was all I could do not to strangle him."

She smiled. "I'm sure he appreciates your restraint."

"*You* probably broke his nose." He grinned.

"I didn't mean to break anything. I practiced those self-defense drills so many times growing up that my reactions are pure muscle memory."

Morgan's father and grandfather had been NYPD detectives. Her dad had been killed in the line of duty fifteen years ago, but clearly the lessons he'd taught his kids had stuck.

She pulled a blue, flowered scarf from her massive purse, in which she seemed to keep everything but a side of beef. She tied the scarf in a fancy knot around her throat to cover the bruises. But he knew they were there.

Her phone buzzed.

"Is that your sister?" he asked, remembering that Morgan's sister was taking their grandfather to the cardiologist that day. Stella was a detective with the Scarlet Falls PD.

"No. His appointment isn't until this afternoon." Morgan read the display. "It's Sharp. He says to hurry back. We have a client."

After the danger they'd faced in the last case they'd worked together and this morning's incident, Lance hoped the new case would be nice and boring.

"He says it's a hot one," Morgan said.

"Of course it is."

Chapter Four

Morgan led the way into Sharp Investigations. The PI firm occupied the lower half of a duplex on a quiet street a few blocks off the main drag of Scarlet Falls. Lance's boss lived in the upstairs unit. Downstairs, the two-bedroom apartment had been converted into professional space. Morgan had taken over the spare office. Though they were separate entities, private attorneys often required the services of PI firms. Being under the same roof was convenient, and the rent was cheap. With a brand-new practice, Morgan's cash flow was tight.

A few sharp barks greeted them. Rocket, the white-and-tan stray dog Sharp had recently adopted, rushed them, wagging and snuffling at Morgan. A bulldog mix of some sort, her sturdy body was filling out nicely with regular meals.

Sharp met them in the foyer. "The client's name is Tim Clark."

In his midfifties, retired Scarlet Falls police detective Lincoln Sharp was fit and wiry. He wore his more-salt-than-pepper hair buzzed short. After twenty-five years on the force and another five running his own private investigation firm, Sharp sized people up with gray don't-mess-with-me eyes that didn't miss a thing. His lean, hawkish features looked tough, but Sharp was a total marshmallow on the inside.

"Clark?" Morgan crouched to greet the dog. "The name sounds familiar."

"It should," Sharp said. "His wife disappeared last Friday. It was on the news."

"Now I remember." Morgan recalled the news report. Young mother vanishing into thin air, her car found in the middle of nowhere.

The case had made headlines only briefly, until a police shooting over the weekend had garnered more public attention.

Morgan and Lance followed Sharp into his office, and he introduced them.

In his late twenties, Tim Clark had messy brown hair that fell to his shoulders. He hadn't shaved in a few days, and his button-up shirt was as wrinkled as a sheet of aluminum foil that had been crumpled into a ball and smoothed out again.

He stood to shake their hands. "Thanks so much for seeing me. I should have called for an appointment, but honestly, I haven't been thinking straight."

Sharp took his seat behind the desk, and Lance leaned on the wall.

Tim eased back into his seat. An infant carrier sat at his feet. From the blue blanket tucked around the baby, Morgan assumed it was a boy.

"How old is he?" she asked.

"Four months." Tim's eyes misted. "His name is William. I'm sorry I had to bring him. My daughter is with my neighbor, but Will is colicky. No one wants to watch him."

"It's not a problem," Morgan said. "I have three kids."

The baby stirred and made a snuffling sound, and Morgan melted a little as she settled in the chair next to Tim.

"What can we do for you, Tim?" she asked.

"I'm not sure." Tim rocked the baby seat with his foot. "My wife went out last Friday night to meet a friend for a glass of wine. She never arrived at the restaurant." His voice faltered. "No one has seen her since."

Morgan leaned forward. "I'm so sorry about what happened, but why are you here?"

His eyes went bleak, and he stared at the baby at his feet. "Because the sheriff has spent more time investigating *me* than trying to find my wife."

On the armrest, Tim's hand curled into a tight fist. His eyes lifted, and behind his despair, a fiery hint of anger flared. "I don't know exactly what I need, but I saw you on the news last month, in that case where the police arrested the wrong man. You proved them wrong. I need you to help me. My wife has been missing for five days, and the sheriff is never going to find her if he refuses to look beyond me for suspects. And that innocent man last month went to jail. I can't afford to let that happen. My kids need me."

The air seeped out of Morgan's lungs, leaving her hollow. She had no way of knowing if Tim was guilty or not. He wouldn't be the first husband to kill his wife and then report her missing.

What if the sheriff was right? One of her greatest fears in practicing private law was that she could be responsible for keeping a criminal out on the street. She knew it would happen eventually. Criminals lied. It was what they did.

Morgan's family sent criminals to jail. They didn't keep them out. But last month's case had eliminated any opportunity of her working in the prosecutor's office. That bridge hadn't been burned. It had been incinerated. She'd been hoping to work mostly civil litigation, but small-town lawyers couldn't afford to be too picky. She could not pay her bills without clients.

The baby made another little noise.

The daylight pouring through the window showcased the deep bags under Tim's eyes. He hadn't slept in a while. Morgan clearly remembered her youngest child's colic. It had seemed endless, even though John had been home to help for most of it. Poor Tim was doing it alone.

And he clearly did need her help.

Every defendant deserved good counsel, and her job as a defense attorney was to represent her clients to the best of her ability. She needed to have faith in the legal system.

She folded her hands in her lap. "So the sheriff has not officially cleared you?"

"I don't know." Tim lifted a shoulder. "He says he's investigating other people, but I don't believe him. They don't seem to have any clues. Maybe if they'd actually tried, if they'd actually investigated someone besides me in the very beginning, they would have found her by now."

Tim's eyes glistened with moisture. He turned away and closed them for a few seconds.

Morgan doubted the sheriff hadn't investigated *anyone* except Tim, but the spouse was always the primary suspect. Sadly, nearly one half of all female homicide victims were killed by their intimate partners. When Chelsea wasn't found within the critical twenty-four- to forty-eight-hour period, any cop holding the case would have investigated Tim.

"Where were you Friday night?" Morgan was blunt.

But Tim didn't miss a beat. "I was at home with the kids."

"Can anyone verify that?" she asked.

"Bella and I had a video call with my in-laws around eight thirty for about fifteen minutes or so. After that, it was just me and the kids."

"How old is Bella?"

"Three."

Too young to provide an alibi.

"So you'll help me?" Tim looked hopeful.

Morgan shared glances with Sharp and Lance. They were both on board. She looked down at the baby. He needed his parents. "Yes."

The decision felt right. Better that she take the risk of representing the wrong client than turn her back on someone who needs her.

"Oh, thank God." Tim relaxed as if the strength had gone out of his body.

"Now, tell us what happened Friday night." Morgan gestured to a legal pad on Sharp's blotter. He handed it and a pen to her.

Tim repeated his opening statement.

"Who was she supposed to meet?" Morgan asked.

"Her friend Fiona West," Tim said. "They've been close since we moved here two years ago."

"How did they meet?" Morgan made careful notes.

"Yoga class," Tim said. "Before Chelsea had William, she went to yoga twice a week. Balanced Yoga. It's next to the bank on Second Street."

Tim took a shaky breath and continued. "When she didn't come home, I called her. She didn't answer. I sent texts and left messages. When she didn't respond, I called her friend. Fiona said Chelsea never showed up at the restaurant. She assumed something had come up like the last time they'd had plans. Then I tracked Chelsea's cell phone to her car. It was parked down the road from the train station in Grey's Hollow. I called 911, then drove up and down that road until the sheriff's deputy came. I didn't see anything. As soon as it got light out, I searched again." He struggled to hold back a tear as he glanced down at his son. "Good thing William likes car rides."

"Is there any reason your wife would have gone to Grey's Hollow or taken the train somewhere else?" Sharp asked.

"No." Tim's face tightened with frustration.

"Why is the county sheriff handling the case and not the Scarlet Falls PD?" Sharp asked.

"I called 911 from Grey's Hollow," Tim explained. "The sheriff's department responded."

Grey's Hollow didn't have a police force. Crimes in that section of the county were investigated by the sheriff's office. Typically, once a department had a case, they kept it.

Tim continued. "Sheriff King says there's no sign of foul play, and it isn't against the law for an adult to leave home. That's why I came to you."

Lance shifted his position. "Has the sheriff's department looked at her phone and computer?"

"Yes," Tim answered. "They have both her laptop and phone. But I already looked at both devices and found nothing. I doubt the sheriff's office has anyone more qualified than me." Arrogance laced Tim's tone.

"They have a protocol to follow," Morgan said.

Tim wasn't giving the county forensics techs enough credit. They were highly qualified.

"What exactly do you do, Tim?" Lance asked.

"I'm a wireless telecommunication engineer," Tim said. "My employer, Speed Net, is working with the university on research to develop the next generation Wi-Fi."

Maybe Tim had a reason to be a little arrogant about his tech skills.

"Must be interesting to work on the cutting edge," Sharp said.

Tim shrugged. "It is. It's also demanding."

"We'll need your employer's contact information," Lance said. "And we'll want to interview your boss and coworkers."

"All the information is in here." Tim slid a file from his diaper bag and set it on the desk.

"I doubt the sheriff will give you her electronics back just yet," Sharp said. "That's too bad. I know you're a computer expert, but we'd still like to look at your wife's digital history. I'm sure you're great with computers, but we know what to look for."

"I'm willing to try anything," Tim said. "Chelsea's laptop and phone both backup to a cloud account every twenty-four hours. I can access everything that was on her computer from mine."

"Perfect. Do you know what kind of initial physical search the sheriff conducted of the area where you found your wife's car?" Lance asked.

Tim sniffed and reeled in his emotions. "The police searched the neighborhood. They drove along all the roads for a few miles in each direction. They put out some sort of alert to other police departments. They brought in a dog."

Sharp rubbed his buzz cut with a palm. "The dog didn't pick up anything?"

Tim shook his head. "Nothing."

"Do you know what the sheriff is doing now?" Sharp asked.

Tim shook his head. "He doesn't tell me much."

"We'll contact the sheriff and get an update," Morgan assured him. "Do you know if the sheriff's department interviewed any of your neighbors?"

"He did," Tim said. "A few people dropped by to let me know."

There were up to ninety thousand active missing persons cases in the United States at any given time, but missing adults often took a back seat to missing kids, homicides, robberies, and assaults. Without clear evidence of foul play, it was unlikely Chelsea's case would take priority.

"Did you check your credit card statements for a train ticket?" she asked. Chelsea's car had been parked so close to the train station.

"Yes. The last charge on her credit card was at the grocery store last Thursday," Tim continued. "The police looked at the surveillance tapes from the train station. They said no one who looked like Chelsea got on the train that night. She never carried much cash. If Chelsea wanted to take the train, she would have bought the ticket online. That's what we usually do."

Unless she didn't want anyone to know where she was going.

But Morgan didn't say it. There wasn't enough evidence to make assumptions. The sheriff's office had made the usual ones, and that by-the-book approach hadn't found Chelsea. It was time for some fresh blood—and brains—on the case. She didn't want Tim to have to live in limbo for the next twenty years.

Morgan glanced at Lance. His face was a tight mask, but emotion clouded the blue of his eyes. Since his father had gone missing many years ago and had never been found, this case would bring up unpleasant memories for him.

Tim tapped the file on the desk. "I brought copies of everything the police asked for: phone records, a list of her family and friends, our employers, bank and credit card statements, social media account information. I copied everything I gave to the police."

The baby began to fuss, starting with bleating cries that quickly escalated to wails.

"I'm sorry." Tim removed a bottle from the diaper bag, unstrapped the infant, and picked him up. He offered the baby the bottle. "But I'm at least grateful that he's decided bottles are OK. The first two days Chelsea was gone were a nightmare. I thought he was going to starve."

The baby drank in greedy gulps. Tim sat back, and Morgan's heart squeezed.

Sharp took the folder and opened it. He thumbed through the papers. "Does Chelsea have an alcohol or drug problem?"

"No," Tim said. "She hasn't even had a glass of wine since she got pregnant with William. Friday night would have been her first. She's fitter than I am. She runs almost every day. She loves to hike. As a couple, we're about as boring as it gets."

Sharp made a note on a legal pad on his desk. "How long have you and Chelsea been together?"

"Five years," Tim said. "We met senior year of college in Colorado."

"Why did you move to New York?" Sharp asked.

"I was offered a job with Speed Net. The move was a little risky, but the company has enormous growth potential. The payoff could be huge. We only had Bella at the time." Tim's gaze dropped to the baby. "In hindsight, leaving Chelsea's family has been really hard."

Morgan stared at the baby for a few seconds, empathy tugging at her. "Tell me about Chelsea's family. Is there any friction there?"

"Not that I know of. Chelsea is an only child. Her father is a chiropractor. Her mother is a teacher."

"Is your family in Colorado as well?" Morgan asked.

"Yes, but I was glad to leave them behind." Tim raised his chin, his jaw tightening. "My parents are alcoholics and drug addicts. My father served time for burglary. Mom sold heroin out of our kitchen, and my brother was in prison for armed robbery when I left the state. I don't want my family anywhere near my wife and kids. That has been the one additional benefit of moving east. Back home, they'd occasionally call or show up at our apartment looking for money. I haven't had any contact with them since we moved here—though I'm a junior so my father's records are constantly crisscrossing with mine."

Morgan made a note to find out if Tim's parents were still in Colorado. Who knew what kind of schemes three criminals in need of cash could hash out? Especially if they resented the one member of the family who'd successfully navigated the straight and narrow.

"Did you bring a photo of your wife?" Sharp asked.

"Yes." Shifting the baby around, Tim reached down and produced a photo from the diaper bag. "This is Chelsea." His hand trembled, just slightly, as he handed it across the desk to Sharp, who studied the picture with a frown.

Tim pushed his hair off his face. Then he squeezed the back of his skull for a few seconds, as if the pressure of his fingers would help hold it together.

Sharp passed the photo to Morgan. Wholesome and fresh-faced, Chelsea was a pretty young woman with long blonde hair, even white teeth, and big blue eyes. In the photo, she stood on a mountaintop. The background was pure blue sky and more mountains rolling into the distance.

"That was taken last year. We were hiking in the Catskills."

Morgan handed the picture to Lance. He took the photo by its edges and studied it.

"How was Chelsea's mental state after William's birth?" Morgan remembered the chaos of her third child's birth. There had been days she'd functioned like a zombie on autopilot. "Did she have any signs of postpartum depression?"

Tim sighed. "The sleep deprivation has been hard on her. I wouldn't call her depressed, but she's definitely frustrated. We both know William's colic is temporary, but some nights it doesn't feel that way."

So, Chelsea Clark was a physically fit, mentally exhausted woman who was making the best of a tough situation.

Until she disappeared into thin air.

Morgan's youngest child had been an infant when her husband had been killed in Iraq. Sophie had no memory of her father. Morgan's middle child struggled to recall him, and even her oldest, now six, studied John's picture every day in fear that she would forget her daddy. Would Tim's children suffer the same way?

Not if she could help it.

Chapter Five

Lance's hands went clammy as he listened to Tim's story. The similarity between Chelsea's disappearance and Lance's own past echoed like shouts in a deep, dark cave. Twenty-three years ago, Lance's father had gone to the store and never returned.

When Lance's father had disappeared, his mother had suffered the exact same scrutiny—and frustration—that plagued Tim now.

But Sharp, who'd been the lead investigator, had quickly eliminated her as a suspect and moved on. Lance remembered being ten years old, sitting in the hallway just outside the kitchen, and listening in on the conversations between his mom and Sharp. His mother crying. Sharp trying to give her hope without making promises. As the weeks, months, and then years passed, those conversations hadn't included any hope at all, and his mother had stopped crying and started fading away. Twenty-three years had gone by, but the memories still brought a sick feeling of helplessness to Lance's gut.

Morgan leaned forward. "Tell me more about Chelsea. She worked before she had William?"

Tim nodded. "Chelsea is an accountant. The name and address of the firm is in the file."

Sharp looked up from the papers he was rifling through. "Has she talked to her boss lately?"

"They talk on the phone about once a week." Tim burped the baby. "He's been really decent about holding her job for her. He's even been letting her work from home part-time."

"Do she and her boss get along? Any disagreements with coworkers?" Sharp asked. "Any unusual calls or e-mails on Friday?"

"Not that I know of." A defeated sigh rolled through Tim. "Frankly, I don't know what she did on Friday. I came home from work late, and Chelsea was mad at me. She didn't have much time to get ready. Bella was already at a neighbor's house. I took the baby. Chelsea changed her clothes and left. We haven't talked much lately. She was exhausted from being up every night." Tim looked away, guilt tightening the corners of his mouth. "I could be a better husband. Having William 24/7 these last few days has made me appreciate what Chelsea has been going through. I should have done more from the beginning. I know I work too much, but I don't know what else to do. My job isn't nine-to-five."

"Do you fight often?" Morgan asked.

"No. It's rare. Most of the time Chelsea just does what needs to be done," Tim said with a sigh of remorse. "But I should have been home on time. Chelsea usually rolls with my schedule. I should have made *her* a priority for once."

Chelsea sounded strong and resourceful. She dealt with her stress by strapping her two kids into a jog stroller and going running every day.

Maybe running had gotten addictive. Maybe she'd run farther away.

But Lance didn't believe his own father had abandoned his family. He had an equally hard time envisioning the young mother leaving her kids behind, even though he knew some women did just that. Either way, they needed to find her.

And if they didn't, Tim would have to live with regret for the rest of his life.

Sharp asked the question on everyone's mind. "Is there any chance your wife simply needed a break and left?"

Tim studied his son's face for a few seconds. "I've asked myself that same question over and over again. Even if she was really mad at me, she'd never leave her kids. She had it all planned out. She nursed him right before she left. She'd have one glass of wine at eight thirty. It would clear her breast milk in two to three hours, and she'd be OK to nurse him by eleven thirty." He lifted his gaze to meet each one of theirs. "She *planned* to be home. Something happened to my wife last Friday night."

The baby began to squirm and squall, and Tim stood, jiggling his son. "We need her."

"We'll do everything we can." Sharp got to his feet.

After Tim left, Morgan went to the kitchen to nuke a cup of leftover coffee. For a major case, they'd use her office as a war room. The whiteboard had hung on her office wall long before it was her office.

"I'm making green tea. Are you sure you want to drink that?" Behind her, Sharp nodded at the microwave. "That stuff will kill you."

"I'll risk it for fully functioning brain cells," Morgan said on the way back to her office.

Lance was already staring at the whiteboard. He'd made copies of Chelsea's picture and used a magnet to fasten the original to the center of the board. He'd started a timeline on one side, noting the time Chelsea left home and when Tim realized she was missing.

Sharp walked into the office, mug in hand. "Where do we start?"

Lance taped up an aerial photo of the place where Chelsea had disappeared. "How did her car get here?"

"Either she drove it or someone else did." Morgan leaned on her desk and sipped her coffee. It was past lunchtime, and her stomach gurgled audibly.

"Or someone forced her to," Sharp added. "One thing we know, if Chelsea had walked away from the car, the dog would have picked up a scent."

"Agreed. It's all but impossible to fool a K-9." Lance made a note on the board with a dry erase marker. "So she left the area in another vehicle."

"She wasn't alone," Morgan said. "Either Chelsea asked someone to leave a car for her, or she was abducted and the kidnapper had a car waiting."

Sharp crossed his arms over his chest. "We need to find out what the sheriff has discovered."

"I doubt he'll talk to either one of us." Lance gestured between him and Sharp. "We both worked for his arch enemy, Horner."

Scarlet Falls Police Chief Dave Horner was a controversial figure. More politician than policeman, Horner had alienated other branches of local law enforcement with his quests to stay in the limelight and to kiss up to the mayor. His focus on good publicity over good policing had angered many of the officers who worked for him.

"I'll go talk to the sheriff," Morgan volunteered. "He might still feel grateful he isn't facing a civil suit for the injuries our previous client sustained on his watch. Besides, I need to put him on notice that I'm representing Tim now."

The sheriff was in charge of the county jail, where their last client had been injured.

Sharp snorted. "The sheriff isn't the grateful type. He's more likely to be suspicious of you for being an attorney."

"Even though we proved the charges were bogus?" Morgan drained her coffee, then shook the cup as if it hadn't been enough.

"Even then," Sharp said.

"She still has a better chance than either of us," Lance pointed out. "She isn't tainted by an association with Horner."

"True," Sharp agreed. "And she's pretty."

Morgan shot him an exasperated look, and he held up a hand. "I know that's a sexist thing to say, but the sheriff is a Neanderthal."

"Wonderful. Is there anything I need to know about him?" Morgan asked. "I've never met him in person. I don't have a good read on him."

"He's hardheaded and short-tempered." Sharp rubbed his chin. "He's a smart cop but a terrible politician, hence the constant head-butting with Horner. My best advice is to avoid a direct confrontation. I've never seen that work for anyone. Sheriff King will just dig in his heels."

"All right." Morgan nodded.

"A missing person's case can require a ton of man-hours. His entire department is overworked and overextended," Lance said. "You might commiserate with him, then try and convince him our help will be an asset."

His dad had disappeared from Scarlet Falls, a town with its own small police force. Even with Sharp working diligently on Lance's dad's case, Victor Kruger had never been found. But twenty-three years ago, the world had been less monitored. Nowadays, it was much more difficult to stay off the radar. Between surveillance cameras and financial records, there had to be a lead if one looked hard enough.

"Good idea," Sharp continued. "If Morgan takes the sheriff, we can dig in to Chelsea's social media accounts and phone and financial records. We also need to scrounge through the recent local news and see if there have been any stories on other missing women."

Lance nodded. "And follow up with Tim about his wife's laptop and phone. I'll let my mom know that we need her help again."

His mother's anxiety issues made her a shut-in. She lived online and was brilliant with computers.

"We need to investigate Tim as well." Sharp drained his mug. "The sheriff isn't wrong. If Chelsea is dead, Tim is the most likely suspect."

"If he killed his wife, why would he come to us to find her?" Morgan asked.

Sharp tossed his glasses onto his desk blotter. "Just because he engaged us doesn't mean he is innocent. He might think hiring a PI firm makes him look innocent. Some criminals are one hundred percent convinced that they are smarter than everyone else. He might think he can play us."

"What would be his motive?" Lance asked.

Morgan pondered his question with a tilt of her head. "What if their marital troubles ran deeper than Tim suggested? Maybe Chelsea was going to leave him. Maybe she wanted to take her kids back to Colorado. Tim is obviously attached to his kids."

"No offense," Sharp said. "But you're supposed to concentrate on proving your client is innocent."

Morgan looked away, her jaw tight. "You're right."

Sharp sighed. "I know you aren't completely accustomed to working in the private sector yet, but making sure everyone accused of a crime gets adequate defense is a cornerstone of our legal system."

"Yes." But she didn't look comfortable with her new role.

Lance considered their client. "Did Tim seem cunning enough to kill his wife, cover it up, and keep his cool during our meeting?"

"Criminals are very good liars," Morgan said.

She had a point.

"Let's keep our eyes on the prize. Our job is to find Chelsea Clark. It's already been five days. The case gets colder by the hour, so let's get busy." Sharp nodded at Lance. "Make it so, Number One."

Sharp was right. They had to focus on the missing woman.

Lance wouldn't wish living with the uncertainty of a long-time missing family member on anyone. Because not knowing was a whole different kind of pain. Every time a body turned up, every time a skeleton was unearthed, or a hiker ran across some bones in the woods, the family of a missing person had their wounds ripped wide-open.

Chapter Six

Chelsea woke to the smell of rust and steel in her nostrils and a thumping pain in her temples. Her vision blurred, and she squeezed her eyelids closed for a few seconds to try to clear it. Confusion fogged her mind. Something was wrong.

She should be hearing William cry. Her overfull breasts ached. Where was the baby? It was past time to nurse. He never went more than a few hours between feedings. He was practically attached to her. Was he sick?

She rolled to the side, coming up against a metal bar. The bed was not familiar. Neither was the silence.

Where am I?

She opened her eyes. For a few seconds, she blinked in the dim light. As she took in her hazy surroundings, bewilderment gave way to fear. It wrapped icy tendrils around her heart, forcing it to beat faster.

Not a nightmare.

The room came into focus in an instant, the truth clicking into place like a key turning in a lock until all the pins lined up.

Reality flooded her consciousness—along with horror as cold and clear as an autumn night. The shock and the sheer unbelievable nature of her predicament passed through her with a shudder.

She'd been abducted.

A vague sense of déjà vu lingered. How many times had she woken, confused and groggy? A memory surfaced.

She stares at her rearview mirror. A streetlight shines on a knife. The blade touches her throat, a sharp, biting pain that vanishes immediately under the numbing onslaught of rushing adrenaline.

"Drink or die," he says.

Her hands shake as she lifts the fast-food cup he hands her. She sucks on the straw. Though initially sweet, the cola has a bitter aftertaste.

Darkness. A clear night sky. Cold air on her face. Wood smoke in her nose. The waving silhouettes of dead cornstalks in the moonlight.

The flash of memory faded, but not before Chelsea gagged.

She ran her tongue over her teeth. Her tongue was dry enough to stick to the roof of her mouth, and she could taste the lingering sweetness of the drugged cola. Vaguely, her brain registered that this was the first time her head had been this clear since she'd been kidnapped. She knew without a distinct memory that the previous times she'd woken, he'd forced more of the cola mixture into her mouth before she was strong enough to object.

How long had she been here?

It felt as if several days had passed.

What else had he done to her while she was unconscious?

Her brain rejected that line of thought and turned to her family instead.

William! Was he eating? He wouldn't actually starve himself, would he? No. Surely hunger would force him to accept a bottle. *Right?*

There was nothing she could do about it from here. Tim might have his faults, but he loved his children. Bella adored him right back. Tim hadn't quite bonded with the baby yet. In his defense, William had wanted no one except Chelsea since the day he was born. A sliver of guilt wormed its way past her fear. She had to accept part of the blame for that. Bella and Tim were so close that Chelsea had felt jealous at times. When the baby had come along and preferred her, she'd enjoyed it.

She'd been selfish and stupid, and William and Tim were no doubt paying the price.

Forgive me.

She took comfort in the fact that her husband was smart, and he would do whatever it took to take care of their baby. William wouldn't starve.

Chelsea closed her eyes for a few seconds, replaying their brief argument Friday night before she'd left. Sure, he'd been late. Tim had no sense of time, and she'd been cranky. She'd wanted to have time to do her hair and put on some makeup. She'd wanted a break. But she regretted her snub of his goodbye kiss. When was the last time she'd told him she loved him?

Tim, I love you. I'm sorry I've been such a lunatic. Sleep deprivation was used as a form of torture for a reason. If only she could get a do-over of the last few months.

Too late now. He couldn't hear her. Would that be their last goodbye? Would she ever get a chance to make it up to him? To tell him that despite her recent exhausted insanity, she loved him.

And there was only one way she was ever going to get back to him.

Putting a hand to her forehead, she lifted her shoulders from the narrow cot. Her head swam with the change in position. She slowed her movements, slowly rising until she was sitting up.

She took stock of her physical condition first. Her body was stiff and cold. A wool blanket was draped over her, but her shoes and coat were gone. She stretched her legs, testing their strength. Something clinked and metal bit into her ankle.

She was chained to an upright barrel that stood next to the cot she lay on.

Her mind reeled.

Chained!

Like a dog.

Terror constricted her throat, the weight of the manacle on her ankle a solid manifestation of the horror of her situation, and the potential that it would get much worse.

This is not helping.

She took two deep breaths and then scanned her body. She was still dressed in the jeans and sweater she'd worn for her evening out with Fiona. Her sweater was damp. Her breasts had leaked, and she smelled of sour milk.

But other than being filthy and uncomfortable, she didn't feel any major injuries. She moved her arms and legs. No broken bones.

Moving on to her prison . . .

The cot was a simple folding type common for camping. A single camp lantern shone weakly from the barrel she was chained to. Her room was about eight feet long and maybe ten feet wide. Corrugated metal walls formed a rectangular box.

Keeping one hand on the cot for balance, she eased to standing. Her feet landed on a plywood floor. When the initial dizziness had passed, she stretched her arms overhead, but couldn't reach the ceiling, which was made of the same corrugated metal as the walls.

Cold, strong steel.

A shudder raced through her.

A shipping container?

She'd never been inside one, but it felt right.

No way to dig or burrow or force her way out. There were no windows, and the space held a persistent chill, a dampness that suggested the container was outside or underground.

Please let it not be underground.

The thought of being buried alive made every inch of her skin itch. Panic hovered around her, buzzing like a swarm of insects.

She pushed it back and felt it fade into the background, lurking, waiting to pounce.

Another flashback slammed into her.

It felt almost like a hallucination, but she knew it was a hazy memory, real in a physical way that a dream couldn't be.

His shoulder jams into her stomach. She can barely control the muscles in her neck, and her head flops against his back. The smell of his sweat clogs her nostrils. He carries her, fireman style, through the darkness.

The second flash ended as quickly as it began, and with the same rush of nausea. She still had no recollection of exactly how he'd abducted her or when he'd brought her into this room.

Maybe the rest of her memories would come back. Maybe they wouldn't. What mattered now was trying to escape. Her family needed her.

The night she'd left her house, she'd been excited about a few hours of adult conversation with Fiona. At the time, an evening free of wiping chins, changing diapers, and explaining to a three-year-old girl why her little brother had a penis and she didn't had seemed glorious.

But now all she wanted was to see her family.

She yearned to walk the floors with William pressed to her shoulder. To inhale the scent of baby shampoo. To snuggle in Bella's bed at nap time and read a picture book while her sleepy daughter's eyelids sagged. To watch her daughter race through a pile of raked leaves or practice awkward, crooked somersaults in the backyard.

To tell her husband she loved him.

Images of her children brought tears to her eyes. She had to get back to them. As long as she drew breath, she would do everything possible to return to her babies. She wiped her face and sniffed. No wasting energy on crying.

Picking up the battery-operated lantern, she walked to the end of her chain. She lifted the light and inspected the far walls and corners of her prison, just out of reach.

A gallon-size plastic jug sat in one corner. A bucket occupied the other.

She dragged the chain behind her as she crossed the space. She picked up the jug, removed the lid, and sniffed. Water?

She was suddenly incredibly thirsty, as if her body had come alive at the scent of the water. She shouldn't dare drink anything he gave her. It was likely drugged. But dehydration would kill her.

She set down the jug and continued her search, moving the light to carefully examine each wall.

On a positive note, she didn't see any obvious cameras.

As terrifying as the situation was, she had to *think*. She had to find a way out. No one was coming for her. She was on her own.

It was her only chance.

The interior brightened suddenly, and a beam of light shone from the ceiling. Sunlight. Chelsea walked under it and stared up. Rust had eaten a hole in the roof the size of a bowling ball. Through it, she could see the sun, patches of blue sky, and a canopy of branches. Clouds drifted in front of the sun, dimming the light.

The knowledge that it was daytime grounded her.

A door stood at the opposite end of the room from the barrel. It was the only way in or out. She reached for the door, but the chain on her ankle wasn't quite long enough, and her fingers fell six inches short of touching the door. Was it even locked? Probably. He'd gone to too much effort to imprison her. There would be a sturdy lock to keep her inside.

She needed to get closer. She needed to free her foot. She tested the manacle around her ankle. It was tight enough to rub her skin when she moved it, far too tight to wiggle her foot free. She followed it to the connection with the barrel. The bolt that secured the chain went right through the metal.

She took the chain in both hands and pulled. The barrel didn't budge, neither did the bolt. She put her weight into the effort, but it was no use. There was zero give. What was inside it? Maybe if she could somehow empty it, she could drag it closer to the door. But then how would she run away with a steel drum attached to her foot?

Maybe if she emptied the barrel, she would be able to disconnect the chain from the inside.

She returned to the barrel. It was an industrial-size metal drum. Rust grew in patches on the sides and coated the seams. On the top was a cap the size of her open hand. A recessed shape in the cap was shaped like a four-leaf clover with flattened leaves. Obviously, there was a specific tool designed to fit into the impression to open the barrel, like the head of a screw was designed for a screwdriver.

Chelsea tried to turn the cap manually. The fit was tight and the edges were rusted. No matter how hard she turned it, the cap didn't budge. Her hand slipped, her fingernail catching on a metal edge.

Maybe if she had other tools—a screwdriver or wrench.

She almost laughed, the hysterical snort of hopelessness. Tools? Why not wish for a whole toolbox? She lowered her hand and clenched her fingers. Blood seeped out from under her torn, dirty nail.

Wait. She looked down at the chain. The links were thick, metal, strong. She gathered up a length of it in her hands. The chain was short. In order to reach the top of the barrel, she had to put her attached foot on the cot. Then she inserted two links into the opposite sides of the clover leaf and tried to use them as levers, but the cap still wouldn't budge. The links were too small.

What did she do when she couldn't open a tightly sealed jar?

She began to strike the side of the cap with a link. She missed. Her fist struck the edge of the cap, and pain shot up her arm. She shook her hand and pressed her stinging knuckles to her mouth. Tears welled in her eyes.

Don't give up!

Desperation fueled a second attempt. The cap shifted slightly. She tried to open it. Not loose enough. Praying no one was close enough to hear, she struck it again and again, until she could turn it with her bare hands. She unscrewed it all the way, lifted it, and peered inside, holding the lantern over the opening.

Pea gravel.

She almost fell backward with disappointment. No wonder it was so heavy. What was the volume of a drum? Fifty-five gallons? How much did fifty-five gallons of stone weigh?

More than she would ever be able to move. She and Tim had done some landscaping when they'd bought the house. They'd moved river rock by the shovelful. They'd barely been able to get out of bed the next morning.

Could she tip the drum over and roll it to the door? She went around to the side near the wall. Bracing her back against the corrugated metal, she put both feet on the barrel and pushed.

Nothing.

On the other side of the door, chains rattled and metal scraped on metal. She jolted at the sound and scrambled to her feet, heart thudding in a dreadful beat. Her gaze went to the barrel. The cap was upside down on the lid of the barrel.

Praying he didn't notice, she pressed her back to the wall. The door swung inward.

And he stepped inside.

A ski mask covered his face. He was average size. Dressed in jeans, work boots, and a heavy sweatshirt that concealed the shape of his body.

He carried a pile of clothes and a greasy paper bag. The scent of hamburger made Chelsea's stomach churn and growl. He walked closer and set the bag and clothes on the foot of the cot. He scanned her from head to toe. Then his head turned toward the barrel. His body stiffened.

"What were you trying to do?" He stalked closer. "Were you trying to escape?"

The first blow caught her on the side of the face and sent her spinning into the wall. Her head ricocheted off the corrugated metal. She crawled onto the cot and cringed, pain and fear congealing in her belly like cold grease.

She heard the chain rattle. She turned toward him, afraid to see what he was doing yet unable to hide her eyes.

"This will be your first lesson. It's a shame you had to learn it the hard way." He yanked hard on the chain. The manacle bit into the thin skin over her anklebone as he dragged her off the cot.

"No! Please." She grabbed for the frame, her fingers wrapping around the cold metal bar for a few precious seconds before his strength was too much. Pain bloomed in her ankle as he pulled harder, and the lightweight cot slid across the floor.

"Come here." The command was quiet, menacing. The icy control of his voice belied the fury in his movements. "You will not speak without my permission."

Her fingers gave way. She landed on the floor on her hands and one knee, the chained leg pulled straight. He kicked out. The toe of his boot caught her in the thigh. Agony ripped through her leg. A fist crashed into the small of her back, the blow radiating white-hot through her spine.

Falling to her side, she curled into a ball as the blows rained down on her. Pain filled every inch of body. She covered her head with her arms and prayed.

He kicked her in the ribs, cutting off her next breath. "Rule number one: You belong to me. You will do what I say without question. You are my property."

Chapter Seven

He could make her love him. He knew it with complete certainty.

Smoke rose in a cloud from the barrel of burning leaves. He waved it away and tossed her jeans onto the fire. At first, the bulk of the material smothered some of the flames, but in seconds, the denim began to burn slowly, starting at the edges and creeping inward. Smoke rose, smelling like burned paper.

Patience.

He added more dead leaves and waited for the flames to rise again. After the fire was reestablished, he set her sweater on top of the pile. Flames curled around the fabric, embracing, and then destroying it.

Unlike Chelsea, who needed to be broken down but left intact.

She'd tried to escape. Fury rose inside him. He breathed through it. Letting the air slowly out of his lungs, he tried to force his muscles to relax. But the tension wouldn't leave him. It built, feeding on his memories like the fire fed on her clothes.

His rage couldn't get the best of him. It needed to be shut down. Chelsea wasn't the only one who needed to change her behavior. He hadn't intended to beat her so badly, but his temper had taken over. He'd barely been able to tear himself away before he'd done permanent damage. He needed another outlet for his rage. He extended his forearm over the fire. The flames licked his skin. The stink of burning hair rose into his nostrils.

But the pain. The pain was a two-headed beast. Ugly as it roared through his arm.

Beautiful as it overran, then released his anger.

He pulled his arm away before the skin blistered. His forearm was red and sore and would be highly sensitive for a few days, a good reminder of the consequences of lack of control. His body would remember the punishment. His brain would learn to avoid it.

Control and reason must rule. He couldn't let his emotions affect his actions. He needed to think clearly. To be objective. To adjust his plan according to Chelsea's progress—not his anger.

He wouldn't make the same mistake again. Losing his temper, not being in control, had cost him too much already.

She would not get away. Her chain was secure. As a backup, he'd used a heavy-duty lock on the door. A wireless door alarm served as a third line of defense. If the door opened, he would get a notification on his phone app. He couldn't be here all the time, but no matter where he was, he'd know if she escaped.

There was nothing to worry about. She wasn't going anywhere.

Besides, he had expected her to rebel. It was part of his plan. If she didn't test the boundaries, he'd be disappointed. And every mistake she made was an opportunity to discipline her, to shape her behavior. He needed a strong woman, not a weak, easily dominated one. But Chelsea would have to adjust her decision-making process. When she was presented with options, she should consider *his* wants instead of her own. Eventually, her instinctive reaction would be *what does he want?*

When he'd first laid eyes on her, he'd known she was the woman for him. His perfect mate, she would be Eve to his Adam.

For him, it had been love at first sight.

Karma, fate, destiny. The label didn't matter. She was going to be his woman. It might take her a while to adjust to the idea, but when her conditioning was complete, she would submit to him as a woman should. And after she learned her lessons, he would cherish her forever.

Chelsea was smart. She was strong. She wasn't going to be easy to break. But that's exactly what he needed to do. He would take her to the root of who she was, and then he would cultivate the characteristics he chose. Like a well-tended hedge, her new personality would grow. And as it bloomed, he would shape it, trimming off her ugly traits and encouraging her desirable attributes until her character was amenable and pleasing to him.

It was simply a matter of working with nature rather than against it.

When a woman's survival was threatened, she tapped into the base instinct that would keep her alive. All humans were programmed for survival. The key would be to find the right combination of discipline and love.

Pain and pleasure.

Stick and carrot.

Stick first, though. Always.

Consequences were the key to any training. They should be severe enough that the subject took no action without careful consideration of the teacher's reaction. At first, she would do it to avoid punishment. She would learn to adapt her behavior to please him. As a reward, she'd be praised, fed, and kept warm. Eventually, she would associate his encouragement with comfort and his criticism with pain.

She would crave his approval like a drug.

He considered how quickly her shock, horror, and disbelief had shifted to acceptance. At first, she'd tried to shield herself from his blows, but then she'd realized it was pointless. He was in control. After she'd stopped defending herself, he'd come to his senses and stopped beating her.

Stick. Carrot.

How long would it take her to make the connection?

Would she remember all the rules he'd given her? Though the severity of the lesson was unintended, her progress pleased him.

He glanced back at the locked door. He'd left her naked, shivering, and cringing in pain. The cot and blanket sat just outside the door, waiting. At the first sign of acquiescence, the simple comforts would be returned, and step one in her transformation would be complete.

He tossed her socks onto the fire and added more dead leaves and dry sticks. The flames reached higher. The fire crackled.

She needed to be completely devoted to him. She must completely let go of the life she'd left behind. She was already beautiful and intelligent—when he was finished with her, she would be perfect.

Next, he'd push her even further.

He rubbed his hands together over the fire. He couldn't wait to continue. But he must be patient. She'd need some time to recover. To reflect on her behavior.

To realize the fruitlessness of any efforts to defy him.

To give up and give herself fully to him.

Chapter Eight

Lance skimmed through the remaining documents in Chelsea's file. Nothing jumped out at him. He closed the file on the card table in his office and sat back, letting the information sink into his head.

Sharp walked into the room. "I made you a shake." He handed Lance a nasty-looking green concoction.

"I will never get used to the way these look." Lance held up the glass and stared at the thick green liquid.

After he'd been shot in the thigh and almost died last year, his recovery had been long, painful, and frustrating. He'd gone back to the police force only to quit when his leg didn't hold up. He'd wallowed in pity at home, seeing little progress with his rehabilitation, until Sharp had convinced him to join his PI firm—and to try his organic-crunchy lifestyle. Several months after Lance had embraced his boss's way of life, his leg was mostly healed.

He doubted it would ever be 100 percent, but he could do most of the things he enjoyed. He'd even returned to coaching the hockey team for at-risk youths he'd volunteered with when he'd been on the police force.

Now instead of heading to the bar when he was stressed, Lance downed a green protein shake and went to bed early.

He was quite the party animal.

"Luckily, these drinks taste better than they look." Lance no longer questioned the ingredients. He'd learned his lesson and simply drank whatever his boss handed him.

To be fair, Sharp was more than his boss. After he'd been unable to find Lance's father, he'd taken ten-year-old Lance under his wing. Over the years, Sharp had driven him to hockey practice, given him the sex talk, and taught him to drive. He was the closest thing to a father Lance had.

Sharp took the empty glass back. "Ready to head over to Tim's house?"

Lance stood and reached for the flannel shirt he'd draped over his chair. "Yes. Want to ride along? We should get a good look at the wife's personal space."

"Let's go." Sharp fetched a jacket from his office.

Lance went to the closet and grabbed a high-capacity USB drive, then met Sharp and Morgan in the foyer.

"I'm off to see the sheriff." She slung her giant purse over one shoulder. She'd changed into what Lance called her lawyer uniform: a fitted navy-blue suit, white silk blouse, heels, and pearls. They all went outside together, and Sharp locked up the office.

Lance thought about kissing her goodbye, but the gesture felt awkward. Their relationship felt awkward, especially in front of Sharp. Instead, Lance said, "Good luck."

They parted on the sidewalk. Lance watched her walk away. The skirt and heels did magical things to her legs. She was all at once lady-like, professional, and unbelievably hot.

At least she was to him.

Morgan got into her minivan and drove off. Lance and Sharp settled in Lance's Jeep.

"What's going on between you two?" Sharp said before he'd even fastened his seat belt.

"It's hard to quantify." Lance started the engine and pulled away from the curb. "Her grandfather has been sick. She has her hands full, and we both know my mom is a lot to manage."

Sharp stared over the console. "Stop overthinking. You are not going to find another woman like that one. Make time for her. Do not fuck this up."

"That isn't my goal."

"You can't possibly manage every single piece of your mother's life forever. You're entitled to some happiness."

"I know." But it didn't feel that simple. His mother's mental health and physical safety required a delicate balance of medication, routine, and vigilance. He'd slacked off during college, and she'd needed inpatient treatment to get back on track. Since then, he'd erred on the side of micromanaging, but that didn't allow much room for a social life.

They drove the rest of the way in silence.

Chelsea and Tim lived in a quiet subdivision. As Lance turned the Jeep onto their street, he slowed to drive around a couple pushing a baby stroller. Ten feet ahead of them, a small child pedaled a tricycle. At three o'clock in the afternoon, grade school-aged kids swarmed a play lot in the center of the cul-de-sac.

Lance parked in front of Tim's house. It was a nice starter home, small but generally well kept. The lawn needed raking, but Lance supposed Tim had had little time or interest in yard work since his wife had vanished.

Two sedans were parked in the driveway, the Toyota that Tim had driven to Sharp Investigations and a late-model Dodge sedan.

Tim answered the door and let them into the house.

"Has the press been hounding you?" Sharp asked.

"They hung around the first day, then they seemed to lose interest." Tim ushered Lance and Sharp into the kitchen. Suitcases crowded a corner of the adjoining family room. "My in-laws just arrived. I don't know how I survived the last few days without them."

He introduced them to a couple in their late fifties.

Chelsea's mother, Patricia, was a tall, fit blonde woman who looked as if she could still hike all day. She wore black yoga pants and a sweater that ended midthigh. She had the sleeping baby draped over one cloth-covered shoulder while she rubbed his back in a circular motion.

Chelsea's dad, Randall, sat at the kitchen table with a little girl of about three perched on his lap. Lance assumed the child was Tim and Chelsea's oldest. Bella and her grandfather were working on a large-piece puzzle.

"We'd like to ask you both a few questions," Sharp said.

Dark circles and worry lined Patricia's eyes as she nodded. She glanced at the little girl on her husband's knee, clearly concerned about the child overhearing the upcoming conversation. "Tim, maybe you could take Bella and William to the playground."

"Yay." The little girl jumped off her grandfather's lap.

Tim did not appear to share his daughter's enthusiasm, but he simply said, "Good idea. Bella, get your coat and shoes. I'll put William in the stroller."

Bella skipped out of the room. The sounds of Tim getting the children ready floated back from the hallway. Bella chattered. The front door opened and closed.

After Tim and the children left, Patricia sat next to her husband at the kitchen table. The older couple joined hands, their fingers intertwining in a show of solidarity Lance admired. This was the way marriages were supposed to work. Couples should lean on each other.

"We usually stay in a hotel. The house is small. But this time . . ." Patricia said, "Tim needs help."

"When was the last time you talked to your daughter?" Sharp settled across from Randall.

Lance took the chair opposite Patricia.

A tear leaked from Patricia's eye. "Chelsea calls us almost every day. I spoke to her Friday morning." She pressed a clenched fist to her mouth. "She was looking forward to going out that night."

The poor woman.

"How was her mood? Did anything seem off?" Lance swallowed his pity and pushed aside memories of his own mother's confusion and grief after his father disappeared. More than two decades later, he could still see her as clear as day in his mind. The tears, the dark circles, the pale skin.

The way she'd seemed to fade away over the following months and years.

Patricia sniffed and wiped a fingertip under her eye. "She's had a rough time since the baby was born."

"It didn't have to be that tough. Tim could have been more useful." Randall scowled.

"So Tim isn't a good husband?" Lance asked.

"That's not fair, Rand." Patricia's knuckles whitened around her husband's. "Tim loves Chelsea. He's a hard worker who's trying to build a future for his family. And he's a nice boy."

"As smart as he is, that's exactly what he is—a boy." Randall didn't look convinced. "He needs to grow the hell up."

"Anyway, we're so glad Tim agreed to hire a private firm," Patricia said. "After speaking to the sheriff over the phone, we didn't have much confidence in his investigation."

"You asked Tim to hire us?" Lance asked.

Patricia's forehead wrinkled. "Not exactly. We were discussing our frustration with the sheriff. No matter how many times I told him Chelsea would never leave her babies, he seemed convinced that she was depressed and left on her own. Tim said he wished he could afford to hire his own investigator, but he didn't have the cash. So we gave him the money."

"Does Chelsea have an agenda book, a calendar, a place where she leaves notes for herself?" Lance asked.

Patricia slid a USB drive across the table. "Tim said he copied everything from her computer and phone onto this. As far as I know, she keeps her calendar and address book on her phone."

Lance pocketed the USB drive.

Of course, having all the information filtered through Tim had its downsides. Tim was skilled with computers. He could have purged any damaging tidbits before he handed the information over. But such was the challenge of working in the private sector. Lance couldn't go to a judge and get a subpoena for Tim's records.

"How about friends?" Sharp asked. "Do you know of any besides Fiona? Someone from back home?"

Patricia shook her head. "She lost touch with everyone back home when they moved here. Young children take up so much time. She has her coworkers, though she never mentioned being especially close to any of them. Randall, did she ever mention anyone to you?"

"Just her boss. What's his name?" Randall tilted his head, thinking. "MacDonald. Curtis MacDonald. She seemed to have a pretty good relationship with him."

"In what way?" Lance asked.

Randall shifted his weight as if suddenly uncomfortable. "Nothing inappropriate. She mentioned he was letting her work a little from home. She was supposed to go back to the office weeks ago, but William hasn't been cooperative."

"Is it all right if we take a look around?" Lance asked.

"Please do." Patricia wiped a teary eye. Randall put an arm around his wife's shoulders, pulled her closer, and kissed her temple. She closed her eyes and leaned into his shoulder.

Lance led Sharp from the room, giving Chelsea's parents privacy. But he glanced back at them over his shoulder. What would it be like to be that close to someone for thirty years? It would be amazing to have that level of comfort and support and love no matter what life threw at him.

Then he imagined having that partner ripped away, which is exactly what had happened to both his mother and Morgan. His mother had never recovered, and it had taken Morgan two years to come out from under her grief.

Everything had a price.

Even love.

Especially love.

In the foyer, Sharp poked him in the arm, breaking his depressing train of thought. "Earth to Lance."

"Sorry." Lance shook off the sad memories. "Where are we starting?"

Sharp opened the hall closet. "I'll go through coat pockets. You want to check out the bedroom?"

Lance turned toward the stairs. "On it."

At the top landing, he glanced in each doorway. One bedroom was an explosion of pink and purple with a clear princess theme. Primary colors and trains decorated the nursery. Lance stopped in the doorway of the master bedroom. A man's watch on the nightstand told him that Tim slept on the right side of the bed.

Lance went to the left side and opened the single drawer. ChapStick. Moisturizer. Pens. Normal stuff. Nothing interesting. The bottom shelf held a few mystery and romance novels, plus a reference book on infant care. Lance picked each book up and made sure nothing was stashed between the pages. The dresser was piled high with clean, folded laundry. Next to the laundry sat a laptop.

Tim's?

No. Patricia said that the computer downstairs was used by both Tim and Chelsea.

Curiosity pulled Lance toward the dresser. He paused and listened for voices. Patricia and Randall were still in the kitchen. Tim hadn't come back yet. Lance raised the lid and turned on the computer.

A few minutes later, he'd determined the laptop was owned by Skyver and MacDonald, the firm Chelsea worked for. Lance tried to poke around, but the files were password-protected. He took his flash drive from his pocket and plugged it in to the USB port. A few keystrokes later, the computer hummed as it copied files.

Had the police looked at the work computer? Probably not. They would need permission or a search warrant, given the confidential nature of accounting. Lance doubted Chelsea's boss would have been able to give access without consulting each and every client whose files were on the computer. And a search warrant wasn't likely to be granted with no link to Chelsea's employer. Hell, the police didn't even have any evidence that foul play of any sort had occurred in Chelsea's disappearance.

Lance left the computer chugging away and searched the dresser and closet. Chelsea and Tim owned mostly casual wardrobes. Lance checked jacket pockets, then sifted through the garbage can for any important notes. He found nothing unusual.

Chelsea and Tim seemed perfectly ordinary, at least on the surface.

"Lance?" Sharp called from the hallway.

Lance relaxed. "In here."

"I've checked most of downstairs," Sharp said from the hallway. "I found two iPads. One must belong to Chelsea." Walking into the bedroom, Sharp glanced at the computer on the dresser and raised his brows. Lance shook his head and put a finger to his pursed lips.

Sharp's mouth flattened with suspicion. "Did you search the bathroom?"

"Not yet."

Sharp went into the adjoining bath. Lance heard cabinets opening and closing.

Ten minutes later, Lance disconnected the hard drive, shut down the laptop, and slid the flash drive back into his pocket just as Sharp emerged from the bathroom.

"Nothing unusual," he said. "Her travel makeup bag is still in there. No interesting prescriptions."

The front door slammed, a baby cried, and a little girl chattered. Lance and Sharp went back downstairs.

In the foyer, Patricia took the baby from Tim, and Randall helped Bella take off her jacket while Tim hung his own in the hall closet. With a quick glance between them, Randall and Patricia led the children toward the stairway.

"Let's read a story." Randall took his granddaughter's hand.

Lance waited until they disappeared at the top of the steps. "Tim, there's another laptop upstairs. Is it yours?"

Tim shook his head. "No. That's Chelsea's work computer. In fact, I have to return it to her office today. I was supposed to do it yesterday, but I got hung up with the kids."

"I don't suppose the police had a look at it?" Lance asked.

"No. They said they couldn't. I don't know why it would matter. There's nothing personal on it. It's all spreadsheets. Chelsea was trying to catch up with her clients' books."

"Then I think we have everything we need for now," Sharp said.

Lance and Sharp left the house and returned to the Jeep.

Sharp slid into the passenger seat. "Drop me at the office before you take Tim's data to your mom."

"We could just drive out there now."

"No," Sharp said. "Morgan is safe enough at the sheriff's department, but if she beats us back to the office, she's liable to head off on her own if the sheriff gave her a lead." Sharp lifted a hand. "Don't give me a bullshit argument about her being able to defend herself. I have enormous respect for her. I don't want you looking for a potential kidnapper on your own either."

"You don't have to convince me. I worry about her more than you do for rational and irrational reasons."

"Glad we're on the same page." Sharp fastened his seat belt. "So whose computer were you copying in the bedroom?"

Once again, Sharp earned his name. He didn't miss a trick.

"It belongs to Chelsea's accounting firm," Lance admitted.

"You know that copying those files was illegal."

Lance started the engine. "Only if I get caught. The operating system's auditing capability wasn't enabled. So there's no record of my activity. No one will know the files were copied."

"Sloppy data security for an accounting firm," Sharp said.

"Definitely," Lance agreed. "If there's nothing suspicious in the files, no one will ever know."

"And if there is?"

"Then we'll cross that bridge when we get to it." Lance drove toward the office. "But I'll go through the computer files myself. I don't want to bring my mom into anything . . . unscrupulous."

"Illegal," Sharp clarified.

"Technicality." Lance felt Sharp's laser gaze on his face.

"This case must bring back painful memories, but you can't let your personal history affect your actions. You've come a long way since your dad disappeared. Don't do something stupid because you can't be objective."

Lance glanced at his boss. "Good thing we have an excellent attorney in the building."

"I mean it."

"OK. OK." Lance held up a hand.

"I will not bail your ass out of jail." Sharp's mouth went tight.

But Lance knew his boss would bail him out in a second. Sharp would be pissed, but he'd be there. As always.

"I'll be careful." To Lance this could never be just a case. A woman's life—and the future of her two children—depended on this investigation.

He would not wish his own life upon those kids. All the years of not knowing. Of wondering if their missing parent was a victim of violence or if they'd been abandoned. Neither option was optimal, but both were better than no closure at all.

He wouldn't be able to live with himself unless he did everything within his power to find Chelsea Clark, no matter how many rules he had to break.

Chapter Nine

The sheriff's office was located near the county jail and municipal complex. After verifying that the sheriff's car was parked behind the building, Morgan opened the glass door and stepped into the lobby. Inside, the ugly brown brick building was old, worn, and thoroughly unattractive, from the scraped linoleum floor to the stained dropped ceiling tiles. The sheriff didn't waste money on decor.

She went to the reception counter. At a desk a few feet away, a woman glanced up from a computer. She looked like a grandma, about sixty years old, soft all over, with dark-brown dyed hair.

But when she crossed the floor to address Morgan, Grandma's voice was sugarcoated steel. "Can I help you?"

Morgan's smile didn't earn her one in return. "I'm Morgan Dane. I'm here to see Sheriff King."

"Is he expecting you?"

"No." Considering their last phone interaction hadn't been entirely pleasant, Morgan had opted not to warn him. Showing up unannounced seemed like her best option. It was harder to ignore someone in person. "But he knows who I am."

Behind her reading glasses, Grandma raised her penciled-on eyebrows. "I'll need to see some ID."

Morgan fished her wallet out of the depths of her tote bag.

Grandma considered Morgan's driver's license for a few seconds before handing it back. "Wait here."

She turned away and disappeared down a hallway. Two additional administrative employees bustled behind the counter, answering phones and working on computers. The sheriff's office of a rural county was always busy.

In addition to regular policing, the sheriff was responsible for the county jail, prisoner transport, and serving warrants. As an elected official, he was also forced to be part politician or face not being reelected.

At least most sheriffs did. King seemed immune to bad press. Last year, his office had been accused of roughing up a prisoner. The sheriff's popularity had soared.

Grandma's soft but firm voice floated back to the lobby. "I will *not* tell her you left. Your car is parked out back, and she can probably hear your voice."

Morgan couldn't make out the sheriff's words, but the deep grumble that answered didn't sound promising. It sounded more like profanity.

"I know you're busy, but you have an election coming up in a few weeks," Grandma said.

More grumbling followed.

But Grandma wasn't fazed. "I'm bringing her back. Be nice."

She returned. "You can go on in." She gestured toward the hallway.

Morgan rounded the counter and went through the doorway. A short corridor opened into a larger room filled with desks and computers. A deputy fielded a phone call and typed on his keyboard.

On the other side of the room, a door opened and a uniformed deputy marched a handcuffed man through a side entrance. The front of his worn jeans and white undershirt were stained with dried blood.

Of all the luck . . .

She had to run into Tyler Green.

His previously handsome face had been transformed by her elbow. Both eyes were blackening. Cotton rolls protruded from his nostrils, and a bandage was taped over the bridge of his swollen nose.

He spied Morgan across the room. A nasty gleam lit his eyes. Morgan's pulse spiked, and her empty stomach cartwheeled as adrenaline flooded her system.

I'm going to get you, he mouthed, his gaze locked on hers. The deputy gave him a not-so-gentle push into a chair.

A tall, broad-shouldered man tossed a file onto the deputy's desk. Sheriff King.

He was at least six feet three inches tall and could have stepped out of an old Western. He wore jeans, a tan uniform shirt, and cowboy boots. Though she knew he was only in his midfifties, he looked older, his skin as weathered and worn as an unpainted fence.

"Hey, Green," the sheriff said in a curt tone. "Shut it." His scowl landed on Morgan, and he gestured toward an open door on the other side of the room. "Come this way."

As they entered his office, she caught sight of a uniform Stetson-style hat hanging on a coat-tree in the corner. Seriously, all the man needed was a horse.

He motioned to a guest chair and left the room.

Morgan slipped out of her trench coat, folded it over the adjacent chair, and smoothed her skirt, grateful that she'd started leaving several changes of clothes and shoes in her office closet. These days, she never knew if she'd have to interview a witness or traipse through a muddy field.

The sheriff returned a minute later with two bottles of water. He perched on the edge of his desk, offered her a bottle, and stared down at her. "So, you're Morgan Dane?"

"Yes." Morgan accepted the water. "Thank you."

She'd seen the sheriff on television, and his reputation had preceded him. He was a hard man, and he looked the part. The tanned skin around his eyes and mouth was deeply lined, as if he squinted and frowned most of the time. His nose was crooked, and a scar bisected one eyebrow. She wasn't surprised at his rough appearance, but his eyes flickered with surprise as they swept over her from head to foot and back again, which was odd. She'd conducted several press conferences during her last case and had no doubt he would have watched them.

"Your appearance is deceiving." He looked at her as if he didn't know quite what to do with her. "Tyler Green obviously underestimated you as well."

Remembering the morning's incident, Morgan flushed.

"Green's nose is broken. He's complaining about headaches and back pain. My deputy was tied up all morning at the ER, and I've been fielding calls from Green's lawyer." King's mouth twisted as he said *lawyer*. "What a pain in my ass."

Me or Tyler?

King's jaw tightened. His tone was all you-don't-belong-here. "You got lucky this morning. He could have hurt you."

Morgan swallowed the retorts on her lips about him being sexist and minding his own business. She needed his cooperation. Butting heads with him wouldn't get it. "I wasn't alone."

"I should hope not."

"And I assure you, my breaking Green's nose wasn't an accident."

Another quick flash of surprise flickered in his eyes, then resignation, and just a little respect. He pushed off the desk and moved behind it. His chair squeaked as he settled his heavy body into it. "So, I hear you officially hung out your shingle. Did you decide criminal defense was more lucrative than working for the prosecutor's office?"

"It isn't about money." Morgan paused. "I come from a family of cops. My brother is NYPD SWAT. My sister is a detective with the SFPD. My grandfather is a retired homicide detective, and my father died in the line of duty. I believe in justice, and I'll fight for it. But I'm afraid my chance to work for the DA has passed."

The sheriff coughed. Was that a grin he was trying to hide with his hand? "Sweetheart, you blew by that chance like Richard Petty."

Morgan's brain stuttered. *Did he just call her* sweetheart?

"So why are you here today?" he asked.

"I'm representing Tim Clark."

The sheriff shifted his weight forward. His forearms landed on his desk. "Tim hasn't been charged with a crime. Why does he need a lawyer?"

"After the publicity of last month's false arrest, he's concerned with your focus on him as a suspect in his wife's disappearance."

King scraped a hand down his battered face. "I assume Sharp and Kruger are on board?"

Morgan nodded. "Yes. Tim wants his wife found."

"We're doing everything we can to find his wife. Since you're from a family of cops, you know I can't talk about an active case." King could share information. He was choosing not to.

"We're both on the same side," Morgan said. "All we want to do is find Chelsea Clark and bring her back to her family."

And protect Tim's legal interests.

"And we are in the middle of our official investigation into her disappearance," King said in an end-of-discussion tone.

"Anything you can tell me would help. I know you're swamped here. You can't possibly give Chelsea's case a hundred percent of your attention. Sharp and Kruger are experienced investigators who can focus solely on finding Chelsea. You don't have the manpower or the budget."

King studied her without responding. Despite his reputation as a good lawman, he was also stubborn and arrogant. Morgan could not force him to cooperate. She needed a new approach, but King wouldn't fall for any bullshit. Her argument would have to be sincere, and something he couldn't argue with. And something that had nothing to do with his department's ability. She needed to throw him off balance, to appeal to him in a human way.

She chose the one thing many men, particularly manly men, weren't comfortable handling: emotion.

"My youngest was an infant when my husband was killed in Iraq."

King blinked. "I'm sorry."

Morgan let her true emotions show on her face. "I know what it's like to be left alone to raise young children. I know what it's like to wish your kids remembered their father. I know what it's like to have to explain, over and over, why Daddy won't ever be coming home. Unless someone finds his wife, Tim Clark won't even have an explanation for his children. Grief is hard enough to survive. I don't want them to have to live with not knowing what happened to their mother."

She had lived under a dark cloud for two long, exhausting years. She was just recently emerging from her depression, blinking at the sunlight, almost as if she'd just discovered that she deserved to have a life. She still missed and loved John but knew that he would have been angry if she wasted the rest of her life being sad.

That she shouldn't feel guilty for allowing herself to be happy.

King glanced away, his expression conflicted, his movements awkward. He got up abruptly and paced the floor behind his desk. His long legs ate up the space with two strides in each direction. He looked like a frustrated predator trapped in a too-small cage. "I don't want to jeopardize our investigation."

"How many leads has your department turned up?"

He stopped. His face hardened. "We both know that most missing adults leave because they want to, and they eventually turn up on their own."

"And you have limited resources. I understand." Morgan used his argument against him.

"I assure you that Chelsea Clark's case is a priority for this department."

"Look, Sheriff, I don't want to step on any toes." But she would if she had to. "I understand your position completely." She shifted her weight, as if ready to leave. "I can always put Tim Clark and his two babies on the news and appeal to the public for help. I'll leave it up to you to explain where you are in your investigation to the press."

Which would publicly highlight his department's lack of progress on a case he'd managed to keep relatively low-key up until this point.

He hooked his thumbs in the front pockets of his jeans and sighed. "We have found no sign of foul play at this time."

"Fingerprints in the car?" Morgan settled back into the chair.

"Sure. Mrs. Clark's and others, but no criminal matches yet."

"You're submitting the prints to local, state, and federal databases?" she asked. In addition to the FBI's national IAFIS system, state and local agencies kept their own records. Typically, it was most efficient to begin with a local search and expand geographically.

"Of course." The sheriff turned to face Morgan head-on. "And the seat was in an expected position for a woman of Chelsea's height."

"Do you really think she was taken or she went willingly?"

"We don't know for certain. There was no blood in the vehicle, and her purse was gone."

"So no sign of a struggle," Morgan said. "What did you find out about the husband?"

"We found nothing suspicious in his background, and his cell phone records indicate his phone was where he said he was last Friday night." King eased a hip onto the side of his desk. "We checked out the friend Chelsea was supposed to meet, and Chelsea's boss. They both have clean records as well. Both seemed upset by Chelsea's disappearance."

"What about the area around her car?"

"We walked a grid. Came up empty. My deputies knocked on doors down the road. Nobody saw anything. According to the surveillance video at the train station, only two people got on the train at the station that night. Neither of them was a young blonde woman."

"Could we have a copy?"

"No."

Morgan opened her mouth to protest, but the sheriff raised a hand to silence her.

"But I will let you view it here," he said.

"Thank you," Morgan said.

If Tim had been arrested and charged in the disappearance of his wife, Morgan would have been entitled to all the sheriff's evidence via the discovery process. But without any formal charges, Morgan would have to accept whatever crumbs the sheriff was willing to toss her way.

"I assume you entered Chelsea in the NCIC?" Morgan asked.

The National Crime Information Center was an FBI database of criminal justice information that included details on everything from fugitives to stolen property to missing persons. If a body or incapacitated person meeting Chelsea's description turned up anywhere in the country, law enforcement would be aware that she was missing.

"I did."

"Did you run a check on similar crimes?"

The sheriff held up a hand. "Of course I did, but there weren't many details to enter. We have no proof a crime was even committed."

"Tim said you brought in a dog."

"Yes. But the dog didn't pick up a scent either, so if she was at the scene, we assume she left by vehicle."

"But you don't know that she was ever there. If someone abducted her, he could have taken her somewhere else and then dumped the car near the train station."

"Or Chelsea had someone pick her up," King added. "It isn't a crime to walk away from your family."

"Why would you think Chelsea walked away from her family? She has two children." Even as Morgan said the words, she knew the weakness in her argument. People did unexpected things all the time.

Terrible, cruel things a normal person couldn't fathom.

"The husband admitted his wife was having a rough time with the second baby, and that he didn't give her much help. I spoke with her parents out in Colorado. Both said how tired their daughter has been, how often she cried over the phone. And her best friend, Fiona West, painted a less rosy picture of Tim and Chelsea's marriage than Tim did."

Morgan put Fiona at the top of her interview list, and doubts about Tim's innocence nagged at her.

"I know it must be hard for you as a devoted mother to think about a woman abandoning her children." The sheriff's tone softened. "But it happens."

Morgan had no difficulty imagining women doing far worse things to their children. She'd prosecuted enough monster mothers. A shudder rippled through her as she remembered a few horrific cases. "You're right. Not all women were born with maternal instincts."

King continued. "Chelsea was feeling neglected and exhausted. Maybe she needed a break and wanted to teach Tim a lesson."

"Let's hope that's the case." Morgan finished the water, tossed the empty bottle in the trash, and stood. "Because I'd like nothing more than to have her show up safe and sound."

"I'll have someone pull up the train station surveillance video so you can watch it before you leave. It won't take long. There's so little activity, you can fast-forward through most of it." Leaning forward, the sheriff tugged the scarf away from Morgan's neck. His eyebrows shot up as the corners of his mouth went down. "Are those from this morning?"

"They look worse than they feel." Morgan turned toward the door. "Thank you for your help. I'll call you if we learn anything."

"Same here." King nodded. "You should be more careful. It would be a damned shame if someone wrung that pretty neck."

Chapter Ten

"Are you sure you want to do this?" Lance rounded the desk in his mother's home office and kissed her on the cheek.

"Of course." His mom tapped her keyboard, blackening her computer screen, then she swiveled her chair to face him. "I like to feel useful."

What had she been doing that she felt necessary to hide?

File in hand, Lance hesitated. Would the case be too much stress for her? The smile on her face didn't resonate in her eyes. She tucked a lock of shoulder-length gray hair behind one ear. Had she lost weight? Her fragile-thin frame couldn't spare an ounce. But since Lance saw her every day, he didn't always notice slight changes, and he couldn't quite quantify what was wrong today.

She wouldn't meet his gaze. Her blue eyes seemed paler, her skin flushed, and her attempt to smile more transparent.

He scanned the tidy room. "No boxes today?"

The modern world of online shopping was an agoraphobic hoarder's dream come true. Lance and his mom had an agreement. She ordered things she didn't need every day. If she wanted to keep a purchase, she had to dispose of an item of equal size. Lance returned or donated the rest. The system was bizarre, but it kept Jennifer Kruger's home relatively sane and safe. Lance would not allow her to live in a firetrap ever again.

"No." She took the file from his hand and spun away from him.

Strange.

But maybe be was being paranoid. With good reason, he was hyper-aware of her behavior.

Clutching the edges of her thick cardigan together, she set the folder on the blotter. "Tell me about the case."

Again, Lance hesitated. Chelsea's disappearance had brought back painful memories for him. How would his mother handle the parallels? Over the years that followed his father's disappearance, she'd retreated into an eggshell of an existence. Her world was self-contained, easily shattered, and impossible to make whole.

"We're looking for someone," he said vaguely. "We need thorough background checks for the people on this list, and we need you to review the missing woman's computer and phone files." He set Tim's USB drive on the desk.

She scanned the first few pages of their suspect list. "This is about that young mother who went missing, isn't it?"

Shit.

"You know about her?" Lance asked.

His mother turned a page. "It was on the news."

His shut-in mother taught online computer science courses and designed and maintained websites. Since she only left her house to go to therapy, she literally lived online. Coverage of Chelsea's case had been limited, but his mom hadn't missed the story.

"Maybe I should do the background checks," Lance said.

"No." His mom put a possessive hand flat on the file as if he were going to snatch it away. "Do you want me to do a deep dig on the husband?"

His mom's precarious mental state often camouflaged her intelligence. She knew Tim would be a suspect despite the fact that he'd hired them.

"Yes," he said.

"Hi, Jennifer." Morgan walked into the room. She'd come with Lance but had been in the kitchen putting away groceries they'd brought. Knowing Morgan, she'd also taken stock of mom's supplies.

Lance's mom's face went as bright as the Christmas tree in Rockefeller Center. He needed to have a talk with her. She was clearly building up unreasonable expectations about his relationship with Morgan.

How could he ever have a real life? There were too many variables to predict his mother's reaction.

Damn it.

He should never have introduced them. His intentions had been good. Morgan would give his mother another person to interact with besides him and Sharp and the package delivery man.

Now if things didn't work out between him and Morgan, his mother was going to be disappointed. Who knew how she would handle it? And what if she got her hopes up about having grandchildren and that didn't pan out. Could she even handle grandchildren?

Why was he thinking about giving her grandchildren?

Suddenly hot, Lance pulled at the neck of his T-shirt. The room felt small. Morgan already had three kids.

Three.

Her life was a 24/7 power play to the kids' advantage. Would she want more? Why was he even thinking about this?

His mom stood, leaned over the desk, and touched Morgan's arm. It wasn't quite a hug, but it was the most physical contact his mom had had with a human other than him or Sharp in a long time.

Morgan returned the touch, as usual letting his mother set the boundaries. "I hope you don't mind. I started a pot of coffee, and we brought apple pie."

Mom beamed. "Of course I don't mind. I love pie."

That, at least, was the truth.

Dropping back into her seat, his mom waved at the file in front of her. "This is just a list of names. Tell me more about the case. Did Chelsea Clark really just disappear into thin air?"

Like his dad.

"We don't have enough information to say yet." Morgan smiled.

His mom nodded, her face grim.

"I could really go for some pie." Morgan shot Lance a worried glance. "Why don't we talk in the kitchen?"

Morgan and Lance took twenty minutes to fill his mom in on the necessary details of the case. His mother ate an entire slice of pie, which eased his mind. Anxiety dampened her appetite. So her being able to eat was a good sign.

"You're sure you don't mind doing those background checks?" he asked his mom.

"I want to do them. I get bored." She kissed him goodbye and then shooed them toward the door.

Outside, Lance stood on the front step and stared at the closed door. The he dug his phone from his pocket and called Sharp. "Would you mind stopping in to see my mom?"

"Tonight?" Sharp asked.

"It's not an emergency." Lance glanced back at the house.

"But—"

"She seemed . . . off." Lance wanted another opinion. Sharp was less paranoid.

"I'll go tonight," Sharp said.

"Thanks." Lance ended the call. He would check on his mom later too.

"What's wrong?" Morgan asked.

"I don't know. Maybe nothing." Unease filled Lance's gut.

"She seemed happy. She ate her pie."

Lance turned and started toward the Jeep. "I know."

"But you're afraid the case will remind her of your father." Morgan fell into step beside him.

"Yes." Though his mom had seemed off even before he'd brought up the case.

"Do you want to stay with her? I can handle the interview with Fiona."

He glanced at her. The scarf around her neck hid the bruises, but he knew they were there, darkening by the hour. After today's incident, he wanted to keep Morgan close. Rationally he knew Tyler Green was safely in custody, but Lance's feelings for Morgan weren't always rational.

"No," he said. "I'll come back tonight and make sure she's all right."

They got into his Jeep, and Morgan read him the address of Fiona West's apartment.

She fastened her seat belt. "How do *you* feel about working on a case so similar to your father's disappearance?"

Lance almost brushed off her question then changed his mind. "I can definitely relate to how Tim's feeling right now."

"I'm sure you can."

He backed out of the driveway and turned the Jeep back toward town. "I still haven't opened Sharp's case file on my dad's investigation."

A few weeks before, Sharp had turned over the information, saying that it was now up to Lance if he wanted to know the particulars of his father's disappearance.

Morgan didn't say anything, but she reached across the console and took his hand.

"I'm afraid I'll be sucked in," Lance said. "Or that my mom will somehow find out. The last thing she needs is anything to bring back memories of those years."

"Do you know any of the details?"

Lance sighed. "I know the basic information. I was only ten when it happened. Sharp shared as much as he thought I could handle. Frankly, there wasn't much to share. Not many leads ever turned up. Those were the days before cell phones, before surveillance cameras were every-where, before E-ZPass and GPS made it hard to disappear. People still used cash in the nineties."

"So why would you dig in to the case?" Morgan asked. "Was there DNA or other physical evidence that could be analyzed with more precision now?"

"I don't think so."

Her fingers squeezed his. "Sharp is a good detective, and you said he worked your father's case for years. I doubt he would have overlooked anything."

"I know." *But did he?* Lance wouldn't know for sure unless he reviewed the file.

"If anything, there will be less evidence now. Memories fade over time. People will have left their jobs. Twenty-three years is a long time."

"You're right." But could he live with not even trying? Uncomfortable, Lance turned the conversation back to the case. "Tell me about Fiona."

Morgan opened a file. "Fiona West is twenty-six years old. She works as a fitness instructor and teaches yoga. She's lived in Scarlet Falls all her life. We don't have our full background check yet, but the sheriff said they found nothing alarming in her history. King wasn't the most forthcoming member of law enforcement I've dealt with. I have no doubt he held back information on the case, but I don't think he'd outright lie."

"Right," Lance agreed. "King is cantankerous and tight-lipped, but he's always been a straight shooter in my dealings with him."

A few minutes later, Lance turned into the entrance to Fiona's apartment complex and parked. He and Morgan walked to a door on the first floor of a plain brick building. Morgan had called ahead. Fiona was home and expecting them.

She opened her door on the first knock. "Come in."

The apartment was a square. A small eat-in kitchen opened to a living room. A hallway presumably led to the single bedroom and bath. Through sliding glass doors, a tiny patio overlooked a strip of grass and the parking lot beyond. No fancy views.

The best word to describe Fiona was *cute*. Dressed in yoga pants and an oversize shirt, she was a little thing—maybe an inch over five feet tall—perky and fit, with big brown eyes and curly brown hair cut short.

After offering them coffee, which they declined, she sat on a futon-type sofa and curled her legs underneath her body in a way that made Lance's knees hurt.

Morgan sat on the futon with Fiona while Lance eased carefully into a modern, metal-framed chair that looked as if it might snap shut at any moment.

"Where did you meet Chelsea?" Morgan started.

Fiona shifted her position and hugged her knees to her chest. "At the yoga studio. I teach there a few nights a week."

Lance leaned forward, resting his forearms on his thighs. "How often did Chelsea come to class?"

"Before she had William, she came three times a week. She practiced right up until she gave birth," Fiona said. "But afterward, she was a mess."

"Babies are a handful," Morgan commiserated. "And I hear William is particularly difficult."

Fiona's lips mashed flat. "Especially if your husband makes no attempt to help. I don't understand why Chelsea put up with him. She did everything."

Morgan tilted her head and nodded.

Tim might not have helped much with the baby, but he clearly went to work and paid the bills. But Lance was not going to argue. He kept his mouth firmly shut. Arguing with a witness wasn't the best way to encourage the free flow of information.

Anger sharpened Fiona's tone. "I stopped by to see her a couple of times a week. All she did was cry. I was worried she had postpartum depression."

"Did you talk to her about it?" Morgan asked.

Fiona nodded, her eyes shining with moisture. She grabbed a tissue from a box on the coffee table and blotted her eyes. "I did. I tried to get her to see a psychiatrist. She said she just needed some sleep." Fiona blew her nose. "In Tim's defense, the baby wouldn't drink from a bottle, and Chelsea refused to be firm. She gave in every time. She's a pushover when it comes to her kids. I kept telling her if she was out of the house, the baby would figure it out." Fiona lowered the tissue to her lap. "And Tim would have to do more."

"You don't think Tim had anything to do with her disappearance, do you?" Lance asked.

Fiona looked horrified. "No. God. No. I didn't mean anything like that. Tim's a perfectly nice guy. He's just clueless and, frankly, a little whiny."

Morgan leaned forward a little. "Fiona, I hate to even ask this, but I have to."

Fiona's eyes opened wide. "What?"

"Is there any chance that Chelsea was so desperate that she needed to get away for a little while?"

"Are you asking me if Chelsea left her family?" Fiona asked.

"Yes." Morgan nodded. "Part of lending fresh eyes to the case means we have to consider every possibility."

Fiona shook her head hard. "No. No way. Chelsea loves those kids to death. She'd never leave them."

"What about Tim? Would she ever leave Tim?" Morgan asked.

"I don't think so." But Fiona didn't seem as adamant. "She excuses everything he does. 'Tim goes to work all day. Tim's tired. He's great with Bella.' That sort of thing. But even as she says it, you can tell she doesn't think he helps out enough. But even if she was mad at Tim, she would never leave her kids."

Morgan nodded. "She sounds like a wonderful mom and wife."

"She is." Fiona sniffed again.

"It's a shame she and Tim were going through a rough patch," Morgan empathized.

"It wasn't just a rough patch." Fiona shook her head. "They were having problems long before now."

Morgan tilted her head. "What kind of problems?"

"Tim worked too much. Last year, Chelsea told me she felt like they were growing apart." Fiona's mouth twisted. "Then she did something really stupid. She got pregnant. I told her another baby would only make their problems worse, but she thought it would bring them together again."

"But it didn't," Lance said.

"No." Fiona sniffed.

"When was the last time you saw her?" Lance asked.

"I stopped by their house on Wednesday," Fiona said.

"Was anything odd about her appearance or behavior?" he pressed.

"She was tired." Fiona tossed her tissue in a wastebasket. "She'd just gotten back from a run. I watched the kids so she could take a quick shower."

"How was William?"

"I tried to do a puzzle with Bella, but I ended up just walking in circles with the baby instead. He cried the whole time she was out of his sight." Fiona picked at a fingernail. "But that's normal for him."

"The crying didn't bother you?" Morgan asked. "My youngest was colicky. The screaming can get to you after hours and hours of it."

Fiona shuddered. "It was nerve-racking, but I wanted to help. I don't know how Chelsea stands listening to him bawl day and night."

Lance added, "But other than the crying baby, nothing seemed abnormal?"

"No." Fiona used her fingertips to swipe a tear from under one eye.

"Were you surprised when she didn't show up on Friday night?" Morgan asked.

Fiona shook her head. "No. We were supposed to meet two weeks ago, but Chelsea was a no-show. I called her and she didn't answer. I worried all night. The next morning, she sent me a text apologizing for blowing me off, saying William had had a bad night. God forbid Tim handle the baby for one evening."

"So Friday night, you assumed the same thing had happened," Morgan said. "When did you talk to Chelsea last?"

"Around seven. She was really excited to see me." Fiona ignored a second tear. Her eyes were bright with tears as she lifted her gaze to Morgan and then Lance. "So where is she?"

"We're going to do everything we can to find her." Morgan asked a few more personal questions about Chelsea, but all of Fiona's answers matched Tim's.

"Please call me if you have any more questions," Fiona said as she escorted them to the door. "I'll do anything to help find Chelsea."

Back in the Jeep, Lance started the engine. "What do you think? Is she being too hard on Tim or is he a self-absorbed jerk?"

"Hard to say." Morgan set her bag on the floor. "Keep in mind, Fiona isn't married and doesn't have kids. From the outside, it may have appeared as if Chelsea was on her own. Who knew what it was really like? When Tim was in our office, he might not have seemed completely comfortable with the baby, but he was hardly incompetent. Clearly, he's handled a baby in the past."

"You're probably right. Their little girl acted very comfortable with him this afternoon." Lance drove toward the office. "What do you want to do for dinner?"

Morgan checked the time on her phone. "We don't have much time before our meeting with Tim's boss at Speed Net."

"You hate to miss dinner with your girls."

"It can't be helped tonight. Gianna will feed them. Maybe I can make it home for bedtime." Morgan had a family friend who insisted on performing live-in nanny duties in return for her keep.

"I know you want to find Chelsea, but we have to eat."

Morgan skipped way too many meals.

"You're right," she said. "I just want to find her. I'll take the Clarks' financial records home with me tonight. I can go through them after the kids go to bed."

"Sharp said he'd work on the phone records. I guess that leaves me with social media accounts." Lance drove toward a deli.

Neither Morgan nor Sharp nor Lance would ever be the kind of professionals who could leave a case like Chelsea's at the office at five o'clock. But on the other side of the equation, they couldn't neglect the loved ones who depended on them. It was going to be a long night—the first of many until they found Chelsea Clark.

Alive or dead.

Chapter Eleven

The lobby of Speed Net reminded Lance of a trendy loft—sleek, industrial, and slightly cold. Building security rivaled that of a bank vault. Instead of glass, the front door was made of steel. Lance and Morgan had been buzzed into the building after speaking to the receptionist via a video intercom.

Lance had expected the start-up tech firm to employ a young, hip receptionist, but the woman sitting at the modern desk was middle-aged and dressed in comfortable navy-blue slacks and a white cardigan. She rounded the desk to greet them, and Lance suspected her heavy-soled black shoes were orthopedic.

The nameplate on the desk read BARBARA PAGANO.

Speed Net was founded by Elliot Pagano. Could this be his mother?

Morgan introduced them and handed the receptionist a business card.

"Hello. I'm Barbara. Elliot is waiting for you." Her smile was a thousand times warmer than the metal-and-glass space around her. Lance half expected her to offer him a cookie.

Barbara stepped in front of a number pad and entered a code. Then she pressed her thumb to a small glass plate. The door unlocked with a soft *snick*, and she opened it. "This way, please."

Lance and Morgan followed Barbara into a large, open industrial-looking room filled with long tables, desks, and computer equipment. At the far end of the room, a few couches and overstuffed chairs were grouped around a large screen TV. Video-game controllers and soda cans littered the sleek coffee table. The ceiling was at least thirty feet high. The people milling around in their jeans and T-shirts and sneakers could have passed for the cast of *American Pie*. They crossed the polished concrete floor to a glassed-in conference room.

Morgan set her tote on the floor and sat in a gray leather chair at the table.

"You're Elliot's mom?" Lance asked.

"I am." Barbara smiled. Her eyes shone with pride. "He doesn't just let me work here; Elliot employs the whole family. There's his dad and brother, Derek." She pointed through the glass. At the far side of the cavernous outer room, two men were installing some sort of conduit along the base of the brick wall. "He'd be furious if he heard me say this, but Elliot is such a good boy. He takes care of all of us. Here he is now."

The door opened and a young man walked in. Elliot wore jeans, sneakers, and a gray *Doctor Who* T-shirt emblazoned with a spinning TARDIS. His hair was short but in need of a trim. A thick chunk fell over his brow. According to their preliminary information, Elliot was a twenty-seven-year-old, self-made multimillionaire. He might be young, but he had the self-assured bearing of a more experienced man.

"Thanks, Mom," Elliot said to Barbara as she bowed out of the room.

Lance held out a hand. "Thanks for meeting with us."

"I'll do anything to help. I can't believe Chelsea is missing." Elliot shook their hands and sat across from Morgan. Lance took the chair beside her. Tim had provided basic information about his employer. Elliot had built the company from the ground up after selling his previous start-up for a huge chunk of change. Not bad for a guy who had dropped out of college at the age of twenty.

"Nice that you let your parents work here," Lance said.

"I tried to give them money, but my father practically burst a vein at the thought of taking money he hadn't earned." Elliot sighed.

"Hard to fault him for having a good work ethic," Lance pointed out.

"This is true," Elliot agreed. "Most of my employees got here by being smart and working hard. Of all of them, I have the most respect for Tim. I grew up poor, but I had the support and love of my parents. Family is everything to me. I don't know how I would have handled my wife's death without my family. Tim didn't have that support network growing up, but I'm glad Chelsea's family is here with him now."

"I'm sorry for your loss," Morgan said.

Elliot was a widower? But then losing a spouse so young could explain Elliot's maturity.

"How much do you know about Tim's background?" Morgan asked.

"Tim was up front about his family's legal issues since his personal information gets mixed up with his father's." Elliot interlaced his fingers and leaned on his forearms. "I'm glad I hired him. He works his ass off, and he's never given me any reason to doubt his loyalty."

"What can you tell us about his wife?" Lance asked.

Elliot shrugged "I really don't know Chelsea that well. We have holiday parties, and several times a year we hold picnics, where we participate in team-building exercises. Spouses are welcome. Chelsea always comes. She seems very sweet. Loves her kids like crazy," Elliot said with a sad smile.

Lance glanced through the glass. Everyone looked young. Very young. Many must be fresh out of college, and apparently not one of them owned an iron. At the ripe old age of thirty-three, Lance felt ancient. A young man in skinny jeans and a knit beanie cruised by on a skateboard. The glass muffled the *click-clack* of his wheels on the polished concrete.

"How valuable is the research Tim's team is working on?" Morgan asked.

"Very," Elliot said. "The technology we're developing has the potential to transform Internet access on a global scale, increasing access to low-cost, multigigabit wireless connectivity."

"Tim is a state-college grad," Morgan said. "I would think a high-tech, cutting-edge firm like Speed Net would want graduates from more prestigious universities."

Elliot steepled his fingers. "I went to a prestigious university. I didn't fit in. Rich, privileged kids weren't and aren't my people. If you've watched your parents struggle to pay bills, if your family has been evicted from their apartment in the middle of winter, if you've made a meal out of government cheese and ketchup packets, you understand the value of success in a way someone who hasn't struggled doesn't. If, in spite of your family's poverty, you've managed to get an advanced college degree, you have my attention."

Refreshing attitude.

Elliot sat back. "Plus, I can't afford MIT grads anyway."

And practical.

"Who is your strongest competitor?" Lance asked.

"Gold Stream," Elliot said with no hesitation. His mouth flattened. "Levi Gold and I used to be partners. We started our first tech company, TechKing, when we were twenty-two. We had a disagreement and sold the company."

"How ugly was your disagreement?" Lance pressed. "Would he hold a grudge or try to sabotage your research?"

Elliot shook his head. "If someone tried to hack our system, I'd look hard at Levi. But kidnapping? No."

"Does anyone here at Speed Net have a grudge against Tim?" Morgan asked.

"No." Elliot frowned, but the wariness that clouded his eyes belied his denial.

"But surely your team members argue?" Morgan suggested. "Stress is high. There's a lot at stake."

"We have our share of disagreements, but we're all professionals here." Elliot said in an almost snippy voice. "I'm the boss. If anyone has earned a grudge, it would be me."

Lance sensed Elliot was holding something back. "Do your other employees know Chelsea?"

"Yes. They would have met her the same way I did." Elliot crossed his arms over his chest and leaned back, putting a few more inches of space between them. One finger tapped on his opposite bicep.

Elliot's body language radiated stress. Lance shared a quick glance with Morgan. The communication between them was silent but swift. Her interest was piqued too. But she also knew the power of silence. A few seconds ticked away, allowing them to hear the muffled sounds of activity on the other side of the glass.

Elliot sighed loudly. "All right. We had a company event about six weeks ago. It was a picnic. Tim and his daughter were running in the three-legged race. It was cute. He's totally hung up on his kid." Elliot took a breath. His brow lowered. "Chelsea was sitting at a picnic table, pushing the baby stroller back and forth. I noticed one of our other engineers on Tim's team, Kirk, watching her."

He paused, a furrow forming above the bridge of his nose. He stared at the wall as if replaying the scene in his mind. "I'm sure it was totally innocent. Chelsea is a very attractive woman. Young guys, particularly nerdy young guys with little experience with women, are bound to notice her." Elliot looked over his shoulder. "If you look through the glass, Kirk is the one with the skateboard."

Lance scanned the office. Beanie boy had emerged from the locked room and was cruising across the space to an open kitchenette. He could have been in high school. He still had pimples. "How old is Kirk?"

"Twenty-three," Elliot said. "Kirk earned his PhD last year. He's brilliant, but he has Asperger's. Emotionally, he's much younger, and social communication is difficult for him. He can talk all day about the challenge of delivering high-frequency, 5G spectrum wireless without a sufficient fiber-optic cable infrastructure. But he can't ask a girl out on a date."

"Has Kirk ever had any negative interactions with female coworkers?" Lance scanned the people on the other side of the glass. More than three-quarters of the employees in sight were male.

Elliot shook his head. "No. Everyone here is a geek. We all speak the same language, and as long as the conversation doesn't venture into personal territory, Kirk is fine."

"Can we talk to everyone on Tim's team?" Morgan asked.

"Of course." Elliot rose. "Do you want me to send them in one by one?"

Lance nodded. "Please."

Elliot hesitated at the door. "You'll be gentle with Kirk?"

"We will." Morgan gave him a sincere, close-lipped smile.

"And understand, they will not be permitted to talk about the project," Elliot said. "It's a general rule."

Lance thought, *Thank God.*

But he said, "Yes. Of course. One more thing. We'd like a list of all your employees."

Elliot frowned. "I don't know. I assure you they were all vetted before they were hired. And the sheriff took a list with him. I assume he was checking everyone for criminal records."

"We know," Lance said. "It's always good to have fresh eyes on any investigation. You'd be surprised what can be missed with an overabundance of information."

"All right," Elliot agreed. "Everyone who works here signs off on periodic drug and background investigations due to the sensitive nature of the business. I don't like to violate my employee's trust, but this is an extraordinary situation."

"Do you remember where you were last Friday night?" Morgan asked casually. "We need to be thorough."

"I understand." Elliot nodded. "I was with my brother at his place."

"What did you do?" Lance asked.

"Nothing really. He was working on his road bike. I watched. We had a few beers." Elliot shrugged. "Derek's girlfriend broke up with him a few weeks ago. He's been depressed."

"I don't suppose anyone saw you there." Morgan looked up from her notes. "Did you order takeout? Run to a convenience store?"

"No. Sorry. If had known I was going to need an alibi, we would have gone out," Elliot said drily. "Let me get Kirk for you."

He left the room. A few minutes later, Kirk shuffled into the conference room, turned his skateboard over, and set it on the table in front of him. Bouncing into the chair Elliot had vacated, Kirk watched his skateboard wheels spin. He flicked quick, almost furtive glances at Morgan and ignored Lance completely.

Morgan gave him a soft smile. "Hi, Kirk."

"Hey," Kirk mumbled. His gaze darted from Morgan's chest to her face, then dropped, and he stared, red-cheeked, at his skateboard.

Morgan began, "We just wanted to ask you a couple of questions about Tim Clark."

Kirk played with a skateboard wheel, brushing it with his fingers and watching it spin. "Sure."

"How long have you worked with Tim?" Lance asked.

Irritation flashed across Kirk's face. His gaze passed across Lance's face for a quick second, then dropped to stare at the center of his chest. "Dunno exactly. Maybe two years."

"Do you and Tim get along?" Lance kept his voice conversational.

One of Kirk's shoulders lifted and dropped. "Sure. Tim's OK."

Morgan set her clasped hands on the table in front of her. "Do you know his wife, Chelsea?"

Kirk's gaze moved to her hands. "Yeah."

"Do you like her?" Morgan pressed.

Despite her gentle tone, Kirk seemed to shrink, his shoulders caving in as his weight shifted back in the chair. "I guess." He swatted the wheel of his skateboard three times. It spun with a soft whir.

"Is she nice to you?" Morgan twirled her thumbs.

Kirk seemed transfixed by the movement. "She's nice to everybody."

Despite his limited social skills, the kid was bright enough to know he was in the hot seat.

"Have you ever talked to her?" Morgan asked.

"Not really." Kirk tugged at the neck of his T-shirt. "Just hi and stuff."

Morgan kept moving her thumbs. "Did you see her at the last company function?"

"Yeah. She brought the kids. I like kids." Kirk's tone brightened.

"Everyone says Chelsea is a great mother," Morgan fished.

Kirk agreed with an emphatic nod. "She is."

"It's such a shame she's missing," Lance said in a tough voice, playing off Morgan's good detective persona.

Kirk's face fell. He looked like he was going to cry.

"We're trying to find her." Morgan unclasped her hands and reached into her bag at her feet. She slid a business card across the table.

Kirk stared at it.

"Would you please call me if you think of anything that might help us?"

Instead of answering, Kirk took the card and slipped it into the back pocket of his skinny jeans.

"Thank you for talking to us, Kirk." Morgan smiled. "Would you let Elliot know we're ready for the next interviewee?"

Kirk grabbed his skateboard and rushed for the exit.

"Oh, Kirk?" Morgan asked. "You don't happen to remember where you were last Friday night, do you? We're asking everyone." She shot him a halogen-bright smile.

Kirk blushed. "I was online playing World of Warcraft."

"People still play that?" Lance asked. "I thought everyone was into Call of Duty, Overlook, and Destiny now."

Kirk nodded. "I play those too."

"Were you playing alone?" Morgan treated him to another smile.

"No. Well, yes." He flushed, his hands clenching the edge of the board. "I was playing online with some friends."

"But you weren't all in the same physical place," Lance clarified.

Kirk shook his head. "No."

"Thanks, Kirk," Morgan said.

Kirk ducked out of the room. Outside the door, he tossed his skateboard onto the concrete and jumped aboard. His body had the finally-free posture of a kid leaving the principal's office.

Lance and Morgan interviewed the remaining five members of Tim's team without discovering anything interesting, other than they all alibied each other.

Lance and Morgan finished with the last interview, and Barbara escorted them to the lobby.

Outside, street lamps cast puddles of yellow light on the parking lot blacktop. The temperature had dropped, and the air smelled of burning wood. Morgan buttoned her coat and hunched her shoulders against the cold as they walked to the Jeep. "Isn't that Elliot's brother, Derek?"

He followed her gaze to a man clad in jeans, a leather jacket, and a knit hat walking across the parking lot. "Yes."

"Shall we ask him about last Friday night?" As she asked the question, Morgan was already veering off course toward him.

"Hi." She flashed him a megawatt smile.

He nodded. "Can I help you?"

Morgan introduced them. Lance kept his mouth shut. Most young men responded better to her than to him, especially when she turned on the charm.

"I know who you are," Derek said. "Everyone inside was talking about you."

"We just wanted to confirm that Elliot was with you last Friday night," Morgan said. "You went out to dinner?"

Lance appreciated her attempt to catch Elliot if he had been lying.

Derek shook his head. "No. We just hung out at my place. I was tuning up my road bike." He glanced back at the building and frowned. "Elliot hasn't been himself since Candace died. I don't like to see him spend too much time alone."

"He must have been heartbroken," Morgan empathized.

"He was." Derek nodded. "I think if you have any more questions about Elliot's wife, you'd better ask him, but I'll tell you right now, Elliot wouldn't hurt anybody. He takes care of people."

Morgan thanked him. Lance led her back to the Jeep, and they got in.

"At least he verified Elliot's alibi. Though they're brothers, so we have to take that into consideration." Morgan closed her door and shivered. "Poor Elliot. Twenty-seven is young to be a widower."

"It would be devastating at any age, but it must have been a huge shock for him. It's a wonder he could function to run his company."

"Maybe he used it as a diversion. It's best to keep busy." Morgan would know. She'd only been thirty-one when her husband had died. No doubt her focus on her children had gotten her through.

He started the engine. "Kirk Armani seemed pretty happy to get away from us."

"He's on the autism spectrum, so I wouldn't read too much into his body language." Morgan fastened her seat belt. "Just being forced to talk to two strangers would be very stressful for him."

"But he got more uncomfortable when we asked about Chelsea."

"True. But given that she's missing, that's natural. He's obviously extremely intelligent. We'll see what turns up in his background check." Morgan cupped her hands in front of her face and exhaled into them. "Do you think there's any possibility that someone kidnapped Chelsea to get information from Tim?"

"Then why would Tim come to us to find his wife?"

"I don't know." She rubbed her palms together. "And we don't have a ransom note."

"No, and it's been five days since Chelsea disappeared." Lance reached across the console and took Morgan's hand in his. Her fingers were freezing. He rubbed her hand between his palms for a few seconds then released it to drive out of the parking lot.

"What if the kidnapper wants to wait until police interest in the case dies down?"

"Typically, the opposite happens. They contact the family immediately to prevent the police from being involved at all."

Morgan's thinking line creased the bridge of her nose. "What's your impression of Elliot?"

"Smart. Ambitious. Workaholic." The air streaming from the vents warmed, and Lance turned the heater on high.

"His only alibi is his brother, though I can't come up with any reason Elliot would hurt Chelsea." Morgan stretched her hands toward the heat vents in the dashboard. "But we should find out more about his wife's death."

"I'll let my mother know, though I'm sure she'll find it on her own." Lance checked the clock on the dashboard. It was almost eight thirty. "I'll drop off the list of Speed Net employees tonight. It'll be a good excuse for the extra visit." He usually stopped to see his mom once a day.

Heat filled the vehicle until Lance was nearly sweating.

But Morgan settled deeper into her seat with a contented sigh. "I doubt his employees get along as well as he claims. There's always workplace drama."

"Throw in high stress levels and a bunch of very young people with outrageous IQs and weak social skills," Lance added. "It was like a high school in there."

"Right?" Morgan laughed. "I felt like such a *mom*."

She crossed her legs, the movement drawing Lance's eye fast enough to treat him to a quick flash of pretty thigh. "I don't think Kirk saw you as a mom."

And neither did Lance, despite the fact that he loved her kids.

"No?" She seemed cheered by his comment.

"No." Lance wasn't giving Kirk a pass because of his autism. The kid had acted weird toward Morgan and even weirder when they'd talked about Chelsea. Until she turned up, no one was getting a pass for any reason except a solid alibi.

Chapter Twelve

Pain surrounded Chelsea. Her entire body hurt. Was there any body part he hadn't battered?

Not that she could find.

She opened her eyes. They were so swollen that all she could manage were slits. Her vision blurred. She lifted a hand to her face and barely recognized its tender contours.

Giving up, she lay still for a while. Her ribs were bruised. Every time she drew in a breath, it felt as if she was wearing a corset of nails.

Pain rolled over her in waves but eased as she breathed more deeply and smoothly.

You can't give up!

Chelsea forced her eyelids open a bit farther and scanned the room as much as she could without moving her head. She was still in the shipping container. Still chained to the barrel. She lay on her side, curled naked on the plywood, in the corner where she'd crawled in a feeble attempt to get away from him.

But there had been no escaping.

As punishment for trying to open the drum, he'd ripped the clothes from her body. He'd taken away the cot, the blanket, and the water and left her shivering in an empty metal box.

After a few minutes, she lifted her head a fraction of an inch. The first movement sent dizziness careening though her. Dehydration? She swallowed. Vomiting wasn't possible. She was so empty she felt hollow. She hadn't had anything to drink since he'd beaten her, and she didn't remember when she'd last eaten.

Still, her stomach heaved as she slowly tested each limb with a tiny movement. She curled her toes and clenched her fingers, bent each knee and elbow. Her muscles protested, but her bones felt miraculously intact. There was no blinding agony to indicate a mortal injury; instead she felt an all-over soreness and exhaustion that made her not want to move at all. But that wasn't an option.

Do something or die.

She put both hands on the plywood and pushed her torso off the floor. The dizziness passed and she sat upright, leaning against the corrugated wall. The metal was cold on her bare back, and she shivered violently.

The cold helped to clear her head as she scanned her body. Her skin was mottled with bruises. She put a hand to her swollen mouth. Dried blood caked her split lips. She found a painful lump on her scalp.

But swelling and bruises seemed to be the worst of it. The rest of her injuries seemed to be superficial. Extensive, but not life-threatening.

As if he knew exactly how hard he could hit her without causing major damage.

As if he'd done it before.

Movement seemed to ease the stiffness in her body a little. She peeled her tongue off the roof of her mouth. Dehydration was the biggest threat. Without water, she wouldn't survive much longer.

There was nothing to do except wait. Rest. Heal. When an opportunity presented itself, she needed to be ready.

She looked up at the hole in the ceiling. The sky was dark. Nighttime. She tried to determine how long she'd been here but couldn't.

The sound of a padlock being opened and chains rattling startled her. She jerked to full alertness, pain jolting through her limbs at the sudden movement.

The door opened, and he stepped inside. The mask made him featureless, and her insides shivered. Her gaze locked on the gallon jug of water in his hand. His other hand was behind his back, and she eyed it with suspicion.

"You're awake." His head tilted as he assessed her. "Finally."

Had he been in before? Had he watched her while she'd slept?

A shudder racked her bones. Her mouth opened to respond to his greeting, but somewhere deep in her mind a warning bell sounded.

Rule number one: Do what he says.

Her mouth automatically clamped shut, as if it had been trained like a dog. Her eyes refused to travel to his face.

Rule number two: Keep my eyes on the floor.

"Do you think you've learned your lesson?" he asked.

Staring at her bare feet, she nodded.

"Good. I knew you were smart." He sounded pleased. He set the jug of water at her feet. "You may drink."

Bending forward, she grabbed for the water. Her weak, bruised arms tapping into some survival reserve. She removed the cap and drank. Water spilled into her mouth and over her chin. The cool liquid soothed her throat and lips. Her body demanded more.

"Wasting what I give you is disrespectful." His tone sharpened.

Fear shot through her. Cringing, she braced for a blow, but it never came. She lowered the jug, wiped her mouth with the back of her hand, and swallowed. Then raising the water again, she sipped slowly.

Neatly.

"That's my girl." His praise was a relief, the way she craved it a horror.

But her instinct told her she had to adapt to survive. Without water, she wouldn't live long. She must do whatever it took to keep him happy . . . so he didn't leave her in here until she shriveled up and died.

Because she knew in her soul that he would do so the moment she was more trouble than she was worth.

What did he want with her?

Water sloshed in her empty stomach. She set the jug on the floor. As much as she wanted to drain it, she feared losing what she'd already drank.

"Since you're being such a good girl, I have something else for you." He brought the hand behind his back around. He held the wool blanket, folded in a neat rectangle. On top of it was another piece of cloth. He set the blanket on the floor and shook out the other item—a bright-yellow dress. He leaned forward and offered it to her. "Put this on."

She scooted forward and took it from his hands. Turning it the right way, she drew it over her head. The dress was long-sleeved, empire-waisted, with a hemline just below her knees. Though the fabric was thin cotton, it was better than nothing. She drew the skirt over her bent knees.

"Do you remember rule number three?" he asked.

Fear curled in her belly as she struggled to remember all he'd shouted at her after the beating. But a blow to the head, the one that had given her the lump behind her ear, had left her ears ringing.

Her hands began to tremble. She bent her fingers into fists. A tear left her eye and dripped down her cheek as she shook her head.

"I'll go over them one more time," he said in a patient voice. "And you will memorize them. Further transgressions won't be tolerated. Understood?"

She nodded.

"Let's review." He crossed his arms. "And pay attention. Memorizing the rules might earn you some food."

At the mention of food, Chelsea's stomach clenched painfully. She strained to listen.

"One, you belong to me. You will do what I say without question. You are my property. Two, when in my presence, you will keep your eyes on the floor. Three, no speaking without permission. Four, disobedience is punishable any way I see fit. Can you repeat those back to me?"

Chelsea nodded but waited for his cue. In her peripheral vision, she saw the cruel smile twist his mouth.

"You may speak." His voice rang with satisfaction.

Mumbling through swollen lips, she repeated his rules.

"You learn quickly." He reached into his pocket and pulled out a protein bar. He held it out to her. She tried to grab it, but he raised it just out of reach at the last second.

With his free hand, he grabbed a handful of her hair. "Know this. I am not fucking around. If you ever try to escape again, I will beat every inch of you bloody, slit your throat, and bury you in the woods. Do you understand?"

Pain seared her scalp. Chelsea's bones shook as she nodded, grateful he hadn't asked her to speak because fear had paralyzed her vocal cords. Terror shook her body down to her bones.

He released her hair and dropped the protein bar in her lap. His hand lingered. His finger stroked her bruised, swollen cheek. "Everything will be all right. You'll see that I know best. I'm going to bring your cot back in. If you continue to behave, I'll bring you more food."

Straightening, he turned and walked toward the door. He returned in a moment, dragging the cot back into the container and leaving Chelsea wondering what else tomorrow would bring and what she would need to do to survive.

Chapter Thirteen

He closed the door, peeled off his mask, and welcomed the cool night air. He could hardly believe how fast she was learning. Pleasure rushed through him like an excited child. Everything was working exactly as he'd planned.

Turning around, he secured the heavy-duty padlock and set the alarm on the door. He couldn't be too careful with his prize. He was a winner, and he intended to keep his spoils. She truly was the ideal woman. He would never let her go.

Chelsea had made so much progress in such a short time. She'd exceeded his best expectations.

Responding to a direct greeting was automatic, yet Chelsea's brain had shut down her normal reaction. He'd seen it happen before his eyes. Her mouth had opened as a reflex, but her brain had intervened and closed it. A protection mechanism no doubt. Defiance equaled pain. Obedience led to physical comfort.

Pavlov could suck it.

Teaching a few caged dogs to drool didn't even compare to his accomplishment. He'd changed more than two decades of learned behavior in just a few days. His appropriate, well-timed, and severe punishment had been enough to rewire her instinct.

Amazing.

She was truly special. This experiment was everything he'd hoped for and more.

Maybe he could speed up his plan. He wanted things from her that she wasn't yet ready to give. He knew men who enjoyed a woman who put up a good fight. For those men, the act of domination was erotic. But he was more refined. He wanted her to kneel before him, to offer herself to him with no reservations. She wouldn't be attractive to him unless she submitted fully. Defiance and disagreement were ugly in a woman.

Surrender.

He reached for the zipper on his jeans. Surrender was hot. He couldn't wait for the day Chelsea willingly yielded to him.

But how long would it take to achieve?

The anticipation was hard to suppress.

Literally.

He lifted his hand. If submission was the most noble and beautiful trait for his woman to achieve, then as her mentor, he should exercise self-control and patience. Discipline should be meted out with love not anger. So far, he'd done his job. The pain he'd given her was all temporary. He couldn't hurt her.

He'd put too much work into her to lose her.

He walked toward his shed. He had big plans for tomorrow, a pivotal lesson for Chelsea and a true test of her progress.

Stick. Carrot.

Pain. Relief.

Especially pain.

He'd take Chelsea to rock bottom. Tomorrow, her soul would be stripped bare. After that, there would be nowhere to go but up. And when he was the one who rebuilt her physically and psychologically, she would be grateful.

She would adore him.

Inside the shed, he set his mask aside. How much longer would he need it? She wasn't leaving him. He wasn't worried about her knowing his identity. But the mask was intimidating. It dehumanized him and terrorized her. Fear generated obedience.

He'd been studying the psychology of torture for months. His arsenal of training techniques was psychological as well as physical, and he wasn't afraid to use every single one. Fear and humiliation were powerful training aids.

Which was why nakedness was one of the consequences of bad behavior. Clothing represented respect, and respect must be earned.

He began gathering his tools. Anticipation hummed through his veins. He had to be patient. The time between sessions was just as important as the actual sessions. Chelsea needed adequate time to reflect, to recover, for her brain to let go of old associations and form new ones.

He selected his blowtorch and put it in his tool bag. But tomorrow was going to be special.

Tomorrow he'd test the extent of her progress and teach her the most important lesson of all.

She belonged to him. Her body. Her soul.

All of it.

Chapter Fourteen

The Jeep pulled into her driveway. Morgan reached for the door handle.

"Morgan," Lance said. The deep tone of his voice pulled at her. "I'd better get my good-night kiss now. Your watchdog, Sophie, will be on duty."

She turned to face him. He leaned across the console, cradled her jaw with one big hand, and kissed her softly. Her eyes drifted closed as his lips lingered. His mouth was warm, with a hint of demand under the gentle press of his lips. She was sorry when he released her.

She caught his hand as it slipped from her face and gave it a tug. His eyes darkened, and he kissed her again. Not as gently. When his lips left hers, she was breathless and hot.

He lifted his head, and his hand slipped from hers.

"Someday, we'll manage to spend a few hours alone." His voice was rough. "Not that I'm complaining. If there's one thing I understand, it's taking care of family."

She exhaled hard. Her girl parts were tired of being set aside for her family's greater good. She'd spent two years with no interest in sex. Now that her hormones had finally reawakened, fate had thrown one roadblock after another in their path.

"It'll happen," she said. But the longer they waited, the more excitement and desire stirred in her belly. And nerves. Those were there too.

She'd slept with one man in the last ten years. One.

And the last time she'd gotten naked for the first time with a man, she'd been a lot younger. One did not have three children without those events leaving a few marks. Anticipation encouraged her insecurities.

"Hey, what's wrong?" Lance asked.

"Nothing. Nothing at all. I was just hoping that someday would be sooner rather than later," she said wryly, studying the brightly lit house through the windshield.

It was natural to be a little nervous at the thought of sleeping with a new man. She had never taken sex lightly. To her, physical and emotional intimacy went hand in hand. She'd never had a one-night stand. Had never wanted one. She'd slept with two men in her entire life, and she'd been married to one of them.

But she'd promised herself that she was going to lead a full life.

And a full life meant taking risks and leaving herself vulnerable.

Lance caught her chin in his hand and turned it toward him. "Are you sure?"

His touch and the connection between them zinged, strong and true as an arrow, slicing through her doubt. She wanted this man. Her emotions were too tender for any admissions of love, but her desire for him went beyond sex. She wanted him in her bed and in her heart.

She above all people should know that love was worth the risk. No matter how great the pain of losing her husband, she wouldn't have given up one second of her time with him to avoid the grief, as soul crushing as it had been.

Meeting his gaze head-on, she kissed him again. The firm press of her lips against his grounded her. *He* grounded her. "I'm positive. Let's go inside."

Morgan barely made it through the front door before she was swamped with three small bodies and a barking dog. The girls were in their pajamas. Their damp hair smelled of detangling spray.

She heard Lance close the door behind them as she crouched to envelop the three little girls in a giant hug. "I missed you."

Having her children in her arms made her think of Chelsea Clark. Would she ever get to hold her babies again?

Morgan released the kids and gave Snoozer, her French bulldog, a scratch behind his ears before standing.

The second she straightened, three-year-old Sophie leaped into her arms. Morgan shifted the skinny child to one hip. Sophie carried her newest favorite toy, a plush Bullseye from Disney's *Toy Story*, by one leg.

"We baked cupcakes with Gianna." Six-year-old Ava grabbed Lance by the hand and tugged him toward the kitchen. "*And* Aunt Stella is here."

Lance let himself be dragged.

Morgan set Sophie down. "Mia, how was your day?"

Five-year-old Mia was the quiet child. "You didn't come home for dinner."

"I know. I'm sorry." Guilt flooded Morgan. "But I'm here now. Can I have a cupcake?"

Mia nodded.

They went into the kitchen. The girls' nanny, Gianna, was loading the dishwasher. Grandpa and Stella sat at the kitchen table. In front of them sat a plate of bare cupcakes, three bowls of white icing and three butter knives.

Morgan's grandfather wiped his mouth with a napkin. A hint of white remained at the corner of his mouth. Morgan pointed to the corresponding spot on her own face, and Grandpa licked his lips.

"Grandpa!" Ava said in a stern voice. "That's your third! You're not s'posed to eat them all, Right, Mommy?"

"Right." Morgan lifted an eyebrow at her grandfather.

Grandpa laughed. "Life is short. Eat dessert."

All three girls looked at Morgan hopefully.

Shaking her head at her grandfather, she turned back to her girls and said, "One cupcake each."

"You were s'posed to watch him," Ava said to Stella.

Stella laughed. "He doesn't listen to me."

Before moving in with her boyfriend, Mac, over the summer, Stella had lived with Grandpa too. Come to think of it, had Grandpa ever had the house to himself? Morgan's older brother, Ian, had been in college when their father had died. Ian had been grown, but Grandpa had helped raise his three younger granddaughters. The man was a saint.

Grandpa reached for another cupcake, his hand trembling.

Stella slid the plate out of his reach. "I doubt your cardiologist would approve."

A saint with a stubborn streak.

"You'd think, at my age, I could do what I wanted," Grandpa grumbled.

"Think again." Morgan kissed him on the cheek. "We love you too much for that."

The girls went back to smearing icing on cupcakes. Ava and Mia worked with slow and deliberate strokes, but Sophie's cupcakes looked like they had been decorated with a fire extinguisher.

Morgan sniffed. The kitchen smelled of roasted meat and vegetables. She turned to Gianna. "That smells amazing. What was for dinner?"

"Pot roast." Gianna dried the slow cooker crock and set it on the counter. "There are leftovers if you're hungry."

"We ate, but I will have a cupcake." Morgan plucked one from the plate.

Though Gianna was still too slender, the dark-haired young woman had put on at least ten pounds and lost her death's-door pallor since Morgan insisted she move in with them four months ago. She still needed kidney dialysis, but her health and quality of life had improved, so much so that she'd insisted on being Morgan's live-in nanny.

Ava carefully smoothed the top of a cupcake and carried it to Lance. "This one's for you."

"Thanks. Vanilla is my favorite." Lance took the cupcake and ate it in three bites. "I'd better go. I'll pick you up at eight thirty?"

They were interviewing Chelsea's boss at nine.

"That's fine." Morgan said, glad she'd kissed him goodbye in the Jeep.

"Where's Mac?" Morgan asked Stella after Lance left.

"At SAR training. Five days in the woods. He's in heaven." Stella often said Mac would never be fully tamed. Totally at home in the wilderness, he had joined the local search and rescue team.

"I'd better go." Stella stood. "I have an early day tomorrow."

"I'll walk you out." Morgan followed her sister to the front door.

"He's really good with kids." Stella donned her coat.

Morgan opened the door for her. "He seems to enjoy them."

"You're lucky to find a second good man."

"I am." Morgan pushed back at the sadness that crept up her throat at the reminder of her late husband. No more lamenting about her loss. It was time to look forward to the future. She followed her sister outside. "How was the cardiologist appointment today?"

"As far as I know, the doctor adjusted his medication. Grandpa wouldn't let me go in with him." Stella tugged her keys from her pocket.

"Why is he so stubborn?"

"Because he's a Dane?" Stella paused to brush a hair off her face. "I'll call you tomorrow."

"Thanks for taking him today."

"Hey, he's my grandpa too. Please don't feel like you have to do it all. We'll manage it together." Stella got into her car and drove away.

Morgan watched her sister's taillights disappear into the darkness. Stella was right. Morgan didn't have to manage everything alone. Why did she always think she did? That whole bringing-home-the-bacon-and-frying-it-up-in-a-pan thing got old fast.

She turned back toward the house. The hairs on her nape rose. Was someone watching her?

She spun around, her eyes searching the darkness beyond the reach of the lights. There was no one in front of the house, and the street was empty in both directions. A gust of wind blew dead leaves along the gutter. Her imagination must be working overtime with Chelsea's disappearance.

But her steps quickened as she hurried toward the front door. She went inside, locked the door, and set the alarm. Grandpa took home security seriously. He'd installed motion lights, surveillance cameras, and a solid alarm system.

Sophie waited in the hallway.

"If you pick a book, I'll read to you," Morgan said. Maybe cuddling with her girls would relax her. She obviously needed some downtime.

"Toy Story!" Sophie ran for the bedroom she shared with her sisters.

Morgan's return to work had made them all a little clingy. Even with Gianna insisting on being her live-in nanny, Morgan preferred to handle bedtime. There was something special about putting her children to bed at night, seeing them safe and warm and content, before she settled herself for the evening.

She read a bedtime story, kissed each little girl, and tucked the covers around their tiny bodies. As always, her heart trembled when the children said good night to their daddy's picture on the dresser in their room. But Morgan was getting better. No more tears. John had been clear about wanting her to move forward and enjoy life.

But damn, the juggling act that had become her life was *hard*. How would she ever make her relationship with Lance a priority?

With no solution to her predicament, it was almost a relief to turn her attention to Chelsea Clark's disappearance.

With the girls in bed, Morgan opened her briefcase at the kitchen table and began to review the Clarks' financial statements. Chelsea and Tim didn't write many checks. Most of their bank transactions were direct deposits and automatic withdrawals for regular monthly bills. Tim paid the utility bills online. Chelsea and Tim had separate credit accounts. Tim's was more active, but nothing stood out as unusual on his statements for the past three months. Most were repeat transactions. Boring purchases like coffee and sandwiches. Morgan skimmed Chelsea's statements.

Grandpa shuffled in and poured himself a glass of milk. "What are you doing?"

"Reviewing my clients' financials. I don't see any red flags, but I'm going to try and trace the wife's recent activities as best as I can. For now, I'm assuming Chelsea was kidnapped. If someone planned her abduction, he saw her somewhere."

Grandpa nodded. "Best to start with the most dangerous hypothesis. If she abandoned her family, she'll be alive to find later."

So many ifs.

"Shouldn't you be using your cane?" she asked.

"I don't need it." But Grandpa kept a hand on the wall or the counter as he moved around the room. "Most women are hurt by people already in their lives so it makes sense to start there. If the crime was random, then finding her will be harder."

With one hand on the back of a chair, Grandpa drank his milk.

Morgan started a list of all the places Chelsea had frequented in the past few months. The statements showed regular activity at a local grocery store, the Walmart, and a gas station. Morgan jotted down the locations. She added less frequent stops at a café, a few small retailers, and an auto-repair shop. There was no recent charge for Chelsea's yoga studio, but Morgan put it on the list anyway. "I'm not finding much."

"Want to tell me about it?" Grandpa was a retired NYPD homicide detective.

"A young mother went out to meet her girlfriend for a drink." Morgan began, then summed up the case for him.

Grandpa reached across the table, picked up Chelsea's photo, and stared at it. "Have you considered human trafficking?"

"Isn't she a little old? Don't they usually abduct teenagers?"

"Yes. But this girl looks young. She also has the wholesome, blonde, all-American look that's very popular in the trade."

"I'll keep it in mind." Morgan turned to her laptop.

Grandpa put the picture down, went to the fridge, and poured a second glass of milk. He set it on the table in front of Morgan, then he took two cupcakes from the container on the counter and handed her one.

"You know my weakness." Morgan bit into the cupcake. Only cop families could eat cupcakes while reviewing a missing person case.

"You were born with a sweet tooth." Grandpa ate his cupcake, tugged a chair next to hers, and sat down, setting his milk on the table.

"Looks like my sweet tooth is genetic. Isn't that your fourth?" She rested her head on his shoulder for a few seconds. She might have lost both her parents and her husband, but Grandpa had always been there for her. "We didn't get a chance to talk earlier. How was your appointment with the cardiologist?"

"My heart is still beating."

She gave his arm a playful swat. "I'm serious. You've been really shaky lately. That's not like you."

"Honey, I know you're worried," Grandpa said. "I'm still on this side of the grass, but someday I won't be."

Morgan's next breath trembled.

"You're stronger than you realize." He patted her hand. "You're going to be all right."

Unable to respond, she nodded.

"I'm not going anywhere just yet, so enough with the long face." He pointed to her cupcake. "Now eat so we can work on your case. I might be old, but I still know a thing or two about criminals."

"You're right." Straightening, Morgan licked icing off her fingertips and turned a page in her file. "I'm going to access the state sex offender registry and see how many possible sexual offenders are in the area."

"Too many."

"Yep." She already knew the number was higher than anyone wanted to think about. There were just under forty thousand sex offenders registered in the state of New York. Considering sexual assaults were severely underreported, the actual number of predators was likely much, much higher. A few keystrokes brought up a list of names. "One hundred sixty-seven convicted sex offenders currently live in Randolph County. This is going to take forever."

"Can I help?"

"Do you want to take the bottom half of the list?" Morgan asked.

"Sure."

"I'll get your laptop." She fetched his computer from his room.

In his mideighties, Grandpa might be shaky on his feet, but his brain hadn't lost any of its sharp edge. He pulled his glasses from the chest pocket of his flannel shirt and set them on the end of his nose. "What do you want to know?"

"Name and home and employer address to start. We'll cross-reference them with the places Chelsea frequents. Then we can get more detail on any that overlap."

The New York State sex offender registry maintained a detailed profile on all level-two and level-three offenders. Home and work addresses, physical descriptions, convictions and sentencing information, photos, vehicle registrations, and specific legal restrictions were listed for all to see.

Morgan didn't find any sex offenders in Chelsea's neighborhood. Nor were there any listed in the immediate vicinity of the spot where her car had been found.

But ninety minutes later, Morgan froze. An address on the registry looked familiar. She went back to her list of Chelsea's activities. A match!

"Chelsea took her car to Burns Auto Shop last month." She shifted her gaze to her list of sex offenders. "The address of the auto shop matches the employer address of Harold Burns, a registered level-three sexually violent offender." She went back to her computer. "Harold is thirty-five years old. He served seven years in state prison for the first degree rape of a twenty-three-year-old woman."

Level-three offenders committed the most serious crimes, both violent and nonviolent crimes against minors and adults, and required lifetime registration with frequent verification of personal information.

"Was the victim a stranger or not?" Grandpa asked. Most sexual predators knew their victims.

Morgan checked the data. "Yes. Stranger. Force used is listed as coercion, threat, and a firearm."

Grandpa's face tightened. "Why on earth a man like this is free is beyond me."

"Prisons are full, and the minimum sentence for first degree rape is only five years. With time off for good behavior, some don't even serve that much time."

"Yeah. Yeah. I know. Still. Burns was a violent man going into his sentence. I would bet that seven years in a state prison didn't magically make him docile."

Morgan shook her head. "No, but he's been out for three years with no arrests, and it seems he's in full compliance with registry requirements."

"So far," Grandpa grumbled. "And no arrests doesn't mean he hasn't committed any crimes. He just hasn't gotten caught."

Harold drove a red Chevy truck. Morgan copied his license plate number. "Since his name is Burns and so is the auto shop's, I'll assume he's related to the owner."

"I can keep plugging away at the surrounding counties tomorrow if you want," Grandpa said hopefully. He missed being a detective.

"Are you sure? It's grunt work."

"I don't mind. Work keeps the mind sharp."

"There is nothing wrong with your brain." She checked the time. Nearly midnight. Too late to call Lance's mom. Morgan sent her an e-mail. Then she copied all of Harold Burns's personal information down into her notes and printed his photo from her computer screen. Tomorrow, Jenny Kruger could dig up more details on him. Morgan fetched the image from the printer in the family room and stared at Harold Burns.

About six feet tall, Harold was dirty-looking. He wore his shoulder-length, gray-streaked brown hair in a ponytail, his bushy beard was unkempt, and his brown eyes were frighteningly emotionless.

Was she looking at the man who had abducted Chelsea?

Chapter Fifteen

The next morning, Lance opened Morgan's front door just as two children shot out past him.

"Hi, Lance," Ava called, running toward the driveway.

Dragging a book bag on the pavement, Mia stopped to give him a quick hug. "Gotta go."

The door opened wider, and Morgan flew by, a piece of paper fluttering in her hand. "Wait!"

She was dressed in gray pants and a matching suit jacket, but she wore no coat and her feet were bare. The hem of her pants was too long and she ran on her toes. The scarf around her neck was more decorative than warm, and he knew it was in place so her kids didn't see the bruises on her neck. Her hair was down and billowed around her head in the wind. The cold reddened her fair skin almost instantly. In his eyes, Morgan was always beautiful, but usually her appearance was polished and perfect. When he caught her in a casual, carefree moment, before she assumed her professional veneer, it felt intimate, and she took his breath away.

She called out, her voice commanding, "Stop!"

Both girls slid to a quick halt.

"Ava! You forgot your permission slip." Morgan twirled her finger in the air.

Ava turned around, and Morgan zipped the paper into the front pocket of her backpack just as a school bus turned the corner. Morgan grabbed her girls' hands and held on until the bus came to a complete stop. Then she kissed each child as they squirmed away and climbed onto the bus.

Once the bus pulled away, she returned to Lance, her cheeks flushed. "I'm sorry. I'm running behind."

She shoved her black mane away from her face. The sight of her smiling up at him froze his vocal cords for a second. Her bare lips looked soft and warm. He itched for their taste. Last night's kiss had left him wanting more.

He leaned forward, but the sensation of being watched stopped him. He glanced around, his gaze catching a figure in the living room window. Sophie. Her skinny arms were crossed over her little body.

Lance straightened. "Your daughter is giving us the stink eye."

As he watched, Sophie turned and fled the window.

Morgan sighed. "I'll be ready in five minutes."

Clearing his throat, he held the door open for her as they went inside. "Take your time. Our appointment with Curtis MacDonald isn't until nine."

She shivered and rubbed her arms. "Thanks."

Lance peered into the kitchen. Art was reading the newspaper. Sophie worked on a pancake, and Gianna was loading the dishwasher. Both girls were in their pajamas. The dog begged at Sophie's feet. The scene was warm and happy, the sink full of dirty dishes the only sign of the bedlam that likely preceded this quiet moment.

If he had told himself a year ago that he'd find this chaos warm and inviting—and that he wanted to be part of it—he wouldn't have believed it.

"Morning," he said.

Art looked up from his paper. "Morning."

"Can I make you breakfast?" Gianna asked.

"No, but thanks." Lance shook his head. "We have to go."

"I'm ready." In the doorway, Morgan buttoned up a black trench-type coat. She stuffed a small umbrella into her big purse.

They went out to the Jeep. Lance slid behind the wheel, started the engine, then turned to Morgan and pulled the scarf an inch away from her neck. The ring of bruises had darkened to a deep purple.

"Does it hurt?" His finger brushed her jaw as he released the fabric.

She tugged the scarf back into place. "It looks worse than it feels."

"I hope so because it looks terrible." Lance drove away from the house.

"Gee. Thanks." Morgan sighed. "How was your mother last night?"

"The same. Maybe I'm just paranoid." But his mom wasn't herself and he needed to keep an eye on her.

"All you can do is your best," Morgan said. "Oh. I have some news on the case. Last month, Chelsea took her car to an auto shop that employs a registered sex offender."

Morgan filled him in on the details of her find.

"You had better luck than I did." Lance drove toward town. The accounting firm of Skyver and MacDonald was local. "Chelsea mainly used her social media accounts to post pictures of the kids. She kept her accounts private and had very few connections. All her online relationships seem to be with family, friends, and coworkers. There were no changes or red flags in her recent posts or comments. There's always the possibility of her accounts being hacked, but I didn't find any obvious clues. Tim doesn't have any social media accounts."

Lance had also hacked into Chelsea's work files, but he didn't mention that to Morgan. He hadn't had time to dig in to the data anyway.

"Should we go see Harold Burns or check with the sheriff first?" Morgan asked.

Lance turned left at a stop sign. "Let's get Sharp's opinion. He's better with local politics than I am."

Morgan put Sharp on speakerphone and gave him the details about Harold Burns.

"Morgan and I were debating whether we should call Sheriff King or stop in to see Harold." Lance steered the Jeep onto the country road that led to town.

Sharp was silent for a few seconds. "Notifying King puts us at the risk of him warning us off without giving us any information. Then we couldn't talk to Burns. Usually, I'm all for stepping carefully around law enforcement, but I think we're better off asking for forgiveness rather than permission in this case. For all we know, King has already talked to Burns and kept it to himself."

"So we'll go talk to Harold after we finish with Curtis MacDonald," Lance said.

"I'd start with a routine inquiry with the manager," Sharp suggested. "Show Chelsea's picture around the shop. See if anyone remembers her and what kind of reactions you get. If or when you confront Harold, do it in private. We don't need to be charged with harassment."

"I'd hate to ruin a sexual predator's day," Lance said, disgusted.

"The law is the law," Sharp answered in a firm tone.

"Yeah. Yeah. I know." But being nice to a predator turned Lance's stomach. Experts could dispute the recidivism rate of sexual offenders all they wanted. Lance would never be convinced any of them could be rehabilitated. He held a grudge against anyone who hurt women or children and he always would.

"Morgan, please make sure he behaves himself," Sharp said.

She laughed. "I'm the one who broke someone's nose yesterday."

"Point taken. Just try and stay out of trouble for one entire day." Sharp chuckled. "Lance, I'll call your mom and put Harold Burns at the top of her list. Let's see if she can dig up more details on him. I'll head to Tim's neighborhood and start knocking on doors. You kids be careful."

Sharp ended the call.

Ten minutes later, Lance parked in front of Skyver and MacDonald. The accounting firm was located in a small business complex at the edge of town. They went inside, and Morgan gave their names to the receptionist.

Curtis emerged in a few seconds. At forty-five years of age, he looked younger than Lance expected. Something about the word "accountant" made him think of old men and dusty ledgers. But Curtis's light-brown hair was streaked with blond, not silver, and he moved like an athlete.

After brief introductions, Curtis asked, "Has there been any news?"

Lance shook his head.

"Please, come into my office." Frowning, Curtis ushered them down a short hallway. He gestured toward a credenza that held a pod-style coffeemaker. "Do you want coffee?"

Lance and Morgan declined and took the two upholstered chairs that faced Curtis's modern desk.

Curtis went behind the desk, but instead of sitting, he faced a window that looked out onto a small green space. "I still can't believe she's missing."

Morgan began, "When was the last time you spoke with Chelsea?"

Curtis faced them, his distress plain in his eyes. "Friday morning."

"Was there anything unusual about the conversation?" Morgan asked.

"Definitely." Curtis rolled the chair out and dropped into it. He picked up a paper clip and twirled it between his fingertips. But he didn't seem nervous, more like a fidgety man with too much energy for a desk job. "She was upset about something she didn't want to tell me over the phone. She was going to come into the office Monday, but obviously that didn't happen."

Lance leaned forward and rested his elbows on his thighs. "So you have no idea what she wanted to talk to you about?"

"No." Curtis's tanned brow furrowed. "She'd been trying to catch up with her clients, but she was having a rough time. I was prepared for her to come in on Monday and quit. I had a counteroffer prepared."

"You didn't want her to quit?" Morgan asked.

"No. She's smart and reliable. I'll admit that her extended maternity leave has put me in a bit of a bind. We have the year-end statements to prepare and tax season right on top of that."

"Seems like it would be easier to replace her," Lance said.

Curtis shook his head. "Turnover is expensive. I already know what I have in Chelsea. She's good at her job. And seriously, I'd feel like a total jerk firing her over a problem with her baby. Her absence has been inconvenient, but it's temporary. We'll survive."

"What has Chelsea been working on?"

"Nothing specific." Curtis said. "Her clients have been spread out among a number of associates. I simply started copying Chelsea on all activity and correspondence so she could get back up to speed. We were both hoping she could start coming in part-time and do some work at home."

Morgan crossed her legs. "Do you normally allow that sort of flexibility?"

Curtis shrugged. "This is the first time maternity leave has come up with anyone outside of administrative personnel. We're not a big firm. But as I said before, turnover is expensive. It costs money to replace key staff. It disrupts client relations."

"Is it possible Chelsea was upset about something else?" Morgan asked.

Curtis dropped the paper clip. It hit the desk with a soft thud. "Like what? She's a good worker, but our relationship is professional. We're friendly, but we're not friends, if you know what I mean. I'm sure if she had a personal problem, she'd take it to a girlfriend."

"What about problems with a client?" Lance asked.

Curtis lifted a shoulder. "Not that I know about."

Lance couldn't think of any further questions. "Do you mind if we talk to the rest of the staff?"

"Not at all." Curtis stood. "Everyone here is really worried about Chelsea."

"What about your partner?" Lance got to his feet.

Curtis shook his head. "Jim Skyver died six years ago. He was the founder of the firm. Changing the name is more effort than it's worth."

Lance followed Morgan out of the office.

There were six junior accountants and a handful of administrative staff. No one at the firm had anything interesting to say. Chelsea seemed genuinely well liked, and her coworkers acted concerned with her disappearance.

Lance and Morgan left the building and got into the Jeep.

"He seems like a nice guy." Lance started the engine.

"He does. Why would Chelsea make an appointment to see her boss if she was going to run away?"

"Maybe she wasn't thinking clearly. Could be depression."

"Maybe." Morgan turned to the passenger window. "But I'm not convinced. She would have had to make arrangements for a car to be left in Grey's Hollow. Where would she get the money? We haven't found any additional friends in her life. She barely had time to see Fiona let alone plan an elaborate vanishing act."

"Could she have had an affair?"

Morgan snorted. "With a preschooler and a baby? I doubt sex was on Chelsea's mind often. With a four-month-old colicky baby, sleep would be a priority, not sex. Besides, no one involved in the investigation has alluded to any indication of infidelity on Chelsea's part."

"What if the affair happened before she got pregnant?"

"We'd have to go back and look at all records from over a year ago."

"Yes," Lance agreed.

A thinking line formed between Morgan's brows. "I still put Chelsea leaving on her own at the bottom of my list of theories. In my opinion, she wouldn't voluntarily leave her children. We'd need to uncover a strong motivation."

But was Morgan projecting her own feelings onto the missing woman?

"Like?"

"Like her presence put her family in danger." Morgan rubbed her forehead. "But we know where she grew up, so she can't be part of witness protection or anything like that, and we've seen no indication of criminal activity."

"So what are we left with? She saw or discovered something she wasn't supposed to?" Lance would spend the evening digging into Chelsea's client files.

"Neither of those possibilities seem likely, but nothing about this case is normal."

"Let's move on to the auto shop." Lance turned the Jeep around and left the lot.

Burns Auto Repair sat on a large piece of land on the outskirts of Scarlet Falls.

They drove out of the town proper. Lance made a left onto a rural route. Forest lined the road on both sides. A few miles later, the woods opened up on the right, and Morgan pointed to a squat, unkempt ranch-style home set back off the road. The three-bay detached garage was larger than the house. "That's Harold's residential address. His brother, Jerry, owns all this property. It's been in the Burns family for years."

The auto shop was a quarter mile down the road. Lance drove into the gravel lot and past the building. A red pickup truck was parked near a side door. Behind the shop, an auto salvage yard stretched across acres of dirt and weeds. Amid the clusters and piles of vehicle carcasses, Lance spotted a few small outbuildings. Thick woods surrounded the property.

Morgan opened Chelsea's file. "The license plate matches. That's Harold Burns's truck."

"Then he's here." Lance parked at the corner of the building, where the Jeep was out of the direct line of sight of the glass-doored entrance.

"Maybe you should wait outside," Morgan suggested.

"No."

"You're intimidating."

"No."

"I'm serious," Morgan said.

"So am I."

"He's an ex-con, and you still look like a cop. He will not talk to you. He'll call his lawyer."

Lance sulked. She was right. But he didn't like it. "He's a predator."

"I've interviewed predators before." She put a hand on his arm. "It's broad daylight and we're in a public place, Lance. I'll be fine."

"OK." He huffed. "I'll walk around back in case Harold suddenly decides he needs to be elsewhere."

She needed to do her job, and he needed to let her, even if he didn't want her anywhere near a violent sexual predator or on a rapist's radar.

Chapter Sixteen

Morgan went inside the small office. A counter faced a waiting area full of plastic chairs. The air smelled of burned coffee, grease, and dust.

A tall, spare man in gray, grease-stained coveralls greeted her from the other side of the counter. His name tag read JERRY BURNS. "Can I help you?"

"Hi, Jerry." Morgan smiled.

Jerry didn't smile back.

Morgan pulled a photo out of her big purse and handed it across the counter. "Have you ever seen this woman?"

Jerry stared at the picture for a couple of seconds. "She looks familiar."

"She had her car repaired here last month."

"Yeah. I remember her." Jerry nodded. "She stayed here for two hours while we fixed her car. Her kid screamed the whole time." He grimaced.

"I'd like to ask your employees what they remember about her."

"Why? Did she do something wrong?" Jerry asked, suspicious.

"She's missing," Morgan said. "I'm surprised you didn't see it on the news. Would she have had direct contact with anyone else here besides you?"

Jerry's gaze flickered to the door behind him that led to the shop, and he licked his lips. "I doubt it. I handle the customers."

"What about the mechanic? It would be so helpful if I could speak with him."

"Let me see who worked on her car." He turned to a computer on the counter and slid the black-smudged keyboard out from under the monitor. He pulled up a few screens, frowned, and scratched his eyebrow. Jerry didn't make eye contact as he said, "The mechanic isn't in today. Can I have him call you?"

The lie was so blatant his coveralls should have spontaneously combusted.

"Could you give me his name?" Morgan asked.

Jerry shook his head. "I can't give out personal information about an employee. Sorry."

"I'd like to show her picture to your employees."

Jerry licked his lips again. "I can't let you in the shop. My insurance company doesn't allow it, but I'll take this in back and show it around." He disappeared through a door. In the brief seconds the door was open, she heard music, voices, and the sound of pneumatic tools being used.

Morgan had interviewed enough criminals and witnesses to know when she was being lied to, and Jerry Burns had told her a whopper when he'd said the mechanic who fixed Chelsea's car wasn't in.

Jerry came back into the office in less than five minutes. He extended the picture over the counter. His chin was lifted, his jaw tight, as if he was forcing himself to look her in the eyes. "Sorry. No one remembers her."

Another bald-faced lie.

Morgan took the photo and composed her game face. "Thank you so much for trying."

She left a card on the counter.

She went outside and walked toward the Jeep. Lance wasn't in it. She was reaching for the passenger door handle when an arm blocked her path. Morgan startled, spun around, and found herself staring up at Harold Burns.

"I hear you're looking for me." He'd changed his appearance. His face was clean-shaven, his hair buzzed short. His brown eyes, which had appeared dead and emotionless in his registry photo, were narrowed and intense.

Morgan took a step backward, then stopped herself. Showing fear to a man like Harold was like dripping blood in a shark tank.

"Did you fix Chelsea Clark's Honda Accord last month?" she asked, remembering that she wasn't supposed to know him on sight.

"Maybe." He stepped forward, eliminating the gap she'd put between them. "I fix a lot of cars. I don't remember each one."

Morgan opened her bag and reached for the photo. While she was in there, she checked the location of her pepper spray—open side pouch, right where it belonged. She showed him the picture. "She needed a new battery. Also had her oil changed and tires rotated."

Harold glanced at it. "Jerry handles the customers. I stay in the back."

He took another step forward.

"Always?" Morgan moved backward. She couldn't help it. He repulsed her on a cellular level. "You're not in the back now."

"You think you're so smart. You know I'm on the sex offender registry." Anger glittered in his eyes. "That's why you're here. If anything bad happens in this town, the cops always come looking for me."

"I'm not a cop."

"No, you're not. But you're a nosy, lying bitch." His lips peeled off his teeth, more snarl than smile. He pressed closer.

The smell of grease clogged Morgan's throat. She retreated farther. Her back hit the side of the building.

She was trapped. Her lungs tightened.

It's fine. It's broad daylight. Lance is around the corner. He'll be back any second.

But no matter what she told herself, her primal instincts wouldn't listen. Under her coat, sweat broke out between her shoulder blades. *Do not show fear.* It would encourage him. As she forced her spine straight, her insides curled into a fetal ball.

"The woman is missing." She stuffed the photo in her bag. Her fingers closed around her pepper spray, and she stepped sideways to go around him.

But Harold mirrored her movement, staying between her and the Jeep.

"Hey," Lance yelled.

Morgan exhaled, her muscles relaxing.

Harold got one look at Lance and backed off. "I don't know anything about a missing woman."

The tendons on the side of Lance's neck had gone rigid. He stalked closer, planting himself between her and Harold.

"You worked on her car." Lance's statement was cut-the-bullshit.

"This is harassment." It was Harold's turn to back up as Lance got in his face.

"Fine." Lance raised his hands, palms out as if he'd given up. "We just wanted to talk to you. But if you'd rather talk to the sheriff, that can be arranged. I'll call Sheriff King now."

He took out his phone.

"Wait." Harold glanced at the auto shop. "I remember her, but I didn't even talk to her when she came in here. Jerry doesn't let me in the office. I stay in the back or I'm fired."

Brotherly love had its limits.

"Maybe we don't have to call the sheriff." Morgan put her hand on Lance's shoulder. The muscles under her palm were hard as concrete. "Let's go."

"Don't come back." Harold spat in the dirt at his feet.

Lance didn't turn his back on Harold as he opened the passenger door for her. He kept one eye on Harold until he went back into the auto shop.

Behind the wheel, Lance faced her. "I can't believe you don't want me to call the sheriff about him."

Morgan stared at him. "Of course we're going to call the sheriff. Harold worked on Chelsea's car. He noticed her. He remembered her. He had access to her address."

"But you told him—"

"I said *maybe* we didn't need to call the sheriff." She set her bag at her feet. "I don't want him to run. I want him to think he's safe."

"Well played."

"I've had lots of experience not showing my utter contempt and disgust in the face of criminals." Morgan fished her phone from her purse and called the sheriff. The receptionist patched her through to his office.

"Yes, Ms. Dane?" Sheriff King sounded irritated.

"Hello, Sheriff. We just left the auto shop where Chelsea Clark had her vehicle serviced last month. The mechanic who worked on her car is a registered sex offender." She gave him the information on Harold Burns. "I wanted to call you right away in case you wanted to interview him."

"I'll send a deputy out to talk to him today," King said, then spit out a grudging, "Thank you."

"You're welcome." She ended the call.

The sheriff could pressure Harold in a way Morgan and Lance couldn't. But would he?

"Do you want to stop for lunch before we drive to Grey's Hollow?" Lance pulled back onto the road and drove toward the interstate.

Morgan plugged the GPS coordinates for the Grey's Hollow train station into her phone. "Let's grab something we can eat on the way. I don't want to waste time. Looks like rain is coming."

Storm clouds darkened the horizon.

They bought sandwiches at a coffee shop and ate them on the drive north. An hour later, Lance exited and threaded his way through the rural roads until they approached the tiny town of Grey's Hollow. On the narrow country road leading up to the station, they passed a smattering of homes. Lance slowed the car as they neared the station. The Grey's Hollow station was basically a platform and parking area. There was no ticket booth, no shelter, no restroom. Nothing except a tiny deli that butted against the platform. Riders bought tickets online or on the train. The small gravel parking lot held six cars.

"She didn't get on the train?" Lance asked.

"No," Morgan answered.

Lance accelerated, and they left the station behind. Chelsea's car had been found a quarter of a mile down the country road. The Jeep came to a stop in the approximate location. Morgan slipped off her heels and put on the cheap flats she kept in her bag for traipsing around in the mud.

She and Lance got out of the vehicle. The wind that whipped Morgan's coat around her legs smelled of rain, and she buttoned her coat. She leaned back inside the Jeep, took her umbrella from her tote, and tucked it into the deep side pocket of her trench coat.

Lance had his camera in hand as they walked to the side of the road.

"This is pretty isolated." Lance stared over a broken fence that ran along the side of the road, separating it from a cornfield. Past harvest, the dry stalks were cut and smashed on the ground. Random stalks that had escaped the tractor blades waved in the wind. "Why leave her car here? Why not in the train station parking lot?"

"Maybe someone didn't want Chelsea's car to appear on the parking lot security cameras."

"Did you look up the weather report for last Friday night?" he asked.

"I did. It was clear, cold, and breezy. The temperature hovered just above freezing."

"So she wouldn't have gone walking if she didn't have to."

"No."

Lance snapped pictures of the surrounding landscape then lowered the camera. They walked along the roadside. Morgan stepped ten feet off the pavement. Lance walked a parallel line ten feet farther away. Eyes on the ground, they continued their trek, their eyes sweeping the ground for anything out of the ordinary. After a hundred yards, they turned around, crossed the road, and went back to the Jeep. Wind stirred dead leaves and dirt into a mini tornado. Morgan's hair blew into her face. She pulled an elastic band from her pocket and secured her hair in a ponytail. They repeated the process in the other direction, not rushing despite the approach of the storm.

Twenty-five yards from the Jeep, thunder boomed. As the first fat raindrops plopped onto the pavement, Morgan opened her umbrella and lifted it high. "You can walk under this too."

"I might miss something." Lance shook his head. "But you can take the camera."

He brought it to her then went back to the line he was searching.

Morgan hung the strap around her neck. The rain turned into a downpour. Lightning flashed, and she startled. The wind caught her umbrella. She bent forward and angled it to keep it from turning inside out.

Ten feet from the Jeep's bumper, in the weeds at the very edge of the pavement, something crunched under her foot. She stopped, squatted, and brushed her fingers through the tall grass. The gleam of wet metal caught her attention. Lifting the camera in a one-handed grip, she snapped pictures from varying angles.

"What is it?" Lance shouted over the rush of rain.

"I'm not sure. A piece of jewelry, I think. Do you have gloves?" She'd left her tote in the Jeep. Setting the camera back on her chest, she searched her pockets but came up empty. Lance went back to the Jeep and then returned to her. He handed her a purple nitrile glove and a tape measure. She moved the weeds to fully expose a small silver pendant.

"Let me hold the umbrella for you." He crouched next to her so she could take more photos.

As private investigators, they followed the same rules of evidence collection as the police. Collecting evidence in a downpour presented challenges. Lance blocked the rain and wind with his body as best he could. Morgan took additional pictures from varying angles and distances. She measured the distance between the necklace and multiple points of reference. Then she used her phone to pinpoint the exact GPS coordinates. When she'd recorded the necklace's position adequately, she picked it up by the chain. They went back to the Jeep.

Lance held the umbrella over Morgan while she got into the passenger seat. Holding the chain, she shivered as he rounded the front of the Jeep. Then the driver's door opened with a gush of wet wind. Lance slid into the seat and tossed the closed umbrella behind him. Rain plastered his hair to his skull and molded his clothes to his body. Below the midthigh hem of her trench coat, Morgan's slacks were soaked. The insoles of her shoes squished.

He wiped water from his face with a hand. "Let's see it."

Morgan lifted the chain. The pendant dangled.

"The sheriff said his deputies searched this area," Lance said.

"It was under the weeds. If I hadn't stepped on it, I wouldn't have noticed it."

The pendant was a bird. Morgan twirled the chain and the pendant rotated. Three letters were carved into the silver on the back: *CJC.*

"What is Chelsea's middle name?" she asked.

Lance took a Ziploc bag from his glove box, wrote the date and time on it with permanent market, and handed the baggie over the console. "Jessica. Her full name is Chelsea Jessica Clark."

CJC.

Morgan lowered the necklace into the Ziploc bag but left the bag open so the pendant could dry. "We need to take this to the sheriff's office."

"Oh joy," Lance said. "He's going to be thrilled that we found something his men didn't."

She studied the necklace. "The chain is broken and there are a few long blonde hairs stuck in the clasp." She unzipped her tote bag and took out her mini magnifying lens. "The roots are attached."

As if the hair had been torn from her head.

Morgan shuddered. Had Chelsea fought?

"So now we know that Chelsea was here with her car."

Morgan held up the plastic bag. "And the broken chain and roots on the hairs suggest the necklace was ripped off her neck. Maybe we finally found an indication of a struggle."

Chapter Seventeen

Lance watched Morgan work the sheriff. She faced Sheriff King over his desk, all big blue eyes and sincerity. She folded her hands in her lap. Her expression was attentive, her posture ladylike, and yet her presence powerful in a way that Lance couldn't quite quantify.

It was confidence, he decided. Every word she spoke rang with truth but was delivered in a quiet way that had King leaning forward to listen. Yes, she had the big, badass sheriff hanging on her every word.

She was good. Very good.

No doubt when she'd been a prosecutor, she'd commanded the jury's attention just as naturally.

King leaned back in his chair and rubbed at his cleanly shaven chin. His eyes drifted to Lance, narrowed just a hair, then returned to Morgan.

Yeah. Lance was not one of his favorite people, which was why he sat back and kept his mouth shut. He would have stayed in the car if he didn't know he needed to sign a statement about the discovery of evidence. Lance wasn't as skilled at hiding his anger as Morgan. Frankly, his disposition was more like the sheriff's.

King dangled the Ziploc bag containing the bird pendant over his desk. "So you found this in the weeds where Chelsea's car was left?"

"Yes. It was buried in the tall grass." Morgan nodded solemnly.

Which was a nice way of saying his men blew it while simultaneously offering an excuse.

The sheriff grunted. Lance had no doubt he was irritated at his
department being shown up, by a woman no less, but Morgan was
so polite and professional and pleasant about the fuckup that King
couldn't get mad, at least not at her.

But his eyes telegraphed his mood. His deputies were going to suffer the blowback from Morgan's discovery.

"We don't know that it belongs to Chelsea Clark," the sheriff said.
"Her husband wasn't very specific when he gave us a list of what she'd
been wearing when she left the house. He said he only saw her for a
couple of minutes, and he was preoccupied with the kids. He couldn't
even tell me what color her boots were."

Morgan nodded. "Actually, I called Tim and asked him if Chelsea
was wearing any jewelry Friday night. He said she has a silver bird
pendant that she wore all the time. I messaged him a photo. He positively identified the necklace as belonging to his wife. He says he has
snapshots of her wearing it. He's looking for one now."

King grunted. "Would have been nice if he'd mentioned it to me."

"I'm sure he just forgot. That night was very stressful." Morgan
continued. "The hairs have roots attached and would therefore contain
DNA. Are you going to have DNA tests run or would you prefer I send
the hairs to a private lab?"

Hair shafts were composed of dead cells and did not contain DNA.
Only the portion of a hair that was located below the skin was connected to the blood stream.

"I'll do it." The sheriff bit each word off like a piece of beef jerky.

"Do you have a sample of Chelsea's DNA?" Morgan asked.

"Yes." The sheriff nodded. "Her husband submitted it when he
filled out the missing persons report."

"Is there anything else we can do to help?" she offered.

"No." The sheriff sighed. "You've done more than enough."

Morgan rose and offered the sheriff her hand over his desk. King shook it gently and thanked her for her help. But all Lance got was a gruff nod that all but said *Don't let the door hit you in the ass on your way out.*

Lance and Morgan exited the station. The storm had followed them and pounded the parking lot with heavy rain. The Jeep was parked just twenty-five feet away. Yet Lance's hair and clothes got a fresh soaking as they raced for the vehicle.

Inside the vehicle, Morgan's teeth chattered. "Where to next?"

He started the engine and then turned the heater on high.

Lance checked the time on the dashboard block. "Dry clothes are next. Then we regroup. Want to make a quick stop at your house?"

"No." She held her hands out to the heat vents. "I have a change of clothes at the office."

"We can update Sharp while we're there. He's going to want to know about the necklace. We've found the first real evidence that Chelsea was forcibly taken."

"I almost wish we hadn't." Morgan's voice was quiet.

"I know." Because now they knew that Chelsea was either being held captive or dead.

The rain stopped as Lance drove to the office. He parked at the curb, and sun burst from the sky in biblical fashion. "Sharp's not here."

"I'll grab my bag." Morgan ran inside and emerged a minute later, garment bag in hand.

Lance had a two-bedroom house in town just six blocks from Sharp Investigations. They went in through the garage, passing piles of hockey equipment.

"How's your team?" Morgan asked.

Lance had coached a team of at-risk youths when he was a patrol officer with the Scarlet Falls PD. He'd bonded with the teens and stayed on after he'd left the police force. "Their skills are improving, their self-control not so much. They could start winning if I could keep them out of the penalty box."

They placed their shoes on the heating vent in the laundry room to dry. Hooking the top of her garment bag over the doorknob, Morgan hung her coat on a peg and then stripped off her socks.

Lance stripped off his flannel shirt and tee. He tossed both into the washer.

"Oh." Morgan was staring at his chest.

"Do you want a hanger for your clothes?"

And would you like me to help you take them off?

She turned to face him.

"You have man candy abs?" She grinned.

Heat rushed to Lance's face. And elsewhere.

She stepped forward, her gaze roaming over his chest, her eyes hungry. With slow, deliberate motions, she unsnapped her pants and slipped out of them. Her sweater hung past her hips, but he could see the lace edges of her dark-gray panties. She held out her pants by a belt loop. "You offered to hang these up."

Holy . . .

Lance's breath caught in his throat. Her legs were slender and long enough to wrap—

You're getting ahead of yourself. Be cool.

Right. He'd been waiting to put his hands, and other body parts, on her skin for months. There was nothing cool about his desire. He shifted his gaze to her face. There was nothing cool about the playful heat in her eyes either.

He took the pants. Without taking his eyes off hers, he grabbed a hanger from the bar over the washer, draped them over it, and hung them from the bar.

"You should get out of those wet pants." She moved closer, her hand reaching for the snap of his cargo pants. He flinched at the brush of her fingers against his belly.

"Are you sure?" He grabbed her hand.

Her face turned serious. "Very. We've been clearheaded and logical about whatever this is between us for weeks. Where has that gotten us?"

"There's nothing wrong with waiting for the right moment."

She smiled. "The right moment is the one that's happening right now. Life isn't perfect. If we wait for all our ducks to be lined up, we'll be waiting for a very long time. My little ducks are tough to herd."

"We do have complicated lives," he admitted.

"I don't want to wait for anything. I want to seize the moment." She smiled. "Or something."

He loved the powerful look in her eyes, and the confident tone of her voice was a huge turn on.

"I could really use a hot shower." She lifted the hem of her sweater, exposing another inch of gray lace. His heart skipped second gear and shifted into third. He ripped his eyes from her tantalizing striptease and focused on her eyes. As much as he wanted her body, he craved the rest of her just as much.

There was no other woman like her. Not for him.

She tugged off her scarf. The bruises around her neck were the color of ripe plums. Lance pictured Tyler Green with his hands around her throat. The quick surge of anger was followed by a cold dash of fear. She could have been killed, that lovely and slender neck broken.

His heart stammered at the thought.

"What's the matter?" Her confidence faltered. She lifted the scarf, as if to put it back on and cover the bruises. She licked her lips. Was she nervous?

The thought disconcerted him. It had been a long time for her, he supposed, but she was so capable that he often forgot about her vulnerabilities.

"Nothing. Nothing at all." He cupped her face in both hands. Her hair smelled of rain and lemons. "This is perfect."

He tilted her head and touched his lips to hers. God, the taste of her . . .

It would never be enough.

With a soft moan, she dropped the scarf, and it fell to the floor at their feet. She slipped her arms around his waist and splayed her fingers across his bare back. She pressed her body against his, all her softness lining up with his hard planes and angles.

He lifted his head. "You're perfect."

"Keep talking like that, mister, and you might get lucky." Her eyes shone with desire, humor—and yes . . . nerves.

"I'm already the luckiest man in the world."

"You asked for it." She wrapped a hand around the back of his neck and pulled him down to kiss her again.

He moved from her mouth to the curve of her neck, nipping lightly at her ear before tasting her collarbone. She groaned, a heady sound of need that slammed him in the gut. Well, below the gut.

"Let's get out of the laundry room." Moving backward, he tugged her into the hallway with him.

He walked backward all the way to the bedroom. Her hands were busy, stroking his back and shoulders. He slid his hands under her sweater and up her back. Her skin was smooth and soft. The backs of his legs hit the bed. He took his hands out from under her sweater to unsnap the holster at his waist. Reaching behind him, he set the gun and holster on the nightstand then got his hands back on her body and his lips on her mouth.

He tugged her sweater off, tossing it over his shoulder. She pressed against him, her skin warm and soft. Reaching behind her, he opened the clasp of her bra. The straps slid down her shoulders. He leaned back, letting it fall to the floor between them and exposing two absolutely perfect breasts. He cupped one, his thumb grazing her nipple. Her eyes drifted closed, and she moaned from deep in her throat.

Lance closed the inches between them, his mouth crushing down on hers. Her hands were at the snap of his pants. This time he helped her. They could not get naked fast enough. There were too many parts of her he wanted to touch and taste.

He lifted his lips from Morgan's, disbelief flooding him. Her eyes opened, the blue of them dark and needy. Finally.

This was actually going to happen.

Annnnnnd the *Magnum PI* theme song sounded from his pocket.

No.

No. No. No.

He froze. The absurdity of the situation rolled over him like a wave of ridiculousness.

They just couldn't get a break.

She leaned forward, resting her forehead against his chest and laughing under her breath.

"That's Sharp. I don't want to answer it." He really, really didn't want to answer that call. Stupid conscience. "But he usually texts unless it's important."

"You have to get it." Morgan sighed, taking a step backward. She rubbed her arms, as if suddenly cold. "What does your phone play when I call?"

"*Charlie's Angels.*" He pulled the phone from his pocket and accepted the call. "What is it, Sharp?"

"Is Morgan with you?" Sharp asked. "She didn't answer her phone."

Lance sighed. "She is."

Her phone was in her bag in the laundry room.

"Put me on speaker," Sharp said.

Lance held the phone between him and Morgan.

"Tim Clark just called looking for you," Sharp said. "There's a deputy at his house. He wants to take him down to the station. Tim sounded upset."

Anger flickered in her eyes. "I don't suppose the deputy told Tim why?"

"No," Sharp answered.

"I'll call Tim right now." She propped a hand on her hip. In just a pair of silk panties, the cocky pose was unbelievably hot.

Nothing short of ice in his shorts was going to cool him off, and Lance lamented the invention of the cell phone.

She ended the call and hurried for the laundry room. She returned a minute later, garment bag in one hand, giant purse in the other. She fished her phone out of her purse. "Tim called five minutes ago."

"You're allowed to have your phone out of reach for five minutes," Lance said.

"I know." But she still felt guilty. Morgan took responsibilities seriously. "It was just bad timing."

"You can say that again." Lance went to the closet for clean clothes. He exited wearing cargo pants and pulling a T-shirt over his head. Morgan put her phone on the bed and unzipped her garment bag while she used voice commands to dial Tim's number.

Lance swallowed with regret as she dressed—stepping into a maroon skirt, tugging a white shirt over her head, and then flipping her hair out of the neck.

"Hello," Tim answered. More than one child cried in the background. The sound set Lance's nerves on edge.

Something major must have happened if the sheriff wanted Tim at the station.

Chapter Eighteen

"What's going on, Tim?" Morgan zipped her skirt.

Still flushed and hot from Lance's touch, she bottled up her irritation. But really, why couldn't the sheriff just work and play well with others? Dressed, she picked up the phone and turned off the speaker.

"I don't know what to do." Desperation raised the pitch of Tim's voice.

"Slow down, Tim," Morgan said in a firm voice. Her client wasn't thinking straight. He needed direction. "What's going on?"

"The sheriff wants me at the station. He refuses to say why." Tim's words were nearly drowned out by crying, too much crying to be made by one baby.

"Who's crying?" Morgan asked.

"Both the kids," Tim answered. "The deputy scared Bella. She thinks he wants to take me away."

Temper heated the back of Morgan's neck. "Where is he now?"

"In the foyer. I'm in the living room, trying to calm down the kids. My in-laws went out to have more flyers printed. They're not answering their cell phones. I told him I needed to wait until they came home, but he said he could call child services to take care of the kids. What am I going to do? Can they really take my kids away?"

Morgan blew a hard breath through her nostrils.

"I want you to ask the deputy if you are under arrest." She seethed. Either the sheriff was holding back a giant piece of information or he was merely trying to intimidate the harried father. Either way, she was done playing nice.

"What?" Tim sounded shocked.

Morgan repeated her instructions in a louder voice. "Trust me. Do it now."

Over the connection, a little girl wailed, "Don't take my daddy!"

Morgan assumed Tim had joined the deputy in the foyer. The baby's cries intensified, each child feeding on the other's hysteria. She barely heard Tim shouting the question. The deputy's reply was drowned out.

"He says no," Tim yelled into the phone.

"Tell him you will meet him at the station as soon as your in-laws come home. Then tell him to leave your house. Be polite but firm."

"Are you sure?" Tim asked.

Morgan answered, "Completely sure."

A few seconds later, a door slammed, the little girl's wails quieted to whimpers, and the baby's cries diminished.

"Thank you." Tim sounded stunned. "I didn't know I could do that."

"Most people don't."

In Morgan's experience, law-abiding citizens didn't know their rights. Criminals, however, were well versed in the legal process.

Morgan said, "I'm on my way over. Don't talk to anyone or do anything without me."

She ended the call. After slipping her feet into her heels, she grabbed her tote bag and headed for the laundry room. "Can I collect my wet shoes when they're dry?"

Fully dressed, Lance was right behind her. "Of course."

She turned. "I wish . . ."

"Yeah. Me too." He leaned down and kissed her softly on the mouth. "At some point, we will have an hour to ourselves. I promise."

"I know." The sigh rolled through her. "But I really wanted it to be today."

The corner of his mouth lifted in a wry smile. "Me too."

She snagged her trench coat from the peg, then slid her arms into the sleeves.

Lance grabbed a jacket from a peg. He was wearing his gun again. "Are we going straight to Tim's?"

"Yes." In the car, she flipped down the mirror in the visor. Her hair was a disaster. She finger-combed it and wound it into a quick twist, digging a few hairpins from the bottom of her bag. She applied fresh lipstick and flipped the mirror closed. "Ready."

"You certainly are." Lance drove to Tim's house.

Tim's in-laws had returned and were in the kitchen with the children when Tim let Morgan and Lance into the house. Chelsea's parents looked shell-shocked.

Patricia shifted the baby over her shoulder. "What's going on?"

"That's what we're going to find out," Morgan said.

Bella cried when Tim said goodbye.

He crouched down and hugged her. "I'll be back soon."

"Promise?" She sniffed and wiped her nose on her sleeve.

"Promise." Tim kissed his daughter on the head then straightened. "Let's go."

He kept his eyes forward until they were outside. They got into the Jeep, and Tim stared at his house from the back seat. "Why would he treat me like this?"

"I don't know." In the passenger seat, Morgan turned to face him. "Here are the rules. If I tell you not to answer a question, don't. You not only cooperated in the sheriff's investigation; you initiated it. In fact, you are the one who is unsatisfied with the way he is handling your wife's disappearance. You've hired a private firm because he hasn't made satisfactory progress on the case."

"OK," Tim said. "But I don't understand. All I want to do is find my wife. Why won't he look for her?"

"I'm sure he is." Morgan tapped a finger on her leg. The sheriff should be sharing more of his investigation with the family, but she suspected something had happened to initiate the sheriff's call to Tim.

Once at the sheriff's station, Morgan, Lance, and Tim were escorted to an interview room by a deputy.

"The sheriff will be back soon," the deputy said.

Sheriff King isn't even here?

Seeing the deputy's grim face as he closed the door sent a chill rippling up Morgan's arms.

What had happened?

Had they found Chelsea?

"I'll get us some coffee." Lance left the room for a few minutes, returning with three Styrofoam cups.

Tim didn't drink his, but he held it between his palms and stared into the cup, barely moving, while they waited. Ten minutes later, the sheriff opened the door and walked in. Tim jumped, the feet of his plastic chair squeaking on the floor with the jerk of his body. His coffee sloshed over the rim of the cup, and he set it down on the table.

The sheriff's boots were muddy, and his hair mussed, as if he'd been outside. The grim set of his face put Morgan on alert.

"I'm sorry to keep you waiting." He settled his bulk in the chair across from Tim. Though his eyes flickered at Morgan with annoyance—no doubt he didn't appreciate her challenging his authority—when his gaze settled on Tim, it was with empathy. "Thank you for coming in, Mr. Clark." He sighed, his big chest expanding and deflating. "I want you to brace yourself."

Morgan stiffened. Next to her, Tim's hands curled around the arms of his chair.

The sheriff continued. "This afternoon, the body of a woman was found by a pair of hikers."

Oh, no.

Morgan's mind spun. Keeping her ears tuned to the sheriff, she turned to her client. Tim blinked. His head shook slightly, as if he didn't believe what he was hearing.

"The first thing you need to know is that we have not identified her yet. We do not know for certain if this woman is your wife," the sheriff continued.

Tim's features were frozen, the color draining from his face until he was the pale gray of day-old snow. When he finally opened his mouth, his voice was a tight rasp. "But it could be?"

"It's possible," the sheriff said. "The age bracket fits, and she was blonde."

The air whooshed out of Tim's body with an almost inaudible moan.

Morgan touched his forearm. His hands clenched his armrests tightly enough to raise the tendons on the backs of them and turn his knuckles white. She leaned closer. "Are you all right?"

Tim didn't react. His eyes were fixed in horror on the sheriff, who was watching him with sympathetic—and assessing—eyes.

And Morgan got it.

Sheriff King had wanted to see Tim's reaction. King had wanted to be the one to deliver the news. So he'd done his best to isolate Tim so he didn't find out another way.

As if he was following Morgan's train of thought, the sheriff said, "I didn't want you to hear this on the news, which is why I sent a deputy to get you immediately. When I left the scene, the first reporters were showing up. It won't take long."

Morgan had proudly worked many cases on the side of law enforcement, but in the last few weeks, she'd seen the flip side of criminal law. How people who were supposedly considered innocent were treated. And what she'd learned so far wasn't pretty.

The sheriff could have gone to Tim's house, or he could have sent another officer. Dragging Tim in hadn't been necessary.

"Do you know how long she'd been out there?" Lance asked.

"Hard to say." The sheriff shook his head. "Coyotes had dug up—"

Tim made a soft, choking noise.

"Sheriff," Morgan said in a reproachful voice.

The sheriff blinked at her. "Sorry."

"Could my client have some water?" Morgan asked, furious. They'd all seen Tim's response to the news. He was obviously shocked. He did not need to know that wild animals had mauled the body.

"Of course." The sheriff got up and left the room.

Tim shoved his chair back, bent at the waist, and buried his face in his hands. His breathing was too fast and shallow.

Morgan put a hand on his arm. "Take a deep breath and hold it for a few seconds. You're going to hyperventilate. There's no point in assuming the worst. Hang on until we get more information."

Without lifting his head, he nodded.

The sheriff returned with several bottles of water that he set on the table. He dropped back into the seat facing Tim.

Tim sat up, his face contorted with the effort of controlling his emotions.

"What do you know about the woman?" Lance asked.

The sheriff lifted a shoulder. "Not much other than she was blonde and the medical examiner thought she was in her twenties."

Tim's eye twitched. He didn't need to hear every detail at this time. Morgan could fill him in on the details when the preliminary autopsy report was finished.

Morgan handed Tim a bottle of water. "Why don't we go into the hall for a couple of minutes?"

Tim twisted off the cap and took a mouthful of water. He seemed to have trouble swallowing. He lowered the bottle and wiped his mouth with the back of his hand. "No. I want to hear everything."

"Are you sure?" Morgan asked. "It's not necessary. You might be torturing yourself for no reason."

Tim pressed his palms to his eyes for a few seconds. When he lowered his hands, he'd regained his composure. "Where was she found?"

"Route 87, in Black Run State Park," the sheriff said. "I know this is hard. I'll let you know as soon as I have more information to share."

"Thank you." The words caught in the back of Tim's throat, and he stared at his water without drinking, seemingly lost.

"Let's get you home before the press shows up." Morgan didn't want Tim to have to run a gauntlet of reporters, cameras, and microphones to get into his house.

Nodding, Tim stood. He wobbled a little and put a palm on the table to steady his balance.

"Oh, Tim," the sheriff said. "Before you leave, I need you to officially state that this belonged to your wife."

He set a small paper evidence bag on the table. Opening the metal clasp, he dumped the contents on the table. The bird pendant slid a few inches across the smooth fake wood surface. "Does this look familiar?"

Tim paled and sucked in a sharp breath. Leaning harder on the table, he reached forward to touch the pendant then paused, his hand hovering a few inches above the silver bird.

"You can touch it," the sheriff said. "It's already been processed."

"It's Chelsea's." Tim picked it up by the chain. He straightened. Draping the necklace across his palm, he stroked the tiny silver bird. "She never takes this off. Her parents gave it to her when she graduated high school." He looked up, his eyes bleak. "This was near where her car was found?"

"Yes," the sheriff answered.

"So she was there, anyway." Tim closed his eyes for a few seconds.

With a quick look at Morgan and Lance, the sheriff added, "Maybe."

The sheriff was holding back. Morgan searched his face. He had more information than he was giving them.

"How long until we know?" Tim asked in a too quiet voice.

"Worst case scenario, we have to wait for a DNA analysis, which could take weeks. But it's possible we'll know much sooner." Could the sheriff be any more vague? But then again, maybe he had good reason.

The police had Chelsea's fingerprints. The body must have been in bad shape if the sheriff wasn't sure that they could be compared. Rodents sometimes nibbled on fingertips. Bears and coyotes dismembered and disseminated bodies. The medical examiner might not even have all of the remains. While Morgan believed in being honest with her client, Tim didn't need to know any of these things. Not yet, anyway. If the body was positively ID'd as Chelsea, then he'd learn all the gruesome details. Until then, what was the point in causing him more distress?

"Oh, no." Tim started for the door. "I have to get home before Rand and Patricia see this on the news."

Her parents would be devastated.

What were the chances that the body of *another* blonde woman would turn up the same week that Chelsea disappeared?

Chapter Nineteen

Morgan bristled as they passed four news vans parked in front of Tim's house.

Damn it!

This is not how Chelsea's parents should have heard about the body being found. The sheriff should have driven out to the house to tell Tim and Chelsea's parents instead of dragging Tim down to the station. Rand and Patricia deserved more respect than finding out via the news.

"Looks like the press found out about the body," Lance said. "The days of carefully controlled press conferences are over. There's more pressure to be first than there is to be accurate."

"I should have called them," Tim said.

"You did what you thought was best," Morgan said.

"You know what they say about good intentions," Tim replied.

Lance parked, and the three of them got out of the Jeep and walked up the driveway. A dozen reporters smoothed their hair and touched up their makeup. Cameramen and sound techs set up equipment.

"There he is!" someone yelled. "Tim!"

A reporter lunged at him. A microphone was thrust into his face. Lance shouldered the reporter out of the way, but a dozen bodies pushed forward.

Angry, Morgan leaned over and spoke in Tim's ear. "Don't answer any questions in this format. Try to ignore them."

But the barrage came from all sides. Morgan and Lance flanked Tim, trying to shield him, but his hands were shaking by the time they reached the top of the driveway.

Then the front door opened, and everyone froze. Chelsea's father stepped outside, his face set in a stony mask of despair. Three seconds ticked by as everyone simply stared. Then the moment of silence passed, and reporters turned away from Tim and rushed for Rand. His eyes were watery and red-rimmed. His body swayed as if he was barely able to stay on his feet.

He knew.

Tim walked closer, through the gauntlet of cameras and eager bodies. Morgan pushed through the throng. "Excuse me."

A reporter stumbled back as she elbowed him aside and fought her way up the three steps toward Rand.

"My wife and I just learned that the body of a young woman was found in the state park." Rand's jaw shifted. Muscles tensed in a face taut enough to shatter. "Until we hear otherwise, we will not simply assume this woman is our daughter. We will continue to look for her, and we hope the sheriff's department will do the same."

Morgan stopped dead. She didn't have the heart to interrupt.

A reporter thrust a microphone in front of Rand. "Are you saying you don't have confidence in the sheriff's investigation?"

Bitterness glinted in Rand's misty eyes. "He hasn't found anything, has he? Hikers found this poor woman."

Another reporter turned back to Tim. "Mr. Clark, do you think the woman who was found is your wife?"

Tim choked.

Morgan grabbed the microphone and pulled it to her. "We're still waiting on word from the medical examiner. There's no value in specu-lating at this point."

Another newsman confronted Tim. "The sheriff's office refuses to clear you as a suspect. How do you feel about that, Mr. Clark?"

Again, Morgan redirected the mic from Tim's face to her own. "Mr. Clark simply wants the sheriff's department to find his wife. He supports the sheriff's efforts to conduct a thorough investigation. Tim has never been accused of having anything to do with his wife's disappearance."

Next to her, Tim cleared his throat. "I just want my wife to come home. I don't care about anything else."

He walked up the steps toward his front door like a zombie.

"Tim's right," Rand said in a stiff voice. "We won't rest until we've brought Chelsea home. Which is why we're offering a ten-thousand-dollar reward for information that leads to finding Chelsea."

Morgan snapped to attention.

Questions burst from the media.

"Is there a hotline number?"

"Can tips be given anonymously?"

"Do you have details on that reward?"

"Is the offer still valid if she's dead?"

Cold bastard!

Rand flinched at the question.

Morgan slid forward and gently eased in front of him. If she'd known he was thinking about offering a reward, she would have tried to persuade him to talk to the sheriff first. Rewards could be helpful, but they could also muddy the investigation. But the offer was out there. No way to take it back. All she could do was manage the fallout. "Details about the reward will be forthcoming from the sheriff's department."

"If the body is identified as Chelsea, then what happens to the money?"

Enough!

Tim stiffened and reached for the nearest microphone. "Please. My family is going through the hardest time of our lives. We ask that you pray for us. And if anyone has any information that might help find my wife, please call the sheriff's department. Please help us bring Chelsea home, and if you don't have any information, then we ask that you respect our privacy."

With that, Tim turned and herded his father-in-law back into the house. Closing the door, he looked out through the narrow window next to the door.

Morgan repeated her statement about the reward. Lance stayed at her side, his body tense, his eyes scanning the group, looking for threats. When she was finished, Morgan ignored follow-up questions. They went inside, hoping the reporters would be satisfied enough to leave.

They found Rand hunched over the kitchen table.

His gaze met Morgan's. "I'm sorry if I messed up. I wasn't thinking. We saw the news about the body on Facebook. Patricia almost fainted."

"I'm the one who should be sorry." Tim sighed. "I was trying to get back in time to tell you in person. I didn't want you to find out that way."

"It's not your fault. It would have been a shock no matter how the news was delivered." Rand's shoulders hunched as if unable to bear the weight of the day.

"Where are the kids?" Tim asked.

Rand pointed at the ceiling. "Patricia took them upstairs. She didn't want Bella to overhear . . ."

"Good thinking," Tim said. He turned to face Morgan. "I'm sorry. I hope I didn't totally screw up out there. I didn't know how to react."

"You did fine," Morgan said. "Your reaction was honest and sincere."

Rand got up and paced the room. "I'm done with that sheriff. He's just going to get mad. He didn't want me to offer a reward in the first place. He's lazy and doesn't want to follow up on the leads. Do we really have to involve him in the reward? I'd rather we handle it ourselves."

"There are legal obligations associated with a reward like this," Morgan said. "It's a verbal contract. And honestly, the sheriff is going to be annoyed, but he's also going to want to retain control of the tips coming in. Handling the phone lines will be a full-time job."

Rand crossed his arms and lifted his chin in defiance. "It only takes one good tip."

"I agree," Morgan said. "But we don't have the manpower or the expertise to handle the sheer volume. But in the end, it's up to you. I'm just asking that you give it serious thought before you decide. Remember, there will be people trying to take advantage. Ten thousand dollars is a lot of money."

"Rand, I know what you're trying to do," Tim said. "But we hired a professional for a reason, right? What's the point if we're not going to listen to her?"

"OK. You're right." Rand nodded, the gesture short and curt and unhappy. He clearly didn't want to give up control. "Let the sheriff handle it."

"Do you want me to talk to Sheriff King?" Morgan offered. The sheriff was not going to be happy, but that was too damned bad. He should have been more sensitive to the family's feelings.

"Is that all right with you, Rand?" Tim asked. "It's your money."

"It's fine," Rand snapped. Then his aggression faded back to grief. "I don't care about the money. I just want my baby back." His voice broke.

"I know." Tim nodded. "But thank you anyway. This wouldn't be an option without your help."

"Now that the reward offer has been made, I'll call the sheriff and let him know," Morgan said. "We'll need to issue a formal statement outlining the terms. The sheriff will have to give us a hotline number. Rand, do you have the money readily available? There could be multiple claimants; though, we'll include an expiration date and language to give us the ability to change or pull the reward if necessary."

As much as Morgan hated to be practical at a time like this, if Chelsea was dead, the family should keep its money. Rand and Patricia appeared to be comfortable but not wealthy. Tim would have new childcare expenses. Raising kids was not cheap. He would be doing it alone. As Morgan well knew, single parenting was hard enough without financial hardship.

She continued. "Also, we might want to consider holding a press conference once the details are worked out. The media will really jump on this. When Chelsea disappeared, coverage had to compete with the police shooting. It would be a good idea to get her picture circulating again and make sure everyone in the area knows she is missing and has a fresh image of her in their minds. We can utilize social media. Criminals will turn on their mothers for ten thousand dollars."

At least, that was what Morgan hoped.

Chapter Twenty

The door opened, and he came in, his black-masked face like a doll with no features.

Chelsea's heart jolted as she scampered off the cot, eyes cast down at her bare toes. Her body was sore, but she'd eaten the protein bar from that morning, sipped water, and moved around enough to prevent further stiffness from settling into her bruised limbs.

The calories and hydration had helped, though she was careful to move as if she was weak and timid. He seemed to like that.

He held a canvas bag in his hand. When he set it down on the floor, it jangled. Not food.

Apprehension stirred in her belly. Something was different in his posture, his attitude.

"I have something special planned for you tonight." Excitement vibrated through his tone.

Chelsea's pulse quickened. Sweat broke out between her shoulder blades and breasts as anxiety blossomed into real fear.

"Say the rules," he commanded, as he had every time he'd come into the container.

She repeated them.

"Repeat number one."

"I belong to you. I will do what you say without question. I am your property."

He opened the bag at his feet. "Lay on the cot, facedown."

She backed to the wall, her bones trembling. "No. Please."

The words barely left her mouth before she realized her mistake.

He straightened, anger tensing his body. "What did you say?"

She slapped a hand over her mouth.

"I thought we'd gotten past that." He shook his head in disappointment as he stepped closer. "Not only did you speak without permission, but you dared to defy me."

The blow came with lightning speed. Delivered with an open hand, the slap stunned and stung without affecting her consciousness. Still, the force of it sent her reeling. She landed on her knees, the impact with the wooden floor ringing pain through her legs.

"I will not repeat myself again." His words were slow and deliberate, menacing. "On the cot. Facedown."

Chelsea's entire body shook, but she couldn't seem to move. Her limbs were useless.

"I guess we still have some work to do." He grabbed the handles of his bag with one hand and took a handful of her hair with the other. Her scalp screamed as he dragged her onto the cot.

"Don't move."

She turned her head to watch as he removed thick leather straps from the bag. Tears streamed down her cheeks, and she couldn't stop the sobs that poured from her mouth.

What is he going to do?

He took one hand and firmly tied it to the leg of the cot. Then he did the same with the other. He pulled her dress up to her waist before strapping her torso and legs down.

Cold air caressed Chelsea's exposed legs and buttocks.

This is it. He's going to rape me now.

145

But he left the room. Minutes passed. She had no idea how much time went by. Her heart thundered. Sweat poured from her armpits. Gooseflesh rippled on her bare skin, and her stomach flipped inside out as she waited.

When the door opened, she startled, her pulse sprinting with a fresh burst of panic. He had a box in his hands. He set it on the floor. From it, he took a piece of gauze and a bottle of rusty-colored liquid. Crouching next to her, he wet the cloth and cleaned her right buttock.

When he pulled on a pair of surgical gloves, she flailed, terror driving her completely out of control. A scream built in her throat, choking her when she couldn't get it out. The lightweight cot jumped.

"Stop it!" He backhanded her across the side of the head. Pain jolted through her. Her ears rang, and her body went slack.

Dimly she heard him rattling around in the box. The sight of the blowtorch and a length of metal brought a groan from her mouth. At the sound, he turned back to her and shoved a thick piece of cloth into her mouth.

The torch fired up with a soft whoosh. He held the metal rod in the blue flame until the metal glowed. When he turned back to her, she knew exactly what he was going to do.

Oh, my God. Oh, my God. OhmyGodOhmyGod.

He was going to brand her.

"Don't. Move."

She couldn't obey. Her brain went into a frenzy. Her body went wild, her limbs tensing and straining against her restraints. With a grunt, he straddled her thighs, his bulk weighing her body and the cot down. He pressed one hand between her shoulder blades to keep her upper body still. Without any hesitation, he pressed the brand into her skin.

Pain blasted through her buttock, the intensity as bright and hot as a rocket. Over the screaming in her throat, she heard his voice, steady and controlled.

"One. Two. Three." He lifted the iron.

The agony radiated from the wound, pulsing with every beat of her heart.

Drenched in sweat, she went limp. She didn't recognize the faint mewling sounds that came from behind the gag. She closed her eyes.

"It's over now." A gentle hand caressed her head. He pulled the gag from her mouth. "Shh. Take a deep breath."

She couldn't. Her breaths came faster and faster. He emptied the bag and put it to her face until she stopped hyperventilating.

"You are a strong one," he said with pride.

He took the bag away. Standing, he repacked his tools and took the bag from the room. Then he applied ointment and a bandage to the burn, finally taping a piece of plastic wrap over the bandage. "It's best to keep the air out."

She didn't move, even after he removed the leather straps. Her body was spent. The horror and pain that filled her left no room for anything else. It filled her until she felt as though she'd burst.

"You rubbed the skin right off your ankle." Then he removed the manacle from one ankle and put it on the other. He treated the abrasion, murmuring soft words that were supposed to be comforting, but they only turned her stomach. Then he offered her two tablets. "These will help."

She couldn't respond. She couldn't do anything. Even her tears and sobbing had stopped. With the heat radiating from her wound, her brain couldn't comprehend what had just happened. Her body and mind were paralyzed with shock.

"I'll leave them here." He set the tablets on the barrel next to the lantern. "You can take them when you've composed yourself. I realize this has been an emotional experience. But now there's no doubt to whom you belong."

He pulled her dress down to cover her legs. Then he went out the door, returning in a few minutes with a white take-out bag. The smell of food wafted across the space, nauseating her.

"I've brought you a special treat. Tonight is special." He set the bag on the barrel then leaned over her. She flinched as he pressed a kiss to her temple. "Tonight, you were marked forever as mine."

Chelsea didn't move as he left. She didn't know how much time passed. She lay on the cot, curled on her side, trembling down to her skeleton, beyond tears.

Almost beyond reaction.

A part of her brain seemed to be shutting down, walling itself off from the horror like scar tissue over a wound. There was only so much fear she could comprehend before descending into madness.

She pictured Bella's smile, her joy, spinning in a twirly dress, skipping across a playground, zooming down a slide.

Running into Chelsea's arms.

And William.

If Chelsea concentrated hard enough, she could smell him, hear his wails, watch his mood shift from despondent to content as he nursed at her breast.

No.

She stirred, levering her upper body off the cot.

She wouldn't . . . *couldn't* give up.

If she did, he won. And she'd never see her children again.

Shivering, she looked for the wool blanket. It had slipped onto the floor. She reached for it, the movement sending a white-hot bolt of pain through her buttock, hip, and thigh. She hadn't seen the brand but knew it was only the size of her palm. Still, her whole body throbbed. She pulled the blanket around her shoulders and breathed.

She spotted a small metal object on the floor near the door. What was that?

A nail.

It must have fallen out of his bag.

Getting to her feet felt impossible. Her body was ravaged by the beating and branding, and by a terror so layered she could barely comprehend its depth. If she sank into that abyss of fear, if it closed over her head, she might never reach the surface of sanity again.

But she'd learned over the past three years that her body could do amazing things. She'd given birth twice. She could do this.

She had to do this.

Shifting her bare feet to the floor, she sat on her uninjured hip. Dizziness swam through her head. She waited, breathing, until it passed. Then she rose to shaky legs. Her knees wobbled, the brand thrummed with waves of heat. Dragging the chain attached to her ankle, she staggered toward the door. The chain ended, and she had to crouch and stretch her hand toward the nail. The tips of her fingers touched it. She pawed it closer, and when her fingers closed around it, a sense of resilience passed through her.

She grabbed the bag of food and returned to the cot, holding the nail in her closed fist as if it were a priceless prize.

Food was necessary for survival. She needed to eat, no matter how awful she felt. She opened the bag. Inside, she found a Coke, chicken fingers, and french fries. Her body perked up at the smell. She took a tentative bite of a fry. When her stomach didn't revolt. She ate another, then moved on to the chicken. She chewed slowly. Who knew when she'd get more food? Everything that went into her belly needed to stay there. She ate every fry and piece of chicken and licked the breadcrumbs from the cardboard box. The Coke settled her stomach. She inspected the two tablets he'd left her. Ibuprofen. There was no need to be in more pain than necessary. She washed them down with Coke. Then she sat back and rolled the nail in her fingertips.

What was she going to do with it?

She curled her knees toward her chest. The manacle on her leg clanked. She inserted the nail into the keyhole, working it gently, feeling her way, prodding, pressing, turning.

Patience! Don't break it.

After what seemed like forever, the lock clicked and dropped open. She flinched, staring.

She'd done it.

A wave of joy swept over her, quickly followed by a burst of terror. What would he do if he found out?

Memories of the beating and branding flooded her. Unable to cry any more, she gagged on her distress. Small, panicked noises sounded in her throat.

Stop!

Bella. William. Bella. William. Bella. William.

She repeated her children's names in a centering and calming mantra. Then she got to her feet again to walk toward the door. She touched the door handle, turned it, and pushed. There was no give. She used all her weight. Resting her forehead against the cold metal, she breathed.

No giving up.

She walked the perimeter of the container again, kicking at each rust spot. Frustration welled in her throat. Her eyes closed, and her head fell back.

This is hopeless.

She was going to die. Or worse. She would be here for a long time, subject to his whims. It would get worse. Every cell in her body knew that he had something truly horrible planned for her.

She opened her eyes. Her gaze locked on the small hole in the ceiling. Through it, she could see a canopy of branches and bits of black night sky. She fetched the camp lantern and held it up. The hole was approximately ten inches in diameter, and the surrounding metal heavily rusted. Could she enlarge it enough to squeeze out? And even if she could, how could she get to the ceiling?

Scanning the container, her gaze settled on the few objects: the chain coiled on the floor, the barrel, the cot. The blanket fell to the floor as she moved toward the cot.

It was a standard camp model. She turned it over. The frame and legs were hinged. When folded, it would fit into a canvas carry bag. At either end, an aluminum bar about two feet long supported the frame. She braced her feet against the bar to pop it out of place. Once she had it loose, she slid it from the canvas sleeve.

Returning to stand beneath the hole, she poked at the edges with the bar. The metal crumbled. She was able to enlarge it several inches all the way around. Large enough that she could probably squeeze through. But she was no gymnast. She couldn't launch her way through the opening.

She dragged the cot under the hole. It wasn't high enough. After reinserting the bracing bar and manhandling it back into place, she turned the cot onto its side. She stooped and picked up the wool blanket, tossing it over her shoulder. She left the lantern behind. She couldn't risk being seen. The shed must appear exactly the same from the outside. Then, carefully placing her foot directly above the center support bar, she pushed up in one smooth motion. The cot wobbled on its side as she straightened her leg and reached for the hole in the ceiling. Close to the ceiling, she was forced to hunch over. She gripped the edge of the hole to steady her balance and keep the cot from toppling. The sharp metal sliced into her hand, the blood that welled up made her grip slippery.

Once her balance was stable, she pushed the blanket through the hole. Her head, shoulders, and arms were next. She pressed her palms down on the roof and pulled the rest of her body onto the roof.

Her breaths came in pants, and her heart jiggled a ragged beat. She rolled to her back and stared up at the sky. The moon shone through a thin veil of clouds. She gulped air. It seemed fresh now, but quickly bit through the thin cotton of her dress. There was nothing she could do about that.

Her heart sprinted in her chest. If he saw her . . .

She stopped herself.

Her mind simply couldn't go there without being paralyzed.

She froze. What now?

She waited, listening and letting her eyes adjust. It didn't take long, though her vision was still a little blurry. In a few minutes, she could make out the outlines of a building. A small house? Cabin?

Whatever it was, it was dark. Was he there? Or did he sleep and live somewhere else? The whole property had an abandoned air. But she didn't have time to contemplate anything. She had to get away. She turned her head and looked over her shoulder. Behind her, on the other side of a meadow, were woods.

She crawled across the flat roof. On the side opposite the house, she tossed the blanket to the ground. She put her feet over the edge and let her body slide until she balanced on her hip bones. The burn on her buttock raged as the muscles tensed. She wiggled farther, until she dangled from her hands. Then she dropped to the ground. Soft knees absorbed the landing.

The container blocked the moonlight. In its shadow, darkness surrounded and concealed her. The ground was cold under the bare soles of her feet. She grabbed the blanket and wrapped it around her, covering as much of the bright-yellow dress as she could.

To get to the woods, she had to cross the open space. A wide, open space. She stepped out of the shadows and started toward the trees. Desperation and hope fueled her steps. She broke into a stumbling jog. Sticks and rocks bit into her feet as she ran for the cover of the forest.

Somewhere behind her, a dog barked. She glanced over her shoulder. A light went on in one of the cabin's windows.

Oh, my God.

He was there!

Chelsea ran faster. One more glance back showed more lights. A door opened, light spilling out.

No more looking back. Adrenaline blocked the pain. Her legs remembered this. Running. She did it every day. Muscle memory carried her toward the trees. She blocked out all thoughts of what would happen if he caught her.

Please.

Bella. William.

Mommy loves you.

The slap of a screen door echoed in the night air.

Chapter Twenty-One

"Enough." He tossed the chained hound a scrap of beef. The dog snapped his reward out of the air and swallowed it whole. The beast knew its job. It had learned.

He scanned the silent yard. Everything looked the same as when he'd gone inside.

The container stood in silence under the thick spread of branches. It had been on the property when he'd purchased it. From the amount of rust on the steel exterior, the metal box had been there for many years. He'd painted the spots of cancer to keep them from spreading.

He crossed the mossy ground and checked the door. Reaching out, he touched the padlock that secured the door. Locked.

But something didn't feel right.

Turning his head, he listened. The snap of a twig reverberated from the darkness of the trees. A deer?

He pulled the key from his pocket, unlocked the padlock, and opened the door. The dim light of the camp lantern shone on an empty box. His gaze took in the chain, the upturned cot, the enlarged hole in the ceiling. Unable to believe what he was seeing, he blinked. But it didn't change reality.

She'd escaped.

Anger spiked inside him, red and hot and sputtering like a thick boiling liquid. He breathed the cold night air deeply into his lungs. Emotions wouldn't find her. A cool head would.

He'd purposefully chosen a smart woman.

Be careful what you wish for.

Pivoting, he sprinted for the house. In the kitchen, he grabbed his jacket from the back of a chair and his flashlight from the counter, then turned back toward the door.

Wait.

He returned to the drawer and withdrew a handgun and checked the load. Then he went back outside and returned to the container. Shining the light on the ground, he found a footprint in the soft earth. Slim arch. Small toes.

Chelsea.

Arcing the light back and forth, he spotted another print and connected the dots. The line pointed straight into the woods. He picked up speed, projecting her trajectory.

"Where are you, Chelsea?" he called. "You can't get away from me. If you come back now, I won't hurt you, but if I have to hunt you down, you'll be sorry."

Very sorry.

Maybe his lessons hadn't been firm enough. He could fix that. When he found her, she wouldn't be able to run away. Hell, she wouldn't be able to walk.

Or crawl.

He started down a game trail, his light seeking and finding a footprint and a spot of dark liquid. He squatted and touched it. Turning over his hand, he examined the bright smudge.

Blood.

Still wet and bright.

She hadn't gotten far.

He straightened, tilting his head and straining for sounds.

She was barefoot, wearing a dress as bright as a beacon. She didn't have a coat, just a blanket to protect her from the fall-crisp air. Though the temperature wasn't low enough to cause frostbite, she'd definitely suffer hypothermia.

No. He'd find her. He had to.

She was his.

He felt for the gun in his pocket. If he couldn't have her, no one could.

Underbrush rustled to his left—and another sound.

Heavy breathing?

He turned toward the sound and broke into a jog. She was close. He could feel her. Smell her. Sense her.

They were connected by a link that could be broken by only one thing: death.

Chapter Twenty-Two

At nine thirty Friday morning, Lance followed Morgan into her office and watched her get settled. "Good morning."

She set her bag and stainless steel travel mug on her desk, removed her coat, and hung it in the closet. Her pants and suit jacket were black, and so were the circles under her eyes.

Worry pulled at him. She'd spent hours the previous day hashing out the details of the reward offered by Rand with the sheriff's department. As predicted, the sheriff was pissed off, but he'd taken on the responsibility. The hotline was supposed to be up and running, and a press conference was scheduled for that evening. Morgan would have spent the night drafting rough statements for Tim and Rand.

No doubt she'd been up late reviewing notes on the case as well. And they'd split the job of writing up the reports on yesterday's interviews. With her grandfather not able to drive, taxiing Sophie to preschool and Gianna to dialysis also fell on her shoulders.

She raised her coffee cup to her lips and drank deeply.

"Are you all right?" Lance asked.

"Sophie had a night terror."

"What is a night terror?"

"She was thrashing around and screaming in her sleep."

"Oh, hell."

"Yes. 'Hell' sums up my night perfectly." Morgan tilted her head back and drained her mug. She crossed the room to the Keurig machine on her credenza. Setting her mug under the spout, she plugged in a pod and pressed the "On" button. "She woke the whole family. I had to bring her into my room for the rest of the night. Sharing a bed with Sophie is like sleeping with an octopus on Red Bull."

Sophie was an unpredictable, sensitive, out-of-the-box child. She experienced life with an emotional meter permanently set to high. She loved powerfully and without reservation. And held a grudge, like the one aimed at Lance for claiming some of her mother's attention, with the steadfastness of a SWAT sniper locked on a target.

"Poor kid. She must have been a mess," Lance said.

"Not at all." Morgan drummed her fingers on the credenza as the coffeemaker gurgled. "A night terror isn't the same thing as a nightmare. She slept through the whole thing and woke up in a great mood surprised to be in bed with me."

A smile tugged at Lance's mouth. "Then poor you."

Morgan sighed. "Night terrors are named appropriately. It was terrifying to watch. I've been awake since three."

"Morning," Sharp said as he walked in, drawing up as he scanned her face. "You look terrible."

"Thanks." Morgan laughed. She lifted her refilled mug and inhaled, her eyes closing in a way that was almost sensual.

"I told you that stuff was bad for you." Sharp lifted his mug. Large red letters on the black ceramic read PRIVATE DICK. It had been a gift from his cop buddies when he'd retired from the force and opened the investigation agency. "Are you sure I can't replace that poison with organic tea and a protein shake?"

Morgan clutched her cup closer, protecting it like a starving wolf standing over a fresh kill. "Hands off the coffee."

Sharp backed away, shaking his head. "Caffeine overloads the adrenal system. In the long run, you'll end up more fatigued. Ask Lance."

"*Lance* is not getting in the middle." Lance turned to face the whiteboard.

Sharp walked up to stand next to him. "Are we still waiting on an ID of the body?"

"I just talked to the sheriff," Morgan said. "The woman's face and hands were badly damaged by animal activity, and her lower jaw is missing. The medical examiner was going to start on the autopsy first thing this morning. He has Chelsea's medical and dental records. If it's not Chelsea, he should be able to rule her out, even if he can't identify the body."

An autopsy could take anywhere from two to four hours. Difficult and damaged remains complicated the process. A preliminary report wouldn't be ready until the next morning, but the county ME would not leave the Clark family hanging any longer than necessary. If he could rule out Chelsea, he'd let them know ASAP.

"The ME likes to get an early start," Lance said. "We'll hear from him in the next couple of hours."

"Are we ready for the press conference?" Sharp asked.

"I need to talk to Tim and Rand this afternoon, but everything is set up with the sheriff's office." Morgan took her place behind her desk. "Now what?"

"We were hired to find Chelsea," Sharp said. "We assume the body isn't hers until we hear otherwise."

"Let me get my laptop and we'll go over the background checks." Lance went to his office and grabbed his computer. Last night, he'd made his first foray into Chelsea's work files. Two hours of reviewing financial statements and tax documents had left his eyes crossed and his head aching. He'd found nothing suspicious, but he'd barely covered 10 percent of the material.

On the way back into Morgan's office, he opened the file his mother had e-mailed him that morning. "We'll start with Fiona West, Chelsea's best friend. There's nothing even remotely interesting in her background. In her interview, Fiona claimed that Tim and Chelsea were having marital problems. Tim worked too much."

"That's what Tim said in our initial meeting," Uncapping a marker, Sharp wrote a note under Fiona's name on the board. "Who's next on your list?"

"Kirk Armani." Morgan opened her file. All her papers were neatly sorted, hole-punched, and affixed in the proper place. "According to Tim's boss, Kirk has a crush on Chelsea."

"Kirk seemed very uncomfortable when we asked him about her." Lance set the laptop on the corner of Morgan's desk.

Morgan shook her head. "The very act of being interviewed would create stress for Kirk. Did your mother find any red flags in his file?"

"No," Lance admitted. "We'll put him aside for now. Moving on to Tim's boss, Elliot Pagano."

Morgan flipped through her paperwork. "What do we know about his wife's death?"

Lance scrolled. "His wife died in a car accident last year. She was under the influence of OxyContin when she got behind the wheel. Not enough to kill her but enough to impair her driving. Her death was ruled an accident, not a suicide. She had family money and did invest some of her funds in Speed Net as a start-up, but most of her estate was tied up in a trust specifically designed to keep spouses from inheriting family money. Elliot didn't receive any of it. Her life insurance policy was held by the family trust."

Sharp's marker hovered over the board. "How tight was his alibi?"

"Vacuum sealed," said Lance.

"Damn." Sharp moved Elliot's name down the suspect list.

Lance continued. "Elliot became a multimillionaire when he sold his interest in TechKing, the company he started with Levi Gold." Lance skimmed the report, pulling out the information his mother had highlighted. "But it's interesting that Speed Net's main competition is Levi Gold's new company, Gold Stream."

"And Elliot mentioned that Levi had a grudge against him." Morgan tapped a pen on her legal pad. "They had a falling-out over the sale of TechKing."

"Did Gold get screwed on the sale?" Sharp asked hopefully.

"No," Lance said. "They both made a hefty profit."

"Crap." Sharp made a note between Elliot and Levi's names and connected it to both men with arrows. "What do we know about Levi Gold?"

Lance clicked on the photo in the file and turned the laptop to face Sharp then Morgan.

Levi Gold was a paraplegic.

"So Levi Gold didn't personally kidnap Chelsea," Morgan said.

Sharp's mouth flattened. "No, but he's rich. He could hire someone to do his dirty work. Where is his company based?"

"New Jersey." Lance rubbed his eyes. He'd worked late and had gotten up well before the sun rose. He eyed Morgan's coffeemaker but decided it wouldn't be worth the argument with Sharp. "My mom is working her way through the list of Speed Net employees, but so far she hasn't found any red flags."

"Do we keep Tim on the list?" Lance asked. "His alibi is a three-year-old."

"Unless he was willing to leave his daughter alone, I don't see how he could have managed it." Morgan shook her head, then stopped suddenly. "Is there any possibility that Chelsea actually disappeared earlier? We only have Tim's word that she left the house at eight."

Lance sifted through Chelsea's phone records. "Fiona talked to Chelsea at seven. The call is verified right here."

"Hold on." Sharp came to stand in front of Morgan's desk. "Can you hand me the report on my canvas of Tim's neighborhood."

"Here." Morgan handed it over.

Sharp flipped to the second page. "Bill Hanks lives two doors down from Tim and Chelsea. Bill was just coming home from bowling when he saw Tim putting the kids in the car. He remembered because he thought it was strange for Tim to be taking the kids out when it was nearly midnight. According to Tim, Chelsea had said she'd be home around ten. There were multiple, verified texts and calls from Tim to Chelsea between ten and eleven. Tim left audible messages. His call to Fiona was also verified. There was no activity on Chelsea's phone, but phone records show that Tim made those calls from home. Some of the location services were disabled on both phones, so we can't determine where they were when they weren't in use."

"So the sheriff was right when he said that Tim was where he said he was Friday night." Morgan finished her coffee and set the mug aside.

"We verified that Chelsea didn't leave her house before seven p.m., that Tim was at home to Skype with his in-laws at eight thirty, that Tim's phone was at home between eleven and twelve, and that Tim left the house close to midnight," Sharp said. "The hours in between eight thirty and eleven are still murky. Can we think of a motivation for Tim to make his wife disappear?"

"It's not money," Lance said. "They don't have much, and her life insurance is minimal."

"What if their marital problems are worse than anyone thought?" Sharp suggested. "Maybe Chelsea was going to leave Tim and take the kids back to Colorado."

"There would be legal issues with her taking the kids to another state," Morgan said.

"But her parents have more money than Tim and can afford better lawyers." Sharp wrote DIVORCE? in black marker under Tim's name on the whiteboard.

"The reports on Tim's family are interesting." Lance scanned a report his mom had flagged. "Both Tim's father and brother have served time in state prison. His mom's drug-dealing charge was pleaded down. She served a year in a county facility for women. Tim's brother missed his last meeting with his parole officer."

Sharp marked their names with an asterisk. "They've asked Tim for money in the past. Maybe they decided he needed to share his newfound success."

Morgan tapped her pen. "Tim hasn't received a ransom demand."

"Maybe they're waiting for the publicity to die down," Lance suggested.

"Or for us to go away," Sharp added. "I know a PI in Colorado. I'll give him a call. I want eyes on Tim's family."

Lance leaned over his laptop and opened another computer file. "Next up is Chelsea's boss, Curtis MacDonald."

"Chelsea wanted to talk to him about something important. We have no indication of what that was." Morgan turned to Lance. "What about the data on Chelsea's computer and smartphone?"

"Nothing unusual," Lance said. "Mostly she was interested in mom-type topics. Colic, infant development, sibling relationships, etc."

"Assuming the dead woman isn't Chelsea, do we still think there's any chance that Chelsea left on her own?" Sharp asked.

Morgan shook her head. "In my opinion, no."

Lance thought of the pretty blonde woman. Was Sheriff King right? Was she hiding out somewhere, depressed, suicidal, angry with her husband and determined to teach him a lesson? "My gut agrees with Morgan. Everyone we asked says Chelsea would never leave her kids."

"The pendant's broken chain and the hairs ripped out by the root support her being forcibly taken," Morgan said.

Sharp nodded, his eyes grim. "Then we're all in agreement on that. Unless Chelsea had some kind of psychotic breakdown, she wouldn't intentionally abandon her family."

Lance returned to his list. "I saved the best for last. Harold Burns?"

Sharp crossed his arms across his chest. "Level-three violent sex offenders aren't magically cured. They're a public threat as long as they're loose."

"Studies are mixed," Morgan argued. "We can't assume he's guilty because he was confrontational."

Sharp widened his stance. "He didn't peep in windows. He committed a violent rape. He used a gun. He threatened and choked his victim."

"I agree. I saw too many repeat offenders of all types to believe any violent criminals should be out on the street. But anyone on the sex offender registry is going to react when an investigator comes calling to talk about a missing woman."

Lance paced, picturing the way Burns had intimidated Morgan. "Even if Burns is likely guilty of something, we can't assume Burns is guilty of *this* crime."

"How far from Burns's home address and the auto shop was the body found?" Sharp asked. "I'm going to get a map."

"I have one right here." Lance clicked through and pulled up a map of the area. He placed a pin on the location near the state park where the body was found. Then, he marked the other two addresses. "The body was found less than two miles from the auto shop. If you went through the woods behind the salvage yard, eventually you'd end up in the state park."

Morgan's phone buzzed. "It's the sheriff."

Lance stopped. Had the ME identified the body?

Chapter Twenty-Three

Holding her breath, Morgan pressed the phone to her ear. "Morgan Dane."

"King here," the sheriff said in a deep grumble.

"Have you heard from the ME?" Morgan asked.

"No. That's not what this is about." The sheriff actually huffed. "I got a call from Harold Burns's lawyer. You and your *investigators* will stay away from him. Consider this your official warning."

"You know he's a level-three violent offender and the woman's body was found less than two miles from Burns Auto Shop?" Morgan's voice was as cold as the icy shiver that slipped through her insides. Burns had gone on the offensive after their visit to the auto shop. She'd expected him to lay low.

"Harassment is illegal, Ms. Dane," the sheriff said in an irritated, frosty voice. "Stay away from Burns, and stay away from his brother's auto shop."

The connection went dead.

Burns had played them.

Shock filled Morgan, then a hefty dose of anger kicked it aside. She lowered the phone. "Did you hear that?"

The grim faces of Lance and Sharp answered her question.

"That son of a—" Lance muttered a curse under his breath.

Morgan got up and paced the narrow space behind her desk. "I knew this was a possibility when we went to the auto shop. I should have done more to prevent it."

Lance punched his palm. "I can't believe the sheriff would side with a violent sexual offender."

"Hold on. I'm sure he isn't taking Burns's side. King might not work or play well with others, but he's a competent cop." Sharp held up a hand. "I'm hoping he's investigating Burns and doesn't want us in his way. If I were him, I might feel the same way."

"Probably isn't enough, and the only reason King is onto Burns is because we found him." Lance scowled.

"Maybe. Maybe not," Sharp said. "We have no idea what the sheriff has been doing."

"Burns is our top suspect in Chelsea's disappearance. How do we ignore that?" Morgan swallowed her disappointment in herself. She was accustomed to working with law enforcement and having the support of the police department. She needed to change her way of thinking, but the whole situation was frustrating. "I know the sheriff isn't obligated to share the details of his investigation with us, but he could at least hint that Burns has actually made his radar in the investigation."

"Look. King is known for holding his cards closely, even with other branches of law enforcement," Lance said. "The man doesn't trust the people who are on his side. I doubt there is any way to make him trust a defense attorney. We are on the opposition in this case."

But Morgan knew they'd handled Burns the wrong way. "We should have approached Burns differently. We should have put him under surveillance without making contact. We showed our hand. Now we can't even watch him without risking a harassment charge."

Sharp got up. "I'm meeting the boys for lunch later. Maybe one of them will have an idea. They're a cagey bunch, and they gossip like little old ladies. I'll find out what they know and get them sniffing around."

The *boys* were Sharp's fellow retirees from the local police force who met regularly at the local tavern.

Morgan checked the time. "Oh. Is it eleven o'clock already? I have to pick up Sophie from preschool and Gianna from dialysis. I'm sorry."

When she'd been a prosecutor, the kids had gone to daycare. John had been deployed more than he'd been home. Morgan had lived like a single parent. But after her husband had died, she'd taken two years off. She'd forgotten how hard it was to juggle work and kids and sanity.

"How long until Gianna gets her license?" Lance asked.

"Her driving test is scheduled for next month, but finding time to let her practice has been tough. Obviously, I'm not going to let her practice when the kids are in the car." And Gianna would have to gain some driving experience before Morgan would allow her to taxi the girls around.

"I can help," Lance offered.

Sharp paused on his way out the door. "Me too. And if you need any help with your grandfather, let me know."

"Thanks. Stella and I are trying to divvy up his doctor appointments." Morgan gathered her things. "I'll be back in an hour."

Shrugging into her coat and hoisting her bag over her shoulder, she went out to her minivan and drove to the preschool. She picked up Sophie at eleven thirty, but Gianna wouldn't be finished with dialysis for another thirty minutes. Seeing no reason to waste a half hour, Morgan drove to the supermarket and parked. Taking Sophie by the hand, she crossed the parking lot and pulled a shopping cart from the lineup. She turned to lift her daughter into the child seat on the front of the cart.

Sophie took a step backward and crossed her arms. Preschool made her tired and cranky. "I wanna walk."

"I need you in the cart today. We have to be quick. Gianna will be finished soon." Morgan picked her child up and set her in the cart.

As much as her youngest did not like being restrained, she also recognized when her mother meant business. Morgan fastened the safety belt.

Sophie obeyed, but not without stating her opinion. "I don't like to sit in the cart."

"I know you don't." Morgan pushed the cart into the store. "What did you do in school today?"

"Can I have a cookie?"

"No. It's almost lunchtime." Morgan headed for the produce aisle and put a bag of potatoes in the cart.

"But I'm hungwy." Sophie wasn't a big eater. If she was asking for food, she must be starving.

"Did you have a snack today at preschool?"

Sophie shook her head, the motion sending her two ponytails swinging. "I wanted to finish my picture."

Typical Sophie. Too busy to eat.

Morgan scanned the aisle for a reasonable option. It would be at least another thirty minutes before they picked up Gianna and drove home. Thirty minutes was a loooong time to spend with a hungry and tired child. "How about a banana?"

"Can I have it now?"

"You can eat it as soon as I pay for it." Morgan walked faster.

"OK." Sophie perked up. Her purple sneakers swung back and forth as she began to sing the theme to *Toy Story*. An older woman smiled as they passed her cart.

Morgan turned down an aisle and collided with a male body. Knocked off balance, she steadied herself with her hand on the cart.

"I'm so sorry." She stepped back and looked up. All the breath left her lungs and fear sent a bolt of adrenaline into her bloodstream.

Harold Burns stared at her, his eyes gleaming with recognition. The basket that dangled from his hand held a single can of tuna fish. "You'd better watch where you're going."

Morgan continued to move away, pulling the cart sideways and trying to step between Sophie and Burns. But the cart nosed into a display of canned peaches. The stacks of cans toppled and rolled across the tile.

Burns didn't move. He just stared at her, his eyes full of malice—and satisfaction.

Had he been following her?

Cans rolled under the cart. Burns's gaze drifted slowly from Morgan to her daughter. A silent alarm rang out in Morgan's head.

Get Sophie away from him!

Next to her, Sophie said, "Mommy?" Her voice was soft and small and scared as she picked up on Morgan's reaction to Burns.

Morgan glanced up and down the aisle. Thirty feet away, the older woman compared prices of Parmesan cheese. Next to her, a young man piled boxes of pasta into a basket on his arm.

They were in a grocery store. In full view of two other shoppers and multiple surveillance cameras, Burns couldn't hurt Sophie.

She's safe. Morgan breathed in an attempt to calm her screaming pulse. But her body responded to Burns's proximity to her child with immediate protest. If she'd been alone, her response would have been completely different, possibly even rational. But her brain simply couldn't override her primitive maternal instinct, the same internal wiring that helped cavewomen keep their offspring safe from predators and ensured the survival of the human race.

There was no arguing with pure and primal instinct.

This violent sexual predator could not be this close to her daughter. The very act of him turning his gaze upon her child was a clear and direct threat.

Morgan grabbed Sophie, pulled her from the cart, and backed toward the exit.

"Mommy, my bananas," Sophie cried, reaching backward as Morgan hurried out of the store. She rushed across the parking lot.

Sophie sobbed quietly as Morgan broke into a jog, opening the side door of the van as she ran toward it. She put Sophie inside, climbed in the side door with her, then closed it behind them. Not even the click of the door locks could temper her panic.

"Get in your seat," Morgan ordered, glancing over her shoulder and dropping her tote bag on the floor.

Harold Burns stood on the pavement just outside the grocery store door, his eyes locked on Morgan's van.

"Mommy?" Sophie climbed into her seat obediently, her voice high with fear, her face streaked with tears.

"It's OK, sweetie." Couched in the small confines of the vehicle, Morgan fastened the safety seat harness and climbed over the console into the driver's seat.

But Sophie clearly knew that it wasn't OK. She sniffed, leaning her face on the headrest and crying quietly.

Morgan started the engine and drove out of the lot toward Sharp Investigations. She was not leading Burns to her home. With an eye on the rearview mirror, Morgan pulled her cell phone from her pocket and called Lance. "Are you still at the office?"

"Yes."

"Can you meet me outside in a few minutes? I'm on my way there. Sophie is with me."

"Morgan, what's wrong?"

"Sophie and I went to the grocery store." Morgan stopped at a red light, her eyes darting between the windshield and all her mirrors. A car pulled up behind her minivan. She exhaled when she saw an older gentleman at the wheel. "Harold Burns was there."

Lance swore. "Where are you?"

"Four blocks away. I'm calling Stella next." She punched "End," then called her sister, giving her a brief explanation. "Gianna needs to be picked up at dialysis."

"OK," Stella said. "I'll get her and meet you at Sharp Investigations."

Morgan drove, checking her mirrors, looking for a red pickup truck.

What was Burns's game? And where had he gone?

Chapter Twenty-Four

Lance paced the sidewalk.

Where is she?

The thought of Burns intimidating Morgan and her little girl stirred a giant pot of rage in Lance's chest. He'd like nothing better than to find Burns and give him back a big dose of his own medicine.

When he'd been a cop, Lance had hated the revolving-door nature of the system. There were people who could be rehabilitated, but there were those who were just bad. Born bad. Made bad. Whatever. It hardly mattered after the fact. Violent men like Burns were dangerous. Occasionally, like now, Lance was appalled at the violence of his own response to them.

But this was personal.

This was Morgan. And Sophie!

Damn it.

Men like Burns shouldn't be allowed to share air with an innocent child.

The heat of fury had climbed into Lance's throat by the time Morgan parked at the curb in front of the office. Her face was as white as a fresh sheet of copy paper. She got out of the driver's seat and opened the sliding side door. Sophie was still crying. Her big blue eyes were scared.

As much as the sight made Lance want to beat Burns senseless, he swallowed and shoved his anger back into its box.

Sophie needed calm.

She needed to feel safe.

God. How do parents do this?

Morgan's hands were shaking so hard she couldn't get the harness unfastened.

Lance stepped in. "Let me."

"Hey, Soph." Lance unfastened her harness, lifted her from the seat, and held her closely. "Everything is OK."

She seemed to forget that she didn't trust him. Her arms went around his neck in a panicked chokehold and her spindly legs wrapped around his waist. She clung to him with a strength that broke his heart.

He made her feel safe.

Morgan grabbed her tote bag from the van, and Lance herded her up the walk and into the office. Holding Sophie in one arm, he locked the door and engaged the alarm. "Are you all right?"

Morgan nodded. But her hands were still trembling and her face had gone from pale to gray.

Sharp emerged from his office, his face grim.

At the clatter of dog nails, Sophie lifted her head from Lance's shoulder. "Puppy."

Morgan smoothed her hair and worked to collect herself. "Sophie, this is Mr. Sharp and his dog, Rocket."

Rocket leaned on Morgan's leg and whined.

Ignoring Sharp completely, Sophie leaned over and reached for the dog. Her tears shut off like a closed tap. "Put me down."

Even Lance couldn't compete with a dog.

Lance cautiously set her on the floor, watching the dog for a reaction. But the stub of Rocket's docked tail wagged. She sniffed then licked the child's hand. Sophie giggled.

"Sit," Morgan said.

The dog planted her butt on the floor and offered Sophie a paw.

Morgan crouched next to Sophie. The dog showed no sign of the timidity she exhibited with strange adults.

"Looks like Rocket likes kids." Sharp nodded.

Sophie turned her huge, teary blue eyes on Sharp. "Can I play with her?"

"You certainly can. Let's go get her ball." Sharp extended a hand toward Sophie.

"I'm hungwy." Sophie was usually distrustful of strangers, or at least she'd always been distrustful of Lance, but she took Sharp's hand without hesitation.

Lance made a note to talk to her about strangers with puppies.

"Let's see if we can find you something to eat," Sharp said.

"We left my banana at the store." The sniff in Sophie's breath tugged at Lance's heart all over again.

"You know what?" Sharp led the little girl down the hall. "Rocket loves bananas too. I have some in the kitchen."

As soon as Sophie and Sharp disappeared into the kitchen, Morgan lost it. Tears began to flow down her cheeks. Covering her mouth, she raced for the bathroom. Lance waited outside, feeling useless. At least he'd been able to hold and comfort Sophie.

When she emerged, her face had been scrubbed and she smelled of mouthwash.

"Do you want some water?"

Morgan shook her head. "Not yet." She was still shaking. "I'm sorry. Tossing our cookies after a stressful situation is a family thing."

With a glance at the kitchen door, Lance led her into her office. He'd finally made progress with Sophie. He didn't want the sight of him hugging her mother to set the kid off again.

Once inside the room, he pulled her to his chest and hugged her hard. She pressed her face to his body.

"He wouldn't have pulled that stunt if you were with me." Morgan was not the damsel-in-distress type, but she wasn't stupid either. "He must have followed me."

"Well, it won't happen again," Lance said. He was sticking closer to her than paint on a wall.

"I need to go home for my gun." Morgan had a concealed carry permit. Feeling that small children and guns didn't mix, she rarely carried it. "For a completely nonviolent incident, that was utterly terrifying. What if he'd done something, and I wasn't able to protect Sophie?"

Lance rubbed her shoulder. "He didn't and Sophie is fine. It serves no purpose to torture yourself with every possible outcome that didn't happen."

Morgan nodded, but she didn't look convinced. "I need to call home and warn Grandpa. What if Burns knows where I live?"

"Your house address is unlisted, right?" Lance asked.

Morgan sniffed. "Yes. But we both know how easy it is to get names and addresses."

Tax records, deeds, and other public records weren't hard to find. Visibility was the downside to all the publicity her last case had garnered.

Someone knocked on the front door.

"I'll get it." Lance went out into the hall and opened the door. Stella pushed past him. "Where's Morgan?"

"In her office." Lance gestured toward the open door. "She's fine. So is Sophie."

Stella and Morgan greeted each other with a tight, sisterly hug.

"Where's Gianna?" Morgan asked, looking over her sister's shoulder. "Is something wrong?"

"No. She's fine. I called her to make sure. Brody went to get her. He's going to take her home and stay there." She leaned back, holding Morgan by the arms and assessing her. "I wanted to get right over here and make sure you were all right. Tell me what happened."

175

"I'm fine." Morgan broke her sister's grip, then closed her office door before describing the incident in the grocery store.

Lance had to work hard to keep his temper in check.

Stella wrote in a small notebook she took out of her pocket. "He didn't say anything else?"

"No." Morgan already knew where her sister's question was leading.

"Unfortunately, there's not much we can do." Stella closed her notebook. "He didn't do or say anything threatening. There are only two grocery stores nearby. He has to shop at one of them. He didn't do anything illegal."

"I know," Morgan said. "But I want my statement on record."

Too many women told themselves they were imagining danger and ended up as victims. If Burns had any ideas about stalking Morgan or her family, it would be vital to have a record of each and every incident.

"OK." Stella nodded, pulling out her phone. "I'll call the store and request a copy of the surveillance tapes." She went into the hallway to make the call.

Morgan's tote bag buzzed from her desk. She fished her cell phone out and read the display. "It's Sheriff King." She answered the call, holding the phone a few inches from her ear so Lance could hear. "Yes."

"What part of stay away from Harold Burns didn't you hear?" King yelled.

Morgan jerked. "Excuse me?"

Apprehension slid an icy fingertip along the back of Lance's neck. Something was wrong.

"I just got off the phone with Harold Burns's attorney," the sheriff said. "Burns says you followed him to the grocery store and harassed him."

"I did nothing of the sort," Morgan said.

The sheriff continued. "He has a photo of you in the store and another of you driving out of the parking lot."

"Did he mention that I was with my three-year-old daughter?" Morgan's voice rose. She breathed, obviously holding back.

"No. He didn't," the sheriff said, his voice turning cautious.

"Do you really think I'd follow a violent sexual predator when I had my child with me?" Morgan was shifting into full mamma-bear mode. On the bright side, her hands had stopped shaking and color flushed her cheeks.

After three heartbeats of silence, the sheriff said, "I'll look into it."

"No need." Morgan's voice chilled, and her tone shifted into I-don't-need-your-useless-ass, even if she was too much of a professional and a lady to say it. "The SFPD has already requested the surveillance tapes, and I'm filing a complaint with them as we speak."

"Who is the responding officer?" Sheriff King asked.

"Detective Stella Dane," Morgan said.

"Of course," the sheriff muttered. "Of course you'd call your sister."

Morgan ignored the comment. "I'll have her send you copies of my statement."

Lance hoped the store's videos had recorded the encounter. But really, what would it show? The way Morgan had described the incident, she'd walked around a corner and straight into Burns. The most they could hope for was that she arrived at the store first, which would back up her claim that *he* followed *her*. If she was lucky, the cameras had caught him looking for her or acting suspicious in some way.

But Lance had a feeling luck wasn't with her today. Every fiber in his being told her that Burns had planned their encounter. And that this was just the beginning of whatever scheme he had in mind.

"Be very careful, Counselor," the sheriff warned. "I don't know what Burns is up to, but he's a very dangerous man."

"Yes. I'm well aware of that." Morgan's lips pressed flat.

"Stay on your toes." The sheriff hung up.

Morgan lowered the phone, her hand shaking. "Did you hear all that?"

"I heard enough." Lance nodded. "Burns is up to something."

"But what?" Morgan shoved a lock of black hair out of her eyes.

"He's setting you up." Lance could feel it in his bones.

Morgan stared at him, her big blue eyes wide. The fear in them an adult version of her daughter's earlier response. The implications of Burns's complaint were sinking in. "But for what?"

"I don't know, but it can't be good."

"Oh, my God. He saw Sophie." She turned toward the door as if to run to her daughter.

Lance caught her by the arm. "She's in the kitchen with Sharp. She's fine."

Morgan nodded. "I know. It's just—" She stopped and took one deep, controlled breath. "I can handle defending myself. But when something threatens my kids, it's different. There's nothing more terrifying."

"I know." Lance was beginning to understand the difference.

The more time he spent with Morgan's kids, the more he thought of them as part of his life. He'd always liked kids. But Morgan's three girls had imprinted on his heart. Their honesty, their inability to bullshit. If they liked you, they didn't hold back. Ava and Mia were free with their affection. They'd lost their father and yet accepted him into their lives with no reservations.

And if they didn't like you, he thought of Sophie's resistance to his relationship with Morgan, at least you knew where you stood.

But even Sophie, or maybe especially Sophie, had wormed herself into his heart. She felt every emotion exponentially. She was a handful, but an honest one. She didn't really dislike him. The way she'd clung to him for reassurance and safety today told him that. She'd had her mother home with her for two years. Now Morgan was back to work *and* forming a relationship with a man. Sophie hadn't yet adjusted to Morgan being out all day. Expecting her to welcome competition for her mother's attention was unreasonable. But Lance would be patient. Eventually she'd accept him.

Probably.

The idea of Burns even standing that close to Sophie shot Lance's anger into the red zone. But the little girl wasn't the one he was most worried about.

"Burns's victim was an adult woman," he said. "His record indicates he's a violent predator, but I didn't see anything to suggest he's a pedophile."

"That's not much of a comfort."

"No. We'll make sure he doesn't get anywhere near your girls," Lance said. "But you'll need to take care too. It's far more likely you're the one he's stalking."

Chapter Twenty-Five

Morgan settled Sophie inside the house with Gianna. Then she stopped in her room and removed her gun from its safe. She changed into a pair of slacks with a belt to accommodate a holster at the back of her hip. Her jacket covered the weapon nicely.

She went outside. Lance stood by the Jeep talking to Stella and Brody. Leaning on his cane in the driveway, Grandpa was wearing his sidearm.

An icy shiver slid though Morgan's belly. All this activity was because of one man, a violent sexual offender who *Morgan* had made contact with.

It was her fault Burns had taken an interest in her.

The former prosecutor in Morgan wanted nothing more than to put Harold Burns under police surveillance until he did something illegal. There was nothing in the man's manner that indicated he was at all interested in being redeemed. In her opinion, it was only a matter of time until Burns gave in to his proclivities.

"Thanks for hanging out here," Morgan said to her sister. "Are you sure it's OK with your boss?"

"It's fine. I've missed the girls." Stella made a shooing gesture with her hand. "Go. Solve your case. I'll be here until you get back."

"Stella and I have this covered." Grandpa tapped his cane on the driveway.

Grandpa had always been an excellent shot. He and Dad had taught all four of the Dane siblings how to handle a weapon. It had been a family ritual. Some families went to church on Sundays. The Danes had gone to the shooting range. But now Morgan wondered if Grandpa's hands were steady enough to hit his target.

And the thought broke her heart.

Stella's partner, Detective Brody McNamara, opened the door to his unmarked car. "I'll head back to the station and see what I can dig up on Harold Burns."

"The sheriff warned us off him," Lance said.

"It's a good thing the chief and the sheriff don't get along," Brody said over the roof of the sedan. "I'll have no problem convincing the chief to investigate Burns in spite of the sheriff's warning."

Or because of it, knowing Horner.

"That's making politics work for you," Lance said.

"For once, right? I'll let you know what I learn." Brody slid behind the wheel and then drove away.

"I'll be inside." Grandpa wobbled as he went up the front walk. Lance went ahead of him, holding the door open as her grandfather navigated the steps and threshold.

"He's really unsteady," Morgan said to her sister.

"I know." Stella sighed. "But at least I convinced him to use his cane outside. I have this covered for today. You've handled the lion's share of his care up until now. It's my turn."

"Actually, up until now, he's taken care of me." Morgan stared at the front of the house. "I'm having trouble with the turnabout."

"I know. He's always been there for all of us." Stella looped an arm around her sister's shoulder. "And now we'll be there for him."

"We will." Morgan nodded. "We need to call Ian and Peyton. They should know what's going on with him."

"If they wanted to know, they would call more often," Stella said.

"Peyton calls now and then, or at least she tries to." Morgan's younger sister was a forensic psychiatrist in California. "And Ian talks to Grandpa at least once a week."

Stella had little patience for their siblings. "Ian lives three hours away. He could visit."

"Ian never lived here. New York City is his home." The Danes had moved to Scarlet Falls after their father had been killed. Ian had already been grown. He'd stayed in the city and followed in the Dane tradition, joining the NYPD. But instead of homicide, he'd chosen SWAT.

"We'll debate family dynamics later." Morgan hugged her sister. "You'll keep everyone inside?"

Stella gave her a look. "Are you kidding me? I'm a police detective. I think I can handle keeping a house locked down for a few hours. Besides, your girls are angels. Most of the time."

"I know." Morgan blinked back a tear. "But I'm not always rational when it come to my kids' safety."

"Everything will be fine here." Stella wrapped her blazer around her body, then turned and went back into the house, passing Lance on his way back to Morgan.

Morgan and Lance got into the Jeep.

"Are you all right?" Lance started the car.

"Yes. No. I don't know." Morgan blew out a hard breath. "Between my grandfather's health and having Harold Burns stalk me and Sophie, I'm feeling guilty for going back to work."

"Stella can handle things here until you get home." Lance had worked with Stella when he'd been on the police force. "She's a good cop."

"I know she is." Morgan's phone buzzed. She read the screen. "It's Sheriff King."

Lance backed out of the driveway.

She pressed answer. "Morgan Dane."

Sheriff King didn't waste time on pleasantries. "The dead woman is not Chelsea Clark."

Morgan felt the air rush from her lungs as the shock rolled through her. Even though they'd been acting as if Chelsea were still alive, she'd feared the worst. "Do you know who she is?"

"Yes. The ME was able to identify her with dental records, but her family has a right to be notified first."

"Of course." Morgan processed the news. "Have you let Tim know that the body isn't his wife?"

"I called him before I called you." The sheriff sounded offended that she would even ask.

"Thank you. I just wanted to make sure." Morgan would still touch base with Tim. The fresh news would generate exposure for tonight's press conference. "How was the woman killed?"

"She'd been badly beaten. She had broken ribs, a broken jaw, a fractured eye socket, and had ligature marks on both wrists," the sheriff said. "She was five months pregnant and suffered a . . ." Papers rustled on the other end of the connection. "Placental abruption." He pronounced the words carefully, as if it was the first time. "Do you know what that is?"

"Yes. It's a separation of the placenta from the wall of the uterus." Morgan let that sink in. "She bled to death."

"That's right," the sheriff continued. "The ME said it's a rare complication that early in a pregnancy. In this case, it was likely caused by a blow to the stomach."

"Whoever held her didn't take her to the hospital when she began to hemorrhage."

"Correct."

"Will the medical examiner be able to use the DNA of the baby to identify the father?" Morgan asked.

"Maybe," the sheriff said. "She delivered, and the baby was not present with the remains. There's another grave somewhere. We're going to search for it. But—" The sheriff paused.

"What else can you tell me?"

"She was close in age and appearance to Chelsea Clark. Blonde. Blue-eyed," the sheriff said. "And she's been missing for eight months."

"Runaway or kidnapping?"

"In the original missing person report, her parents said she had no reason to run away. She was a college student. Doing well in all her classes." The sheriff sighed. "Like I said, the ME found marks on her wrists consistent with long-term use of restraints."

"So she was kept prisoner all that time. How long has she been dead?" Morgan's mind turned the information over and over, trying to stay detached from the details, which wasn't easy with such a horrifying case.

"A week to ten days. Animals had been at the body, but the intact portions were in good condition. Cold nighttime temps preserved the remains somewhat. But we don't know that this case has anything to do with Chelsea Clark. Yet."

"Chelsea's case is odd enough that I wouldn't rule anything out at this stage," Morgan said. "Do you have any other information for me, sheriff?"

"Harold Burns was working in the auto shop the night Chelsea disappeared."

"Let me guess," Morgan said. "His brother is his only alibi."

"Yes. They don't have surveillance video in the shop. Only in the office."

"Convenient." Morgan was almost surprised the sheriff had shared the information.

"I thought so," King agreed. "I'll let you know if I have anything else that I can share."

"Thank you for the update, Sheriff."

He grumbled something that sounded like "you're welcome" and the line went dead.

"The sheriff was a regular Chatty Cathy today," Lance said.

"That was a lot of sharing," Morgan agreed. "I'm waiting for the other shoe to drop, right on my head."

"Does this woman's death have anything to do with Chelsea's disappearance? They were approximately the same age with similar physical characteristics."

Morgan looked out the window. Trees rolled past. "This woman was held captive for eight months by someone who raped, impregnated, and beat her. Then she died."

"Whoever was holding her might need a replacement." Lance followed her train of thought.

"All speculation."

"One hundred percent," he agreed.

"But a thin theory is better than no theory." Morgan stared out the window as they drove to the Clarks' house.

Chelsea could still be very much alive. Where was she?

Tim answered the door, the baby asleep, draped over his shoulder. He gestured for them to follow him back to the kitchen. The house was quiet, a countertop TV muted. He laid the baby in a bassinet. William didn't stir.

"He's quiet today." Morgan peered at the sleeping infant and felt her hormones stir. *No! Down!*

"The pediatrician said the colic should start to improve between four and six months. He was right." Tim gestured to the coffeemaker. "I just made a fresh pot of coffee. Can I offer you some?"

Morgan and Lance declined.

"Where are your in-laws?" Lance asked.

"Patricia is upstairs reading to Bella. Rand is taking a nap, or so he says. He was looking pretty rough." Tim frowned. "The call from the sheriff took a toll on all of us, which is the opposite of what you would think, right? We should be jumping for joy, yet we're a mess."

Morgan empathized. John's death had devastated her, but how would it feel to never know what had happened to her husband? To never have closure? Like Lance. "I don't think there's any right or wrong way to feel. This is a horrible situation no one should have to handle."

Tim poured himself a mug of coffee and then eased into a chair with his back to the TV. Morgan sat across from him. Lance paced the kitchen.

"Are you ready for the news conference?" Morgan asked Tim.

"I don't know. I'm not good on camera. Maybe it would be better to let Rand talk."

"Rand's reward offer and his heartfelt plea as Chelsea's father will help, but the public will want to hear from you too. You are Chelsea's husband. The father of her children. They need to hear how much you and the kids miss her and need her back. Whenever a woman disappears or is killed, the husband or boyfriend is always the primary suspect. If you and Rand present a united front, it will help shape public opinion."

Tim looked up. "I don't care about public opinion. I just want my wife back."

"Rand is offering money for the help of the community. He wants their help. It would seem very odd if you didn't speak." Morgan couldn't help but jump ahead. What if the next body that turned up *was* Chelsea? With or without evidence, Tim would be a suspect in the public's eye.

Next to her, Lance stopped. His body stiffened. Morgan followed his line of sight to the small TV. On it, a shaky camera recording, taken through a windshield, showed a blonde woman staggering on the side of the road. She wore a dirty yellow dress and had a blanket wrapped around her shoulders. She was barefoot. Blonde hair fell in a dirty wave to her shoulders. Her face was bruised and swollen.

A car pulled onto the shoulder, followed by the vehicle in which the person filming the scene was riding.

Morgan stood. "Turn on the sound."

But Lance was already on it.

Tim spun in his chair. "Oh, my God."

The audio played on the TV. They heard traffic sounds, then a man's voice. "It's a woman. She appears to be hurt."

Yet the man continued to film rather than help her.

The woman collapsed onto the asphalt. A man in the car ahead got out of his sedan and hurried to her side, dropping to his knees on the road. A few seconds later, he took off his jacket and wrapped it around her, then turned and gestured to the man taking the video. "Stop filming and call an ambulance!"

The "you idiot" was implied.

Morgan's gaze shifted from the screen to Tim.

He hadn't moved. His face was frozen in shock. "It's Chelsea."

Chapter Twenty-Six

He paced the plywood floor of the storage container. The door was open, and daylight flooded the space. No point in closing it now.

She was gone. No. Not gone. She'd left him.

This was his first chance to examine the evidence. He'd tried to find her all night. And this morning he'd had other things to do.

The distinction hit him squarely in the chest with an ache of betrayal. How could he have been so wrong about her? Why didn't he foresee her deception?

The mistake was his, not hers. He'd challenged a superior female, and she'd risen to the test. Overconfidence had been his error. It wouldn't happen again. When he took her the next time, it would be final. She'd know there would be no getting away.

And he would eliminate any reasons for her to escape, which meant he'd need to eliminate her family.

But first he needed to know how she'd defeated him. He scanned the evidence in front of him. Squatting, he picked up the chain. The lock was opened, not broken, so she'd picked it somehow. She could have had a pin in her hair that he hadn't seen. Next time he'd search her hair carefully.

The cot was on its side under a hole in the roof. When he'd left her the night before, the hole had been too small for a person to squeeze through. He'd made sure of it. But Chelsea had enlarged it. Rust had weakened the structure of the ceiling. She'd seen this and taken advantage of it. Then she'd used the cot to boost herself to the roof. If she hadn't been able to fit, she would never have managed it.

Maybe she was too smart.

She'd certainly outsmarted him. He should have shored up the hole. He'd left it so she could see the passage of time and have a small amount of fresh air. Obviously, that had been a mistake. Next time he would use complete darkness and disorientation as an additional tool.

He'd failed. And if he didn't get Chelsea back, all his work was for nothing.

That couldn't happen.

Fury built inside him, and no deep-breathing exercise was going to settle it down. It raged in his chest like an animal in a cage, grabbed his ribs, and shook them like bars. He needed to release his anger or he wouldn't be able to think clearly.

He went to his shed and picked up a knife. Pulling up his sleeve, he cut the skin of his forearm. Blood welled, but the slice was clean and sharp, the pain not enough to scramble his emotions. He needed the equivalent of a defibrillator to his emotions.

He fired up his blowtorch and heated the branding iron he'd used on Chelsea. The infinity symbol, because she was going to be his forever. The reminder stoked his rage higher. If he didn't short-circuit it, he'd go into a red zone. A category-five hurricane of fury was building in his head. It couldn't be contained. He had to decide how to release it.

His hand trembled with anger and anticipation as the iron began to glow. He rolled up his pant leg and pressed the orange-hot iron into his skin. The smell of burning flesh rose. Sweat poured from his pores. The pain burst, bright and beautiful and clear. It seared through his leg in a blinding explosion.

He lifted the iron. As the pain reached a crescendo and ebbed, the anger faded. He tossed the iron into the dirt to cool. Sweat soaked his shirt, and pain throbbed in his leg.

But his head was cool.

With the same first aid kit he used on Chelsea, he applied ointment and bandaged the wound. The lingering pain would help keep him centered on his task.

He pulled his pant leg down over the bandage, straightened, and walked outside. With renewed purpose, he continued his examination of Chelsea's escape.

Just a few barefoot prints led toward the meadow and woods. Last night he'd followed her into the forest, but she'd gotten away in the dark.

This could all be fixed. He knew where she lived. He'd taken her from there once before. He could do it again. This time, she would be forewarned. The police would be watching her. The bar would be higher. But if he was patient, everyone would let down their guard eventually.

No one could remain completely vigilant for an extended period of time. It wasn't natural. When nothing happened, they would become complacent.

But waiting was not one of his strengths. Maybe he should find another woman and hone his methods.

Chelsea was still meant to be his, but there was no reason she had to be his *only* woman. But what if she remembered too many details about the container? What if she led the police right back to his doorstep? There had to be some way to get to her.

He had to get her back.

And if he couldn't, she'd pay the ultimate price.

Chapter Twenty-Seven

Chelsea rested her head on the pillow. Nerves hummed through her like electrical currents. Her body refused to accept that she was safe. They'd put her across from the nurses' station to keep her under close observation. But it was the hub of the floor, crowded and noisy. Every bang of a metal tray or slam of a drawer startled her. The doctor, a tiny Asian woman with a calm demeanor, had said she was stable. But she didn't feel very stable.

According to the doctor, her body was still in flight mode. They'd offered her a sedative, but she'd said no. Why would she want to be drugged and helpless again?

She shivered, tugging the heated blanket up to her chin. Would she ever be warm again?

Her entire body ached, from her torn-up feet to her beaten face. Her eyeballs hurt if she moved them too quickly. There wasn't an inch of her that wasn't cut, bruised, abraded, or exhausted.

But she was here.

Alive.

She'd won.

A sound in the doorway made her jump.

Tim.

Her heart stuttered at the sight of him. She hadn't thought she'd ever see him again.

He walked into the room. As much as he tried not to stare, she felt his shock at her appearance. She hadn't seen her face in a mirror, but she knew she looked awful. Her lip was split, both eyes blackened, her nose broken. She was dehydrated and hypothermic. Her skin felt raw and tight, as if it belonged to someone else.

At the foot of the bed, a nurse wrote on a chart and talked in a soothing monotone. "It's going to rain tonight."

Tim shuffled into her room. He stopped, as if afraid to approach her. As if he didn't want to frighten her. "Hey, Chels. It's me."

Emotions choked Chelsea. She didn't know what to feel first. Love. Relief. Gratitude.

She'd wanted to live—to see her husband and her children again—and she had.

Now what?

The nurse hung the chart from a hook and moved to Chelsea's side to take her pulse. "I was just telling your wife how happy everyone is to see her."

The artificial pleasantness of the nurse annoyed Chelsea. She swallowed, her throat dry.

"Tim." Her voice was a croak.

He let out an audible breath.

How did he feel? He must have thought she was dead.

"I'll give you a few minutes alone." The nurse handed Tim a plastic cup of water. "I'll be right outside if you need me." With a reassuring nod, the nurse left the room.

Tim put the straw between Chelsea's lips. She closed them around it and winced as a scab cracked. How could she even react to a pain so slight after what she'd been through? But her body seemed overly sensitized. Could a person use up her supply of grit?

"I want to hug you, but I'm afraid I'll hurt you." Tim's eyes shone. Was he crying?

"It's OK," she said, the words slurring through her swollen lips.

He leaned over the bed and studied her face. "I want to kiss you, but I don't know where."

A tear slipped from her eye and ran down her temple. She took her arm out from under the covers. Tim took her hand, the warmth radiating between them familiar and comforting. She held on.

This is what she'd prayed for.

Tim wiped a hand across his eyes. "I don't have the words for how I feel right now. I didn't think I'd ever see you again."

She squeezed his fingers. "Same here."

"I love you." Tim looked into her eyes. "You are the strongest person I know."

His words warmed her from the inside out. "I love you too. The whole time I was . . . there, all I could think about was getting home to you and the kids."

"Is there anything I can do to help you?"

"Just be here?" Her next breath shook her to the core. From the scattered, panicked emotions flitting through her mind, she knew that her psychological recovery was going to be harder than her physical healing.

"I'm not going anywhere." Tim perched on the edge of the bed.

She almost couldn't believe she'd made it.

A knock startled them both. Chelsea recoiled, a reflex she couldn't control.

In the doorway, the sheriff cleared his throat. "Mrs. Clark. I'd like to talk with you for a few moments."

"It's OK, honey." Tim shot the sheriff a look of warning. "This is Sheriff King."

Tim nodded toward a plastic chair against the wall. "Why don't you sit down, Sheriff?"

The sheriff turned the chair to face Chelsea's bed and sank into it. Then he pulled a notebook out of his pocket. "Do you remember what happened last Friday night?"

Chelsea inhaled, a hitched and unsteady sound that reminded her of William as he came down from a crying jag. She shook her head. "Not exactly. I have flashbacks." She squeezed her eyes shut for a few seconds, memories crowding, intimidating, terrifying her. She pushed them aside. The sheriff would want to find the man who'd kidnapped her. She had to dig deep for courage to help him. "I think he was in the back seat when I got into the car."

He'd been waiting for her in her own driveway.

"He told me to drive to Grey's Hollow. After we passed the train station, he made me stop the car and drink something. I was in and out of it for days."

The doctor had said that the drug had likely affected her memory.

The sheriff frowned. "What's the first thing you remember *after* Friday night?"

Chelsea remembered waking in the storage container. Her body began to tremble.

Tim stroked her arm. "It's OK. You're safe now."

She shook her head. Tears welled up in her eyes and spilled down her cheeks. "He. He. He." She couldn't get the words out between gasps for air. She inhaled and held her breath for a few seconds, then exhaled. "He chained me."

The infected sore on her ankle throbbed.

"Can you describe him?" the sheriff asked.

Chelsea clung to Tim's hand as she shook her head, feeling weak and helpless and pathetic. No one was going to find him if she couldn't even answer a few simple questions. She forced her lips to form the words. "He wore a mask."

The sheriff frowned. "Anything you can tell us will help."

Tim raised his voice. "My wife—"

"No, please, Tim. The sheriff is trying to help. I want him caught." Chelsea tugged on Tim's hand. "I don't want *him* still out there."

Above all, she wanted *him* to be the one who was imprisoned and *her* to be the one who was free.

"All right, but tell me if it's too much," Tim said.

She released his hand and picked up her water, taking a slow sip. The water slid down her throat, cool and soothing. She could do this. She lifted her chin and met the sheriff's gaze. "He wore a ski mask. But he was about six feet tall, maybe a little taller, and strong."

"What about his voice?" the sheriff asked. "Was it familiar in any way?"

"I don't think so."

"No accent?"

"No."

"What about the place you were held?" the sheriff asked.

"It was an old shipping container in the woods." Chelsea described the inside of the container then detailed how she'd gotten out through a rust hole in the ceiling. "There was a cabin or small house about a hundred feet away."

As she talked, her voice grew weaker, her pauses for breath longer. She was physically and emotionally depleted, but she wanted to give the sheriff as much information as she could. "He chased me." The last three words quivered. "But I just ran. I ran as fast as I could. When I had to stop and catch my breath, I didn't hear him behind me anymore. I rolled in the dirt. The dress was such a bright yellow. I was afraid he'd see the fabric."

Probably why he'd chosen such a bright color, she realized with a cold knot in her belly. Maybe a sedative wasn't a bad idea.

She sipped more water. "The trees are so bare and gray this time of year. After that, I just kept moving. I don't know how far I went, but I knew that if I stopped, I'd stiffen up. I wasn't sure I'd be able to get going again."

"Smart," the sheriff said.

"Plus, it was getting colder, and all I had was that blanket." Chelsea's hands—and the rest of her body—shook violently.

The sheriff wrote notes. "Did you see a vehicle?"

"No." Chelsea pictured the cabin and container in the clearing. "There should have been, though. He must have had transportation."

"What time did you escape?" he asked.

"I don't know," Chelsea said.

"Do have any idea how far you ran?" the sheriff pressed.

She shook her head. The night had been a blur of pain and exhaustion and terror. "I don't know."

Tim took his wife's hand again. "Chelsea runs almost every day. She's very fit."

The ability to outrun her captor had no doubt saved her life.

Frustrated, the sheriff tapped a pen on his notepad. "How far do you usually run?"

Chelsea rested her head back against the pillows, spent.

Tim jumped in. "Anywhere from five to fifteen miles, and she's fast too."

Sheriff King exhaled hard. "And you didn't follow a trail or stream?"

"I just ran. It was dark. Eventually, I had to walk, but everything looked the same in the woods." Chelsea's words and memories blended together, the pitch of her voice rising as exhaustion weighted her.

"Did you hear anything while you were in the container or while you were running away?" the sheriff asked. "Any little detail might help us locate him."

"No. I don't know." Chelsea blinked. Tears spilled from her eyes, and her voice cracked in frustration. "I don't remember."

"Was there a road or could the container be seen from above?" the sheriff asked.

Chelsea pictured it in her mind. "I didn't see a road, and there were tree branches overhead, so I don't know. Maybe? I'm sorry. It was dark and I was more interested in getting away than remembering every detail."

The doctor came into the room and frowned at the sheriff. "That's enough. After she rests, she might be able to recall more information. But you've clearly pushed her far enough for now."

The doctor held a syringe in her hand. "I know you didn't want a sedative earlier, but you haven't slept and you really need to. I think the rest will help."

Since the emotions scurrying in Chelsea's mind were overwhelming, she agreed. "All right." She turned to Tim. "If you'll stay?"

"I'll be here when you wake up." He stroked her forehead.

The doctor injected clear liquid into the IV.

Within seconds, the tension in Chelsea's body eased. Her fingers relaxed in Tim's hand and the room blurred. She barely noticed as the sheriff ducked out of the room.

The doctor's voice floated to Chelsea. "As I mentioned earlier, I'm also going to order a psychiatric evaluation. There are techniques that might help her remember details, but right now, she's been through enough."

The sheriff's voice followed, "I'll put a deputy outside your wife's door for tonight. We'll reassess the situation tomorrow."

Chelsea shivered. Her kidnapper had held her for almost a week. He'd tortured her.

He might not give her up so easily.

Chapter Twenty-Eight

Lance and Morgan sat in the hospital waiting room. Morgan silently contemplated the dark-gray carpet. She hadn't said a word since a nurse had come for Chelsea's parents ten minutes before. Morgan's eyes were dark and far away, and Lance wondered what difficult memory was playing in her mind.

Several hours had passed since they'd seen the video in Tim's kitchen. A few phone calls had verified that Chelsea had been taken to the hospital. A neighbor had been called to watch the children so that Tim, Patricia, and Rand could go to the hospital.

Lance reached for Morgan's hand, interlacing their fingers. Hers were cold. "Are you all right?"

"When the chaplain came to the house to tell me that John was dead, I was alone. The girls were there, but I was the only adult. Sophie was still a baby. I don't even remember the next couple of hours. I don't know who took care of the children. Maybe the chaplain. Maybe the army officer who came with him. Maybe me." She paused for a slow breath. "Someone called Grandpa because he and Stella just showed up at the house. I have no memory of the rest of that day. Except for John's funeral, the next few weeks are hazy."

Lance squeezed her hand, the pain in her voice breaking his heart. "Maybe that's for the best."

"Maybe it is."

"Chelsea is alive."

"I know." Morgan's voice was soft. "I was just thinking how good it was for Tim to have support. To not be alone. Chelsea is alive, but we have no idea what happened to her. What she went through."

Lance was betting it had been pretty horrific. Even without seeing her in person, he'd seen her face on that recording. She'd been filthy and battered, her bruised face the color of a raw steak, her features swollen. It had taken Tim a few seconds to recognize her, and he'd been blown away.

A shadow darkened the doorway.

"There you are." The sheriff walked in. He went to the portable coffeemaker on a table in the corner and brewed himself a cup. He took a chair across from Morgan and Lance. His eyes were troubled, and he held the cup in both hands, but Lance could see the ends of his fingers trembling.

Sheriff King wasn't easily disturbed. He'd undoubtedly seen many terrible things in his decades in law enforcement. But Chelsea had gotten to him. Discomfort stirred in Lance's chest. What had Chelsea told the sheriff?

"How is she?" Morgan asked.

"She's in rough shape, but she's alive." The sheriff paused to drink his coffee. "Unfortunately, her captor wore a ski mask, so she can't describe him other than to say he was six feet tall, maybe a little more, and strong. She didn't recognize an accent, so maybe he's from the general area."

"That description fits Harold Burns," Lance said.

The sheriff shrugged. "Her description fits a good percentage of the male residents of Randolph County."

"Do you have men out searching the woods for the place where she was held?" Morgan asked.

The sheriff nodded. "We do, but we have no idea how long or how far she ran. From the injuries to her feet, we think she covered some ground. Miles. It might have been a house or cabin in the woods, and she was held in a shipping container. It'll be hard to narrow down the search unless we can get more information from her. We're looking at satellite photos of the area to see if we can see the container, but Chelsea said there are branches that might conceal it." His big chest rose and fell. He stared into his coffee. The attempted interview had troubled him. "I wish she remembered more details."

"She's traumatized."

"Yes." He composed his face back into its usual stony mask. "We sent the blanket and the dress she was wearing to forensics. They'll try and find trace evidence or DNA, but given how far she ran in the woods, I'm not sure how much help anything the techs find will be. When you talk to her, please take notes. Any small piece of information could help us find this guy."

"Thanks for the update," Lance said.

The sheriff tossed his empty cup in the trash on his way out.

"What now?" Morgan stood and stretched.

"I don't know." Lance got to his feet. "Sharp and I were hired to find Chelsea, and she's no longer missing."

"I'm not sure Tim will be needing a lawyer at this point. I don't know where I stand either." Morgan paced the room. "Let's give Tim a little more time."

They didn't have to wait long. Tim walked into the room; his eyes looked as if *he'd* been traumatized. "I only have a few minutes. I want to get back to Chelsea."

"Of course you do," Morgan said. "Don't feel like you need to give us a report. Go back to your wife."

"She's . . ." He glanced away, then turned and eased into a chair. Resting his elbows on his knees, he dropped his head into his hands and shoved both hands into his hair.

Morgan moved to take the chair next to him. Without speaking, she put a hand on his back. Tim's shoulders shook as he cried silently. He lifted his head a few minutes later, his eyes still shocked.

"She was shaking when I went in to see her. So hard." Anger glittered in his tear-filled eyes. "But she's strong. Stronger than I ever realized." Tim leaned back and wiped his sleeve across his face. His eyes were bleak as he said, "He branded her."

"What?" Lance asked.

"A brand. It looks like an infinity symbol." Tim sighed. "The doctor said a plastic surgeon will look at it. What if they can't remove it? Every time she sees it, she'll be reliving her captivity all over again. She'll never be able to put it out of her mind." Tim jumped to his feet and paced the small room. His gaze landed on random spots in the room and flittered away without seeming to register what he was seeing, as if his mind couldn't process the last few hours. Tim was a man on the edge of the breaking point. "I have to go back to Chelsea. I don't know what to say to her."

Morgan answered, "There's nothing you can say that will undo what's been done. Just tell her you love her. She's going to need you."

"You're right. Thank you." He headed toward the door.

"Is there anything we can do?" Lance was just as worried about any immediate physical threat to Chelsea's life. "Is the sheriff putting a guard on her?"

Tim nodded. "He's posting a deputy outside her room tonight."

Hopefully, the sheriff would be willing to continue to protect her until the man who kidnapped her was caught.

"What do you want to do about the press conference?" Morgan asked. "It's scheduled for seven o'clock."

Lance checked the time on his phone. It was after six. His stomach rumbled, as if it had just learned it was time for dinner. Had they eaten lunch? The day was a blur.

Tim looked unsure. "The sheriff said he'd handle updating the press, but he suggested someone be there to represent the family. I don't really want to leave Chelsea, and her parents aren't in any condition to be on camera. But what happens to the reward now that she's been found?"

"The primary purpose of the press conference was to appeal to the public for help in finding her. The details of the reward were never publicized, so we can just pull the offer now that she's been found," assured Morgan.

Tim shook his head. "Chelsea's dad wants the reward to remain in place for information leading to the arrest and conviction of the man who kidnapped Chelsea."

"All right," Morgan said. "I'll rewrite the statement we drafted earlier."

"So, you'll handle the press conference for us?" Tim asked.

"Yes," Morgan said.

"Thank you. Very much. We really appreciate your help. None of us are thinking clearly right now." Tim left.

"I need to get to the press conference." Morgan picked up her bag.

"I'll take you." He wasn't happy that she was, once again, volunteering for publicity. But she was going to do her best for her client. And Lance would stick close.

They left the hospital, making their way through the parking lot. Back in the Jeep, Lance started the engine. "Do you need to stop at the office?"

"There's no time." Morgan opened her bag, combed her hair, and fixed her lipstick. "This should be quick. I'll give a simple statement about the family being joyful over Chelsea's return and appeal to the public to respect the family's privacy. The sheriff will have to field questions about the actual investigation."

Lance drove to the municipal building, where the sheriff had arranged for a room for the press conference. By the time they arrived, the press was already gathering and setting up. At least a dozen stations were represented. Chelsea's disappearance hadn't garnered this much attention, but then how many kidnapping victims escaped their abductors. Having been missing for a week, no doubt most people had written Chelsea off as dead.

Morgan walked toward the front of the room. Lance took a place near the wall, out of the line of media fire but close enough to be supportive.

Sheriff King stepped up behind a podium. Morgan took her place next to him. They tested microphones, and then the sheriff took the lead, introducing himself and Morgan, then reading a prepared statement. "Chelsea Clark was found on the side of Breakneck Road this morning by a passing motorist. The sheriff's department is grateful that she is alive and reunited with her family. We are still investigating her disappearance, and we're determined to bring her kidnapper to justice."

The press jumped in with questions immediately. "What is her condition?"

The sheriff answered. "Mrs. Clark is stable."

A reporter in the front row stood. "Where has she been all week?"

"It appears that she was kidnapped and held captive by an unknown person," the sheriff said.

"Was she released? Did she escape?" another reporter asked.

The sheriff leaned closer to the mic. "It appears that she escaped."

"What does that mean?" the reporter sounded almost hostile.

The sheriff tensed. "It means I can't give any further information about an ongoing investigation."

A tall thin man pushed his way to the front of the crowd. "Is this case related to the woman's remains that were found in Black Run State Park?"

"No." The sheriff looked taken aback. He wasn't openly challenged often. "At this time, we have no evidence to link the cases."

Thin Man continued. "Do you have a description of who took Chelsea Clark?"

Clearly irritated with the reporter's relentlessness, the sheriff stiffened his shoulders. He inhaled, inflating his chest and sitting taller. He tried to stare down Thin Man, but the reporter's expression remained smug.

When the sheriff spoke, his words were careful, measured, and full of authority. "Chelsea Clark was abducted last Friday night and held for six days by a man wearing a mask. She never saw his face."

Thin Man changed the target of his inquiry. "Ms. Dane, as the family's legal representative, can you divulge any details? The public has a right to know if they're in danger."

"Chelsea's family is grateful to have her back and are focused on her well-being. They ask for the understanding and prayers of the community," Morgan said. "If you want details about the case, ask the sheriff."

Thin Man wasn't deterred. "Is there a serial killer in Randolph County?"

The sheriff leaned close to the mic. "We don't have evidence to suggest the cases are connected or the inclination to leap to such a conclusion at this time."

Except that two women, approximately the same age and physical description, had been kidnapped and beaten.

Chapter Twenty-Nine

A child's scream startled Morgan from a dead sleep. Her heart stuttered in her chest. The bed was cold. After being woken too many nights, Snoozer had abandoned Morgan to sleep with her grandfather. A second small cry floated through the open doorway.

Sophie.

Morgan listened intently for another sound. Her eyes drifted to the clock on the nightstand. Just after midnight. She'd slept barely thirty minutes after staring at the ceiling and worrying about the case for an hour.

Maybe the night terror will pass.

The previous two episodes lasted at least ten minutes each, but the doctor had said their duration could be a short as a minute or so. It was possible that they'd get lucky and Sophie would settle on her own. A thumping noise verified that this would not be the case tonight.

Bleary-eyed, Morgan tossed the comforter aside and stumbled out of bed. A chill swept over her. Grandpa liked to turn the thermostat down at night, and the old house could use new insulation.

Her bare feet hit the freezing hardwood. Where were her slippers? Not beside her bed where they should be. No time to look for them. She grabbed a sweatshirt and headed for her daughters' room, still half-asleep and hoping she could remove Sophie before the screaming woke

Ava and Mia. They were both sound sleepers, but if Sophie really got going, her screams could wake the dead.

Drawing the shirt over her head, she hurried into the dark hall. A night-light, plugged into a wall socket, cast light downward onto the floor, just enough to keep one from tripping over a toy on their way to the bathroom. The hallway led to the foyer, living room, and kitchen at the front of the house. Moonlight streamed through a window, cutting a swath of light through the darkness.

The light also silhouetted two dark figures, one child and one adult, at the other end of the hall. Morgan stopped in her tracks. Did Gianna or Grandpa wake up and see to Sophie?

Her eyes continued to adjust to the dimness.

The adult figure was much larger than Gianna and definitely male. The child's shadow wiggled.

"Grandpa?" she called softly, but as the word left her lips, she knew the figure didn't move like an old man.

He spun to face her. Morgan's blood chilled to ice water. Definitely not her grandfather.

A strange man stood in her hallway.

An intruder.

A hood shadowed his features. The small form next to him struggled, but he held her firmly by the arm, her back pressed against his body, one of his hands covering her mouth.

Sophie's eyes were opened so wide that the whites showed in the dark corridor.

Morgan's brain processed the scene in front of her with horror. She looked for a weapon. But both of his hands were visible and occupied. The chill in her body transformed itself into a cold and furious calm.

"Release my daughter." Morgan didn't recognize her own voice. It was full of a menace she'd never felt before. She'd secured her gun in its safe when she'd arrived home and set the alarm. Not that she'd risk firing a shot with the intruder using her daughter as a shield. TV shows aside, pistols were not accurate enough to fire over a child's head, especially in a dark hallway with adrenaline mainlining through Morgan's bloodstream.

So what could she do?

She took a step closer.

He moved his hand from Sophie's arm to her chin. "If you take one more step, I'll snap her neck." His voice was an unidentifiable whisper.

Morgan assessed his hold on her daughter. With one hand across her face and the other cupping her, could he scissor his hands with enough force to break her neck?

Sophie was tiny and fragile, and Morgan couldn't take the risk.

Fear and adrenaline flooded her veins, but Morgan's mind felt strangely detached. Some primitive instinct kept her concentrated on getting her child away from the intruder without giving in to her terror.

"What do you want?" she asked. She didn't recognize her own voice. The calm inside her was steely and determined and pissed off beyond measure. It waited, biding its time, until it could be unleashed upon this man who dared to touch her baby.

"You're coming with me."

"Done." She would do whatever it took to get him away from her child. Sacrifice herself, kill him with her bare hands, claw his eyes out. There was no price too high, and no act beyond consideration. "Let go of her."

He chuckled, a low and mocking sound that rippled along the goose flesh covering Morgan's arms under her sweatshirt. He was enjoying himself. "It's not going to be that easy."

"Tell me what you want me to do." She waited for his response.

"She's coming too."

Sophie turned her head and bit him. He jerked his hand away from her face. "Ow. You little . . ."

His hand rose, as if he was going to smack the child. But she didn't give him the chance. Her little body pivoted to face him, her arms flailing wildly to keep him from getting a fresh grip.

The hallway seemed to grow longer as Morgan rushed forward.

Six feet still separated them as Sophie kicked out. Her bare foot connected with his leg. One flailing fist struck his groin. He doubled over, and Sophie broke away, running behind her mother.

The flash of relief was fleeting.

The man got to his feet. They were too close now. Barely five feet separated them. Sophie clutched Morgan's thigh, inhibiting her movement.

His head turned toward the doorway on his left. The girls' bedroom.

Morgan wanted to put herself between him and her other two children. Without lowering her gaze, she pushed Sophie backward. "Go in Mommy's room and lock the door."

Crying softly, Sophie clung to Morgan.

"Do it now." Morgan kept her gaze firmly on the intruder, watching his head, hands, and hips for signs of his intended movements.

Sophie let go. Morgan heard her whimpering and her bare feet slapping the hardwood as she ran down the short hallway. Her heart bled for the child, but she had to protect her first. Comfort would have to come later, when they were all safe. A door slammed shut. A lock clicked.

But Morgan knew that flimsy interior door wouldn't keep her daughter safe for long. And now her older two children were also in danger.

"Don't move." Grandpa's voice came from the shadows behind the intruder. Light glinted off the pistol in his hand. "I promise that I will shoot you without hesitation."

Morgan breathed.

Thank God.

Grandpa was in the dark and smart enough to stay there. Moving any closer to the intruder would show how old and frail he was, plus closer quarters would give the intruder the opportunity to disarm him.

The intruder froze for a few long seconds, then turned and bolted for the front of the house. He unlocked the door, opened it, and disappeared outside. The security lights illuminated as his footsteps thudded on the concrete stoop. Gun in hand, Grandpa shuffled after him, stopping on the front stoop and scanning the brightly lit front yard.

Morgan hesitated. Part of her wanted to follow Grandpa. He wouldn't be able to catch the intruder, and she hated the thought of him getting away. She didn't even know his identity. But Grandpa would make sure the man was gone. She needed to check on each member of her family.

She turned around. Sophie was locked in Morgan's bedroom, alone and no doubt terrified.

"What happened?" Gianna stood in the doorway across the hall from the girls' room.

"We had a break-in." Morgan rushed for her room. "Could you call the police, and then make sure Ava and Mia are OK?"

Her older daughters were quiet. Hopefully, they hadn't woken.

Morgan knocked softly on her bedroom door. "Sophie? It's Mommy. Open the door, sweetie. Everything is all right now. The man is gone."

Nothing.

Morgan tried the door. Locked. She reached for the top of the door frame and swept her hand along the molding. Her fingers found the thin key she kept there in case one of the kids locked themselves in a room.

As Sophie had done multiple times.

Morgan unlocked the door and opened it slowly. "Sophie? Where are you?"

She crouched to check under the bed and found only her slippers. There was only one other place to hide. She crossed the room to open the closet door. At first, she didn't see anything. She moved her hanging clothes aside and almost burst into tears.

Sophie was huddled on the floor of the closet.

Morgan squatted down to her level. "It's OK, sweetie. You can come out."

She held out her arms, and Sophie leaped into them, sobbing. The child's pajamas were wet, and she smelled like urine. Morgan stood, lifting her baby in her arms. She grabbed her cell phone from the nightstand and called Lance as she walked back out into the hallway.

He answered, sounding wide-awake and anxious. "What's wrong?"

"We had an intruder in the house."

"I'll be there in ten minutes."

She ended the call, shoving the phone into the pocket of her pajamas.

Gianna was coming out of the girls' bedroom. She held a finger to her lips. "Unbelievably, they are both still asleep," she whispered. "I called 911 and Stella."

"Thank you." Morgan walked toward her. "Sophie needs dry pajamas."

Gianna slipped back into the bedroom, emerging a minute later with a clean nightgown and panties. She handed them to Morgan, then headed for the kitchen. "I'll put on some coffee."

It was going to be a long night.

Morgan set the shivering little girl down, stripping the wet clothes off her body. She set them aside in case the police wanted them as evidence.

"I'm sorry, Mommy." Sophie's voice was thin and small and helpless. "I was going to the baffroom, and I saw him. He grabbed me. I was sca-wed."

"Of course you were, honey." Morgan's heart cracked, visions of her baby confronting an intruder breaking her in pieces. Sophie shivered, and Morgan wanted to rip the intruder to shreds.

And maybe set the shredded bits on fire.

Drawing in a calming breath, she tugged the flannel nightgown over Sophie's head. "You were very brave. Grandpa chased him away."

Her children were all right. If she focused on that fact, she'd get through this.

Once dressed, Sophie wrapped all four limbs around Morgan and clung hard. Her three-year-old was surprisingly strong—inside and out.

"It's all right now," Morgan soothed, staggering to her feet with the additional weight.

"Morgan!" Gianna's shout came from the front door.

Heart clutching, Morgan carried Sophie out onto the stoop. Three concrete steps led to the front walkway. Grandpa was sprawled at the bottom.

"Stay calm," he said in a breathless whisper. "I'm still alive." But his words were strained, his face was drawn, and one leg was bent at an impossible angle.

Chapter Thirty

"Don't move, Grandpa." Morgan used her cell to call for an ambulance. Then she brushed her daughter's hair from her face. "Sophie, I need you to go inside with Gianna."

Sophie hugged her harder. For a second, Morgan thought she'd have to peel the frightened child from her body, but Sophie seemed to understand the gravity of the situation. She released Morgan and allowed Gianna to take her from her mother. Gianna carried the child back in the house.

Morgan ran inside and grabbed a blanket from the back of the living room sofa. Back outside, she dropped to her knees beside her grandfather, tucked the blanket around his trembling body, and took his hand.

"Twenty years ago, I would have chased that son of a bitch. Ten years ago, I would have shot him," Grandpa wheezed, pain creasing his face. "But my hands are so shaky now, I was afraid I'd miss and hit you by accident."

Morgan held beck her tears. "You still saved us all tonight."

As always.

"I wish I wasn't so damned old." Grandpa's breaths shortened. "I can't believe I fell down a couple of steps."

The next ten minutes seemed to take ten hours to pass, but the ambulance and paramedic vehicle finally arrived, just a minute apart. Morgan stood aside to give the medics room to work.

Lance's Jeep sped down the street and parked at the curb. A few seconds later, he jogged across the grass to stand next to her. He took off his leather jacket and wrapped it around her.

Morgan hadn't realized she was freezing until the warmth of it enveloped her. It smelled like him, a cedar scent that now comforted her. Her knees, her whole body, felt weak. She leaned into him, grateful for his presence and support.

His arm wrapped around her shoulders, and he pulled her close. "What happened?"

"Grandpa fell chasing the intruder." She watched the paramedic start an IV and assess her grandfather's injuries while she briefly recapped the details of the break-in for Lance.

A minute later, Stella drove up to the house and parked behind Lance's vehicle. She ran up to one of the paramedics and peered over his shoulder. "I'm here, Grandpa."

Stella turned and joined Morgan and Lance on the lawn. She hugged Morgan. "How did he get inside?"

"I don't know," Morgan said. "I'm absolutely positive I set the alarm as soon as I got home and again after I took the dog out."

Stella rubbed her arm. "Brody is on his way. He'll review the surveillance feed. He'll find out what happened."

The paramedics loaded Grandpa onto a gurney. His face was as white as the pillow under his head, and worry roiled in Morgan's belly.

"I need to go to the hospital, but I don't want to leave Gianna and the girls here, not after the break-in." Morgan brushed her hair out of her face. Would she ever feel safe in her own home again? She didn't know who had broken into her house or why.

"Mac is on his way home," Stella said. "But he won't be here for a few more hours."

Morgan turned to Lance.

"What can I do?" he asked.

"Can you take the girls and Gianna to your place?" She had complete faith that he'd protect them.

"Are you sure?" he asked. "I hate to leave you alone right now."

Morgan hated to give up his support too, but . . . "My kids come first. They were in danger tonight. I can't function if they aren't safe. Gianna will help you get their stuff together." She looked into his eyes. "Please, I need to know they're safe." Her gaze drifted to the ambulance pulling out of the driveway.

"Or course I'll take care of them. I'll do anything you need." Lance rubbed her arms.

"Thank you. I have to go inside and get my purse. I'll get you the keys to my minivan." She started toward the house, still feeling dazed. "I can take Grandpa's car to the hospital."

"No need. I have my Jeep," Lance said.

"I doubt two car seats and a booster will fit in it." Morgan moved toward the house.

"I'm going to follow the ambulance. Are you all right to drive yourself to the hospital?" Stella asked.

"Yes. I'll be a few minutes getting the girls ready." Morgan had thought juggling three young children and an aging grandfather was difficult before. Handling an intruder and a probable broken leg for her grandfather seemed overwhelming.

"You'd better get dressed too." Stella took her keys from her pocket.

Morgan looked down at her bare feet, which would be freezing if she weren't numb with shock. She'd forgotten she was in her pajamas. "Right."

The ambulance pulled away, lights flashing red in the darkness. Stella followed in her car.

Morgan went inside and got dressed, then helped Gianna pack a change of clothes for each of the girls. Lance carried Mia and Ava to the van with a brief explanation about Grandpa being hurt. Gianna grabbed some dog food, snapped Snoozer's leash to his collar, and carried him to the minivan.

"Mommy, don't weave me." Sophie clutched Morgan's thigh.

Morgan crouched. "I have to go with Grandpa to make sure he's OK. Lance will keep you safe."

Sophie's gaze drifted toward the open doorway to Grandpa's bedroom. How much did she understand? Between being attacked and seeing her beloved Grandpa lying on the concrete in obvious pain, poor Sophie was traumatized. "Pwomise?"

"Promise." Morgan hugged her daughter. She wished she could be two people right now. How could she possibly take care of three children and her grandfather? The answer was, she couldn't, at least not alone. She needed help.

She needed someone to lean on, to trust, to share the burden, and she knew without a doubt that Lance was that person. Together, he and Gianna were perfectly capable of caring for the girls. But it still broke her heart to put Sophie in her car seat, shut the minivan door, and watch it drive away.

Brody and two patrol cars arrived at the house just before Morgan left. She gave Brody an abbreviated statement and left him to his investigation. When she was finally ready to go to the hospital, her hands trembled on the steering wheel of Grandpa's Lincoln Town Car. She blasted the heat for the entire drive but was still shaking when she parked her car in the emergency lot. Stella was waiting outside a cubicle in the ER hallway.

"How is he?" Morgan unzipped her coat.

"His vitals are strong," Stella began. "But his leg is badly broken. He's going to need surgery to repair it. Do you have a list of his medications?"

"I do." Morgan opened her tote bag and unzipped the side pouch. She withdrew a notecard. She kept several printed copies in her bag and a backup note in her phone. Grandpa usually carried a copy in his wallet, which he hadn't had on him in the middle of the night. Stella walked the card to the nurses' station and handed it to the doctor.

"Is he going to be OK?" Morgan asked when her sister returned.

"The surgery will be hard on him at his age, but he's tough." Stella chewed on a nail. "And we really don't have any options."

A nurse emerged through the sliding glass door. "We're going to take him upstairs in a few minutes. Do you want to see him first?"

Morgan and Stella went to his bed. Morgan did not allow herself a reaction. Grandpa lay surrounded by beeping monitors and dripping IVs. He looked as if he'd shrunk. Just a few months ago, before his blood pressure had suddenly spiked, he'd been a robust, active man. The sheer stillness of his body shocked Morgan.

He opened his eyes and held out a hand. "My girls."

They went to his side. Morgan took his hand, taking comfort that his grip was strong despite his obvious frailty.

"I called Peyton and Ian," Stella said. "They're both going to come as soon as they can."

"No need for them to travel all this way," Grandpa rasped. "The surgery will be over before either one of them can get here."

"That's not the point." Morgan gave his hand a gentle squeeze. "We all love you."

Peyton and Ian hadn't been around much in the past few years, but that didn't mean they loved him less.

"I love you too, but don't look all glum," he ordered. "I'm not ready to die yet. I have things to do."

The nurse tapped on the door frame. "We're going to take him up now."

Morgan and Stella each gave him a kiss on the cheek before retreating to the hallway. They followed posted directions to the surgical waiting room.

In the small, ugly mauve room, Stella made a cup of coffee on a pod machine in the corner. "He's tough. Try not to worry too much."

"I know." Morgan would rather talk about anything except the surgery. And silence amplified her worry. "When are Peyton and Ian coming?"

"I don't know. Peyton checked for flights, but they were all full. She's going to get on the standby list." Stella sank into a plastic chair. "I left a message for Ian."

"He must be working. It's not like he can return a call when he's busy with a hostage situation or serving a high-risk warrant."

"He should visit more." Stella lifted her Styrofoam cup. "Want one?"

Morgan shook her head. Her stomach was roiling from the earlier adrenaline dump. "He should be thinking about settling down. As far as I know, he doesn't even have a steady girlfriend. Or a plant."

"He will, as soon as he's done with SWAT." Stella sipped her coffee and made a face. "You were ready to settle down young. The rest of us took longer to mature."

"Does that mean you're settling down?" Morgan asked. The night seemed surreal. Too many shocks for her brain to absorb. She wanted normal for a little while, even if it was just an ordinary conversation. "My kids could use some cousins."

Stella choked on her coffee. "I'm not *that* settled yet. Please. Mac and I have only been living together for a few months."

"But you've thought about it?"

"Of course I've thought about having kids in the future. Keyword: future. Could you imagine having a few mini-Mac wild boys running around? Any kids Mac fathers are guaranteed to be a handful."

"But adorable."

"Yeah." Stella's sigh was just a little wistful. "That too."

They distracted themselves with more inane small talk until Brody walked in a short while later.

"Any news?" he asked.

Stella updated him. "We're waiting. What did you find out about the break-in?"

"This guy knew what he was doing." Brody sat across from Morgan and Stella. "Older security systems were easily beaten by burglars. They simply found the siren wire and the telephone line and cut them. The system couldn't summon the police and the siren didn't go off. Newer systems use wireless technology as a workaround."

"Our system is wireless," Morgan said. "With a backup battery in case we lose electricity."

"But wireless systems aren't foolproof either. Every time there's an advance in security technology, criminals find a way to beat it. It's a vicious cycle." Brody scratched his chin. "We believe the intruder used a jammer to interrupt the radio frequency of the wireless system. The alarm never sent a signal to the central monitoring station or the siren. Once he beat the alarm, he took his time picking the lock."

"Not an amateur." Stella huffed.

"No. Definitely not." Brody swept a hand through his short hair. "I contacted the unit watching Burns's house."

"You have a unit watching Harold Burns?" Morgan was surprised.

"We do, but because of Burns's legal maneuvering, they've been told to keep their distance and stay off his property." Brody's face tightened with a frown. "We haven't seen any movement or lights at Burns's house. His car has not left the garage. But his house is surrounded by forest, and he only lives a half mile from his brother's auto shop. He could easily walk there through the woods and help himself to a car. In short, we have no way of knowing for certain if he's actually inside."

Chapter Thirty-One

It was after one in the morning when Lance lugged three backpacks into his house. Then he went back to the Jeep and carried Ava and Mia inside, one by one, and tucked them into his guest bed. Gianna and Sophie walked in under their own steam. Unbelievably, Morgan's littlest was still awake. Snoozer shuffled into the house, jumped up on the sofa, and curled into a ball.

"The girls can sleep in the guest room. I can give you mine," Lance said to Gianna. He'd sleep on the couch.

After he moved the dog.

Gianna shook her head. "I'll share with the girls. That way, if they wake up and don't know where they are, I'll be there."

"Will all four of you fit?" Lance's guest bed was a queen size but still . . .

"They're small." Gianna hadn't bothered to dress. In her flannel pajamas and oversize sweatshirt, the eighteen-year-old looked much younger. Even with the pounds she'd gained since moving in with Morgan, Gianna was still slender, though less frail and much healthier than when she'd lived alone.

"OK. I have a blow-up mattress. I'll put it in the bedroom in case you need more room." Lance went into the garage and used his compressor to inflate the twin mattress. Then he wedged it between the wall and the bed. The second bedroom in his compact house wasn't large. Neither Ava nor Mia stirred. Amazingly, they hadn't objected to being roused from their beds in the middle of the night, though Morgan had only told them that Grandpa was hurt. She didn't want to frighten them.

Sophie was scared enough for all three children.

"I'm going to use the bathroom." Gianna carried a small bag toward the hall bath. "Are you OK, Soph?"

Nodding, Sophie wandered around the living room, inspecting Lance's few pieces of furniture.

"I don't wanna go to bed." Sophie hugged a toy horse tightly against her face. The sight stabbed Lance in the heart. The child was always a handful but not typically whiny. She'd had a rough, frightening night.

"How about a glass of milk?" he asked.

She nodded and followed him toward the kitchen. Passing the piano, she stopped. "Can I touch it?"

"Sure. But softly, OK? Mia and Ava are sleeping," Lance said.

Sophie sat down on the piano bench and raised a hand over the keyboard. She pressed a key, her touch light and hesitating, almost reverent. A soft middle *C* sounded through the dining room.

Lance sat down next to her.

"Can you play a song?" She plunked another soft key.

"It's too late." Lance's gut wrenched as she turned and blinked her big blue eyes at him. "But I promise I'll play for you another time. In fact, I can even teach you a song."

She nodded hard and sniffed.

"How about we get you to bed, Soph?" Gianna walked into the room and held out a hand. Sophie scrambled off the bench, took it, and let Gianna lead her into the guest room.

Lance drank the milk himself. Then he hauled his exhausted body to his bedroom, stripped off his clothes, and took a quick shower. He'd still been up, unable to sleep, when Morgan had called. It was now two a.m.

He usually slept naked. It was more comfortable, and creating dirty laundry while sleeping never made much sense to him. But with four female guests, it didn't feel appropriate. He didn't own pajamas and settled on a pair of athletic shorts and a T-shirt. Good enough.

His cell phone buzzed from the nightstand. He read Morgan's text: THE BREAK IS BAD. GRANDPA GOING INTO SURGERY. RISKY BUT NO OPTIONS. HOW ARE THE GIRLS?

He responded: GIRLS ARE IN BED AND FINE. SORRY TO HEAR ABOUT ART.

Lance hesitated. He wanted to tell her he loved her, but was this really the right time? No. Telling a woman you loved her for the first time in a text was lame.

He typed: THINKING OF YOU. Which felt weak, so he added: I'M UP. CALL ME IF YOU WANT TO TALK.

Morgan: OK. GOTTA GO. THX.

Well, damn.

Art's condition didn't sound good.

He set the phone down. Poor Art. And poor Morgan. Art was old for surgery, and Lance hated thinking of Morgan in the hospital, worrying. For years, her grandfather had been mother and father to her. She'd already lost both her parents and her husband. She did not need any more tragedy in her life.

Lance crawled into bed. He'd rather be with Morgan, but she'd entrusted him with her kids. He'd do his best to take care of them. He lay still, staring at the ceiling, wondering who had broken into Morgan's house and why and coming up with few answers.

It felt as if he'd barely closed his eyes when something woke him. Not a noise. A feeling. The hairs on his neck went rigid.

He was being watched.

All his senses went on alert. He stared into the darkness at his open doorway, listening, not moving, waiting for his eyes to adjust. His gun was on top of his armoire, out of the children's reach but also out of his immediate reach.

Scanning the room, he startled when he made out the small shadow standing at the foot of his bed, staring at him.

"Sophie?" He reached for the light and switched it on.

Tears streaked the little girl's face. "I had a bad dream. He was there." She sniffed and inhaled three sharp breaths.

Lance sat up. "It's OK. You're safe now."

"I'm scaa-wed." She pronounced the word in two syllables as she crawled up onto the bed and knelt in front of him, still clutching her stuffed horse. "Can I sweep with you?"

Her tiny voice broke, and his heart did that Grinch thing again. She trusted him to keep her safe.

How could he say no?

"Ah. Sure." He lifted the covers next to him and she scooted under them. But she wasn't content to occupy the other side of his king bed. She pressed her small body against his from her head to her feet, as if every inch of her needed reassurance that he was there to protect her.

Oh, what the hell?

Lance turned on his side and threw an arm over her. A contented sigh escaped her mouth as she drifted off to sleep.

The room was still dark when Lance woke again. Silence filled the house, and exhaustion blanketed him. Why was he awake? He checked the clock. He'd only been asleep for an hour. No wonder he was still tired.

A scream split his left eardrum, and he automatically lurched a few inches away from its source.

A small fist smacked him in the head, and the night came rushing back. Next to him, Sophie thrashed, then settled onto her back. She stared straight up at the ceiling, her big eyes wide-open but unseeing. She let out a scream, the plaintive, panicked pitch disturbing Lance right down to his soul. The hair on his arm rose, and goose bumps rippled along his skin.

Was this a night terror?

Must be.

It was pretty freaking terrifying.

What should he do?

She rolled suddenly. Her heel struck his thigh in the exact spot where he'd been shot the previous year. Pain burst in Lance's leg. He reached down and rubbed the scar tissue.

Sophie shouted, "No." Her limbs flailed, and she screamed a few more times over the next ten minutes. Lance's gut twisted as he watched, helpless, hoping she didn't wake the other girls. Morgan hadn't said whether she'd roused Sophie or not. Somewhere in the back of his mind he recalled something about not waking a sleepwalker, but had no idea if the tidbit was fact or fiction. Just when he was considering waking her, the episode seemed to pass, and she relaxed back into the pillow. One little foot stretched across the mattress to touch his leg.

But Lance would never get back to sleep now. Sophie's screams still echoed in his head.

Would he disturb her if he got up? He eased away, inch by inch, until he slipped off the side of the bed and fell on his ass. After tucking the blankets up to her chin, he slipped his phone into the pocket of his shorts, went into the kitchen, and started a pot of tea, wishing it were coffee. There was no way Sharp's green tea was going to cut through the haze of one hour of sleep with a screaming three-year-old. The dog didn't even crack an eyelid as he walked by the sofa. Snoozer was no watchdog.

Obviously.

Lance checked his messages. No updates from Morgan. He debated texting her, but he wouldn't want to wake her if she'd dropped off to sleep.

A brushing sound caught his attention. A second later, Sophie appeared in the doorway.

"You weft me." Her lip quivered, and she clutched her stuffed horse. Her eyes were huge, full of tears, and underscored by deep, dark circles.

Oh, geez.

Guilt speared him through the belly.

This babysitting gig was going to take some practice. Lance felt like someone had dropped him in the middle of the ocean without so much as a compass to tell him which way to swim. He'd have to rely on instinct. Kids didn't bullshit, right? So the truth was probably best when possible.

Lance squatted to her level. "I'm sorry. I didn't want to wake you."

She walked right into him and rested her head against his shoulder. Her body trembled with a huge sigh, and Lance's heart melted like a stick of butter in a hot pan. He wrapped his arms around her and picked her up as he straightened. Carrying her, he went back into the kitchen and poured a cup of tea one-handed. Then he started to assemble the ingredients for his morning protein shake, only to realize there were still several hours until dawn and that there was no way he could run the blender without disturbing his other three guests. He returned the frozen berries to the freezer.

Sophie's body was totally limp. Lance glanced down. She was sound asleep against his chest, her little butt perched on his forearm, her tiny hands clutching her stuffed horse.

Lance eased into his living room chair. He set his tea on the end table. Sophie curled up against him.

Now what?

The child was exhausted and wouldn't sleep unless she was with him. Shifting to one side, he drank tea, checked his e-mail, and waited. He must have drifted off at some point, because when Gianna, Mia, and Ava emerged from the bedroom, dawn flooded the room with light and

Lance's neck felt like someone had beaten it with a stick. He lifted his head from the back of the chair and rolled his shoulders.

Ava and Mia's chatter woke Sophie, who crawled out of Lance's lap. He stood and stretched his stiff back, a pins-and-needles sensation flooding his legs.

"We're hungry." Ava bounced toward the kitchen, with Mia and Sophie at her heels.

Lance grabbed his mug and followed them. This was going to be a two-cup, maybe a three-cup morning. He opened the refrigerator. "How about some eggs?"

The three children stared up at him like he'd said *poison*.

Gianna laughed. "Do you have bread? I can make them French toast."

"In the freezer." Lance pointed.

She pulled the loaf out.

"Ew. It's brown." Ava wrinkled her nose.

"It's oat bread," he said. "It's good for you."

None of the children looked convinced.

"What are those *things* in it?" Mia poked at the frozen loaf.

"Sunflower seeds," Lance said with a sinking feeling. What did kids eat?

Mia frowned. "They look like bugs."

"How about pancake mix or flour?" Gianna asked.

"Sorry." Since he'd embraced Sharp's crunchy and organic diet, Lance's kitchen was full of eggs, vegetables, seeds, and nuts.

Someone knocked on the front door. Lance checked the time. Who would be visiting at seven thirty in the morning?

"Wait here." He went to the front door and looked through the narrow side window.

Stella's boyfriend, Mac Barrett, held a bag of groceries. Lance opened the door.

"Sorry. Just got in a couple of hours ago." Mac walked in. "I brought child-friendly food."

"Thank you," Lance said, grateful.

"You're welcome." Mac handed Lance the bag and took off his leather jacket. "Been there, done that with my nephew and niece."

"Mac!" Ava and Mia raced to hug him. Even Sophie seemed pleased to see him.

Gianna took the grocery bag. "Oh, good. Pancake mix." She went back to the kitchen.

The hungry girls trailed after her like baby vultures.

Mac hung back in the living room and spoke in a low voice. "Have you talked to Morgan this morning?"

"No. I was going to call her, but I've been busy." Lance nodded toward the crowded kitchen.

"I'll bet. I stopped at the hospital earlier. Art is out of surgery. He had a few complications because of his age, so they put him in ICU." Mac pushed his shaggy hair out of his face. "He hadn't regained consciousness yet when I talked to Stella last. It's been a long night for Stella and Morgan."

Lance's phone vibrated and he checked the display. "That's Morgan now."

He turned away to answer the call. "Hey."

"Hey yourself. How are the girls?"

"They're fine. Gianna is making them pancakes."

Morgan updated him on her grandfather's condition. "Stella is still trying to get a hold of Ian. She'll stay at the hospital for now."

"What are you doing?" Lance asked.

"I want to find the man who broke in to my house." Morgan sounded determined. "This wasn't a random event. Whoever bypassed our security system knew what he was doing."

"Harold Burns?" Lance asked.

"Maybe. The intruder said he wanted me. He wasn't looking for cash or drugs."

"Just tell me how I can help."

"Mac is going to take the girls to his brother's house after breakfast. They've been there before."

"What do you want me to do?" Lance asked.

"Help me. I'm going to grab a shower, stop in to see the girls at the Barretts' house, and then head to the office. This break-in was related to Chelsea's case, I just feel it. None of us are safe until we solve it."

Chapter Thirty-Two

He paced the yard between the storage container and the shed. The morning chill hung in the damp air, but rage warmed his blood to boiling.

Chelsea. Chelsea. Chelsea.

Grabbing his head between his hands, he pressed on his skull, but his brain continued to whisper her name.

What had he done?

He'd gone to the hospital, intent on seeing Chelsea, to figure out how he was going to get her back. Instead, he'd found a sheriff's deputy at her door. The image of the lady lawyer at the press conference had popped into his head, and all of his rage had landed on her with the force of a speeding truck. As the family's lawyer, she would be able to get to Chelsea. If he could force her to help him.

Women were weak, he'd reasoned. It was too easy to use their children as leverage against them. That had been his plan. The lawyer lived with three small children, a sickly girl, and an elderly man. How hard could it be?

But he'd failed. He hadn't expected the old man to be armed. He hadn't expected the kid to fight back.

He hadn't planned the break-in beyond circumventing the alarm system. He'd rushed. He hadn't done any surveillance. Foolishness had nearly ruined his entire plan.

Anger reared its head like a serpent in his chest. The lawyer and her brat could use lessons in being submissive females. If he ever got his hands on them . . . but they were not his problem. Chelsea was.

And he was never going to come up with a new plan until he regained control. Rage tunneled his vision and blocked his common sense.

He turned to the shed and rammed a fist into the side. His skin split on impact, blood bursting from his knuckles. But the pain that throbbed through his hand wasn't enough to drown out the whispers.

He had to get her back, but how?

By not being stupid!

Chelseeeeeeea.

Stop it!

He ran into the shed, his gaze bouncing from the workbench to the corkboard of tools. He grabbed a hammer and slammed the flat end into his calf, right where he'd branded himself. Agony, blessed and beautiful, erupted from the burn, leaving no room for emotions. Pain cleansed his focus, swept aside his fury, and clarified his thoughts.

His knees buckled. He braced a hand on the wall to steady himself. The weakness was a relief. In a few moments, he'd recover. He'd drink. He'd eat. He'd redress his wound.

Once his body was restored to order, his mind would follow.

He turned toward the cabin, a plan already spinning in his mind. He would get Chelsea back if it was the last thing he ever did.

If it was the last thing either one of them ever did.

Chapter Thirty-Three

"The girls seemed happy with Mac's brother." Standing in the doorway of Lance's office, Morgan lifted a gigantic cup of coffee to her lips and drank. It was her third, but there just wasn't enough caffeine to jump-start her brain today. They'd dropped off Grandpa's car and Morgan's minivan at her house and picked up Lance's Jeep.

"They were excited to go to the house with the creek and the big, sloppy dog," Lance clarified.

"It's a relief to know they're safe."

Mac's brother was a former army officer.

"You look exhausted," Lance said.

She gave him a wry smile. "You don't look so chipper yourself."

"I slept more than you did." Lance stood. "And Sophie might actually like me now."

Sometimes the little lifts in life helped get you over the big hurdles.

"Here." Sharp walked down the hall. He handed her a protein shake and gave one to Lance.

"Thank you." Morgan sipped the shake.

"If neither of you will sleep, this is the best I can do." He frowned at her coffee cup. "How many of those have you had?"

"I'll plead the fifth on that question." Morgan tossed the empty cup in the trashcan. She was more than tired. Worry for her kids and her grandfather was eating a hole through her.

"We need a strategy meeting," Sharp said.

"Definitely." Morgan retreated to her office. Lance and Sharp followed her inside.

She settled in her chair, leaned on the desk, and stared at the case whiteboard. "I ran into Tim at the hospital this morning. Chelsea is being released later today. The sheriff has agreed to post a car at her house."

"For now," Sharp said.

"Tim has no faith in the sheriff," Morgan said. "He wants us to keep working the case. The reporter's suggestion of a possible serial killer in the area spooked him. Plus, he says Chelsea will never have peace until the bastard who kidnapped her is caught."

"We should interview Chelsea," Lance said.

"Yes," Morgan agreed. "Tim is going to call me as soon as they get home. He thought she might remember more details if she was in a familiar setting."

Sharp faced the whiteboard, crossed his arms over his chest, and stared at it. "First question, was the break-in at Morgan's house related to Chelsea Clark's case?"

"Chelsea escaped. Her captor was pissed. Then Morgan appeared on that press conference representing the family," Lance said. "The correlation is logical. Was it Burns?"

"Burns stalked Morgan," Sharp added. "But that doesn't necessarily mean he kidnapped Chelsea."

"Right," Morgan said. "Burns followed me *after* Lance and I confronted him at the auto shop."

Everything about this case felt so convoluted.

A strand of hair landed on her nose. She brushed it back and smoothed her ponytail. She lowered her arm, and her holster dug in to her hip. She was carrying her handgun until she knew the intruder had been apprehended.

"Do we have any evidence that the body found at the state park is related to Chelsea's kidnapping?" Sharp asked.

Morgan shook her head. "As far as I know, the only thing that ties the cases together is the physical appearances of the victims. They were both young and blonde."

"That's not enough." Sharp rubbed his jaw. "I nosed around for information yesterday. The dead woman was identified as Sarah Bernard. She went missing from the university last February. She was twenty-two years old and a history major."

"He held her for eight months." Morgan's stomach went queasy thinking about the poor girl's fate. "She was five months pregnant. The girl died of a placental abruption. She bled to death." She set her shake aside. "Instead of getting her medical attention, he let her die."

"If we assume Chelsea was his replacement," Lance said. "Could he now be focused on Morgan?"

"I'm not blonde," she said.

"But he might feel a personal connection with you, since you represented the family in that press conference," Lance suggested.

"And he might be flexible on his target profile," Sharp added. "Having two similar victims doesn't mean he has a type. The fact that they were both blonde could have been a coincidence."

Morgan leaned back in her chair. "Who are our best suspects?"

"Let's start with Burns." Lance pushed off the wall and studied the whiteboard.

Morgan started. "SFPD had a car down the road from his residence. He's already complained of harassment once, so they kept their distance. His car stayed at the house. They saw no sign that he'd left. But there's no way they'd know if he went out the back door and walked through the woods to the auto shop. There are plenty of cars there to borrow."

"We don't know if he was there all night," Lance said.

"No." She took a breath. "I talked to my sister this morning. She and Brody knocked on his door to see if he was home. No one answered. The auto shop is closed on weekends. They have zero evidence to support a search warrant for either property. Burns has registered and complied with all legal requirements."

"Damned lawyers." Sharp glanced at Morgan. "Present company excluded. What about Levi Gold?"

"Spoke to my mom an hour ago." Lance shook his head. "Gold is in London right now. He's off the list."

"Kirk Armani?" Sharp's gaze moved down the list of suspects on the board.

"Mom finished checking the list of Speed Net employees and came up mostly empty, though we found a restraining order filed against Kirk Armani a few years ago. A female student accused him of stalking her. There were no subsequent complaints, and the order eventually expired."

"We should talk to Kirk again," Morgan said. "We have his home address."

"Let's do it." Lance paced. "Sarah Bernard was a university student. Kirk finished his PhD, but does he have a current relationship with the university?"

Morgan searched her bin for the correct file. "No, but in our original interview, Tim said Speed Net works with the university."

Anxious to take any kind of action, she started shoving files into her tote.

"Hold on!" Studying the board, Sharp held up a hand. "What about the mysterious message that Chelsea needed to speak with her boss about something too sensitive for e-mail or text?"

Lance answered, "We've come up empty with Curtis MacDonald and everyone else at the accounting firm."

"Chelsea can answer that question for us." Morgan rubbed the ache in her temples. "I'll call Tim." She picked up her cell and scrolled to

Tim's number. "No answer. We'll have to wait. But what if the answer doesn't lie in the data within her files? I wish we had a list of her clients."

Lance and Sharp shared a look.

"What?" Morgan raised her head.

Lance glanced away. "I might have copied the hard drive of Skyver and MacDonald's laptop when I was at Tim's house copying the Clarks' digital data."

"Chelsea's work computer?" Interest stirred life into Morgan, along with a healthy dose of apprehension.

"It was in her bedroom," Lance answered.

"Why didn't I know about this?" she asked.

"Because it's illegal." Sharp flashed an accusing glare at Lance.

Lance's shoulder twitched, not quite a shrug. "And the files are password-protected. I had to hack into them."

Morgan's elbows hit the desk and her head dropped into her hands. "Evidence discovered illegally isn't admissible. We could all lose our licenses."

"We could go to jail," Sharp added.

"All true," Lance admitted. "I'll take all of those risks on my shoulders. Neither of you had anything to do with my decision. You didn't touch the original computer, and you haven't touched the flash drive. It's all on me." The muscles in Lance's face shifted as he ground his teeth. "I'm tired of having my hands tied while criminals hurt people. Cops put them in jail, and the system lets them out."

"I know." Morgan knew that frustration was one of the reason he'd left the force. "But we're still bound by the law."

She wasn't sure if she was annoyed that he'd done something illegal and possibly put both professional firms in jeopardy or because he hadn't told her.

Or because—at that moment—she felt the exact same way. Everything was out of hand. No matter how many times she told herself that all citizens had the same rights, and that criminals deserved fair representation, when you were a victim, the legal system didn't seem fair.

For a long minute, she longed to be back in the prosecutor's office, working for the state rather than a person, not floundering through a messy, active investigation.

She missed her convictions. She missed the certainty that a defendant was guilty. She missed having a clear path: assemble evidence, present to court, take another criminal off the street.

On the private side, everything was painted a million shades of murky gray. It was as if her world had gone from narrow to panoramic, forcing her to view the limitations of every side: accused, victims, law enforcement. She'd once seen the legal system as a tunnel. Now it was a maze.

"I'm sorry if you don't approve, but I took what I thought were prudent precautions. If I hadn't grabbed that data at the time, I wouldn't have gotten another chance." Lance sighed, his broad chest deflating. "Just pretend you didn't hear any of this. I'll handle it. So far, I haven't found anything unusual, but I've only gotten through a small portion of the files. If we're lucky, Chelsea will tell us what we need to know, and we can all pretend we never had them."

"Until we hear from Tim, your mom and I can dig around." Sharp turned toward the door. "Give me that flash drive, and I'll head over to your mom's house and help her however I can." He took the slim black rectangle from Lance's hand, then left the room, muttering, "We are so screwed if this goes sideways."

"Sharp?" Lance called.

Sharp poked his head around the doorway. "What?"

"The sheriff's office is using satellite images to try and locate the place where Chelsea was held," Lance said. "A clearing with a small house or cabin and a shipping container that may or may not be visible from above. Maybe you can try to track shipping container purchases?"

"I'll see what kind of satellite photos I can dig up too. If the container has been there awhile, maybe it was visible in older images." Sharp disappeared.

Morgan had spent her whole life defending the law, but at this point, she'd been pushed over the line. No. That wasn't true. She was running over it. Her children had been threatened. That superseded all legal requirements. There wasn't anything she wouldn't do to protect them.

Which was interesting because when she'd been an assistant district attorney, she'd prosecuted several vigilante-type crimes with a *no exception to the law* inflexibility that now seemed naive. Her stomach rolled, and she fished in her bag for a roll of antacids, popping two in her mouth.

"Are you all right?" Lance asked in a concerned voice.

"I am." Morgan reached for a bottle of water on her credenza. She chased the antacids down with two ibuprofen tablets from her desk drawer. "Let's go find this bastard before he hurts anyone else."

Sharp reappeared in the doorway. "Too late."

Morgan's belly clenched.

"A woman named Karen Mitchell was reported missing this morning. She left her parents' house to go for a run in the state park. She never came home. She's young. And she's blonde."

Chapter Thirty-Four

"So, what have you been up to, Kirk?" Lance asked.

Inside the fish-bowl conference room at Speed Net, Morgan sat at Lance's left. Kirk Armani and Elliot Pagano, who insisted on being present, had taken seats across from them.

Lance leaned back in his chair and tried to act casual.

But apparently, he wasn't a very good actor.

Kirk Armani held his upturned skateboard in his lap and spun the wheels with trembling fingers. The kid looked like hell. His clothes were wrinkled. He refused to make any eye contact at all.

He and Morgan had knocked on Kirk's apartment door. When no one answered, they'd driven over to Speed Net to talk to him.

Lance scanned the main room through the glass. Despite it being a Saturday afternoon, Speed Net was humming with activity.

Elliot crossed his arms over his chest. "What is this all about? I thought Chelsea had been found."

"We are not law enforcement officers. Kirk is under no obligation to talk to us," Lance said. "But another woman went missing."

Elliot straightened. "That's terrible, but I'm still confused as to why you are here this morning. Are you still working for Tim?"

"We are. Tim and Chelsea want to know who kidnapped her," Morgan said. "And last night someone broke in to my home and threatened me and my family. We think it might have been the same person who kidnapped Chelsea."

"I'm sorry," Elliot said. "That must have been terrifying."

"Yes. It was." Morgan interlaced her fingers on the table. "Kirk, we know about the restraining order that was filed against you."

Kirk paled. "I didn't mean to harass her. I wasn't stalking her. I promise."

Sweat broke out on his forehead. He stopped spinning the skateboard wheels and gripped the edges of the board with both hands.

"It's OK, Kirk," Elliot soothed. "This is old news. Kirk didn't mean any harm."

Kirk shook his head almost violently. "She never asked me to stop talking to her. I didn't know."

"He was working here at the time?" Lance asked.

"Yes. He was really upset. I helped him sort it all out." Elliot's mouth tightened. "The young woman gave Kirk hints that she wasn't interested in him. Kirk didn't read those hints. When he asked her out on a date, and she turned him down by saying she had to clip her cat's toenails, he took her at her word."

"I didn't know." Kirk's breaths came harder and faster.

"Calm down, Kirk. It's fine." Elliot leveled a hard glare at Lance and Morgan in turn. "Kirk has trouble with social cues. If the young woman had just told him she didn't like him, he would have backed down. But she didn't. She was snarky and sarcastic—two things Kirk has trouble interpreting well. He kept asking her out, thinking eventually her schedule would clear."

Disappointment flashed through Lance. Not that he wanted this kid to be guilty. He felt bad for Kirk. But he wanted to find the man responsible.

"We're so sorry we brought this all up, Kirk," Morgan apologized. "I'm frightened for my children. I'm just trying to keep them safe."

"I'd never hurt a kid. I like kids." Kirk sniffed and wiped the back of his hand under his nose. "Kids are nice to me."

As opposed to adults . . .

And Lance felt like he'd just kicked a kitten.

He rubbed his sternum, where frustration burned like a bad case of heartburn. Another dead end.

"Besides, I was here all night." Kirk finally lifted his gaze and briefly let it connect with Lance's, like a moth bouncing off a hot light bulb. "Me and the team worked late. We ordered pizza and played Overlook most of the night. I fell asleep on the couch."

"You've been here all night?" Lance clarified. "With your team members?"

Kirk nodded.

"I'm so sorry we bothered you." Morgan stood. "Thank you for clearing that up for us."

Elliot escorted them to the lobby. "Next time you want to talk to me or one of my employees on corporate property, you'll have to go through my attorney."

He watched them exit. The door closed behind them with a solid and final thud. Lance and Morgan stepped out into the parking lot. The temperature had dropped since they'd gone inside.

"Well, I feel like a total bully." Lance unlocked the Jeep.

"Me too." Morgan climbed into the passenger seat. After he settled behind the wheel, she said. "This case has me feeling all sorts of terrible. Since when am I willing to harass law-abiding citizens or ignore the law?"

"Since the threat became personal." Lance started the engine and drove out of the lot. "That kid will be OK. You did what you had to do. Surely, you were hard on witnesses and defendants when you were a prosecutor?"

"When necessary, yes." She pushed her hair off her face. "But their involvement in the case was always established beforehand. For the most part, I already knew what they were going to tell me."

"The police sorted through the witnesses for you. This is what it's like when you're chasing down leads."

"Yes. You're right. As an ADA, I didn't get involved in cases until arrests were made." She pressed her fingertips to her temples. "This is frustrating."

"You haven't slept. You haven't taken a break. You didn't even finish that protein shake Sharp made you, and now it's lunchtime." Lance glanced over, worried. The circles under Morgan's eyes were dark enough to match the bruises around her throat. Her home had been invaded, her family threatened, and then she'd spent the night in the hospital waiting room.

Lack of sleep was making *him* punchy, *she* must feel ten times worse.

"Have you checked in on your grandfather?" he asked.

She pulled her phone out of her enormous bag. "I haven't heard from Stella for a while. I'll call her."

She pressed the phone to her ear and conferred in a low, anxious tone for a few minutes before lowering the cell to her lap. "There's no change in his condition. He hasn't woken up yet."

"Do you want to stop by and see him?"

Morgan nodded. "Yes. We're at an impasse with this investigation. The SFPD is watching Harold Burns. I haven't heard from Tim, but there's a county sheriff's deputy assigned to protect Chelsea. I don't know what else to do at this point." Her voice broke. "And I think I should see him, just in case."

The break in her voice implied "in case it's my last chance."

Lance drove toward the hospital. He dropped Morgan at the door, then parked the Jeep. When he caught up with her in the ICU waiting area, she was talking to her worn-out and wrinkled sister.

Stella's eyes were red-rimmed, and her nose was red, as if she'd been crying. She handed Morgan a book, a popular crime fiction paperback. "I don't know if he can hear me, but I've been reading to him."

Morgan took the paperback and smiled sadly. "He loves to criticize police procedurals."

"I was hoping he'd wake up and rant about all the errors." Stella hugged her sister. "I'm going to have a shower and a nap. Then I'll be back."

"Still nothing from Ian?" Morgan asked.

"No." Stella took her keys from her pocket. "But Peyton got on a flight a few hours ago. She should be here by dinnertime. So maybe she can take over the night shift."

Stella left. Morgan and Lance were buzzed through the double doors into the ICU. They went into Art's glassed-in room. He looked small, and the machines surrounding him were intimidating.

Morgan went to his side, leaned over to kiss his cheek, then found his hand under the blanket and gave it a gentle squeeze. A tear rolled down her cheek. She sniffed and brushed it away.

A nurse came in and checked his vital signs. "Try not to panic."

"But he hasn't woken up," Morgan said, her face pale enough to break Lance's heart.

"His body needs rest." The nurse wrote on his chart. "We haven't seen a repeat of the blood pressure issue or heart arrhythmia that occurred during the surgery. He's been stable all day. Give him some time. At his age, his body won't bounce back from the injury or the anesthesia quickly."

"Thank you," Morgan said.

"I'll be right outside the door if you need me." The nurse left. Grandpa's room was across from the nurses' station.

Morgan settled in a chair by the bed. Lance pulled a chair up next to hers. She opened her giant bag and pulled out a stack of files.

"You're not going to read to him?"

"I'll read him our case notes. That'll interest him more than anything else." She handed Lance a stack of reports. "Maybe he'll wake up and point out a clue we missed."

The sheer volume of information was staggering. But four hours later, they'd reviewed most of their case notes and found nothing.

Her phone vibrated. "It's Stella." She answered the call. The conversation was brief. She ended the call with an angry stab to her phone screen. "The SFPD has been ordered to stay away from Harold Burns. His lawyer filed a harassment suit against the township."

"Now he can do whatever he wants without anyone knowing about it."

"Yes." Morgan lowered the phone and paced the hospital room. "The DA had no choice but to rein Horner in, especially after the disaster last month."

Morgan's neighbor had almost died in jail after being falsely arrested and imprisoned.

"The press was relentless on the DA and Horner," Lance said.

"They don't have any options." Morgan stopped pacing and pressed her palms to her eyes. "There's no evidence against Burns. None."

"Morgan?" A low voice came from the doorway.

Though he'd never met Peyton, Lance had no doubt the young woman who entered the room was Morgan's younger sister. Peyton had the same black hair and blue eyes as Morgan and Stella, though she was a head shorter. Age-wise, at thirty-two, Peyton was sandwiched between her sisters. She wore dark jeans, knee-high boots, and a black sweater.

The sisters hugged, teary-eyed.

Morgan introduced them, and Lance felt Peyton's scrutiny. The third Dane sister might not be a cop, but as a forensic psychiatrist she was no less assessing.

Peyton went to her grandfather's side. She kissed his cheek, then stood back and scanned the monitors before picking up his chart and flipping through the pages.

"I'm so glad you're here." Morgan stood next to her sister. "The doctor should be in soon. You'll understand the medical terms better than me."

"I checked at the desk," Peyton said. "He'll be here in about twenty minutes."

Morgan peered over her sister's shoulder. "How does he look?"

"The fact that he's been stable is a good sign." Peyton took her grandfather's hand. "I miss him."

"He understands." Morgan rubbed her sister's shoulder.

"I know, but that doesn't change the fact that I haven't seen him in ages." Peyton shook her head and turned to Morgan. "You look terrible. Go home. Have some dinner. Get some sleep. I'll stay with him tonight. I promise I will text you immediately if there's any change in his condition."

"All right." Morgan stepped back and gathered her files, stuffing them into her big bag.

They said their goodbyes, then Lance escorted her down the hall and through the secure doors to the main hallway. They didn't speak until they were in his Jeep.

Darkness had fallen. At seven in the evening, the parking lot was bathed in the white glow of overhead lights.

"You need to eat." Lance had eaten a couple of protein bars in the hospital, but Morgan had refused.

Morgan's phone buzzed. "It's Tim."

She answered the call. "How's Chelsea?"

Lance could hear Tim's response over the connection. "She just woke up. I'm sorry. I missed your earlier message. I had to give Chelsea a sedative. She freaked out as soon as we pulled into the driveway."

Where she'd been abducted . . .

"How is she now?" Morgan asked. "We'd like to stop by and ask her a few questions."

"Hold on." A pause suggested Tim was asking his wife. A moment later he came back on the line. "She says yes."

"We'll be there in about fifteen minutes." Morgan ended the call. "Let's go see what Chelsea remembers."

Chapter Thirty-Five

"We'd like to ask you a few questions." Morgan studied the Clarks over the coffee table in their living room. Dressed in a cozy sweater and yoga pants, Chelsea held her baby in her arms. Tim and Bella flanked her on the sofa. Bella curled up into her mother; Tim's shoulder pressed into his wife's.

Their connection went beyond physical touch. Morgan could feel their bond, their unity, from across the six feet of space that separated her and Lance from the family.

"Bella, it's time for your bath," Chelsea's mother called from the doorway and held out her hand toward the little girl. Chelsea's father stood behind his wife, looking lost, as if he didn't know what to do.

Bella hesitated, looking up at her mother, and Morgan's heart bumped in her chest. The poor child was confused and vulnerable.

Chelsea gave her daughter a one-armed hug. "Go with Grandma. I'll read you a story after your bath."

The little girl obeyed, casting a reluctant glance back at Chelsea as she left the room with her grandmother.

"Dad, would you take William?" Chelsea asked.

"Of course. He's starting to like me." Her father seemed relieved to have a task. He took the baby. "We'll hang out with Bella and Grandma."

After her father and son had left the room, Chelsea turned back to Lance and Morgan. "We're taking it one day—sometimes one moment—at a time. I'm grateful to be home."

The damage to Chelsea's body was easy to assess. Every inch of exposed skin was mottled with swelling, healing abrasions, and bruises in varying shades of purple and green. But despite her damaged face, behind the fear and anger, determination shone from her eyes.

He'd beaten her body, but not her spirit.

"Reporters were outside when we came home." Tim reached for his wife's hand. "The sheriff made them leave."

For once, Morgan appreciated Sheriff King's intimidating and unyielding nature.

"I want him caught. I don't want to spend the rest of my life looking over my shoulder," Chelsea said. "I don't know if I can take that."

"You should invest in a good security system," Lance said. "We can give you some recommendations."

"Please," Tim said.

"We might want to move." Chelsea's gaze wandered to the window. "I don't know if I can stay here after . . ."

After she'd been abducted from her own driveway.

Chelsea shook her head. "Now what do you need to know? I'll try to answer the best I can."

"What do you remember about the man or the place you were held?" Lance asked.

"I was in a storage container." Chelsea described finding a nail, picking the lock on her chains, and escaping through a rust hole in the roof. "The container was in a clearing, but there were tree branches overhead and a cabin or small house nearby." Chelsea closed her eyes for a moment. "I'm sorry. It was dark. Once I was out, and I heard him coming after me, I just ran."

"How about sounds?"

"I heard a dog barking."

"No traffic sounds?" Lance asked.

"No." Chelsea drew her knees up under her chin. She curled her body into a defensive ball. "I wish I could tell you more. I feel useless."

"Don't. You did exactly the right thing. You got away," Morgan said. "Can you tell us anything about your captor?"

Chelsea stared down at her knees. "He wanted to train me. To teach me to be submissive. If I obeyed, he fed me. If I didn't, he punished me."

"What did he look like?" Morgan asked.

"He wore a mask, so I didn't see his face," Chelsea's brows lowered. She gave them a very basic description of an average-size, white male. No distinguishing accent. "He was strong."

"So probably not too old," Lance said. "How about visible tattoos or scars?"

Chelsea shook her head.

"Did he wear cologne?" Lance asked.

"I was so scared; I wasn't paying attention." Chelsea froze. "Wait. There was a smell. Something . . . sharp. Almost oily."

"Was it motor oil?" Lance asked.

"No. It wasn't that strong." She shuddered. "I'm sorry. I just can't." She pressed a fist over her mouth, clearly fighting for control.

Morgan changed the topic. "Your boss said you wanted to talk to him about something. What was it?"

"One of my clients has statements that don't reconcile." Chelsea tilted her head. "I can't give you his name, but he can't possibly be connected to this. It's a tax issue, and he would have no way of knowing that I'm aware of it."

And this was obviously not the crime of a tax evader.

"But it was important enough that you didn't want to e-mail your boss or explain the problem over the phone?" Lance asked.

"I don't have a secure server at home, and the baby was always crying. The last time I talked to Curtis over the phone, I could barely hear him," she explained. "I thought it would be easier to discuss the problem in his office."

Morgan stood. "If you remember anything else, please call us right away. It doesn't matter how small of a detail it is. You never know where it might lead."

"I will." Chelsea rested her chin on her knees. "Thank you. For everything."

Tim showed them to the door. "I hope she sleeps tonight. Last night, in the hospital, she was up all night. Every noise . . ."

"It's going to take time," Morgan said.

Tim nodded and opened the door for them.

"What does the brand look like?" Lance asked in a low voice.

Tim paled. "It's an infinity symbol."

Forever . . .

Morgan and Lance went back to the Jeep and climbed inside.

"Well, that was disappointing," Lance said. "Though we confirmed that it's unlikely the kidnapping is related to her client files."

"He drugged her, so that likely affected her recall." Morgan couldn't imagine. Not only did Chelsea have to deal with the horrifying events she remembered, but she would no doubt wonder and fear what she'd forgotten. Would other memories continue to return? And for how long?

Lance started the engine. "This feels like a personal crime. No one tortures and psychologically conditions a woman to avoid being caught cheating on his taxes."

"No," Morgan agreed. "This was personal, sick, and twisted. Now what?"

He pulled out of the driveway. "Can you call Sharp and let him know what we found out? He and my mom can stop reviewing financial statements and concentrate on getting background info on Chelsea's clients. It's still possible one of them fixated on her."

"*Someone* did." Morgan made the call. Sharp was relieved to give up the financial statement review.

"Where do you want to go? No matter what we do, we need to get some food in you." Lance declared after she'd put her phone away.

"You're going to think this is nuts."

And he wasn't going to like it one bit.

"What?" His voice turned suspicious as he drove away from the Clarks' house.

"I want to snoop around Harold Burns's house."

Lance frowned. "Not nuts, risky."

"All our other leads have run dry. Burns is all we have left. And Chelsea mentioned that oily smell, though she said it didn't smell like motor oil."

Lance shrugged. "Mechanics use different kinds of oil."

Morgan stared through the windshield. Despite her exhaustion, seeing what Chelsea had endured made her more determined to catch the man responsible. "What if he has that girl, and no one can save her? What if he wants more time to kill her and dispose of her body?"

"That's a lot of speculation."

"It is," Morgan said. "But hear me out. The police think that the woman found in the state park had been held captive for eight months. She'd have to be kept somewhere that no one would hear her scream. Burns's house is in the middle of nowhere."

"So is the auto shop."

"Yes, but the auto shop has too much foot traffic to hold a woman captive."

"It's a big piece of property, and there were outbuildings. It would be a great place to hide a storage container," Lance said. "The woods behind the junkyard connect to the state park."

"True," Morgan agreed. "But the police did a compliance check on Burns's house three months ago. If he was holding a woman in his house, they would have heard or seen something."

"Probably. His house is small," Lance said. "We don't know that she was kept in the same place for the entire eight months."

Morgan pictured Harold Burns's property. "Remember that huge detached garage behind Burns's house?"

"I do." Lance turned on the heat. "That was big enough to house all sorts of illegal activity."

Morgan spread her fingers in front of the vents. "If we find anything, we'll make an anonymous phone call to the police and report that we heard a woman screaming."

"We'll need to wait until later. We want Burns to be asleep." Lance turned onto the main road. "We'll need to gear up too. We should call Stella or Brody and let them know what we're planning."

"No." Morgan wouldn't ruin her sister's career over a hunch. "That wouldn't be fair to them. What we're going to do is completely illegal."

Not to mention dangerous.

Chapter Thirty-Six

A few minutes before midnight, Lance drove past Harold Burns's one-story house. A quarter mile down the road, he steered the Jeep off the side of the road and parked behind a few evergreens. If Burns had slipped out of his house while the SFPD was watching him, he would have gone through the woods to the auto shop. What was good for the goose, in this case, could also be used for the goose hunters.

"You ready?"

In the passenger seat, Morgan checked the weapon in her holster and zipped her black jacket closed over it. "Yes."

Lance slid some extra ammunition into the thick pocket of his dark cargos. Though he wasn't cold, he tugged a black knit cap over his bright-blond hair. Morgan's hat was for warmth. She tucked a flashlight into her pocket. He did the same, then loaded the rest of his equipment, including a pair of night vision binoculars, into a small backpack.

They got out of the Jeep and walked along the edge of the woods so they could duck into the trees if a car approached. Thick clouds drifted overhead, and snow flurries floated in the chilled air. His breath fogged in front of him. The ground was dark, but he wanted to preserve his natural night vision and didn't want to risk using a flashlight. There wasn't much out here. Burns would be able to see a light from far away.

Next to him, Morgan tripped.

Lance steadied her by the elbow. "You OK?"

"Just a rock. I'm fine." She got her feet back under herself. "I don't know how Chelsea went miles and miles through the dark woods."

"She was literally running for her life. I doubt she was even thinking at that point. She kept moving on instinct. The fact that she's an avid hiker and runner probably saved her life."

"Remind me to start exercising," Morgan said. "I doubt if I could run two miles without collapsing."

They'd stopped for takeout earlier. Energized by the thought of taking action, Morgan had polished off every fry in her bag. Lance was glad to see her eat.

The greasy burger and fries might be unhealthy in the long run, but his body had appreciated the calories as well. He didn't remember the last time he'd had a Coke, but the sweet, fizzy drink had hit the spot. The sugar practically vibrated in his system.

Just before Burns's house, the woods cut away. They followed the edge of the forest, arcing around the back of the property. Ahead, the detached garage and house lay dark.

Lance removed his night vision binoculars from his bag and scanned the backs of the buildings. "No windows on the garage and I don't see his truck." He also didn't spot any security cameras.

"Maybe he's not home."

"Or his truck is in the garage."

There was only one way to find out. They were going to have to break in to the garage.

They jogged across the open space, keeping the garage between them and the line of sight of the house. Even so, Lance was glad for the absence of the moon and the exceptionally dark night. Unfortunately, the entry door was on the side of the garage that faced the house. They crept around the corner of the building. Despite the sharp chill in the air, sweat dripped between his shoulder blades. Approaching a building with unknown occupants felt much more dangerous since he'd been shot and nearly died in such a situation. And fear for Morgan's safety drove his apprehension levels through the roof.

He motioned her to wait in the shadows as he drew his lock picks from his pocket. The lock was surprisingly simple, and a slight tingle of doubt crept into Lance's gut. If he were keeping a woman prisoner, he'd use a complex security system.

Stepping into the open, Lance inserted the two thin blades into the lock. In less than twenty seconds, he felt the gentle click of tumblers sliding into position. He turned the knob and opened the door, slipping inside. For a few seconds, he listened for a chirp that would indicate an alarm system, but he heard nothing. Morgan's body bumped him as she entered the garage behind him. She closed the door and absolute blackness fell over them.

Though his eyes had adjusted to the night, inside was far darker. There were no windows in the building. His night vision binoculars required at least scant light to function. They'd be useless in the pitch black of the garage's interior. Lance risked the flashlight. He clicked it on, aiming a narrow beam of light on the floor. The garage was one large open space filled with junk. Disappointment welled inside him as he surveyed the clusters of discarded furniture and boxes. Even before they'd made a complete circuit, he knew the missing woman wasn't here and that Chelsea hadn't been held there either. There wasn't enough security. No setup for even keeping a captive.

Morgan led the way back outside. Lance carefully locked the door as they left, and they retraced their steps back to the woods. The sound of an engine floated on the cold air.

"I hear a car." He tugged Morgan behind a few trees. They crouched and waited as headlights approached then taillights faded before resuming their trek. Burns's house and the auto shop were only a quarter mile apart. They passed the place where the Jeep was hidden and continued along the edge of the woods until the forest ended and the cleared space of the auto shop and salvage yard began.

They stood at the edge of the woods and surveyed the landscape, all dirt and shadows in the darkness. Ahead, a soft light shone from the exterior of the auto shop and one office window glowed pale yellow.

"Did he leave a light on or is someone there?" Morgan asked.

"Impossible to say without getting closer." Which might give them away.

"Do you see Burns's red truck?"

"No." Lance used the binoculars to search the darkness behind the shop. "But it could be inside."

The auto shop had multiple bays and overhead rolling doors. But there was no need to search it. Creeps did not usually keep prisoners in buildings frequented by customers. Holding a woman for eight months required privacy.

"Then we'd better be quiet and quick." Morgan turned away from the office and toward the scrap yard. They skirted the forest until they reached the rear of the property.

"I don't see any cameras back here."

"Guess we'll find out."

They entered the scrap yard. Most of the land was open. Rusted vehicle carcasses were piled and clustered seemingly at random. Dirt-and-weed tracks large enough to drive on meandered around them. A small area was enclosed by a six-foot-tall chain-link fence. The vehicles inside looked like later models, some heavily damaged by accidents but likely still worth money for parts.

No moon lit the way, but Lance couldn't risk using the flashlight out in the open.

"We'll take it slow. Watch where you step." He steered Morgan around a rusted fender.

Passing the severed front half of a crushed and rusty Volkswagen Beetle, she tapped her scarred forearm. "Good thing I've had a tetanus shot recently."

They stopped at the chain-link fence. Most of the vehicles within its enclosure were intact and organized into rows, more like a parking lot than a junkyard. In the center, stood a large metal shed.

"You wait here. I'll climb in and check out the shed," Lance whispered. "The gate is around front, behind the shop. I don't want to go in that way."

"I don't like splitting up," Morgan said. "But I'd just slow you down."

Lance removed his lock pick from the backpack and tucked it into a pocket. Then he handed the bag to Morgan. "I'll be quick. Back before you know it."

He scaled the fence and dropped off the other side. Adrenaline hummed in his bloodstream as he glanced back at Morgan, standing alone in the dark. Her dark clothes had blended well in the woods, but out in the open, she was a clear human shape. He didn't like to leave her alone.

"Watch your back," he said.

"I'll watch yours too." She pivoted to put her back to the fence.

Turned back to his task, Lance crept through the rows of vehicles. There were too many places to hide in and around the cars. He strained for sounds in the darkness but heard nothing unusual.

He approached the shed. It was longer than it had appeared. A few snowflakes drifted down to the dirt, but the ground had not yet frozen, and they melted on contact. The only entrance to the building was a set of metal rolling doors secured with a chain and padlock. Lance could probably pick the lock. If not, he had a set of bolt cutters in his backpack, but he'd prefer not to leave evidence of their search or damage any property.

Broken windows were spaced out along the side of the shed, but they were two feet above Lance's head. He looked for something to climb on. Spotting a cluster of barrels near the back of the building, he climbed on one and peered through the filthy, spider-cracked glass.

All he could see was darkness.

He lifted the binoculars from his chest and used them to scan the interior. The space was full of vehicles and engines. A few long workbenches were stacked with car parts. There were no rooms inside in which Burns could have kept a woman captive.

Lance jumped down from the barrel and retreated to the fence. Morgan crouched where he'd left her. He scaled the fence in a few swift motions and landed softly next to her.

"Anything?" she asked in a low voice.

He shook his head.

They resumed their search. Lance's pulse thudded in a steady, highly tuned beat as they crept around piles of junked vehicles. Near the back center of the scrap yard, they came upon a single trailer set on cinder blocks. The rectangular structure was rusted and dented. Instead of steps, a single cinder block stood just below the narrow door, which was secured by a heavy-duty padlock. A dim yellow bulb glowed next to the door.

The hair on the back of Lance's neck quivered. "I wonder what they're keeping in there."

"That's an awfully big padlock," Morgan said. "Is that a camera above the door?"

Lance nodded. "I see a motion detector too."

"So how do we get a look inside?"

Lance scanned the structure. "The windows are covered."

They circled around to view the trailer from the other side. Boards were nailed over both windows on this side as well.

"This doesn't look anything like Chelsea's description of where she was held," Morgan said. "Do you see a hole in the roof?"

"Not from here." But the trailer was setting off all Lance's alarms. The trailer was more secure than the office and auto shop. "I'm going to get closer. Wait here."

"I don't want to wait here."

"Someone needs to call the police if I get caught," Lance argued. "Harold Burns is a violent man. If I've found his next victim, he's not going to call the police on me. He's going to bury me in a shallow grave in the state park."

Morgan blew a hard breath out through her nose. "All right."

Lance handed her the binoculars. "Watch my back?"

"Always."

Lance jogged across the dirt. When he reached the trailer, he checked the padlock. It could be picked, but not quickly, and he'd rather not stand out in the open for any length of time. He'd look for an easier way in first. Then he went from window to window looking for a weakness but found none. The boards were nailed or screwed from the inside. He dropped to the ground and slid under the trailer but found no easy points of entry.

He was going to have to do this the hard way.

His options were to pick the lock or cut it off with the bolt cutters. Did he want to leave evidence of entry? Not really. He slid along the ground to get out from under the trailer. Bits of gravel rolled under his back, making more noise than he intended.

A scratching sound came from inside the trailer. He froze, straining his hearing.

There it was again. Scratching. Tapping. Crying?

And holy shit. Was that a sob?

"Is someone in there?" he called out.

"Yes," a woman's voice cried out. "Please help me."

There was someone in the trailer, and they weren't happy about it.

Lance scooted out from under the trailer. He'd get the bolt cutters from Morgan and be inside in a few seconds. He climbed to his feet. A long shadow fell over him. As he turned to confront the dark figure, a board swung toward his head.

Chapter Thirty-Seven

A scream sounded from the trailer. Morgan dialed 911 and gave the salvage yard address. She shoved the phone into her pocket and searched the clearing for Lance.

A man swung a board at Lance. He spun and ducked to evade it. The board struck him across the back of the shoulders. He fell to the ground, stunned, and lay still. His attacker dropped the board and jumped on top of him.

No!

Morgan pulled her gun from its holster and ran forward.

The attacker straddled Lance's chest and threw a punch at his face. Lance wrapped his arm around his head to block the incoming fist.

Morgan stopped ten feet away and aimed the gun at the fighting men. "Freeze!"

The attacker ignored her and punched Lance in the ribs; Lance recoiled from the blow.

The man reached for the gun in Lance's holster. Lance clamped both hands over his opponent's, keeping the gun secure. They struggled for control of the weapon. Lance bucked and rolled.

And Morgan had no clear shot.

She changed her angle but still couldn't shoot.

Damn it!

She had to do something. She couldn't—wouldn't—let Lance get hurt. Heart hammering, she scanned the ground, looking for a weapon.

The two-by-four!

Holstering her weapon, she raced forward and snatched it off the ground. The fighting men came to a stop, the attacker on top. Morgan rushed forward, desperation lending her strength. Two-handing it, she swung it like a baseball bat and hit him across the back.

He collapsed. Lance bucked hard and bridged over one shoulder, rolling his attacker onto his back and reversing their positions.

Morgan dropped the board. With Lance in control, relief surged through her, the rush of adrenaline making her light-headed.

He flipped the man onto his belly and twisted his arms behind his back. "Get some zip ties."

Morgan ran back to retrieve the backpack. Returning to Lance's side, she handed him a plastic tie, and he used it to secure the man's hands.

Then he rolled the man to his back, and Morgan shone a flashlight on his face.

Harold Burns.

"You're trespassing!" Harold spat.

"Then you should have called the police, Harold." Lance climbed to his feet. "But I bet you didn't."

"*I* did," Morgan said.

From inside the trailer, a woman cried. "Who's out there? Please help me."

The woman!

Morgan grabbed the bolt cutters from the backpack. While Lance secured Harold's ankles with a second set of zip ties, Morgan cut the padlock, opened the trailer door, and shone her flashlight inside.

The trailer was one open space. The only furnishing was a filthy mattress in the center. A large, dark stain in the center of it turned

Morgan's stomach. A woman huddled on the edge of the mattress. She was chained to a ring bolted into the floor.

The space was warmer than outside, so the trailer must have heat. Morgan felt along the wall by the door for a light switch. Finding one, she flipped it.

A light bulb suspended from the center of the ceiling shone weakly on the woman. She huddled at the end of her chain. Handcuffs bound her wrists. She raised her hands in front of her face, shielding her eyes from the light.

In one sweeping glance, Morgan took in the woman's shivering, naked body, the blood and bruises and battered face. Shaking off her shock, she lifted her foot to step through the doorway.

"Not so fast," a man said behind her.

Morgan turned.

Jerry Burns stood fifteen feet away, a pistol in his hands pointed directly at Morgan.

Her stomach flipped.

"Get down here." Jerry's head jerked toward Lance, who knelt over Harold's prone body. "You, cut my brother free or I will put a bullet in this bitch's pretty face."

This couldn't happen. Morgan and Lance had to save this woman and themselves.

Morgan glanced at Lance. Harold was incapacitated. There was no way Lance was going to release him. He and Morgan would never survive against both of the Burns brothers. And neither would the woman chained in the trailer. If they were going to get out of this alive, they needed to act now. Allowing themselves to be taken prisoner by the Burns brothers would get them all killed. She weighed the bolt cutters in her hand. She was too far away to use the tool as a club. Jerry's gun was pointed at her. She wouldn't get closer before he reacted. Nor did she have time to drop the bolt cutters and draw the weapon under her jacket.

There was only one option.

Morgan would have to get out of the way and pray that Lance could take Jerry down before he could turn the gun on him.

She was fifteen feet away. Outside of television, handguns weren't that accurate beyond eight to ten feet.

There were no options.

Her eyes met Lance's. A silent agreement passed between them. From his position, kneeling on the small of Harold's back, Lance extended three fingers on his thigh.

Two.

One.

Morgan dove through the doorway and covered her head with her arms. Her flashlight rolled across the floor. The bolt cutters landed with a thud. A gunshot rang out. Jerry's shot went low, hitting the floor. Wood splintered. The thin walls of the trailer wouldn't stop a bullet. A second shot boomed. Morgan drew her weapon and belly-crawled toward the open trailer door.

Her heart vibrated inside her chest. Had Lance shot Jerry or vice versa?

No.

Lance just had to be all right. He'd almost died by gunfire last year. He couldn't—she shut down that thought. Her brain couldn't go there and still function.

The woman in the trailer needed saving.

Inching forward, heart hammering, Morgan peered around the bottom of the door frame and took in the scene with profound and surreal shock.

Jerry lay on the ground, a bloodstain spreading across his shoulder. Behind him stood Sheriff King and two deputies. The gun in the sheriff's hand was still pointed at Jerry.

Her gaze found Lance, still kneeling on the ground, his hand on his weapon holster as if prepared to draw his gun. Obviously, the sheriff had beaten him to it.

261

"Get handcuffs on this scumbag." The sheriff stepped around Jerry and started toward Morgan.

Relief and surprise rolled through Morgan. There was no way he could have responded to her call that quickly. But she didn't have time to question the sheriff's presence. The traumatized woman sobbed in the darkness behind her. Morgan glanced at Lance once more, verified that he was whole and alive, then scrambled to her feet and turned to the victim.

She picked up the bolt cutters.

"I'm going to free you now." Not wanting to frighten her any further, Morgan approached her slowly.

The woman continued to cry, her words unrecognizable, her voice as rusty as her prison.

Behind her, the trailer creaked as the sheriff stepped inside. "Oh, my God."

Morgan severed the chain with the bolt cutters. The woman stumbled forward, sobbing, into Morgan's arms. She slid off her jacket and put it around the woman's shoulders.

"There's an ambulance on the way." The sheriff stood back, his face drawn, as he scanned the interior of the trailer.

"Out." The woman pushed to her feet, her words desperate. "Get me out. Please. I have to get out of here."

Who wouldn't?

Morgan wrapped an arm around her shoulders and steadied her balance.

Lance peered through the doorway. "I'll get a blanket."

Morgan helped the woman limp toward the door. The sheriff stepped aside, allowing them to pass.

"What's your name?" Morgan asked.

"Karen. Karen Mitchell," she said, her voice growing stronger with each step toward freedom.

The missing woman.

They stepped through the opening. The trailer, while not cozy, had been warmer than the air outside. Karen shivered, her body quaking from head to toe. A frigid wind kicked up. Morgan blocked it with her body as best she could.

Lance appeared with an outspread blanket. As he enveloped Karen in it, her legs gave out. Lance caught her and swept her off the ground, and Morgan tucked the blanket around the woman's bare feet.

Two sheriff's deputy cars drove through the salvage yard, their headlights illuminating the trailer. The cars parked, and the deputies got out of their vehicles.

"This is Karen Mitchell," Lance said.

"I've got her." One of the deputies retrieved a first aid kit and another blanket from his trunk. "Put her in the car. It's warm. The ambulance will be here soon."

Lance put her in the back seat of the police car "You're safe now."

Talking in a calm voice, the deputy squatted in the door opening, covered her with the second blanket, and lifted the lid of his first aid kit.

Morgan's face felt hot in the cold air. She was simultaneously freezing and sweating as her heart rate dropped back to normal. Nausea rose in throat. She bent over, resting her hands on her thighs. She sucked in some cool night air.

Lance turned back to her. "If you need to puke, move away from the scene."

"I think I'm OK. It's an irritating reaction to the rush of adrenaline."

He walked over and handed her a bottle of water. "You get the job done first. That's what matters."

"I guess." Morgan took an experimental sip. The cold water soothed her stomach.

Lance put a hand between her shoulder blades. "We saved that woman's life. That's worth a little puking."

"Says the guy who doesn't get sick."

"It'll catch up with me," Lance said.

"Kruger and Dane. Over here. Now." Sheriff King pointed at Lance and Morgan and jerked his thumb away from the growing crowd of law enforcement. Morgan's legs felt like rubber bands as she and Lance joined the sheriff.

Sheriff King propped his hands on his hips. "Let's get this straight. I am pissed as hell at both of you. You were trespassing on private property." The sheriff stabbed an angry finger at Lance. "I expect you to risk your own life, but endangering a woman?" He pointed at Morgan.

"It was her idea." Lance crossed his arms over his chest. "She's a lot tougher than she looks."

The sheriff threw his hands into the air. "You could have both been killed. I should have known you'd pull a stunt like this."

"But we weren't killed," Lance said. "And Karen Mitchell is alive because we pulled this *stunt*."

The sheriff glowered at Lance, then redirected his anger at Morgan. "And *you*, Counselor, you should know better. The very first thing the Burnses' defense attorney is going to do is claim all the evidence in that trailer could have been planted and is therefore inadmissible against them in court."

Morgan cut him off. She'd had enough. She and Lance had taken over the situation and saved Karen Mitchell. The sheriff's misdirected anger was not her problem. "We both know that isn't going to happen. Karen Mitchell will provide testimony. There will be physical evidence on her body, and as a previously convicted sex offender, Harold Burns and his brother will be hated by any jury they are put in front of. Nor do I know any judge who will give them any leeway. If my suspicion is correct, the very large bloodstain on that mattress is from victim number one, Sarah Bernard. The Burns brothers will be charged with two counts of kidnapping and one count of murder, along with as many lesser charges as possible."

The sheriff huffed. "I could charge you both with trespassing."

Morgan didn't care about a ridiculous trespassing charge. Exhaustion and her adrenaline crash were catching up to her with the speed of a freight train. "Are you going to arrest us?"

"Not at this time." The sheriff frowned at her. "I need statements from you both. Now."

"When we talked with Chelsea earlier, she mentioned an oily odor."

"And you didn't call me?" The sheriff chewed his molars.

"She specifically said it didn't smell like motor oil, but it made us think hard about Burns." With a glance at Lance, Morgan gave a very abbreviated version of their search of the property. She didn't mention their trip through Harold's garage. If asked, she wouldn't lie. But there was no point in volunteering the information. When she was finished, she asked, "How did you get here so quickly?"

"We've been watching Harold and Jerry all night," the sheriff said. "Chief Horner called me to tell me the DA forced him to cease his surveillance. Considering that we've been searching for Ms. Mitchell, I decided we should focus on this area. But we had no good reason to search the property until you called in that scream."

"You're welcome," Lance said drily.

The sheriff glared.

Lance finished describing the events of the night. The sheriff released them with a threat of arrest if they didn't report to his office first thing in the morning to cross *t*'s and dot *i*'s. The walk back to the Jeep was only a few hundred yards, but it seemed like miles.

"I don't like it." Morgan crawled into the passenger seat.

"What?"

"I can't explain it. Something feels unfinished."

"We still have to deal with the sheriff again tomorrow." Lance started the engine. "I'm tired of his controlling bullshit."

"He didn't arrest us for trespassing."

"But he wanted to. He wishes he was the one who found Karen Mitchell." Lance drove out onto the road. "He's been chomping at the bit all night, wanting to search the property but without enough evidence for a warrant."

"The laws exist for a reason." Morgan pressed her head to the back of the seat.

"We saved that woman's life tonight," Lance said. "Who knows if she would have still been alive in the morning? The Burnses could have killed her and buried her out in the woods before the sheriff accumulated enough evidence to satisfy a judge that there was probable cause. Would you rather Karen Mitchell have spent the night in that trailer? I would rather go to jail."

"So would I," she said. "Which is why we did what we did tonight."

"Plus, I'll bet forensics will find evidence that the first victim and Chelsea were both held in that trailer. Chelsea will be able to go on with her life knowing that the men who kidnapped her are behind bars. Your family can rest easy too."

"I know." But uneasiness stirred in Morgan's belly. It didn't feel over.

"Do you think they'll get a plea deal?" Lance asked.

"I doubt it. After what happened last month, the DA needs to save some face, and he's up for reelection next month. He's going to promise to bring the hammer down. A high-publicity case against a previously convicted sex offender and his brother is media fodder. Plus, New York no longer has a death penalty. What can the DA offer the Burns brothers in exchange for a guilty plea? This is a particularly heinous crime. The Burns brothers kidnapped and held a woman captive for eight months, impregnated her, and then beat her to death. The beating also killed her unborn baby. They are going to prison, probably for life."

"So what's wrong?"

"I don't know. Something doesn't feel right."

"We'll know more after we talk to the sheriff tomorrow. The forensics team will be in that trailer all night. Let's see what they find and then reassess the case." Lance drove toward town. "We're both too tired to think straight. We need food and sleep. We've been running on adrenaline all night. The most useful thing we can do is get some rest and look at the facts with fresh eyes in the morning."

"You're right." She was wired. Her blood was still humming even though her eyelids were as gritty as sandpaper.

There was something lurking in her exhausted brain, a connection she was too tired to make.

Were adrenaline and stress stimulating her paranoia? Or was her subconscious issuing her a warning?

Chapter Thirty-Eight

Morgan paced Lance's guest room, her cell phone pressed to her ear as she talked to her sister. Her nerves were still frayed by what happened with the Burns brothers that night—and by the sight of Karen Mitchell chained up in that trailer. But rescuing Karen was worth every drop of clammy sweat and rush of adrenaline-induced nausea.

If only Grandpa would wake up.

"So there's no change?" she asked Peyton.

"No." Behind Peyton's low voice, a monitor beeped in a steady rhythm. "He's stable. Please try to get some sleep."

"When do you think he'll wake up?"

"I'm a doctor, not a psychic, Jim," Peyton said in her best Dr. McCoy voice.

Morgan appreciated her sister's attempt to lighten her mood, but she didn't have the energy to laugh. "You'll call me if anything happens?"

"I promise." Peyton's tone grew sincere again. "I will watch over him all night. I've got this covered. Go. To. Sleep."

"OK."

"And Morgan?"

"Yes?"

"Grandpa is tough," Peyton said. "Don't give up on him yet. He's not going down without a fight."

"Thanks, Peyton. Good night." Morgan ended the call, crossed the hall to the bathroom, and turned on the shower. She undressed as the water warmed. The instant Morgan stepped into the heat, her tightly reined emotions burst. She leaned against the tile and let herself cry. She was too damned tired to hold back any longer.

Her sister meant well, and as a doctor, Peyton was a far better judge of Grandpa's medical condition, but Morgan was afraid to let herself hope. She'd just crawled out of a seemingly bottomless pool of grief and now felt the need to brace herself. To prepare. To gather her energy against the possibility of another devastating loss.

Hope raised the platform from which she'd fall if the worst happened.

She had children to care for.

When her husband had died, they'd been too young to understand, and John had been deployed more than he'd been home. Their world hadn't been disrupted. But this time, they were old enough to grieve for the great grandfather who'd willingly stepped up to fill the role of a father.

Just as he had for Morgan and her siblings.

Grandpa had been her rock. Without him, she'd never have gotten through the deaths of her parents and then John. She couldn't imagine losing him.

Who did you turn to when your source of comfort was gone?

But someday that would happen, even if it wasn't today. No one lived forever. And when that day came, her girls would need Morgan to be strong. *She* would have to be *their* rock. She couldn't allow herself to sink again.

She turned the water to cold and stuck her head under the spray, letting the shock of freezing water jolt her out of her heartache. Shivering, she shut off the water and dried herself.

Morgan emerged from the bathroom, her damp hair hanging down her back and soaking the borrowed T-shirt. Her eyes were raw, and her face felt tender from crying. No matter how much resolve she mustered, the despair inside her refused to back down.

She'd never felt so alone.

In the bedroom, she stepped into the sweat pants Lance had given her, tying the drawstring tight to keep them from falling down. Returning to the hall, she glanced into his room. The decor reflected him: all masculine, nothing fussy.

His furniture was modern and clean-lined. A dark-wood dresser and leather headboard. The king-size bed was covered in a solid navy-blue comforter. A single nightstand held a clock, a lamp, and a book. The entire room smelled faintly of his cedar-scented body wash. She sniffed her skin. So did she.

She'd slept in his guest room once before. But that's not where she wanted—or needed—to be tonight.

The sounds of soft piano chords floated down the hall. The poignant lyrics of "Tears in Heaven" pulled her into the living room. Lance sat at the piano. He wore gray sweatpants and a snug black T-shirt. His short hair was still damp from his shower. A tumbler of whiskey occupied a coaster on top of the gleaming mahogany.

She knew he used music to express emotions he couldn't verbalize. Sadness poured out of him. Was he thinking about the suffering of the woman they'd rescued? Her grandfather, his own long-missing father, or the damage his disappearance had done to his family?

If anyone understood her grief, it was Lance.

She crossed the room and sat next to him on the bench.

He paused, hands over the keys. His eyes grew worried as he scanned her face. "Are you OK?"

"Please, don't stop." She leaned her head against his shoulder.

He continued. His voice was soft and gentle, doing justice to the pure and simple anguish in the song.

When he'd finished, he turned his head to plant a soft kiss on her head. "Did you call Peyton?"

She nodded. "She says he's the same, and she'll call if that changes. Did you talk to Sharp?"

"I did. He's still at my mom's house. He's too tired to drive home and is staying there tonight."

Lance craned his neck to view her face. "It's been a long few days. You should get some sleep. Are you sure I can't feed you? Scrambled eggs or toast maybe?"

"I'm not hungry." And she wasn't ready to settle either. Restlessness pawed at her. "Do you believe in heaven?" Morgan had lost her father, her mother, and her husband. With her grandfather's life in jeopardy, she wanted to think they were somewhere, waiting for him.

That he wouldn't be alone.

He picked up his whiskey and drank. "I don't know. I hope so. I hate to think this is it."

And on that note, she reached for his glass.

He held the glass tight. "Remember what happened last time?"

"I'm not going to get drunk." She had no tolerance for alcohol, something she'd demonstrated to him in the past. "I could get a call at any time. But I need the warmth."

"I could make you a cup of tea," he said as he released the glass.

"This is fine." She took a small sip and handed it back to him. The whiskey burned a path down her raw throat. "Do you think your father is alive?"

He touched a key and pressed it softly. "Whatever happened, I can't believe he'd just walk away from us."

"How do you deal with not knowing?" Morgan asked.

His face went tight, his voice pained. "It wasn't a choice."

"No. It wasn't." The sigh that rolled through her grated like shards of broken glass. Pain welled up in her chest until she felt as if her heart would crack. Her next breath vibrated with it.

She reached for his face with both hands, cupping his jaw between her palms and drawing his face close enough to press her lips to his. The kiss started out soft and gentle then shifted to needy.

She needed him.

Her hands slid down to his shoulders.

"Morgan," he said against her mouth, his words more breath than words.

She deepened the kiss.

He grabbed her wrists and broke their lip lock. "You don't know what you're doing."

A quick flash of anger shot through her. "I know exactly what I want."

"You're vulnerable."

"What's the alternative? Not to care about anyone? That's not really living."

"That's not what I mean." He shook his head. "You're hurting. I want to be here for you, but I don't want to take advantage of you because you need to release some emotions."

"I don't want a release." Morgan shook her hands free, frustrated. "I'm scared." Her voice softened. "And I don't need *sex*. I need *you*."

When she'd lost her husband two years before, she thought her heart was too damaged to love again. She'd been wrong. She wasn't sure if she loved Lance or not, but there was heat and longing and a connection that was all at once familiar and unique.

What she felt for him was different. Not less. Not more. It was unique and separate and belonged to them and them alone. There was no comparison, just as there was no need to compartmentalize one love from the other.

Lance froze. The honor and determination in his eyes heated into something else.

Hunger, she realized with a shock.

He needed her as much as she needed him.

"You've been a good friend, Lance." She reached out and cupped his jaw. "I want more, but if you can't give it, I understand."

He covered her hand with his, turned his head and kissed it. "You have no idea how long I've waited to hear those words. I'm here for you." He lowered his head. "For as long as you want me."

Their lips met.

This kiss was different than others they'd shared. This kiss was knowing. This kiss brimmed with anticipation and discovery and even friendship.

Her body pressed against his as if telling her brain to shut up. She looked up into his eyes. They were dark and intense and entirely focused on her. Heat bloomed over her skin and desire unfurled in her belly.

His hand slid down her arm to grip her hip and pull her even harder against him. His thumb brushed an exposed strip of skin between her T-shirt and the sagging waistband of the sweatpants. She surged forward, other body parts demanding attention.

She twisted, intending to crawl into his lap, but her knee struck the piano. The keyboard cover slammed down with a crash.

Lance shoved the piano bench backward. He turned and lifted her. In one smooth motion, he picked her up and turned her around so she could straddle him. She was no tiny waif, and as superficial as it was, the ease with which he maneuvered her body was a huge turn-on.

All those muscles weren't for show.

She wrapped her legs around his waist, bringing her core down against his.

Yes.

Definitely *yes*.

Breathless, he lifted his mouth from hers. "As much as the thought of making love to you on my piano is hot, the actual orchestration eludes me."

She laughed against his mouth. "We would probably wreak havoc on the keys."

"It would be worth it. I can get a new piano. But as it's our first time, I'd rather have some room to do my best work. I'll only get one chance to make a first impression."

"Wow. No pressure, right?" A sudden burst of nerves shook her. It had been so long for her. She splayed a hand over his heart, taking comfort in the steady thud of it under her palm. "I haven't had sex in years. I hope it's like riding a bike."

"I hope it's *nothing* like riding a bike." His brows shot up with mock indignation. "I want to rock your world."

"OK, then." She slid off his lap. She'd seen Lance almost every day for months. Her sudden shyness was unexpected.

Smiling, he stood and offered her his hand. "Trust me."

"I do." She took it and let him lead her to his bedroom. Standing next to his bed, he turned her to face him. He switched on the night-stand lamp. The glow was soft, just enough to see the intensity of desire in his eyes.

A flush heated her skin.

She stepped forward, crushing her body to his, feeling his warmth everywhere she was cold. His mouth roamed from her lips down her neck and to her shoulder without coming up for air, as if he couldn't taste enough of her.

Leaning back, she grabbed the hem of his T-shirt, pulled it over his head, and tossed it aside. His body was thick and powerful, with heavy ridges of well-defined muscles on top of muscles. His sweatpants rode low, exposing an impressive V of lower abdominal muscles.

She wanted to run her hands over every inch of him. "Can I touch you?"

He made a choking sound and then cleared his throat. "You can do anything you want."

For once, she let impulse have its way like a teenager after prom.

She reached out a hand and placed it on his hip, running her fingertips over his abs. His skin was smooth and warm, solid under her fingers. His body vibrated as she stroked her way to his broad chest, and she reveled in the sheer masculinity of him.

Then he moved.

His hands were on her biceps, sliding up to her shoulders, cupping her face and stroking her cheekbones with his thumbs. His mouth came down on hers. No hesitation this time. The kiss was all hunger and need and months' worth of pent-up desire.

Pulling his mouth from hers, he lifted the hem of her shirt and drew it off her body. He hooked his thumbs in the waistband of the sweatpants and dragged them down her legs. Then he leaned back and took a good, long look, licking his lips in anticipation. "You're perfect."

He backed her against the bed and eased her onto it, stretching his body out alongside hers. His lips roamed from her neck, down her collarbone, and across the tops of her breasts. Every touch of his mouth, every stroke of his fingertips, stoked her need higher.

He lifted his head, watching her with intimidating concentration as he slid a hand between her legs. Her body arched under his touch, and he smiled, obviously pleased by her response.

"That's it," she said.

When she reached for him, he pulled his hips out of her reach. "Ladies first."

Tension built inside her, spiraling higher and higher, until she writhed.

"Now," she gasped. She'd been waiting for what seemed like forever for this moment.

"But you're so beautiful like this," he murmured against her face. "I could watch you all night."

But Morgan couldn't wait another second. Her body and her soul wanted to be part of him. This man who had turned her life around. He'd shown her she could be happy again.

That she could *live* instead of simply existing.

She reached for him again, her hand trembling with need. This time he didn't resist. Her fingers closed around him, and his eyes practically rolled back in his head.

"Now," she said in a firmer voice.

His chest shook with a low chuckle. "Yes, ma'am."

His confidence settled her nerves, and she clung to him.

He reached for the nightstand, opening the drawer and removing a condom. After sheathing himself, he slid on top of her, nestling between her thighs. His hands cradled her face, framing it, and his gaze studied her, as if he was deliberately preserving this moment in his memory.

He slid inside her, filling her body and soul. Fully seated, he froze and stared down at her. The connection between them seemed to transcend time for a few seconds.

"I'd love to stay like this forever." Sweat broke out on his forehead. "But I can't."

"Nothing lasts forever." Morgan hitched her legs around his waist and pulled him deeper. "Better to make the most of every moment."

But she would remember every precious second and hold it tightly in her heart.

They moved together, instinct guiding their bodies. Tension built, ebbed, built again, until Morgan finally spiraled out of control. Her orgasm was a free fall that left her dizzy. Lance shuddered and collapsed on top of her.

Sweating and panting, she poked him in the ribs. "You're crushing me."

But inside, her heart felt full, as if he had filled its cracks.

"Sorry." He rolled off her and onto his back, out of breath.

She rolled onto her side, throwing a leg over his and resting a hand on his powerful, bare chest. "Consider my world rocked."

He put his hand over hers and squeezed gently. "I think my heart exploded."

Her gaze went lower, to the thick angry scars on his thigh from where he'd been shot the previous year. He'd almost bled to death. For a second, she couldn't bear to think about a world without him in it. "You almost died." The words choked her, and a tear rolled down her cheek.

"But I didn't."

She squirmed lower on the bed and pressed her lips to it.

He tugged her back into his arms. "Life doesn't come without risk."

"I'm sorry." She wiped her cheek. "I'm an emotional mess tonight."

"You need sleep. It's a wonder you're still conscious. Close your eyes. Whatever happens in the morning, we'll face it together."

Exhausted and spent, she rested her head on his shoulder. His arm wrapped around her shoulders and held her close. Despite the uncertainty that lurked outside the door, here and now, in his arms, she felt safe and whole for the first time in years.

What she felt for Lance was as strong and simple and pure as a beam of sunlight cutting through storm clouds.

Was it love? It just might be.

She was certain about one thing. Anything bad that happened to her would be more bearable because of his presence. She was stronger with him than she was alone.

She lifted her head. His eyes were closed, and his chest rose and fell in a deep rhythm. She closed her own eyes. Thoughts of love shifted to Tim and Chelsea. The sheriff had said he would call them to let them know about the arrests of the Burns brothers. Morgan wondered how Chelsea was taking the news. Was she relieved? Did she believe it was over? Was she being comforted by her husband tonight?

Even in sleep, Morgan's brain refused to let go of the inconsistencies of the case that she'd noted at the salvage yard.

A few hours later, she woke. Morning had broken. Pale sunshine filtered through the blinds, casting stripes of shadow and soft light across the bed.

Something wasn't lining up so neatly in her mind.

She slid out of bed, donned the borrowed sweatpants and T-shirt, and tiptoed into the kitchen. She scanned the counters. No coffee machine. Why hadn't she noticed the absence in her previous visits to Lance's house? He didn't drink coffee regularly, but surely he must have a machine somewhere in case of an emergency.

Like now.

Her head ached for caffeine. Yes. She was an addict.

She checked his cabinets but found no sign of coffee. She'd have to wait until he woke up. With a sigh, she gave up, took her files into the living room, and spread them across the coffee table.

The answer was in here somewhere.

Chapter Thirty-Nine

The bedroom was bright with daylight when Lance woke. He rolled over to find the bed next to him empty and cold. For a few seconds, he wondered if he'd dreamed making love with Morgan. But her scent on the pillow next to him assured him it had happened. The memory gave him a rush of lust, quickly doused with concern.

Where was she? Why wasn't she in bed?

He stepped into his sweatpants and padded barefoot into the living room. Morgan sat on his couch, the case files spread across his coffee table. He glanced at the clock. Eight a.m. He'd slept maybe four hours.

"Did you sleep at all?" he asked. He was still groggy. She'd slept even less than he had over the past few days.

"I did. I've only been up about an hour." Over the dark circles, her eyes were bright with interest. She wore his sweatpants and T-shirt, and her hair tumbled around her face in a tousled wave that made him want to scoop her up and take her back to bed. Even if it was just to make her sleep.

But he recognized the dog-on-a-scent look on her face. There was no way she was going back to bed. She was onto something.

He sat down next to her on the sofa. "What did you find?"

"At least one thing that doesn't add up already." She shuffled a few pages. "Chelsea escaped from her prison through a hole in the roof. I don't remember seeing a hole in the roof of that trailer last night. Plus, Chelsea never mentioned a bloody mattress in the container."

"Maybe the police will find a shipping container somewhere on the property. I hate to say it, but the Burns brothers could have had multiple places they held women." Lance stood. "I need food. I can't think straight. I'm making eggs. I can't make you sleep, but you will eat. We have to go to the sheriff's office today."

"Oh, joy."

"Hopefully, he'll have some information about what they found at the scene overnight."

"But will he share it with us?" Morgan asked.

"Stranger things have happened," Lance said. "I'm hoping some of his attitude was for show. Secretly, he has to be at least relieved that we found Karen Mitchell, and hopefully, the Burns brothers also killed Sarah Bernard, kidnapped Chelsea Clark, and broke in to your house."

"I'll feel better if Chelsea's DNA turns up in that trailer or somewhere else on the property."

"Me too." Lance went into the kitchen. He scrambled half a dozen eggs with olive oil, basil, and spinach, and then toasted four slices of the organic, gluten-free oat bread Morgan's kids had refused to touch. He brewed a pot of strong green tea and piled the food onto two plates.

"Here." He set a plate in front of Morgan.

She pushed it aside. "Thank you."

Lance put the plate back in front of her. "Stop working and eat before you make yourself sick."

"You're right." She leaned back and lifted the fork from the plate. "What's the green stuff?"

"Spinach. You need the vitamins." Did he sound exactly like Sharp? Yes. Yes, he did.

That was what happened when you cared about someone. And he definitely cared about Morgan.

He loved her. Was she ready to hear that?

Probably not.

She finished her food. Lance put the dirty plates in the sink and brought her a cup of green tea.

"Thanks." She sipped without looking up from the page she was reading, then froze and looked up at him in horror. "You really don't have coffee? I mean I looked for it earlier, but I assumed you'd have an emergency stash somewhere."

"Sorry. Sharp purged my kitchen of everything he considered to be a 'toxic' substance over the summer. He practically needed a dumpster. I'm lucky I saved the whiskey."

"I would never have parted with my coffee machine."

"I can hardly argue with his lifestyle. It healed me." Lance took his place on the couch next to her and drank his tea. She was right. It was a sad substitute when proper rest wasn't an option. "We'll stop for coffee on the way to the sheriff's office."

"Damned straight."

"Hand me a few files. Let's see if we've overlooked anything else."

They passed files back and forth. A few hours later, Morgan said, "This can't be right."

He pressed his shoulder to hers. "What?"

She sifted through her mound of files. Opening one, she flipped through the pages of one of her meticulous files. Her fingertip slid down a page and stopped. She started reassembling her files. "We need to check with the sheriff."

"What did you find?"

"It's not what I found, but what I didn't find." She opened a file. "This is the list of Speed Net employees Elliot Pagano gave us."

"OK. We checked them all out. They were all clean except Kirk Armani. Did you find something else on him?"

"No. But Elliot didn't include his brother, Derek, on this list."

"Maybe he forgot to include his family?"

Morgan shook her head. "His mother and father are here, and so is every member of Tim's team. The janitor is even listed. But not Derek. I'd like to ask the sheriff if Derek is included on his list. It's probably just an oversight." She reached for her cell phone, frowned when the call went to voice mail, and left a message.

"Considering the scope of last night's crime scene, the sheriff might still be there. Or he's interviewing Harold Burns," Lance said. "Either way, he'll call back. We should drive over to my mom's house. She'll make quick work of Derek Pagano's background."

"OK. I need to stop at the office for my laptop. I have clothes there too." Morgan stretched.

"I'm going to grab a quick shower. Then we can go to the office." Lance headed toward his bedroom. He glanced back at her, all tousled and gorgeous. "The sheriff still hasn't returned your call. Want to join me?"

Her smile brightened her eyes. "I do."

The shower wasn't as quick as he'd intended. But the extra time was well spent.

Very well spent.

An hour later, Morgan still looked tired, but her posture was much more relaxed as they headed to Sharp Investigations. She changed her clothes and grabbed her computer. Lance made protein shakes, but Morgan still insisted they stop for coffee. He went through the drive-through, succumbing to the smells emanating from the coffee shop and ordering one for himself. He handed her the vat she'd ordered, and she nearly purred when she sipped it.

The sun was high over the trees as they drove to Lance's mother's house. Morgan slung her bag over her shoulder and carried her giant coffee up the walk. Lance followed. A bark greeted them as they went inside. Rocket rushed into the foyer and butted Morgan's legs with her head. Morgan leaned down and stroked the dog's head.

"I've been thinking." Sharp appeared in the kitchen doorway. "You should take her home with you. She likes kids, and that little purse pup of yours is worthless as a watchdog."

"But she's your dog." Morgan straightened.

"Not from where I'm standing." Sharp snorted. "Rocket barks when someone is at the door, and she proved she'd protect you last month."

"I'll talk it over with Grandpa." Her smile faded.

"How is he?" Sharp asked.

"I talked to my sister this morning. There's been no change."

"No change can be good." Sharp turned up his nose at their coffee cups. "Come back to the office. Let's get caught up."

Lance automatically scanned his mom's living room. No packages. Lance didn't remember a week where he hadn't had to return or give away a Jeep full of merchandise to keep his mom from sinking back into hoarder status. How long had it been since she'd indulged her unrestrained shopper? Was it possible she'd finally learned to control her impulses, after more than two decades of indulging them? Lance was afraid to be hopeful. Her history with change wasn't promising.

They left their coats in the living room and went back to the office. Lance rounded the desk and kissed his mom on the cheek. "You look tired."

His mom came out from behind the desk to greet Morgan with a hug.

A hug!

Mom hadn't hugged anyone except Lance or Sharp in decades. What the hell was going on?

Rocket followed them into the office. Mom's two cats perched on a shelf, staring down at the dog with disdain.

A kitchen chair sat across the desk from his mother. Sharp's laptop was on the desk, facing the chair.

Lance explained about Derek Pagano's name not being on the list of Speed Net employees. "It might just be an oversight, but I'd like to learn everything we can about Derek ASAP."

His mom cracked her knuckles over the keyboard. "OK. Let me get to it."

Since she'd started doing background checks for their firm, his mom had set up search engine software that simplified much of the process of tracing a person's address history, obtaining a credit report, checking driving records, and verifying educational credits.

Sharp sat in his chair and opened his laptop. "We can speed this up. I'll start on the criminal searches. What county is he in?"

Lance's mom said, "I'll have that for you in a minute."

There was no way for them, as private investigators, to run a national criminal history search. Only law enforcement agencies had access to the National Crime Information Center, the FBI's national database of crime data. The next best option was a criminal records search in each of the counties where the individual had lived. They were lucky that Randolph County maintained its most current records online. Sharp would start with Derek's current county of residence and work backward after the social security trace had identified any previous addresses.

"Excuse me. I'm going to call my kids," Morgan said as she left the room.

Lance waited until his mom and Sharp found Derek's Pagano's address and social security number. Then he went looking for Morgan. She was sitting on the living room sofa, her phone in her lap. Her head rested against the sofa back. Her eyes were closed and her breathing deep and even. He picked up a folded afghan from a chair and spread it over her.

Confident that Sharp would wake him if they discovered anything interesting, Lance stretched out in the chair with his feet on the ottoman and closed his eyes. The room was dark when someone shook his shoulder. He looked over at the couch. Morgan was curled on her side, one hand under her cheek.

Sharp stood next to his chair. "We found it."

"Found what?" Morgan opened her eyes and sat up, tucking her legs alongside her body.

"Derek Pagano is registered as a sex offender in Meeker County," Sharp said.

"But my grandfather checked the surrounding counties." Morgan's voice was sleepy. "He wouldn't have missed the name Pagano. It isn't very common."

"Derek is a level one," Sharp clarified. "He wasn't on the website. I had to call to find out he was on the list."

Level-one offenders were considered to be at low risk of committing future crimes and were afforded more privacy than more serious offenders. By law, their names could not be included on the registry list. But if an individual called the sex offender information line with a specific name and address or social security number, they could find out if that person was registered.

"What did he do?" Morgan rubbed the side of her neck. One side of her face was lined from being smashed into the seam on the couch cushion.

"Voyeurism was the official charge." Sharp perched on the edge of Lance's chair. "I'm trying to get more information. I left a message for the detective who handled the case, but it's Sunday. I don't really expect a call back today."

Morgan blinked hard, as if to clear the sleep from her eyes. "Do you know the stats on voyeurs escalating to violent offenses?"

"There are two ways to look at it," Sharp said. "Only a small percentage of voyeurs go on to commit more serious offenses, but many rapists and serial murderers display voyeuristic tendencies."

Morgan balled up a fist on her knee. "I can't believe we didn't notice he wasn't on the list."

"That list had forty-nine names on it," Sharp said. "We checked each one. If you hadn't seen Derek at Speed Net, we would never have known he worked there."

Lance could see her brain firing up. "We shouldn't get ahead of ourselves."

"Derek owns one property in Meeker County, the one he lists as his address," Sharp said. "We didn't find any secret real estate holdings of any of the Pagano family other than those listed as their official addresses. Derek's property is rural, so it's the most promising."

"Does Derek have any other arrests on record?"

"Not that we found," Sharp said. "But we tried to call the girl who recently broke up with him. She moved to London."

"Maybe to get away from Derek." Morgan's eyes brightened as she mulled over the information. "And if Derek isn't guilty of anything, then why did Elliot leave him off the list?"

Chapter Forty

"Have you checked on Chelsea Clark?" Morgan asked. She and Lance faced the sheriff across his desk.

"I talked to Tim right after you called me." The sheriff leaned back in his chair. "She's doing as well as can be expected."

He and his deputies wore wrinkled uniforms and smelled like they'd been working for thirty-six hours straight.

Morgan explained what they found out about Derek Pagano. "Is he on your list of Speed Net employees?"

With a long-suffering sigh, the sheriff tipped his body forward. He swiveled his chair and pulled the file from a bin on his credenza. Pivoting back to his desk, he opened the file on his blotter, flipped though pages, and scanned lists. He frowned. "I don't see his name here."

"You didn't know he was a sex offender?" Morgan asked.

"No. But we've found evidence that Harold and Jerry Burns have been very busy. There were photos of other women, chained, beaten." He paused. "Dead. We found pictures of Sarah Bernard."

"So, they definitely killed her?" Morgan asked.

The sheriff nodded. "As we speak, there are cadaver dogs searching the woods around the salvage yard and the area of the state park where Sarah Bernard's body was found. We expect to find additional bodies."

"But you didn't find a picture of Chelsea?" Lance asked.

"No." The sheriff shook his head. "But we didn't find any photos of Karen Mitchell either. Maybe photography came later in the Burns brothers' fantasies."

"Was either Karen Mitchell or Sarah Bernard branded?" Morgan asked.

The sheriff shook his head. "No."

Morgan rolled the evidence in her mind for a few seconds. "Did you find a piece of metal to match the brand used on Chelsea?"

The sheriff's mouth turned down at the corners. "Not yet."

"Elliot left his brother's name off his employee list. I can't see how that was anything except an intentional omission. Doesn't that bother you?" Lance asked.

"It does, but we have our man," the sheriff said. "Or in this case, men."

"The prosecutor will want the information on Derek," Morgan pointed out. "The defense attorney will pounce on any inconsistencies in your reports."

The sheriff dropped his elbows onto the desk and massaged his temples for a few seconds. Looking up, he considered Morgan with bloodshot eyes. "If I promise to send an officer out to talk to Derek Pagano, will you get out of my office and stop calling my cell phone?"

"Yes," Morgan said, not exactly pleased with his lackluster response. "When will you do that?"

"As soon as I can." The sheriff rested both palms flat on his desk and pushed to his feet. "I have some loose ends to tie up before I can go home to a shower, a meal, and my bed. You should both do the same. You look like shit."

"Thank you, I think." Morgan stood and offered her hand across the desk.

The sheriff took it, albeit grudgingly. "You're OK, Counselor. But don't get in my way again."

"Good night." Morgan smiled politely, but she made no promises.

She and Lance left the sheriff's station. Light from overhead lamps puddled in yellow circles on the asphalt. A blast of cold air swept across the parking lot. Mid-October felt more like winter than autumn.

Morgan clutched the lapels of her coat together. "I'm not sure what to think of the sheriff. Sometimes he seems competent, but his department definitely dropped the ball a few times on this investigation."

Lance walked closer, his body shielding her from the wind. "He probably should have called the state police for help on a case that clearly strained the resources of his department, but that's against his nature. Maybe next time he pulls a case of this magnitude, he will."

Morgan doubted it. Old dogs could learn new tricks, but she didn't have the same faith in humans.

Her phone buzzed. She dug it out of her bag. Her sister's name was displayed on the screen.

"It's Stella." She answered the call, nerves jangling. "Hello?"

"He's awake," Stella said.

Morgan put a hand to the center of her chest. Her heart thumped hard and relief weakened her legs. "I'm so glad."

"I thought you'd want to know right away."

"God, yes." Morgan could barely catch her breath. "Where's Peyton?"

"She's talking with the doctor. Grandpa is already ornery. He's asking for bacon and eggs. Ian just got here too. But Grandpa is kicking us all out tonight. He said he doesn't need a damned babysitter and that we all look worse than he does."

"I can't believe it."

"Stop by and see him," Stella said. "You'll feel better."

"I will." Morgan ended the call and slid into the passenger seat of the Jeep.

Lance took her hand over the console and squeezed it. His hand warmed hers. "Your grandfather is all right?"

"Yes. Awake and hungry." She drummed her fingers on the armrest. "I'm going to call Tim on the way and make sure he and Chelsea are OK."

Morgan called Tim's cell number. He didn't answer, and she left a message. "Let's drive by Tim and Chelsea's house."

"Why?"

"He didn't answer his phone."

"Maybe he's busy." Despite his argument, Lance turned in the direction of the Clarks' neighborhood.

"Nothing would make me happier than the county forensics team finding DNA in a storage container in the salvage yard. I really want this to be over for Tim and Chelsea."

"But?"

"But there's no physical evidence linking the Burns brothers to Chelsea's kidnapping."

"The sheriff said he'd send an officer to talk to Derek Pagano."

"He didn't say when," Morgan pointed out. "And what is Sheriff King going to do without any evidence?"

"We don't *know* that Derek did anything. Unfortunately, the police can't get a search warrant based on gut instinct."

"Elliot lied." Six years as a prosecutor had given Morgan an excellent lie detector. Yet she hadn't picked up Elliot's omission. Either he was very good or he had simply made a mistake.

"He omitted information," Lance clarified. "Maybe he was just trying to protect his brother."

Morgan fastened her seat belt. "Let's drive by Derek's house."

"The sheriff said he'd do it."

"He didn't say when, and we didn't promise not to pay Derek a visit," Morgan said.

"Good point."

Meeker County was a twenty-minute drive from the sheriff's station. Lance followed the GPS until it led them to a narrow county road in the middle of the woods. Not a streetlight in sight.

"What is the house number?" Lance asked, slowing the vehicle and squinting through the windshield. The houses were spaced very far apart on the rural route. The last mailbox had been nearly a mile back.

Morgan scrolled on her phone. "Two hundred thirty-eight."

Lance stopped the Jeep. "That's two fifty and the last house was number two twenty-seven.

"How can there be no house?"

"The address is wrong." Lance turned the Jeep around. "Could be a simple error."

"Or not." Morgan set a hand on her stomach, where anxiety burned like a smoldering match. "I don't like this at all. Elliot omits his brother's name from the list and doesn't mention the fact that his brother is a convicted sex offender. Then Derek's home address is listed incorrectly?"

"This isn't right."

"No."

"Would you call Sharp and put him on speakerphone?" Lance asked.

Morgan held the phone between them as they waited for Sharp to answer.

"What's up?" Sharp asked.

Lance explained the error regarding Derek's address. "Could you double-check the house number and pull up a satellite photo of the area?"

"I'll will. I'll call you when I have something." Sharp hung up.

"We need to talk to Tim and Chelsea," Morgan said. She checked her phone. Tim hadn't called her back yet.

"Do we really want to upset her when we really don't have much information?" Lance asked. "We have no backup. The sheriff is convinced the Burns brothers kidnapped Chelsea. We have no proof Derek is the one who actually took her."

"No. We don't. We also have no evidence that he's going to come after her again."

"But you think he will?"

"Yes," she said. "If we're right and the sheriff is wrong, then Chelsea's kidnapper is still out there. What if whoever broke in to my house wanted to get to Chelsea through me? Chelsea and Tim deserve to be warned."

Derek Pagano was the center of too many coincidences. Morgan remembered the man who'd broken into her house. He'd threatened to take Sophie for insurance that Morgan would cooperate. Had that been Derek? If so, he was willing to go to great lengths—and hurt children—to get what he wanted.

Chelsea.

How would they protect her? All they had was a hunch that her kidnapper wanted her back.

Morgan straightened. "Turn the Jeep around."

"What are you thinking?" Lance asked in a suspicious voice as he made a U-turn.

"Head for Tim and Chelsea's house." Morgan reached for the armrest as the vehicle lurched. "We need to talk to them."

"OK." Lance pressed the accelerator, and the vehicle surged forward.

"He branded her with an infinity symbol." The brand was the one thing that separated Chelsea from the other two women. It was unusual. Personal. Intimate. "Chelsea's kidnapper intended to keep her *forever*. He won't let her go easily. He'll know about the arrest of the Burns brothers, and that the sheriff considers the case closed."

"And that the sheriff will pull the car sitting in her driveway," Lance finished.

Morgan tapped her phone with a fingertip. The fact that Tim hadn't returned her call worried her.

"We need to make a stop. I have an idea," Morgan said. "You're not going to like it."

"Wonderful."

Outside the car window, clouds obscured the moon. Night smothered the landscape.

Was he hiding out there? Waiting for Chelsea to assume she was safe and drop her guard?

Chapter Forty-One

Chelsea woke with a start. The darkness suffocated her. She drew in a gasp of air, and her heart leaped into a full panicked sprint.

"Hey, Chels. It's OK." A light clicked on. Tim was sitting in a chair by the window, an electronic tablet on his lap. He got up and moved to the side of the bed. He put a hand on her forehead. She flinched.

"I'm sorry." She couldn't help it.

"Don't worry about it." He smiled to cover the hurt in his eyes. "You can't expect to go through what you did and not be affected. We'll get through this."

He put his hand out on the bed, palm up, and waited for her to take the initiative. She didn't want to. She didn't want to be touched at all. Her body hurt. From her face to her feet, there wasn't an inch of her that didn't ache.

She shifted her legs under the blanket. The burn on her buttock blazed. Agony shot from the brand, radiating like a starburst into her hip and thigh.

"I don't feel safe here." She'd been taken from her own driveway. How would she ever feel safe in her home again?

"The doctor said we should try to wait a few months before we move."

"I know." But Chelsea wanted to run away from this house—this town, this state—as fast as she could. When they'd returned home, there had been reporters outside.

In the container, all she'd wanted to do was get home. Now that she was home, she didn't want to be there.

"What about going to a hotel for a few days?" She wanted to be somewhere no one knew her.

She wanted to hide.

"Do you want to talk to the psychiatrist?" Tim asked. "He gave me his cell number."

The same psychiatrist who'd recommended keeping her routine as normal as possible.

"No." Even Chelsea knew she was hiding from her own shadow and that she had to face reality.

"Do you need a pain pill?" Tim asked.

Across the hall, William began to cry.

She nodded. At least William had accepted bottle feedings so she could take medication. Between the drugs, the beatings, and the dehydration, her breast milk had dried up while she'd been gone.

It hurt to think the words: Kidnapped. Held captive. Beaten. Branded. The psychiatrist had said she should expect nightmares and panic attacks. They were normal reactions to the trauma she'd suffered. The only bright spot had been that he hadn't raped her.

But hiding from her pain wasn't going to help. She needed to face it, and she was too exhausted to do it alone.

She laid her hand in Tim's. His fingers closed, the connection between them familiar and comforting.

William grew louder, and Chelsea automatically started to rise.

Tim squeezed her hand. "It's OK. Your mom will get him."

"No. I want to feed him. The doctor said normal activities will help." She should strive for moments—even seconds—of normal activity. Take each day one minute at a time. All she'd been able to think about when she'd been in the container was getting back to her kids. That, at least, made her feel sane.

"I'll get him for you then." Tim released her hand and stood. "Your dad took Bella out for ice cream. She was restless. Will you be all right for a few minutes alone? I have to warm up a bottle."

She wasn't really sure, but she nodded. Tim walked out of the room. Chelsea eased to her feet. Her soles were bandaged and sore from running miles in the woods barefoot.

She hobbled to the bathroom. Even though she'd seen her reflection earlier, the sight of her black-and-blue face startled her. She shivered. She still couldn't get warm. She'd lost eight pounds in nine days but had no appetite. She gently brushed her teeth. Her bruises would fade. The swelling would go down. In a few weeks, she'd look normal.

Except for the brand.

The doctors wanted her to wait until she was fully recovered before undergoing plastic surgery to remove it. But they warned that it was deep. No matter what they did, she would have a scar. A permanent reminder of her captivity.

She could deal with that. She was alive. She'd held her baby and read to Bella. Thankfully, Chelsea's mom had prepared the little girl by telling her that Mommy had fallen and landed on her face, just like when Bella had fallen off the slide and scraped her knee a few weeks before. So after a long, hard look, Bella had pointed to her knee and decided her mommy would get better soon too.

The sheriff had called to say they'd caught her captor and rescued the blonde woman he'd kidnapped the day before. It was really over.

Everything was going to be all right. Her mom and dad and husband were taking care of her.

So why did her hands continue to shake?

William cried louder. Chelsea was afraid to pick him up. She was still weak. But she couldn't stand to listen to him cry. She brushed her teeth gingerly, then washed her hands.

Where was Tim?

A loud thud downstairs turned Chelsea's blood to ice. Her knees shook as she walked toward the hall.

Chapter Forty-Two

Moonlight lit his way. He cruised past the Clarks' house. No police car. The sheriff's department thought they had Chelsea's kidnapper and had pulled their deputy from his babysitting duty. Tim's Toyota was parked in the driveway, but the Dodge rental car was gone. Chelsea's parents must have left as well.

This was exactly what he'd been hoping for.

Perfect timing.

He parked at the curb in front of a house catty-corner from the Clark residence. The neighbors had teenagers and cars coming and going at all hours. No one would notice one more vehicle.

Last time he'd come here, the night he'd brought her home with him, he'd ridden his road bike and hidden it behind some bushes. Tonight, she'd be coming with him in his car.

Anger rose in his throat.

She'd left him to return to Tim. This time, he'd make sure Chelsea had no husband to return to. She would never choose another man over him again.

Tim had to go.

The kids too. Chelsea would never let go of her old family and embrace him while they lived. As much as it pained him to hurt two children, he had no choice. He'd be merciful. Their deaths would be quick and painless.

But not Tim's. He had to pay, and Chelsea had to watch. She had to know that Tim's suffering was her fault. That everything that was going to happen tonight was her doing.

After tonight she'd never fuck with him again. She'd do what she was told. She'd finally understand that he owned her.

The mark he'd left on her body was a permanent reminder.

He checked his pockets before he got out of the car: knife, duct tape, nylon rope.

He scanned the street in both directions before crossing it and jogging up the driveway. Coming and going would be the riskiest. Once he was in the house, he had confidence he'd be able to overpower Tim quickly. Once Tim was restrained, the rest would be a cakewalk.

Chelsea wasn't in any condition to fight back. That he knew.

Once he entered the shadows on the side of the house, he breathed easier. There were enough mature trees and shrubs that the neighboring houses couldn't see him. At the back of the house, he climbed onto the air-conditioning unit to peer through the window into the kitchen.

The house was dark. He could see through into the adjoining family room. No one was there. The TV was off.

They were probably sleeping.

He crept to the sliding glass door. Chelsea and Tim didn't have an alarm system. He lifted the door at the handle, jiggling it until the latch opened. Most people had no idea that the latch on a standard sliding glass door was useless.

Sliding the door open, he stepped inside and listened for a few seconds. The house was quiet. He'd never been inside, but the house was small and the layout fairly obvious. A night-light in the electrical socket at knee level lit his way. He had a small flashlight in his pocket but preferred not to use it.

His sneakers were silent on the tile as he crossed the kitchen. In the adjoining family room, he entered the hall and walked to the foyer at the front of the house. The living room and dining room flanked the foyer. Both were empty and dark.

Where was Tim?

A floorboard overhead creaked. His nerves sat up straighter. Someone was awake upstairs.

The stairwell was dark as he crept up the steps. He stopped just shy of the landing and scanned the second floor. Two doorways on the left. A bathroom straight ahead. And another door on the right. Only one door was open.

Another floorboard creaked and the sound of a baby crying came from the opened doorway. Who had woken to tend to the baby?

Chelsea or Tim?

He slid the knife from his pocket and turned it over in his grip.

Moving slowly, he stole up the last few steps. On the landing, he wavered. Should he go into the nursery and confront whoever was in there? Or should he find the master bedroom?

A sleeping adult would be easier to overpower. But the person who was already awake was more likely to hear him.

He would deal with the conscious adult first and hope he didn't wake the sleeper.

Putting his back to the wall, he sidled to the doorway and peered around the frame.

His heart stuttered. There she was.

Chelsea.

Her back was to him, so he took a minute to watch her.

Moonlight poured through the window and turned her blonde hair silver. It fell down the back of her thick robe. She was leaning over the crib and picking up the baby, her voice soft, more murmurs than words.

She was perfect.

From the first time he'd seen her he'd known. She was the one for him. Sure, he'd thought that before, and he'd been wrong *that* time. But this was different; this time he knew for sure.

Chelsea was wholesome and sweet. Most women ignored him, but she always smiled. She talked to him like he was normal.

His fingers tightened around the knife as he edged closer. They were going to be together again. And this time she'd never leave him. She'd learn her lesson.

He stepped into the room, planning his attack. He didn't want her to hear him and call her sleeping husband. He needed to incapacitate and silence her. He lifted his left hand, prepared to slap it over her mouth. Once she was tied up, he'd go after Tim.

The children he could deal with at his leisure.

Then it would be just him and Chelsea. She'd be his forever.

Just a few more steps.

The floor squeaked under his sneaker. She turned around. He raised the knife.

Shock stopped him in his tracks.

Chapter Forty-Three

"Put your hands on top of your head." Lance stepped out of the closet in the nursery, both his gun and the beam of his flashlight pointed at Derek Pagano. Lance hadn't liked Morgan's plan one bit, but her instincts had been dead-on.

Standing in front of the crib, wearing a blonde wig and Chelsea's robe, Morgan pointed her own weapon at the intruder.

Derek stopped, slack-jawed for a few second. "You!"

Morgan pulled the wig off her head and tossed it into the crib. It landed next to the cell phone playing a recorded sound of a baby crying. Lance hadn't liked her idea to trap Derek by pretending to be Chelsea, but he had to admit the plan had worked brilliantly. Chelsea had been upstairs when Morgan and Lance had arrived at the house. Lance's knock on the door had scared Chelsea, and she'd been easy to convince that getting her family out of the house and letting Morgan take her place was their best chance to catch her kidnapper.

Derek's eyes darted to the door, to Lance's weapon, then to Morgan.

"Drop the knife, Derek," Lance warned.

Derek turned toward Morgan, the shift in his posture drawing Lance a step forward. He didn't want to shoot the nutcase—OK, maybe he did, just a little—but he wouldn't pull the trigger unless it was absolutely necessary.

But Derek turned and ran out the door.

Damn it!

Lance couldn't shoot a man in the back. He shoved his gun into his holster and sprinted after him. He heard Morgan behind him talking to the police.

At the bottom of the stairs, Derek hooked one hand on the bannister, skidded through a one-eighty in the foyer, and ran for the back of the house. Lance followed him down the hall and through the family room into the kitchen.

Derek slid to a stop at the sliding glass door. He flung it open and bolted through the opening into the back yard. Lance ran straight through. The pause to open the slider had allowed him to catch up. He was only a few feet behind him.

What he wouldn't give to still be on the force. He'd fry this bastard with a stun gun in a heartbeat. But it was illegal for a private citizen to own a Taser in New York State.

Lance threw everything he had into a tackle. He pushed off one foot and dove for his running target. His arms wrapped around Derek's legs. They crashed to the ground. Derek grunted as his body bounced on the grass. He kicked to free his legs. A heel struck Lance in the head. Stars blinked in his vision, and he lost his grip on Derek for a second.

A second was all Derek needed.

He scrambled away, kicking at Lance. Another foot connected with Lance's face. Pain speared through his forehead and blood trickled into his eye. He grabbed for Derek again but missed.

Derek got a leg under his body and stood. His steps were unsteady as he broke into a jog and headed across the yard. Lance lurched to his feet, the old wound in his thigh screaming and reminding him why he'd left the force.

Hoping his leg held out, Lance ignored the pain and sprinted after him.

Derek ran for the corner of the house. Lance kicked his stride into full gear. But his thigh burned with every step, and Derek drew a few feet farther ahead.

He was going to lose him.

Shit!

Lungs on fire, leg on fire, Lance gave the chase one last burst of energy. It was now or never.

No doubt Derek had left a car on the street somewhere. If he reached it . . .

Derek glanced over his shoulder as he ran through the shadows of the side yard. Just as he cleared the house and leaped onto the driveway, a tree branch swung from out of nowhere.

The branch clotheslined Derek. His head snapped back. His legs continued forward, and he landed on his back in the dark.

Panting, Lance stopped next to the prone body. He grabbed Derek's arm and rolled him onto his face. A quick pat down of his pockets turned up duct tape and rope. Lance planted a knee into Derek's lower back to pin him in place. He pulled a set of zip ties from his own pocket and used them to secure Derek's wrists behind his back.

When Derek was restrained, Lance looked up at the shadow.

Morgan stood in the moonlight, her black hair gleaming, her face set in a determined mask.

"Thanks," he said.

"I was hoping he would head for the street." Morgan crossed her arms and rubbed her biceps. "The police are on the way. Are you all right?" She pointed to her own eyebrow.

Lance touched his forehead. His hand came away sticky and wet. "He kicked me in the head. It's nothing."

"Let me go!" Derek squirmed. "You're not cops. You can't keep me here."

"I'm making a citizen's arrest." Lance leaned a little more weight on his knee. His thigh throbbed. "You broke in to a home armed with a weapon. And I'll bet the police are going to find some interesting things when they search your house. You're in big trouble, Derek."

"They can't search my house. Elliot will call his lawyer. Elliot fixes everything." Derek spat at the ground. "You'll be sorry."

"Your brother can't get you out of this one." But Lance wondered how many other crimes Derek had committed.

"Why did you do it, Derek?" Morgan asked.

"I love her." Blood trickled from the corner of Derek's mouth. "She's mine."

"She's married to Tim," Morgan said.

"Chelsea was unhappy." Anger fueled Derek's words. "Tim doesn't know how to keep a woman. I do. Women need to be dominated. They can't make decisions. They don't know what they want."

"Is that why your girlfriend broke up with you?" Morgan asked.

"She's a stupid bitch," Derek snapped. "I tried being nice to her, but that didn't make her happy. Women don't want a nice man. They want a man who takes control. They want decisions made for them."

Morgan's head tilted. "You tried that with your girlfriend."

"If I could have kept her for a few weeks, I could have turned her attitude around. But the bitch ran off to London." Bitterness clipped Derek's words.

"She ran away from you," Morgan clarified.

"Women can't commit to anything. They let their emotions control them instead of logic. Look what happened to Elliot. He loved Candace. He tried to get her help, and what did she do? She threatened to leave him rather than do what was best for her."

The truth fell on Lance like a cartoon anvil.

Derek had killed his brother's wife.

Morgan clearly made the connection as well. Her posture stiffened. "Candace didn't know what was good for her."

"Just another example of women needing caretakers." Derek turned his head to stare at Morgan over his shoulder. "Candace was killing

305

herself with her addiction. Elliot loved her enough to try and stop it. But beating her addiction would have been hard, and she wasn't willing to do the work. Elliot should have put his foot down, but he didn't. He was weak."

"What did you do?" Morgan asked.

Derek's lips peeled off his teeth. "I tried to make her, but Elliot had let her get away with her bad behavior for too long. It was ingrained. If I could have isolated her for a month or so, I could have turned her around."

Silence pulsed in the night for a few seconds.

Derek shook his head. "Her addiction was out of control. I went there to save her. To save Elliot. He was unhappy." He took a breath, anger narrowing his eyes. "But she wouldn't let me fix her. I tried. I tried my hardest."

"You killed her," Lance finished.

"She fell and hit her head." Derek spat out the words. "It was an accident."

Lance pressed him harder. "Then why did you cover it up?"

Derek's lips pressed into a colorless line.

"Was she dead when you sent her car over that embankment?" Lance asked.

Derek didn't respond, but his flat gaze lifted goose bumps on Lance's arms.

It hadn't mattered to Derek. In his mind, she was worthless. Her life simply didn't matter. Lance didn't believe for one second that her death was an accident. Derek could have called for an ambulance. Instead, he chose to cover up her death.

"You failed with Chelsea," Lance prodded.

"I can fix *her*." Derek's voice rose. "She's sweeter. More pure of heart and soul. Not jaded and ruined by drugs."

"She has children," Morgan said.

"She can have more children. *My* children." Derek's face reddened. "I can make her love me. It just takes time."

"You tortured her." Lance wanted to find that brand and hear it sizzle in Derek's skin. The man deserved to feel the pain he'd inflicted on Chelsea.

"I *taught* her," Derek interrupted. "There's a difference. A blend of positive and negative reinforcement to show her that being submissive to a man would make her happy."

Lance had nothing left to say. There was no point. A man that far gone, that demented, could never be turned around.

Sirens floated on the cold air.

Now it was over.

Chapter Forty-Four

Thirty minutes later, Morgan stood in front of Chelsea and Tim's house. She wrapped her arms around her waist. Her initial nausea after the showdown with Derek had faded. Adrenaline had deserted her, leaving her limbs shaky and weak.

Derek's revelations had not been a complete surprise. But she was too spent to fully process what he'd told them. Lance thought his story was bullshit. Morgan didn't know what to believe.

"Morgan!" Stella's voice pierced the busy scene.

Morgan braced herself for her sister's fury.

Stella weaved her way through a foursome of patrol officers and sheriff's deputies. Both departments had responded to the 911 call.

Stopping in front of Morgan, Stella propped her hands on her hips. "What the hell were you doing?"

Morgan hugged her body against the night chill. She'd ditched Chelsea's robe in the house so she could move faster. "What did you want me to do? Call you and tell you we had a hunch that Derek Pagano was Chelsea's kidnapper, and we were planning to camp in their house until he showed up for her?"

"Yes!"

Morgan shook her head. "We didn't know when or if he'd come. It could have been days from now."

It hadn't taken much to convince Tim and Chelsea they were at risk. Chelsea had jumped at the chance to get out of her house. The family had packed a few bags. Sharp had whisked them off to the hotel where her parents were registered and stayed to watch over them.

"You should have told me," Stella huffed. "At least I would have had a patrol car in the area."

"What if he didn't come tonight? Or tomorrow night? Would the SFPD have continued to babysit us?" But Morgan had expected him to come quickly, before any evidence surfaced to make the sheriff doubt the Burns brothers had kidnapped Chelsea.

Stella glared. "I could have done it off duty."

"So, no. The SFPD wouldn't have babysat us for a hunch." Though Morgan knew she probably *should* have called her sister.

Morgan and Lance had agreed to give her plan three nights. As it turned out, they'd needed only one.

Lance came out of the house, where he'd been walking the responding officer through the events of the evening. He held a gauze pad over the cut on his eyebrow.

Morgan reached up and lifted the corner of the gauze. "You need a couple of stitches."

"Probably." He shrugged.

Morgan took his arm. "I'll drive you."

He opened his mouth to protest, but she shook her head and shot him a *look*. Morgan wanted to give her sister some time to cool off. She steered Lance toward the Jeep and held out her hand for the keys.

"I can drive," he protested.

"Seriously? You'll get blood all over your vehicle."

He handed her the keys and cursed under his breath as he stared over her shoulder. "It's the sheriff. Quick. Get in. We can pretend we didn't see him."

"Kruger! Dane!" Sheriff King's voice boomed over all the other law enforcement activity.

Morgan turned to face King. "Can I help you, Sheriff?"

The sheriff's face was red enough that she thought *he* might need to go to the ER. He led Lance and Morgan away from the other officers.

King folded his arms over his chest. "I sent a car to Derek Pagano's address, but there was no driveway or mailbox. We found a back entrance to the property. Derek has an old cabin back in the woods. The deputy took a walk around the property looking for Derek. Behind the cabin, he found a rusty old shipping container. Someone had busted a hole right through the roof."

"That's where Chelsea was kept," Morgan said.

"Forensics will have to do its thing, but I think it's reasonable to theorize that Derek kidnapped Chelsea. I'll be heading over there when I'm finished here. I'll let you know what we discover." The sheriff coughed into his fist and looked away. "Thank you for your help. If you two hadn't been so persistent, tonight would have turned out very different for Chelsea and her family."

"You're welcome," Morgan said. "Keeping the Clark family safe was our only goal. You're going to pick up Elliot too, right? He gave his brother an alibi for the night Chelsea went missing. He also left Derek's name off the list of Speed Net employees."

"I already sent a deputy to his house," the sheriff confirmed.

"Now that I think about our first visit there, we saw Derek by chance," Morgan said. "It was their mother, Barbara, who pointed Derek out to us. If she hadn't done that, we would never have known that Derek worked at Speed Net."

Morgan shivered. Lance put an arm around her shoulders.

"I'll need you both in my office tomorrow to sign formal statements." With a nod, the sheriff backed away.

Morgan drove Lance to the hospital and walked him to the ER waiting room.

"Would you mind if I snuck upstairs to see my grandfather?" she asked.

"Or course not, but it's one a.m. Do you think you can get in?"

"They have a twenty-four-hour visitation policy for critical patients." She rose on her toes and kissed him on the mouth. "Later, we'll process what happened tonight. Right now, I'm just very, very happy that we're both in one piece, and that Chelsea, Tim, and their kids are safe."

"Go check on Grandpa." Lance gestured toward the four people sitting in the waiting room. "I'm going to be here for a while."

Morgan made her way to the ICU ward. She stopped in the hallway and glanced through the doorway. A monitor beeped in a low, steady rhythm. A nurse stood next to the bed, checking the machines and recording information on a clipboard. She spotted Morgan and crossed the room to join her in the corridor.

"He's doing really well," the nurse said. "We're moving him to a regular floor in the morning. And he's awake. Go on in."

"Thank you." Morgan went into the room.

Grandpa opened his eyes and smiled at her. His hand slipped out from under the white blanket. His fingers curled in a beckoning gesture.

"Hey." Morgan took his hand, her chest tightening with gratitude and relief.

"I told you I wasn't dead yet." Grandpa's skin was pale, and his focus appeared fuzzy. "You need to have faith."

"You're right." She squeezed his fingers. "Are you in pain?"

"A little, but don't worry. The nurses are taking good care of me," he said. "Did you solve your case?"

"We did." Morgan gave him a condensed rundown of the last two days.

"Atta girl." He gave her hand a weak shake. "I knew you'd figure it out. It's in your genes." His eyelids drooped.

"I have to go collect Lance in the ER." She leaned over and kissed his cheek. "I'll see you tomorrow?"

"Ian and Peyton are in town too." His voice slurred. He'd protested calling them, but his sleepy smile said he was pleased that they'd come.

"I love you."

"Love you more." Grandpa's eyes closed.

Despite Morgan's exhaustion, her step was light as she left the room. Grandpa wasn't getting any younger, but he was still with her. She was going to enjoy every day he was in her life and try not to worry about the future.

She returned to the ER. A nurse directed her to Lance's ER bed, where a young doctor was finishing stitching his cut. When the wound was closed and bandaged, Lance checked out.

"It's too late to pick up the kids," she said.

"Stay with me the rest of the night?"

"Yes." She wanted to spend the night with him without any major trauma.

Ignoring his complaints that he was perfectly fine, *she* drove back to his house. A short while later, she stripped off her clothes and climbed into his big bed.

Lance lay down next to her. He opened his arms. "Come here."

She was too exhausted for sex, but his body was warm beside her, and she curled up against him.

"I know I didn't love your plan," he said. "But we did good tonight."

"We're a great team." She nestled into his shoulder.

"We are."

No matter what happened, it was easier to handle with him at her side.

Chapter Forty-Five

Monday morning dawned brightly—too brightly for someone who'd slept only a few hours. Morgan squinted through her sunglasses and clutched her extralarge coffee like a security blanket as Lance escorted her across the parking lot of the sheriff's station.

"I owe Mac's brother a favor or ten," Morgan said. Grant Barrett had volunteered to drive the girls to school and drop Gianna at dialysis that morning. "I'm not sure how I'll ever repay them."

"I doubt he's looking for repayment. Mac said they just wanted your kids to be safe."

"Well, I'm eternally grateful."

Everyone in the sheriff's department looked ragged. The deep bags under Sheriff King's eyes said he'd been up all night, but he'd shaved and his clothes were fresh.

She probably didn't look much better.

"Come this way." Sheriff King waved Morgan and Lance into a conference room. "Elliot Pagano was here most of the night. He gave a full confession. Do you want to watch his interview?"

"Yes." Morgan concealed her surprise at the offer.

A monitor had been set up on the table. The sheriff sat down in front of it and typed on the keyboard. He gestured to the chairs opposite him, and Morgan and Lance sat.

The sheriff turned the monitor to face them. A picture on the screen appeared to be the same room. Sitting at the table, Elliot Pagano looked like he'd aged ten years in a few days. He waived his right to an attorney. His eyes looked lost. Beaten.

Almost dead.

On the video, the sheriff sat across from Elliot. Another officer sat to his left. The fourth man, who sat next to Elliot, had "lawyer" written all over him from his Hermès tie to his David Yurman cuff links.

"We know your brother kidnapped Chelsea Clark and that he killed your wife," the sheriff said.

Elliot folded his hands on the table. "He did it for me."

"Why?" the sheriff asked.

Elliot lifted a shoulder in the careless gesture of a man who doesn't have anything else to lose. "She was leaving me. I wanted her to go into treatment for her drug addiction. We fought. She wanted a divorce. I made the mistake of telling Derek. She contributed a portion of the start-up capital. If she divorced me, she might have been entitled to half of Speed Net."

"Derek couldn't let that happen," the sheriff said.

"He didn't intend to kill her." Without meeting the sheriff's gaze, Elliot shook his head. "It was an accident."

"Was it?"

"Yes!" Elliot's eyes snapped to the sheriff's for a moment. "She fell and hit her head."

"So Derek put her in her car and sent it over a cliff. Did you help him?"

"She was already dead; it hardly mattered. Why should he go to prison over an accident?"

"If it was an accident, why cover it up?"

Elliot stared down at his hands in silence.

The sheriff leaned closer. "Are you sure she was dead when he put her in that car?"

"Derek wouldn't lie to me." Elliot's voice was flat, lifeless. "We're family."

"He killed your wife."

"No!" But Elliot's voice broke, as if the night had shaken his trust in his brother, and he couldn't bear it. "Derek wanted to help Candace. She was self-destructing. He thought he could break her addiction, but she wouldn't cooperate. They fought. She fell and hit her head. That's what happened." His eyes drifted. He wasn't talking to the sheriff anymore, but to himself. As if trying to convince himself that his brother's story was true.

The sheriff changed tack. "Did you know he took Chelsea?"

"Not at first. He confessed to me the next morning." Elliot looked away. "I encouraged him to let her go, but he couldn't. He loved her."

A muscle in the sheriff's jaw twitched. "He kidnapped and beat her."

Elliot let out a breath. "He wanted a woman who would never leave him. He hadn't had any luck finding one, so he decided to make his own."

"Did you help him?" the sheriff asked. "He needed to drop a car at the train station. He got to Chelsea's house somehow."

Elliot shook his head. "Derek used his bike to get to Chelsea's house. He hid it in the woods and retrieved it later. He took the bike with him to Grey's Hollow. He left his car there and rode his bike back. Twenty miles is nothing for him. Some of his road races are over a hundred."

"How did he know Chelsea would be going out that night?"

"Early Friday morning, I asked Tim if he could work late. He said no, that his wife had plans. Derek overheard." Elliot's absence of emotion lifted goose bumps on Morgan's arms.

"He's so . . . flat," she said.

The sheriff reached forward and turned off the monitor. "No trace of remorse."

"No trace of humanity," Lance said.

Morgan rubbed her biceps. "The only thing he seems to care about is believing what his brother told him."

"Maybe he *needs* to believe that Derek didn't murder Candace," Lance added.

"I hope they don't try for an insanity defense. Derek's body is covered with scars, including a brand on his leg that matches Chelsea's and cuts on his arms and legs that look self-inflicted." The sheriff rubbed the back of his neck. "Their parents seem pretty normal. They refuse to even consider the idea their sons committed any crimes, but they did verify that the two men have always been extremely close. Derek wasn't a good student. Elliot got him through school. On the other hand, Elliot was scraggly as a kid and got beat up a lot. Derek always came to his defense. Mr. Pagano told a story about Derek beating up a neighborhood bully who tormented Elliot. Mr. Pagano tried to make light of the incident, but apparently, Derek pushed the kid off an overpass. He broke both his legs. There's no official record, but I'll bet if we dig in to their childhood enough, we'll find some teachers who remember more disturbing incidents involving the Pagano brothers."

"They both likely suffer from some kind of psychopathy," Morgan said. "But to be criminally insane, they have to be unable to determine right from wrong. Elliot and Derek are too cold and calculating. They took steps to prevent Derek from being caught. They clearly knew what he was doing was wrong. They just didn't care about anyone but themselves."

"Let's hope the judge and jury agree with you." The sheriff sat back.

"What are they charging Elliot with?" Morgan asked.

"Everything the DA can think of." Anger flared in the sheriff's eyes. "That bastard knew where Chelsea was on Saturday. He could have gotten her rescued. Instead, he let his brother torture her for nearly a week—"

The sheriff paused, visibly getting himself under control. "The ME pulled Candace Pagano's autopsy report. That embankment she went over is steep. The car rolled all the way down to the bottom. Without a seat belt to hold her in place, she bounced around enough that the initial head trauma was covered up by the crash. Derek got lucky when the car caught fire. Her purse, containing a bottle of illegal OxyContin, was flung from the vehicle, and the autopsy showed the drug in her bloodstream. She took it every day. I don't know if he'll be able to find any proof that she was dead or alive when she was put in that car, but we have a confession. And forensics is having a party over at Derek's place. In the workshop where he fixes his bike, they found a metal infinity symbol that matches the brand on Chelsea Clark. The storage container looked exactly like she described, and her fingerprints and Derek's were all over the unit. Also, he repaired his road bike in his shed. The oil he uses on his bike has a funky smell. Chelsea recognized the odor immediately."

The sheriff paused for air. "Derek Pagano isn't going to see the outside of prison walls for a very long time. If we're lucky, he'll never be free again. Hopefully Elliot will be locked away for a long time too."

"I hope so." Morgan stretched her neck. The nastiness of the case was wearing on her. All she wanted to do was hug her kids.

"I spoke to Derek's former girlfriend on the phone this morning. She broke up with him because he creeped the hell out of her. Started checking her phone messages, trying to control who she hung out with, et cetera. The girl was so nervous about him that when a job offer came up in London, she took it. She was afraid to come back."

The sheriff shook their hands. "Thank you for your help on this."

The words sounded as if it pained him to say them.

Morgan couldn't believe Elliot had sat across from them, knowing where Chelsea was, and lied so smoothly. Chelsea had been beaten and branded. Elliot could have prevented much of her suffering, but he chose not to. Did he have no soul?

"What about the Burns brothers?" Lance asked on the way out.

The sheriff reached for the doorknob. "Jerry came out of surgery, but we haven't been allowed to question him yet. Doesn't matter, though, because we have them cold for kidnapping Karen Mitchell and murdering Sarah Bernard. The cadaver dogs have found two more bodies in the state park, and they aren't finished yet. There's a lot of ground to cover. We're not sure how many other woman they might have killed."

As if three weren't enough.

The sunshine felt warm and clean as they stepped out of the building.

Morgan turned her face to the heat. "That feels good."

Lance squinted at the light. "I hope the Burns brothers and the Paganos are all in cold, dark cells."

Chapter Forty-Six

"I brought ice cream." Sharp walked into Lance's house.

"I'm sure the kids will love it," Lance said.

Sharp froze. "Wow. This is different."

Lance's stark, minimalistic decor had been revamped. Toys littered the floor, girly backpacks were piled by the sofa, and coloring books and crayons covered his coffee table. Mia and Ava knelt on the carpet, playing a game of Candy Land.

Rocket followed Sharp inside.

"My house is a little tight for six people, but we're making it work." Lance closed the door. It's only for a couple of days. The alarm company is updating the entire system."

Morgan and the girls were staying with Lance until her security rivaled that of the White House.

Gianna, Mia, and Ava were sleeping in Lance's room. Morgan and Sophie had the guest room. Until Sophie outgrew her night terrors, she couldn't share a room with her sisters. Lance was bunking on the couch. Even without Sophie's night terrors, Lance knew there'd be no sleeping together with the kids in the house.

"It's chaos." Sharp laughed.

"But a good kind of chaos." In truth, as crowded as the house was, it felt more like a home than it had in the past. Lance didn't even mind the clutter of stuffed animals, dolls, and tiny socks. And glitter. Lance had even found silver flakes in his scrambled eggs.

Sharp handed him a brown paper bag. Lance glanced inside. Organic ice cream.

"I don't know what kids eat." Sharp stooped to take the leash off Rocket's collar. The dog trotted into the living room. Snoozer hopped off the couch, and the dogs went through a sniffing and wagging routine.

"They love each other." Sophie clapped her hands, joining the dogs in a circling frenzy.

"Hold on. I want to tell you something," Sharp said. "I found out why your mom has been acting differently."

Lance held his breath.

"She has a boyfriend." Sharp grinned.

"What?" Of all the things Lance had braced himself to hear, that wasn't on the list.

"Yep," Sharp said. "They met in group therapy. He has anxiety issues too. The last week or so, she'd been messaging with him online at night instead of shopping."

Lance didn't know how to feel about his mother having an online relationship. "OK."

"Don't look so glum." Sharp slapped him on the shoulder. "This is a good thing for her."

"Until they break up." And Lance had to clean up the fallout.

Sharp shook his head. "Don't borrow trouble. Be happy for her. She's in a better place than I've ever seen. It's about time she's had something positive in her life."

"You're right." Lance would be happy for her, but he'd also keep a close eye on her. "Do you want some tea?" Lance asked.

"No. I'm not staying. It looks crowded enough in there." Sharp backed toward the door. "I just came to drop off the ice cream and the dog."

"You're leaving the dog *now*?" Lance asked.

"Yes." Sharp chuckled. "Rocket is bored at my place. She belongs with Morgan and the kids."

Lance glanced into the living room. Rocket had planted herself between Ava and Mia.

What was one more warm body?

"Thanks," Lance said.

Sharp couldn't fool him. He'd been worried about them.

"You all have a nice night." Sharp left.

Lance locked the door behind him. He took the ice cream to the kitchen. Gianna was loading dishes into the dishwasher. Morgan was drying a baking pan, which they'd gone out to buy because Lance's hadn't owned one.

He did now.

"Wance." Sophie tugged on Lance's hand. "You pwomised to teach me a song."

Lance crouched to her level. "You know what? I learned a song just for you."

Her eyes widened. "Yay."

He let her pull him to the piano bench. He sat next to her, and she watched, rapt as he spread his fingers over the keys and played the opening notes. Her feet swung back and forth, in perfect time. When he started singing "You've Got a Friend in Me," she joined in after the first few lines. Her voice soft and surprisingly on key.

By the time they finished the song together, Mia and Ava were peering over their shoulders, singing along.

"Again!" Sophie shouted.

"How about I teach you to play it instead?" Lance plunked out the first few lines of the melody.

Sophie picked the tune up fast, and after fifteen minutes, was content to practice on her own. She played the notes over and over with a determination and patience Lance would not have expected of a three-year-old.

"OK, girls, bath time," Gianna called.

The room emptied out, and Morgan and Lance spent the next fifteen minutes clearing the clutter. But with so little room and so much stuff, there was only so much they could do.

Lance took advantage of the empty room. He tugged Morgan to him and planted a kiss on her lips.

She wrapped her arms around his neck. "I've never heard you play happy music before."

"I guess I do lean toward the moody and broody when it comes to music." Lance glanced around at the jumble of pink in his house. "I'm feeling pretty happy."

He was an only child, and after his father had disappeared, his life had deteriorated. He didn't remember ever feeling the sense of family that being with Morgan and her girls gave him. The kids added fun and wonder to his life. He was loving every crowded, glitter-bombed moment of having them at his house. The idea of stepping in as a parent to three little girls was daunting, but they were worth the work. His house was going to feel empty when they were gone.

And he couldn't quantify everything Morgan meant to him without choking up.

Tomorrow, he'd go over to her place and meet with the alarm company to check on the progress. She wanted to be home when her grandfather was released in a few days. There was no way one more person was going to fit in Lance's two-bedroom ranch.

"You really don't mind us all invading your house?"

"Not at all." He wasn't looking forward to them leaving. If she'd have asked him that question the year before, his answer would have been entirely different. But only because he hadn't realized what he'd been missing.

"Still, I can't thank you enough. Stella and Mac's place is much smaller than yours."

"It's fine. I'm enjoying it. Bachelor life is boring." He silenced her with a kiss.

"This case was so horrible." Morgan reached for Lance's hand. "I don't know how I would have handled it without you."

Lance closed his fingers around hers. He wanted to say something romantic back, but the words stuck in his throat. He wasn't skilled at expressing his feelings, especially to her. But he had to get better at that.

"No matter how complicated our personal lives are, we need to prioritize our relationship from now on," she said. "That is, if you want to."

Lance smiled down at her. Finding his voice, he said what was in his heart. "There's nothing I want more."

He'd been waiting to hear those exact words.

"All right, then." She rose onto her toes. "From now on, we are officially us."

Acknowledgments

As always, credit goes to my agent, Jill Marsal, and to the entire team at Montlake Romance, especially my managing editor, Anh Schluep, developmental editor, Charlotte Herscher, and author herder/tech goddess Jessica Poore.

Special thanks to Leanne Sparks for her patience and help with some of the procedural elements of this story. She saved me weeks of research.

About the Author

Wall Street Journal bestselling author Melinda Leigh is a fully recovered banker. A lifelong lover of books, she started writing as a way to preserve her sanity when her youngest child entered first grade. During the next few years, she joined Romance Writers of America, learned a few things about writing a novel, and decided the process was way more fun than analyzing financial statements. Melinda's debut novel, *She Can Run*, was nominated for Best First Novel by the International Thriller Writers. She's also garnered Golden Leaf and Silver Falchion awards, along with nominations for a RITA and three Daphne du Maurier Awards. Her other novels include *She Can Tell*, *She Can Scream*, *She Can Hide*, *She Can Kill*, *Midnight Exposure*, *Midnight Sacrifice*, *Midnight Betrayal*, *Midnight Obsession*, *Hour of Need*, *Minutes to Kill*, *Seconds to Live*, and *Say You're Sorry*. She holds a second-degree black belt in Kenpo karate; teaches women's self-defense; and lives in a messy house with her husband, two teenagers, a couple of dogs, and two rescue cats.